FROM THE EARTH TO THE MOON

It was a goal of the imagination long before the Apollo missions made it a reality. Now on the thirtieth anniversary of the leap from imagination to reality, some of today's bold explorers of futures yet to come offer us fascinating new looks at our closest companion on our journey through the solar system:

"An Apollo Asteroid"—It had taken a new way of perceiving the universe to make travel to the Moon an everyday event. Would a celestial catastrophe make us abandon the Moon—or give us the universe?

"Ashes and Tombstones"—Anyone who learned what he had done would think it was a monument to the wealthy dead. But what exactly had he sent to the Moon?

"The Last Man on the Moon"—He had agreed to help them create their virtual reality version of Armstrong's trip to the Moon, but could he live with the way they were rewriting history?

MOON SHOTS

MOON SHOTS

Edited by Peter Crowther

DAW BOOKS, INC.

DONALD A. WOLLHEIM, FOUNDER

375 Hudson Street, New York, NY 10014

ELIZABETH R. WOLLHEIM
SHEILA E. GILBERT
PUBLISHERS

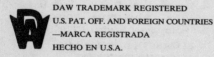

ACKNOWLEDGMENTS

CONTENTS

INTRODUCTION

by Ben Bova

She hangs there in the sky almost every night and blesses us with her radiance. The Moon was a goddess to the ancients: Diana, Hecate, Luna, Mama-Kilya, Nsongo, Selene, Tecciztecatl, Thoth.

To us, the Moon is a goal, a destination, an end and a beginning. There are human bootprints on her dusty surface. I'd like to see the lights of human cities up there.

As I was growing up in the row houses and narrow streets of South Philadelphia, the Moon was one of the few astronomical objects we could see in the night sky. When I was ten or eleven years old, I went to the Fels Planetarium and saw their thrilling version of what a trip to the Moon might be like. That hooked me. I've been a "lunatic" ever since.

When the U.S. government announced that it would try to launch an artificial satellite into orbit around the Earth, I quit my job as a newspaper reporter and talked my way into a position as a technical editor on the Vanguard project. Getting a satellite into Earth orbit was the first step toward getting to the Moon, you see.

Vanguard turned out to be the third program to orbit a satellite, not the first, but that didn't matter. We were on our way. Washington created the National Aeronautics and Space Administration, NASA, and a few years later a new president launched the Apollo program.

1

I did not participate directly in Apollo, although by then I was working at a research laboratory whose parent corporation built the heat shields for the Apollo return capsules. Our lunar astronauts returned safely to Earth, thanks to the research on reentry physics that our lab had done.

We got to the Moon. We did it so superbly well that most people still think it was easy. It wasn't. Men died along the way. The Soviet government did its best to beat us to the Moon, and once they saw that they had failed, Moscow claimed that they had never tried. Sour grapes. Once the Soviet Union collapsed and their carefully-hidden files were opened up, we saw that they'd tried their damnedest.

The big surprise was not that we reached the Moon. The big surprise was that we stopped going there. Washington had achieved its political objective and shown that Western technology was superior to the Soviets'. End of story, as far as the politicians were concerned. All the bright, shining plans that the scientists and engineers (and science fiction folks) had for building permanent bases on the Moon were tossed in the ash can.

Yet the dream lived on.

I continued to write about the Moon: *Millennium* in 1976, and its prequel, *Kinsman,* three years later. In 1987, with the help of ambitious but frustrated engineers who were fellow "lunatics" and the brilliant artist Pat Rawlings, I wrote *Welcome to Moonbase,* a nonfiction book organized as an employees' manual for people who would work on the Moon.

It seemed clear to me that the government's efforts in space would always be dictated by political considerations. No great strides in space were planned by Washington because no politician's election depended on space accomplishments. Just the opposite. Apollo 17 astronaut Harrison Schmitt was elected to the U.S. Senate after returning from the Moon, but was defeated in his reelection bid by an opponent whose slogan was, "What on Earth has Jack Schmitt done for you?"

By the time I wrote *Welcome to Moonbase,* it seemed clear to me that private enterprise would be the driving engine that returns us to the Moon.

Why? Because the Moon can become the resource center for factories in space. Because the Moon can be the main transportation node for travel through the solar system and beyond. Because scientists want to study the Moon to unlock the origins of the solar system. Because the Moon is an excellent platform for astronomical observations. Because the low lunar gravity will make the Moon a marvelous place for retirees and people too physically infirm to lead active, useful lives on Earth.

Because people can make money on the Moon.

Because it's the frontier. It's exciting. It's new. Frontiers—both the physical and mental types—are where the new ideas come from, the new inventions, the new social creations, the new lifestyles. And the new wealth.

Thus I began the *Moonbase Saga,* a series of novels spinning the tales of how humankind establishes a permanent base on the Moon, and how that base grows from a small, struggling, dangerous outpost into a full-fledged, and fully free, major city.

Moonrise, the first novel in the *Moonbase Saga,* was published in 1996, *Moonwar* in 1998. There are more to come.

As you will see in this anthology, the Moon is an excellent inspiration for fiction. The lunar goddess still calls forth the muse and sets writers' minds to create sparkling new tales.

But the Moon is more than a distant source of imaginative storytelling. It is a goal for each of us, waiting for our return, ready to serve as the foundation for the next wave of human enrichment.

In 1962, President John Kennedy said:

"We choose to go to the Moon in this decade . . . not because [it is] easy, but because [it is] hard, because that goal will serve to organize and measure the best of our energies and skills, because that challenge is one that we are willing to accept, one we are unwilling to postpone, and which we intend to win."

Now we are ready to return. The next time you look up at the Moon, realize that it could become your home one day. Imagine standing there and gazing back at Earth. Dream grand dreams, then work to make them come true.

AN APOLLO ASTEROID

by *Brian Aldiss*

Everything has changed. Back at human beginnings, perception was locked in a shuttered house. One by one, the shutters snapped open, or were forced open, revealing the real world outside.

We can never be sure if all the shutters have yet snapped open.

At one time, it was well known that the caves of Altamira in northern Spain had been accidentally discovered by a girl of five. She had wandered away from her father. Her father was an archaeologist, much too busy studying an old stone to notice that his daughter had strayed.

It is easy to imagine the fine afternoon, the old man kneeling by the stone, the young girl picking wildflowers. She finds blue flowers, red ones, and yellow. She wanders on, taking little thought. The ground is broken. She attempts to climb a slope. Sand falls away. She sees an opening. She has no fear, but plenty of curiosity. She climbs in. Just a little way. She is in a cave. There she sees on the wall the figure of an animal, a buffalo.

That does frighten her. She climbs out and runs back to her father, crying that she has seen an animal. He goes to look.

And what he finds is an extensive gallery of scenes, painted by Paleolithic hunters or magicians, or hunter/magicians. The great artistry of the scenes changes

human understanding of the past. We came to believe
that we comprehended that sympathetic magic when
we had in fact failed to do so. We accepted a scientific,
mathematical model into our heads, and had to live
by it.

Clues to a true understanding of the universe lie
everywhere. One after another, clues are found and,
when the time is ripe, are understood. The great rep-
tiles whose bones lie in the rocks waited there for
millions of years to be interpreted, then to expand
greatly humanity's knowledge of duration and the
planet's duration. Frequently women are associated
with such shocks to the understanding, perhaps because they contain magic in their own persons. It was
a Mrs. Gideon Mantell who discovered the bones of
the first reptile to be identified as a dinosaur.

All such discoveries seem little short of miraculous
at the time; then they become taken for granted. So
it has proved in the case of Bagreist's Shortcut.

It has been forgotten now, but an accident similar
to the Altamira accident brought Joyce Bagreist to
understand the signal of the Northern Lights, or au-
rora borealis. For untold years, the lights had been
explained away as the interaction of charged particles
from the sun reacting with particles in the upper atmosphere. True, the signal was activated by the charged
particles: but no one until Bagreist had thought
through to the purpose of this activity.

Joyce Bagreist was a cautious little woman, not particularly liked at her university because of her solitary
nature. She was slowly devising and building a computer that worked on the color spectrum rather than
on mathematics. Once she had formulated new equations and set up her apparatus, she spent some while
preparing for what she visualized might follow. Within
the privacy of her house, Bagreist improvised for herself a kind of wheeled space suit, complete with bright
headlights, an emergency oxygen supply, and a stock

of food. Only then did she track along her upper landing, along the measured two-point-five meters, and through the archway of her apparatus.

At the end of the archway, with hardly a jolt to announce a revolution in thought, she found herself in the crater Aristarchus, on the Moon.

It will be remembered that the great Aristarchus of Samos, in whose honor the crater was named, was the first astronomer to correctly read another celestial signal now obvious to us—that the Earth was in orbit about the sun, rather than vice versa.

There Bagreist was, rather astonished, slightly vexed. According to her calculations, she should have emerged in the crater Copernicus. Clearly, her apparatus was more primitive and fallible than she had bargained for.

Being unable to climb out of the crater, she circled it in her homemade suit, feeling pleased with the discovery of what we still call Bagreist's Shortcut—or, more frequently, more simply, the Bagreist.

There was no way in which this brave discoverer could return to Earth. It was left to others to construct an Archway on the Moon. Poor Bagreist perished there in Aristarchus, perhaps not too dissatisfied with herself. She had radioed to Earth. The signal had been picked up. Space Administration had sent a ship. But it arrived too late for Joyce Bagreist.

Within a year of her death, traffic was pouring through several Archways, and the Moon was covered with building materials.

But who or what had left the signal in the Arctic skies to await its hour of interpretation?

Of course, the implications of the Bagreist were explored. It became clear that space/time did not possess the same configuration as had been assumed. Another force was operative, popularly known as the Squidge Force. Cosmologists and mathematicians were hard put to explain the Squidge Force, since it resisted formulation in current mathematical systems. The elaborate mathematical systems on which our global civilization was founded had merely local application: they did not extend even as far as the heliopause. So while the practicalities of Bagreist were being utilized, and people everywhere (having bought a ticket) were taking a short walk from their home onto the lunar surface, mathematical lacunae were the subject of intense and learned inquiry.

Two centuries later, I back into the story. I shall try to explain simply what occurred. But not only does P-L6344 enter the picture; so do Mrs. Staunton and General Tomlin Willetts, and the general's lady friend, Molly Levaticus.

My name, by the way, is Terry W. Manson, L44/56331. I lived in Lunar City IV, popularly known as Ivy. I was General Secretary of Recreationals, working for those who manufacture IDs, or individual drugs.

I had worked previously for the Luna-based MAW, the Meteor and Asteroid Watch, which was how I came to know something of General Willetts' affairs. Willetts was a big consumer of IDs. He was in charge of the MAW operation, and had been for the previous three years. The last few months had been taken up with Molly Levaticus, who had joined his staff as a junior operative and was shortly afterward made private secretary to the general. In consequence of this closely kept secret affair—known to many on the base—General Willetts went about in a dream.

My more serious problem also involved a dream. A golf ball lying forlorn on a deserted beach may have nothing outwardly sinister about it. However, when that same dream recurs every night, one begins to worry. There lay that golf ball, there was that beach. Both monuments to perfect stasis and, in consequence, alarming.

The dream became more insistent as time went by. It seemed—I know no other way of expressing it—to move closer every night. I became alarmed. Eventually, I made an appointment to see Mrs. Staunton, Mrs. Roslyn Staunton, the best-known Ivy mentatropist.

After asking all the usual questions, involving my general health, my sleeping habits, and so forth, Roslyn—we soon lapsed into first names—asked me what meaning I attached to my dream.

"It's just an ordinary golf ball. Well . . . No, it has markings resembling a golf ball's markings. I don't know what else it could be. And it's lying on its side."

When I thought about what I was saying, I saw I was talking nonsense. A golf ball has no sides. So it was not a golf ball.

"And it's lying on a beach?" she prompted.

"Yes. An infinite beach. Stony. Pretty bleak."

"You recognize the beach?"

"No. It's an alarming place—well, the way infinity is always pretty alarming. Just an enormous stretch of territory with nothing growing on it. Oh, and the ocean. A sullen ocean. The waves are heavy and leaden—and slow. About one per minute gathers up its strength and slithers up the beach."

"Slithers?" she asked.

"Waves don't seem to break properly on this beach. They just subside." I sat in silence thinking about this desolate yet somehow tempting picture which haunted me. "The sky. It's very heavy and enclosing."

"So you feel this is all very unpleasant?"

With surprise, I heard myself saying, "Oh, no. I need it. It promises something. Something emerging . . . Out of the sea, I suppose."

"Why do you wish to cease dreaming this dream if you need it?"

That was a question I found myself unable to answer.

While I was undergoing three sessions a week with
Roslyn, the general was undergoing more frequent
sessions with Molly Levaticus. And P-L6344 was rushing nearer.

The general's wife, Hermione, was blind, and had
been since childhood. Willetts was not without a sadistic streak, or how else would he have become a general? We are all blind in some fashion, either in our
private lives or in some shared public way; for instance, there are millions of Earth-bound people, otherwise seemingly intelligent, who still believe that the
Sun orbits the Earth, rather than vice versa. This, despite all the evidence to the contrary.

These sort of people would say in their own defense
that they believe the evidence of their eyes. Yet we
know well that our eyes can see only a small part of
the electromagnetic spectrum. All our senses are limited in some fashion. And, because limited, often mistaken. Even "unshakable evidence" concerning the
nature of the universe was due to take a knock, thanks
to P-L6344.

Willetts' sadistic nature led him to persuade his
fancy lady, Molly Levaticus, to walk naked about the
rooms of his and his wife's apartment, while the blind
Hermione was present. Commentators, confronted by
this fact, variously saw Molly either as a victim or as
a dreadful predatory female. The question seemed to
be whether she had been trapped in her innocence by
the power of the general, or whether she had schemed
her way into his office and bed.

Nobody considered that the truth, if there was a
unitary truth, lay somewhere between the two poles:
that there was an affinity between the two, which is
not as unusual as it may appear, between the older
man and the younger women. She undoubtedly had
her power, as he had his weakness. They played on
each other.

And they played cat-and-mouse with Hermione

Willetts. She would be sitting at the meal table, with Willetts seated nearby. Into the room would come the naked Levaticus, on tiptoe. Winks were exchanged with Willetts. She would circle the room in a slow dance, hands above her head, showing her unshaven armpits, in a kind of *tai ch'i*, moving close to the blind woman.

Sensing a movement in the air, or a slight noise, Hermione would ask mildly, "Tomlin, dear, is there another person in the room?"

He would deny it.

Sometimes Hermione would strike out with her stick. Molly always dodged.

"Your behavior is very strange, Hermione," Willetts would say, severely. "Put down that stick. You are not losing your senses, are you?"

Or they would be in the living room. Hermione would be in her chair, reading a book in Braille. Molly would stick out her little curly pudendum almost in the lady's face. Hermione would sniff and turn the page. Molly would glide to Willetts' side, open his zip, and remove his erect penis, on which her fingers played like a musician with a flute. Then Hermione might lift her blind gaze and ask what her husband was doing.

"Just counting my medals, dearest," he would reply.

What was poor Hermione's perception of her world? How mistaken was it, or did she prefer not to suspect, being powerless?

But he was equally blind, disregarding the signals from MAW, urging immediate decision on what to do to deflect or destroy the oncoming P-L6344.

Willetts was preoccupied with his private affairs, as I was preoccupied with my mentatropic meetings with Roslyn. As our bodies went on their courses, so, too, did the bodies of the solar system.

The Apollo asteroids cross the Earth/Moon orbit. Of these nineteen small bodies, possibly the best

known is Hermes, which at one time passed by the
Moon at a distance only double the Moon's distance
from Earth. P-L6344 is a small rock, no more than
one-hundred-and-ninety meters across. On its previous
crossing, the brave astronaut, Flavia da Beltrau do
Valle, managed to anchor herself to the rock, planting
there a metal replica of the Patagonian flag. At the
period of which I am speaking, the asteroid was coming in fast at an inclination of five degrees to the plane
of the ecliptic. Best estimations demonstrated that it
would impact with the Moon at 23:03 on 5/8/2208. But
defensive action was delayed because of General Willetts' other interests.

So why were the computers not instructed by others,
and the missiles not armed by subordinates? The answer must lie somewhere in everyone's absurd preoc-
cupation with their own small universes, of which they
form the perceived center. Immersed in Recreationals,
they were, in any case, disinclined to act.

Perhaps we have a hatred of reality. Reality is too cold
for us. Perceptions of all things are governed by our own
selves. The French master, Gustave Flaubert, when asked
where he found the model for the central tragic figure of
Emma in his novel, *Madame Bovary,* is said to have replied, "Madame Bovary? C'est moi." Certainly Flaubert's
horror of life is embodied in his book. The novel stands as
an example of a proto-recreational.

Even as the Apollo asteroid was rushing toward us,
even as we were in mortal danger, I was looking—
under Roslyn's direction—to find the meaning of my
strange dream in the works of the German philoso-
pher, Edmund Husserl. Husserl touched something in
my soul, for he rejects all assumptions about existence,
preferring the subjectivity of the individual's perceptions as a way in which we experience the universe.

A clever man, Husserl, but one who said little about
what things would really be like if our perceptions
turned out to be faulty. Or, for instance, if we did not

perceive the crisis of an approaching asteroid soon enough.

Running promptly on timetable, P-L6344 struck. By a coincidence, it impacted in Aristarchus, the very crater in which Joyce Bagreist had emerged on the Moon.

The Moon staggered in its orbit.

Everyone fell down. Hermione, groping blindly for her stick, clutched Molly Levaticus' moist and hairy little pudendum and shrieked, "There's a cat in here!"

Many buildings and careers were ruined, including General Willetts'.

Many lunarians took the nearest Bagreist home. Many feared that the Moon would swan off into outer space under the force of impact. I had my work to do. I disliked the squalid cities of Earth. But primarily I stayed on because Roslyn Staunton stayed, both she and I being determined to get to the bottom of my dream. Somehow, by magical transference, it had become her dream, too. Our sessions together became more and more conspiratorial.

At one point I did consider marrying Roslyn, but kept the thought to myself.

After the strike, everyone was unconscious for at least two days. Sometimes for a week. The color red vanished from the spectrum.

One strange effect of the asteroid strike was that my dream of the golf ball lying on its side faded away. I never dreamed it again. Oddly, I missed it. I ceased visiting Roslyn as a patient. Since she no longer played a professional role in my life, I was able to invite her out to dine at the Earthscape Restaurant, where angelfish were particularly good, and later to drive out with her to inspect the impact site when things had cooled down sufficiently.

Kilometers of gray ash rolled by as the car drove us westward. Plastic pine trees had been set up on either side of the road, in an attempt at scenery. They ceased a kilometer out of town, where the road forked. Distant palisades caught the slant of sun, transforming them into spires of an alien faith. Roslyn and I sat mute, side by side, pursuing our own thoughts as we progressed. We had switched off the radio. The voices were those of penguins.

"I miss Gauguins," she said suddenly. "His vivid expressionist color. The bloody Moon is so gray—I sometimes wish I had never come here. Bagreist made it all too easy. If it hadn't been for you . . ."

"I have a set of Gauguin paintings on slides. Love his work!"

"You do? Why didn't you say?"

"My secret vice. I have almost a complete set."

"You have? I thought he was the great forgotten artist."

"Those marvelous wide women, chocolate in their nudity . . . the dogs, the idols, the sense of a brooding presence . . ."

She uttered a tuneful scream. "Do you know '*Vairaumati Tei Oa*'? The woman smoking, a figure looming behind her?"

". . . And behind them a carving of two people copulating?"

"God, you do know it, Terry! The sheer color! The sullen joy! Let's stop and have a screw to celebrate."

"Afterward. His sense of color, of outline, of pattern. Lakes of red, forests of orange, walls of viridian . . ."

"His senses were strange. Gauguin learned to see everything new. Maybe he was right. Maybe the sand is pink."

"Funny he never painted the Moon, did he?"

"Not that I know of. It could be pink, too. . . ."

We held hands. We locked tongues in each others' mouths. Our bodies forced themselves on each other. Craving, craving. Starved of color. Cracks appeared in the road. The car slowed.

My thoughts ran to the world Paul Gauguin had discovered and—a different matter—the one he opened up for others. His canvases were proof that there was no common agreement about how reality was. Gauguin was Husserl's proof. I cried my new understanding to Roslyn. "Reality" was a conspiracy, and Gauguin's images persuaded people to accept a new and different reality.

"Oh, God, I am so happy!"

The road began to hump. The tracked vehicle went to dead slow. In a while, it said, "No road ahead," and stopped. Roslyn and I clamped down our helmets, got out, and walked.

No one else was about. The site had been cordoned off, but we climbed the wire. We entered Aristarchus by the gap which had been built through its walls some years previously. The flat ground inside the crater was shattered. Heat of impact had turned it into glass. We picked our way across a treacherous skating rink. In the center of the upheaval was a new crater, the P-L6344 crater, from which a curl of smoke rose, to spread itself over the dusty floor.

Roslyn and I stood on the lip of the new crater, looking down. A crust of gray ash broke in one place, revealing a glow beneath.

"Too bad the Moon got in the way . . ."

"It's the end of something . . ."

There was not much you could say.

She tripped as we made to turn back. I caught her arm and steadied her. Grunting with displeasure, Rosalyn kicked at what she had tripped on. A stone gleamed dully.

She brought over her handling arm. Its long metal fingers felt in the churned muck and gripped an object—not a stone. It was rhomboidal—manufactured. In size, it was no bigger than a thermos flask. Exclaiming, we took it back to the car.

The P-L6344 rhomboid! Dating science showed it to be something over 2.5 million years old. It opened when chilled down to 185.333K.

From inside it emerged a complex thing which was, at first, taken for a machine of an elaborate if miniature kind. It moved slowly, retracting and projecting series of rods and corkscrewlike objects. Analysis showed it to be made of various semimetal materials, such as were unknown to us, created from what we could have called artificial atoms, where semiconductor dots contained thousands of electrons. It emitted a series of light flashes.

This strange thing was preserved at 185.333K and studied.

Recreationals got in on the act because research was funded by treating this weird object from the remote past as a form of exhibition. I was often in the laboratory area. Overhearing what people said, as they shuffled in front of the one-way glass, I found that most of them thought it was pretty boring.

At night, Roslyn and I screamed at each other about "the tourists." We longed for a universe of our own. Not here, not on the Moon. Her breasts were the most intelligent I ever sucked. And not only there.

Talking to Roslyn about this strange signaling thing we owned, I must admit it was she who made the perception. "You keep calling it a machine," she said. "Maybe it is a kind of a machine. But it could be living. Maybe this is a survivor from a time when the universe did not support carbon-based life. Maybe it's a prebiotic living thing!"

"A what?"

"A prelife living thing. It isn't really alive because it has never died, despite being two million years in that can. . . . Terry, you know the impossible happens. Our lives are impossible. This thing delivered to us is both possible and impossible."

My instinct was to rush about telling everyone. In

particular, telling the scientists on the project. Roslyn
cautioned me against doing so.

"There must be something in this for us. We may
be only a day or two ahead of them before they, too,
realize they are dealing with a kind of life. We have
to use that time."

My turn to have a brain wave. "I've recorded all its
flashes. Let's decode them, see what they are saying.
If this little object has intelligence, then there's a
meaning awaiting discovery. . . ."

The universe went about its inscrutable course. People lived their inscrutable lives. But Roslyn and I
hardly slept, slept only when her sharp little hips had
ground into mine. We transformed the flickering messages into sound, we played them backward, we
speeded them up and slowed them down. We even
ascribed values to them. Nothing played.

The stress made us quarrelsome. Yet there were
moments of calm. I asked Roslyn why she had come
to the Moon. We had already read each other, yet did
not know the alphabet.

"Because it was easy just to walk through the neighboring Bagreist, in a way my grandparents could never
have imagined. And I wanted work. And."

She stopped. I waited for the sentence to emerge.
"Because of something buried deep within me."

She turned a look on me that choked any response
I might make. She knew I understood her. Despite
my job, despite my career, which hung on me like a
loose suit of clothes, I lived for distant horizons.

"Speak, man!" she ordered. "Read me."

"It's the far perspective. That's where I live. I can
say what you say, 'because of something buried deep
within me.' I understand you with all my heart. Your
impediment is mine."

She threw herself on me, kissing my lips, my mouth,

saying, "God, I love you, I drink you. You alone understand—"

And I was saying the same things, stammering about
the world we shared in common, that with love and
mathematics we could achieve it. We became the animal with two backs and one mind. . . .

I was showering after a night awake when the
thought struck me. The prebiotic semilife we had uncovered, buried below the surface of the Moon for
countless ages, did not require oxygen, any more than
did Rosalyn's and my perceptions. What fuel, then,
might it use to power its mentality? The answer could
only be: *Cold!*

We sank the temperature of the flickering messages,
using the laboratory machine when the place was va-
cated during the hours of night. At 185.332K, the messages went into phase. A degree lower, and they
became solid, emitting a dull glow. We photographed
them from several angles before switching off the
superfrigeration.

What we uncovered was an entirely new mathematical mode. It was a mathematics of a different existence. It underpinned a phase of the universe which
contradicted ours, which made our world remote from
us and from our concept of it. Not that it rendered
ours obsolete: far from it, but rather that it demonstrated by irrefutable logic that we had not understood
how small a part of totality we shared.

This was old gray information, denser by far than
lead, more durable than granite. Incontrovertible.

Trembling, Roslyn and I took it—again at dead of
night, when the worst crimes are committed—and fed
its equations into the Crayputer which governed and
stabilized Luna. It was entered and in a flash—

Groaning, we climbed out of the hole. Here was a
much larger Bagreist. As we entered into the flabby

light, we saw the far perspective we had always held
embedded in us: that forlorn ocean, those leaden
waves, and that desolate shore, so long dreamed
about, its individual grains now scrunching under our
feet.

Behind us lay the ball which had been the Moon,
stranded from its old environment, deep in its venerable
age, motionless upon its side.

We clasped each other's hands with a wild surmise,
and pulled ourselves forth.

HAS ANYBODY SEEN JUNIE MOON?

by Gene Wolfe

The reason I am writing this is to find my manager. I think her name is really probably June Moon or something, but nobody calls her that. I call her Junie and just about everybody else calls her Ms. Moon. She is short and kind of fat with a big wide mouth that she smiles with a lot and brown hair. She is pretty, too. Real pretty, and that is how you can be sure it is her if ever you see her. Because short, fat ladies mostly do not look as good as Junie and nobody thinks, "Boy, I would really like to know her like I did that time in England when we went in the cave, so she could talk to that crabby old man from Tulsa because Junie believes in dead people coming back and all that."

She made me believe it, too. You would, too, if you had been with Junie like I have.

So I am looking for a Moon just like she is, only she is the Moon that I am looking for. The one she is looking for is the White Cow Moon. That is an Indian name and there is a story behind it just like you would think, only it is a pretty dumb story, so I am going to save it for later. Besides, I do not think it is true. Indians are nice people except for a couple I used to know, but they have all these stories that they tell you and then they laugh inside.

I am from Texas, but Junie is from Oklahoma.

That is what started her off. She used to work for a big school they have there, whatever it says on that sweatshirt she wears sometimes. There was this cranky old man in Tulsa that knew lots of stuff, only he was like an Indian. He would tell people, this was when he was still pretty young, I guess, and they would never believe him even if it was true.

I have that trouble, too, but this cranky old man got real mad and did something about it. He changed his name to Roy T. Laffer, and after that he would tell things so they would not believe him or understand, and then laugh inside. Junie never said what the T. stood for, but I think I know.

Do you know what it says on the tea boxes? The ones with the man with the cap on them? It says honest tea is the best policy. I know what that means, and I think that cranky old Roy T. Laffer knew it, too.

He gave big boxes full of paper to the school Junie worked for, and Junie was the one that went through them and that was how she found out about White Cow Moon. He had a lot of stuff in there about it, and Junie saw her name and read it even if his writing was worse even than mine. He had been there and taken pictures, and she found those, too. She showed me some.

It goes slow. Junie said that was the greatest secret in the world, so I guess it is. And there were pictures of a big old rock that Roy T. Laffer had brought back.

One picture that I saw had it sitting on a scale. The rock was so big you could not hardly see the scale, but then another picture showed the part with numbers, and that big old rock was only about a quarter ounce. It was kind of a dirty white like this one cow that we used to have.

Maybe that was really why they call it that and not because a cow jumped over it like those Indians say. That would make a lot more sense, only I did not think of it till just now.

I ought to tell you things about me here so you understand, but first I want to tell more about Junie because I am looking for her, but I know where I am already, which is here in Florida at the Museum of the Strange and Occult. Only it is all big letters like this on our sign out front, THE MUSEUM OF THE STRANGE AND OCCULT, ADMISSION $5.50, CHILDREN $2, CHILDREN IN ARMS FREE, SENIORS $3 or $2 WITH ANOTHER PAID ADMISSION. The letters are gold.

Junie had been to college and everything and was a doctor of physic. When she got out, she thought she was the greatest since One Mug. That is what she says it means, only it is German. I do not remember the German words.

So she went to work at this big laboratory in Chicago where they do physic, only they had her answer the phone and empty the wastebaskets and she quit. Then she went back home to Oklahoma, and that is why she was at the big school and was the one that went through Roy T. Laffer's papers. Mostly I do not much like Oklahoma people because they think they are better than Texas people, only Junie really is.

So if you see her or even just talk to somebody that has, you could come by and tell me, or write a letter or even just phone. I will be glad any way you do it. Dottie that works in our office here is putting this in her computer for me and printing it, too, whenever I have got a page done. She says you could send E-mail, too. That would be all right because Dottie would tell us. I would be very happy any way you did it. Dottie says www.Hercules@freaky.com.

My name is not really Hercules, that is just the name I work under. My name is really Sam and that is what Junie calls me. If you know her and have talked to her and she said anything about Sam, that was me. If you want to be really formal, it is Sam Jr. Only nobody calls me that. Most people I know call me Hercules. Not ever Herk. I do not like it.

Let me tell you how bad I want to find Junie. Sometimes there is a man in the tip that thinks he is stronger. I really like that when it happens because it is usually fun. I will do some things that I figure he can do, too, like bending rebars and tearing up bottle caps. Then if I see the tip likes him, I will say something hard and let him win.

A week ago maybe there was this one big guy that thought he was really strong, so I did him like I said. I threw him the two-hundred-pound bell and he caught it, and when he threw it back to me, I pretended like I could not catch it and let it fall when I had my legs out of the way and everybody was happy. Only yesterday he came back. He called me Herk, and he said I was afraid to go up against him again. The tip was not with him then. So I said all right, and when he could not lift my five-hundred-pound iron, I did it with one hand and gave it to him. And when he dropped it, I picked him up by his belt and hung him on this high hook I use for the pulley. I left him up there until everybody was gone, too, and when I took him down, he did not say a word. He just went away.

Well, I want Junie back so bad that if he was to tell me where she was, I would let him win anytime he wanted.

I do not make a lot of money here. It is just five hundred a month and what I make selling my course, but they have got these trailers out back for Jojo and Baby Rita who is a hundred times fatter than Junie or anybody. So I have one, too, and it is free. I eat a lot, but that is about all I spend much on. Some fishing gear, but I have got a real good reel and you do not need much else.

Well, you do, but it does not cost the world.

So I have a lot saved and I will give you half if you tell me where Junie Moon is and she is really there when I go look.

This is the way she got to be my manager. I was in

England working at a fair that they had at this big
castle where King Arthur was born, and Junie was in
the tip. So when it was over and they were supposed
to go see Torchy, Junie would not go. The steerer said
she had to, but she kept saying she wanted to talk to
me and I could tell she was American like me. So
after a while I said she probably knew that if she
really wanted to talk to me all she had to do was meet
me out back. So then she went.

When I went out back, which was where the toilets
were, I did not expect to see her, not really, even if I
had let her feel my arm which is something I do sometimes. But there she was, and this is what she said,
with the little marks around it that you are supposed
to use and all of that stuff. Dottie, help me with this
part.

"Hercules, I really need your help. I don't know
whether I was really one of the daughters of King
Thespius, but there were fifty of them, so there's a
pretty good chance of it. Will you help me?"

That was the first thing Junie ever said to me, and
I remember it just like it was a couple of days ago.
Naturally I said I would.

"You will! Just like that?"

I said sure.

"I can pay you. I was going to say that. A hundred
pounds right now, and another hundred pounds when
I'm over the fence. I can pass it to you through the
fence. Look." She opened her purse and showed me
the money. "Is that enough?"

I explained how she did not have to.

"You'll be in danger. You might be arrested."

Junie looked really worried when she said that, and
it made me feel wonderful, so I said that was okay. I
had been arrested once already in England besides in
America and to tell the truth in England it was kind
of fun, especially when they could not get their hand-
cuffs to go around my wrists, and then they got these

plastic strap cuffs and put those on me and I broke
six pairs. I like English people, only nothing they say
makes any sense.

Junie said, "Back there, you threw an enormous
barbell up in the air and caught it. How much did you
say it weighed?"

I said, "Three hundred. That was my three-hundred-
pound bell."

"And does it actually weigh three hundred
pounds?"

I said sure.

"I weigh only a little more than half that. Could
you throw me, oh, fifteen feet into the air?"

I knew I could, but I said I did not know because
I wanted to get my hands on her.

"But you might? Do you really think you might be
able to, Hercules?"

I sort of raised up my shoulders the way you do
and let them drop.

"We—if you failed to throw me high enough, I
would get a severe electric shock." She looked scared.

I nodded really serious and said what we ought to
do was try it first, right now. We would measure something that was fifteen feet, and then I would throw
her up, and she could tell me if I got her up that high.
So she pointed to the temporary wires they had strung
up for the fair, and I wanted to know if those were
the ones. She said no. They were not fifteen feet either. Ten or twelve maybe. But I said okay only do
not reach out and grab them or you might get killed,
and she said okay.

So I got my hands around her which was what I
had been wanting to do and lifted her up and sort of
weighed her a couple times, moving her up and down,
you know how you do, and then I spun around like
for the hammer throw, and I heaved her maybe ten
feet higher than those wires, and caught her easy when
she came down. It made her really scared, too, and I

was sorry for that, but I got down on my knees and hugged her, and I said, "There, there, there," and pretty soon she stopped crying.

Then I said was that high enough? And she said it was.

She was still shaky after that, so we went back inside and she sat with me while I waited for the next tip. That was when she showed me the pictures that Roy T. Laffer had taken up on the White Cow Moon and the pictures of the rock that he had brought back, a great big rock that did not hardly weigh anything. "He let a little boy take it to school for a science show," Junie told me, "and afterward the science teacher threw it out. Mr. Laffer went to the school and tried to reclaim it the following day, but apparently it had blown out of the dumpster."

I promised her I would keep an eye out for it.

"Thank you. But the point is its lightness. Do you know why the Moon doesn't fall into the Earth, Hercules?"

I said that if I was going to throw her around, she ought to call me Sam, and she promised she would. Then she asked me again about the Moon and I said, "Sure, I know that one. The moonbeams hold it up."

Junie did not laugh. "Really, Sam, it does. It falls exactly as a bullet falls to Earth."

She went and got a broom to show me, holding it level. "Suppose that this were a rifle. If I pulled the trigger, the bullet would fly out of the barrel at a speed of three thousand feet per second or so."

I said okay.

"Now say that you were to drop that weight over there at the very same moment that the rifle fired. Your weight would hit the ground at the same moment that the rifle bullet did." She waited for me to argue with her, but I said okay again.

"Even though the bullet was flying along horizontally, it was also falling. What's more, it was falling at virtually the same rate that your weight did. I'm sure you must know about artificial satellites, Sam."

I said I did, because I felt like I could remember about them if I had a little more time, and besides I had the feeling Junie would tell me anyhow.

"They orbit the Earth just as the Moon does. So why doesn't the bullet orbit it, too?"

I said it probably hit a fence post or something.

She looked at me and sort of sucked on her lips, and looked again. "That may be a much better answer than you can possibly be aware of. But no. It doesn't orbit Earth because it isn't going fast enough. A sidereal month is about twenty-seven days, and the Moon is two hundred and forty thousand miles away, on average. So if its orbit were circular—that isn't quite true, but I'm trying to make this as simple as I can— the Moon would be traveling at about three-thousand-five-hundred feet a second. Not much faster than our rifle bullet, in other words."

I could see she wanted me to nod, so I did.

"The Moon can travel that slowly." Slowly is what she said. Junie is always saying crazy stuff like that. "Because it's so far away. It would have to fall two hundred and forty thousand miles before it could hit the Earth. But the bullet has to fall only about three feet. Another way of putting it is that the closer a satellite is, the faster it must move if it is to stay in orbit."

I said that the bullet would have to go really fast, and Junie nodded. "It would have to go so fast that the curve of the Earth was falling away from it as rapidly as the bullet itself was falling toward the Earth. That's what an orbit is, that combination of vertical and horizontal motions."

Right then I do not think I was too clear on which one was which, but I nodded again.

Then Junie's voice got sort of trembly. "Now suppose that you were to make a telephone call to your

wife back in America," is what she said. So I explained I did not have one, and after that she sounded
a lot better.

"Well, if you were to call your family, your mother
and father, your call would go through a communications satellite that circles the Earth once a day, so that
it seems to us that it is always in the same place. It
can do that because it's a good deal lower and going
a great deal faster."

Then she got out a pen and a little notepad and
showed me how fast the bullet would have to go to
stay in orbit just whizzing around the world over and
over until it hit something. I do not remember how
you do it, or what the answer was except that it was
about a jillion. Junie said anything like that would
make a terrible bang all the time if it was in our air
instead of up in space where stuff like that is supposed
to be. Well about then is when the tip came in for the
last show. I did my act, and Junie sat in the front row
smiling and cheering and clapping, and I felt really
swell.

So after it was all over, we went to Merlin's cave
under the big castle and down by the water, and that
was when Junie told me how King Arthur was born
there, and I told her how I was putting up at the King
Arthur, which was a pub with rooms upstairs. I said
they were nice people there, and it was a clean and
cheap, which is what I want anywhere, and the land-
lord's name was Arthur, too, just like the pub's. Only
after a while when we had gone a long ways down the
little path and got almost to the water, I started to
sort of hint around about why are we going way down
here, Junie, with just that little flashlight you got out
of your purse?

Maybe I ought not say this right here, but it is the
truth. It was scary down there. A big person like I am
is not supposed to be and I know that. But way up
on the rocks where the fair was the lights kept on

going out and you could see the fair was just sort of
like paint on the old walls of that big castle. It was
like somebody had gone to where my dad was buried
and painted all over his stone with flowers and clowns
and puppies and kitties and all that kind of thing. Only
now the paint was flaking away and you could see what
was underneath and he had run out with his gun when
the feds broke our front door and they killed him.

Here is what I think it was down there and what
was so scary about it. King Arthur had been born
there and there had been knights and stuff afterward
that he was the head of. And they had been big strong
people like me on big strong horses and they had gone
around wearing armor and with swords and for a while
had made the bad guys pay, and everybody had loved
them so much that they still remembered all about
them after a hundred years. There was a Lancelot
room in the pub where I was staying, and a Galahad
room, and I was in the Gawain room. And Arthur
told me how those men had all been this king's
knights, and he said I was the jolly old green giant.

Only it was all over and done with now. It was dead
and gone like my dad. King Arthur was dead and his
knights were, too, and the bad guys were the head of
everything and had been for a long, long time. We
were the paint, even Junie was paint, and now the
paint was getting dull the way paint does, with cracks
all over it and falling off. And I thought this is not
just where that king was born, this is where he died,
too. And I knew that it was true the way I meant it.

Well, there was a big wire fence there with a sign
about the electricity, only it was not any fifteen feet
high. I could have reached up to the top of it. Ten
feet, maybe, or not even that.

"Can you pick me up and throw me over?" Junie
said.

It was crazy, she would have come down on rocks,

so I said I could only she would have to tell why she wanted me to so much or I would not do it.

She took my hand then, and it felt wonderful. "People come back, Sam. They come back from death. I know scientists aren't supposed to say things like that, but it's true. They do."

That made me feel even better because it meant I would see my dad again even if we would not have our farm that the feds took anymore.

"Do you remember that I said I might have been one of the fifty daughters of Thespius three thousand years ago? I don't know if that's really true, or even whether there was a real King Thespius who had fifty daughters. Perhaps there was, and perhaps I was one of them—I'd like to think so. But this really was Merlin's cave, and Roy T. Laffer was Merlin in an earlier life. There were unmistakable indications in his papers. I know it with as much certainty as I know Kepler's Laws."

That got me trying to remember who Kepler was, because I did not think Junie had told anything about him up to then. Or after either. Anyway I did not say much.

"I've tried to contact Laffer in his house in Tulsa, Sam. I tried for days at a time, but he wasn't there. I think he may be here. This is terribly important to me, and you said you'd help me. Now will you throw me over?"

I shook my head, but it was really dark down there and maybe Junie did not see it. I said I was not going to be on the other side to catch her and throw her back, so how was she going to get out? She said when they opened in the morning. I said she would get arrested, and she said she did not care. It seemed to me that there were too many getting arrested when she said that, so I twisted on the lock thinking to break the shackle. It was a pretty good lock, I broke the hasp instead. Then I threw the lock in the ocean and

Junie and I went inside like she wanted. That was how she found out where White Cow Moon was and how to get on it, too, if she wanted to.

It was about two o'clock in the morning when we came out, I think. I went back to the King Arthur's and went to bed, and next day Junie moved in down the hall. Hers was the Lancelot room. After that she was my manager, which I told everybody and showed her off. She helped me write my course then, and got this shop in Falmouth to print it up for us.

Then when the fair was over, she got us tickets home, and on the airplane we got to talking about the Moon. I started it and it was a bad mistake, but we did not know it for a couple of days. Junie had been talking about taking pictures and I said, "how can you if it goes so fast?"

"It doesn't, Sam." She took my hand, and I liked that a lot. "It circles the Earth quite slowly, so slowly that to an observer on Earth it hardly seems to move at all, which was one of the things Roy T. Laffer confided to me."

I said I never had seen him, only the lady with the baby and the old man with the stick.

"That was him, Sam. He told me then, and it was implied in his papers anyway. Do you remember the rock?"

I said there had been lots of rocks, which was true because it had been a cave in the rocks.

"I mean the White Cow Moon rock in the picture, the one he lent to the science fair."

I said, "It didn't hardly weigh anything."

"Yes." Junie was sort of whispering then. "It had very little weight, yet it was hard to move. You had to pull and pull, even though it felt so light when you held it. Do you understand what that means, Sam?"

"Somebody might have glued it down?"

"No. It means that it had a great deal of mass, but very little weight. I'm sure you haven't heard of anti-

matter—matter in which the protons are replaced by
antiprotons, the electrons by positrons and so on?"

I said no.

"It's only theoretical so far. But current theory says
that although antimatter would possess mass just as
ordinary matter does, it would be repelled by the gravitational field of ordinary matter. It would fall up, in
other words."

By the time she got to the part about falling up,
Junie was talking to herself mostly only I could still
hear her. "Our theory says a collision between matter
and antimatter should result in a nuclear explosion,
but either the theory's mistaken or there's some natural means of circumventing it. Because the White Cow
Moon rock was composed of nearly equal parts matter
and antimatter. It had to be! The result was rock with
a great deal of mass but very little weight, and that's
what allows the White Cow Moon to orbit so slowly.

"Listen to me, Sam." She made me turn in my airplane seat till I was looking at her, and I broke the
arm a little. "We physicists say that all matter falls at
the same rate, which is basically a convenient lie, true
only in a hard vacuum. If that barbell you throw
around were balsa wood, it wouldn't fall nearly as fast
as your iron one, because it would falling in air. In
the same way, a satellite with great mass but little
weight can orbit slowly and quietly through earth's
atmosphere, falling toward the surface only as fast as
the surface falls away from it."

"Wouldn't it hit a mountain or something, Junie?"

"No, because any mountain that rose in its path
would be chipped away as it rose. As light as the
White Cow Moon must be, its mass has got to be
enormous. Not knowing its orbit—not yet—we can't
know what mountain ranges it may cross, but when
we do, we'll find it goes through passes. They are passes because it goes through them."

Junie got real quiet for a while after she said that,

and now I wish she had stayed quiet. Then she said, "Just think what we could do, Sam, if we could manufacture metals like that rock. Launch vehicles that would reach escape velocity from Earth using less thrust than that of an ordinary launch vehicle on the Moon."

That as the main trouble, I think. Junie saying that was. The other may have hurt us some, too, but that did for sure.

We were flying to Tulsa. I guess I should have written about that before. Anyway, when we got there, Junie got us a bunch of rooms like an apartment in a really nice hotel. We were going to have to wait for my bells to come back on a boat, so Junie said we could look for the White Cow Moon while we were waiting, and she would line me up some good dates to play when my stuff got there. We were sitting around having Diet Cokes out of the little icebox in the kitchen when the feds knocked on the door.

Junie said, "Let me," and went, and that was how they could push in. But they would have if it had been me anyway because they had guns. I would have had to let them just like Junie.

The one in the blue suit said, "Ms. Moon?" and Junie said yes. Then he said, "We're from the government, and we've come to help you and Mr. Moon."

My name never was Moon, but we both changed ours after that anyway. She as Junie Manoe and I was Sam Manoe. Junie picked Manoe to go with JM on her bags. But that was not until after the feds went away.

What they had said was we had to forget about the Moon or we would get in a lot of trouble. Junie said we did not care about the Moon, we had nothing to do with the Moon, what we were doing mainly was getting ready to write a biography about a certain old man named Roy T. Laffer.

The man in the blue suit said, "Good, keep it that

way." The man in the black suit never did say anything, but you could see he was hoping to shoot us. I tried to ask Junie some questions after they went away, but she would not talk because she was pretty sure they were listening, or somebody was.

When we were living in the house, she explained about that, and said probably somebody on the plane had told on us, or else the feds listened to everything anybody said on planes. I said we were lucky they had not shot us, and told her about my dad, and that was when she said it was too dangerous for me. She never would tell me exactly where the White Cow Moon was after that, and it traveled around anyway, she said. But she got me a really good job in a gym there. I helped train people and showed them how to do things, and even got on TV doing ads for the gym with some other men and some ladies.

Only I knew that while I was working at the gym Junie was going out in her car looking for the White Cow Moon, and at night I would write down the mileage when she was in the living room reading. I figured she would find the White Cow Moon and go there at least a couple of times and maybe three or four, and then the mileage would always be the same. And that was how it worked out. I thought that was pretty smart of me, but I was not going to tell Junie how smart I had been until I found it myself and she could not say it was too dangerous.

I looked in her desk for Moon rocks, too, but I never found any, so that is why I do not think Junie had been up there on the White Cow Moon yet.

Well, for three days in a row it was just about one hundred and twenty-five on the mileage. It was one hundred and twenty-three one time, and one hundred and twenty-four, and then one hundred and twenty-six. So that was how I knew sixty-three miles from Tulsa. That day after work I went out and bought the biggest bike at the big Ridin' th' Wild Wind store. It

is a Harley and better for me than a car because my
head does not scrape. It is nearly big enough.

Only that night Junie did not come home. I thought
she had gone up on the White Cow Moon, so I quit
my job at the gym and went looking for her for about
a month.

A lot of things happened while I was looking for
her on my bike. Like I went into this one beer joint
and started asking people if they had seen Junie or
her car either. This one man that had a bike, too,
started yelling at me and would not let me talk to
anyone else. I had been very polite and he never
would say why he was mad. He kept saying I guess
you think you are tough. So finally I picked him up.
I think he must have weighed about three hundred
pounds because he felt like my bell when I threw him
up and banged him on the ceiling. When I let him
down, he hit me a couple of times with a chain he
had and I decided probably he was a fed and that
made me mad. I put my foot on him while I broke
his chain into five or six pieces, and every time I broke
off a new piece I would drop it on his face. Then I
picked him up again and threw him through the
window.

Then I went outside and let him pick himself up
and threw him up onto the roof. That was fifteen feet
easy and I felt pretty proud for it even if it did take
three tries. I still do.

After that, two men that had come out to watch
told me how they had seen a brown Ford like Junie's
out on this one ranch and how to get there. I went
and it was more than sixty-three miles to go and Junie's brown Ford was not there. But when I went back
to our house in Tulsa it was sixty-eight. Not a lot else
happened for about two weeks, and then I went back
to that ranch and lifted my bike over their fence real
careful and rode out to where those men had said and
sat there thinking about Junie and things that she had

said to me, and how she had felt that time I threw
her higher than the wires back in England. And it got
late and you could see the Moon, and I remembered
how she had said the feds were building a place for
missiles on the other side where nobody could reach
it or even see it, and that was why they were mad at
us. It is supposed to be to shoot at other countries
like England, but it is really to shoot at us in case we
do anything the feds do not like.

About then a man on a horse came by and said did
I want anything. I told him about the car, and he said
there used to be a brown car like that parked out
there, only a tow truck cut the fence and took it away.
I wanted to know whose truck it had been, but he did
not know.

So that is about all I have got to say. Sometimes I
dream about how while I was talking to the man on
the horse a little white moon sort of like a cloud came
by only when I turned my head to look it was already
gone. I do not think that really happened or the little
woman with the baby and the old man with the stick
in the cave either. I think it is all just dreams, but
maybe it did.

What I really think is that the feds have got Junie.
If they do, all they have got to do is let her go and I
will not be mad anymore after that. I promise. But if
they will not do it and I find out for sure they have
got her, there is going to be a fight. So if you see her
or even talk to anybody that has, it would be good if
you told me. Please.

I am not the only one that does not like the feds.
A lot of other people do not like them either. I know
that they are a whole lot smarter than I am, and how
good at telling lies and fooling people they are. I am
not like that. I am more like Roy T. Laffer because
sometimes I cannot even get people to believe the
truth.

But you can believe this, because it is true. I have

never in my whole life had a fight with a smart person or even seen anybody else have one either. That is because when the fight starts the smart people are not there anymore. They have gone off someplace else, and when it is over, they come back and tell you how much they did in the fight, only it is all lies. Now they have big important gangs with suits and guns. They are a lot bigger than just me, but they are not bigger than everybody, and if all of us get mad at once, maybe we will bring the whole thing crashing down.

After that I would look through the pieces and find Junie, or if I did not find her, I would go up on the White Cow Moon myself like Roy T. Laffer did and find her up there.

ASHES AND TOMBSTONES

by Brian Stableford

I was following Voltaire's good advice and working in my garden when the young man from the New European Space Agency came to call. I was enjoying my work; my new limb bones were the best yet and my refurbished retinas had restored my eyesight to perfection—and I was still only 40 percent synthetic by mass, 38 percent by volume.

I liked to think of the garden as my own tiny contribution to the Biodiversity Project, not so much because of the plants, whose seeds were all on deposit in half a dozen Arks, but because of the insects to which the plants provided food. More than half of the local insects were the neospecific produce of the Trojan Cockroach Project, and my salads were a key element in their selective regime. The cockroaches living in my kitchen had long since reverted to type, but I hadn't even thought of trying to clear them out; I knew the extent of the debt that my multitudinous several-times-great-grandchildren owed their even-more-multitudinous many-times-great-grandparents.

When I first caught sight of him over the hedge, I thought the young man from NESA might be one of my descendants come to pay a courtesy call on the Old Survivor, but I knew as soon as he said "Professor Neal?" that he must be an authentic stranger. I was Grandfather Paul to all my Repopulation Kin.

The stranger was thirty meters away, but his voice carried easily enough; the Berkshire Downs are very quiet nowadays, and my hearing was razor-sharp even though the electronic feed was thirty years old and technically obsolete.

"Never heard of him," I said. "No professors hereabouts. Oxford's forty miles thataway." I pointed vaguely northwestward.

"The Paul Neal I'm looking for isn't a professor anymore," the young man admitted, letting himself in through the garden gate as if he'd been invited. "Technically, he ceased to be a professor when he was seconded to the Theseus Project in Martinique in 2080, during the first phase of the Crash." He stood on the path hopefully, waiting for me to join him and usher him in through the door to my home, which stood ajar. His face was fresh, although there wasn't the least hint of synthetic tissue in its contours. "I'm Dennis Mountjoy," he added as an afterthought. "I've left messages by the dozen, but it finally became obvious that the only way to get a response was to turn up in person."

Montjoie St. Denis! had been the war cry of the French, in days of old. This Dennis Mountjoy was a mongrel European, who probably thought of war as a primitive custom banished from the world forever. It wasn't easy to judge his age, given that his flesh must have been somatically tuned-up even though it hadn't yet become necessary to paper over any cracks, but I guessed that he was less than forty: a young man in a young world. To him, I was a relic of another era, practically a dinosaur—which was, of course, exactly why he was interested in me. NESA intended to put a man on the Moon in June 2269, to mark the three-hundredth anniversary of the first landing and the dawn of the New Space Age. They had hunted high and low for survivors of the last space program, because they wanted at least one to be there to bear witness to their achievement, to forge a living link with history. It didn't matter to them that the Theseus

Project had not put a single man into space, nor directed a single officially-sanctioned shot at the Moon.

"What makes you think that you'll get any more response in person than you did by machine?" I asked the young man sourly. I drew myself erect, feeling a slight twinge in my spine in spite of all the nanomech reinforcements, and removed my sun hat so that I could wipe the sweat from my forehead.

"Electronic communication isn't very private," Mountjoy observed. "There are things that it wouldn't have been diplomatic to say over the phone."

My heart sank. I'd so far outlived my past that I'd almost come to believe that I'd escaped, but I hadn't been forgotten. I was surprised that my inner response wasn't stronger, but the more synthetic flesh you take aboard, the less capacity you have for violent emotion, and my heart was pure android. Time was when I'd have come on like the minotaur if anyone had penetrated to the core of my private maze, but all the bull leached out of my head a hundred years ago.

"Go away and leave me alone," I said wearily. "I wish you well, but I don't want any part of your so-called Great Adventure. Is that diplomatic enough for you?"

"There are things that it wouldn't have been diplomatic for *me* to say," he said, politely pretending that he thought I'd misunderstood him.

"Don't say them, then," I advised him.

"Ashes and tombstones," he recited, determinedly ignoring my advice. "Endymion. Astolpho."

There were supposed to be no records—but in a crisis, everybody cheats. Everybody keeps secrets, especially from the people they're supposed to be working for.

"Mr. Mountjoy," I said wearily, "it's 2268. I'm two hundred and eighteen years old. Everyone else who worked on Theseus is dead, along with ninety percent of the people who were alive in 2080. Ninety percent of the people alive today are under forty. Who do you think is going to give a damn about a couple of itty-bitty rockets that went up with the wrong payloads to the wrong destination? It's not as if the Chaos Patrol was left a sentry short, is it? Everything that was supposed to go up did go up."

"But that's why you don't want to come back to Martinique, isn't it?" Mountjoy said, still standing on the path, halfway between the gate and the door. "That's why you don't want to be there when the Adventure starts again. We know that the funds were channeled through your account. We know that you were the paymaster for the crazy shots. You probably didn't plan them, and you certainly didn't execute them, but you were the pivot of the seesaw."

I put my hat back on and adjusted the rim. The ozone layer was supposed to be back in place, but old habits die hard.

"Come over here," I said. "Watch where you put your feet."

He looked down at the variously-shaped blocks of salad greens. He had no difficulty following the dirt path I'd carefully laid out so that I could pass among them, patiently plying my hoe.

"You don't actually eat this stuff, do you?" he said, as he came to stand before me, looking down from his embryonically-enhanced two-meter height at my nanomech-conserved one-eighty.

"Mainly I grow it for the beetles and the worms," I told him. "They leave me little for my own plate. In essence, I'm a sharecropper for the biosphere. Repopulation's put *Homo sapiens* back in place, but the little guys still have a way to go. You really ought to wear a hat on days like this."

"It's not necessary in these latitudes," he assured me, missing the point again. "You're right, of course. Nobody cares about the extra launches. Nobody will mention it, least of all when you're on view. All we're

interested in is selling the Adventure. We believe you
can help us with that. No matter how small a cog you
were, you were in the engine. You're the last man
alive who took part in the pre-Crash space program.
You're the world's last link to Theseus, Ariane,
Apollo, and Mercury. That's all we're interested in,
all we care about. The last thing anyone wants to do
is to embarrass you, because embarrassing you would
also be embarrassing us. We're on *your* side, Professor
Neal—and if you're worried about the glare of publicity encouraging others to dig, there's no need. We
have control, Professor Neal—and we're sending our
heroes to the Sea of Tranquillity, half a world away
from Endymion. The only relics we'll be looking for
are the ones Apollo 11 left. We're not interested in
ashes or tombstones."

I knelt down, gesturing to indicate that he should
follow suit. He hesitated, but he obeyed the instruction eventually. His suitskin was easily capable of di-
gesting any dirt that got on its knees, and would
probably be grateful for the piquancy.

"Do you know what this is?" I asked, fondling a
crinkled leaf.

"Not exactly," he replied. "Some kind of engi-
neered hybrid, mid-twenty-first-cee vintage, probably
disembARked fifty or sixty years ago. The bit you eat
is underground, right? Carrot, potato—something of
that general sort—presumably gee-ee augmented as a
whole-diet crop."

He was smarter than he looked. "Not exactly whole-
diet," I corrected. "The manna-potato never really
took off. Even when the weather went seriously bad,
you could still grow manna-wheat in England thanks
to megabubbles and microwave boosters. This is head-
stuff. Ecstasy cocktail. Its remotest ancestor produced
the finest melange of euphorics and hallucinogens ever
devised—but that was a hundred generations of mutation and insect-led natural selection ago. You crush

the juice from the tubers and refine it by fractional distillation and freeze-drying—if you can keep the larvae away long enough for them to grow to maturity."

"So what?" he said, unimpressed. "You can buy designer stuff straight from the synthesizer, purity guaranteed. Growing your own is even more pointless than growing lettuces and courgettes."

"It's an adventure," I told him. "It's *my* adventure. It's the only kind I'm interested in now."

"Sure," he said. "We'll be careful not to take you away for too long. But we still need you, Professor Neal, and *our* Adventure is the one that matters to us. I came here to make a deal. Whatever it takes. Can we go inside now?"

I could see that he wasn't to be dissuaded. The young can be very persistent, when they want to be.

I sighed and surrendered. "You can come in," I conceded, "but you can't talk me 'round, by flattery or blackmail or salesmanship. At the end of the day, I don't have to do it if I don't want to." I knew it was hopeless, but I couldn't just *give in.* I had to make him do the work.

"You'll want to," he said, with serene over-confidence.

The aim of the project on which we were supposed to be working, way back in the twenty-first, was to place a ring of satellites in orbit between Earth and Mars to keep watch for stray asteroids and comets that might pose a danger to the Earth. The Americans had done the donkey-work on the payloads before the plague wars had rendered Canaveral redundant. The transfer brought the European Space Program back from the dead, although not everyone thought that was a good thing. "Why waste money protecting the world from asteroids," some said, "when we've all but destroyed it ourselves?" They had a point. Once the plague wars had set the dominoes falling, the Crash was inevitable; anyone who hoped that ten percent of the population would make it through was considered a wild-eyed optimist in 2080.

The age of manned spaceflight had been over before I was born. It didn't make economic sense to send up human beings, with the incredibly elaborate miniature ecospheres required for their support, when any job that needed doing outside the Earth could be done much better by compact clever machinery. Nobody had sent up a payload bigger than a dustbin for over half a century, and nobody was about to start. We'd sent probes to the outer system, the Oort Cloud, and a dozen neighboring star systems, but they were all machines that thrived on hard vacuum, hard radiation, and eternal loneliness. To us, there was no Great Adventure; the Theseus Project was just business—and whatever Astolpho was, it certainly wasn't an Adventure. It was just business of a subtly different kind.

Despite the superficial similarity of their names, there was nothing in our minds to connect Astolpho with Apollo. Apollo was the glorious god of the sun, the father of prophecy, the patron of all the Arts. Astolpho was a character in one of the satirical passages of the *Orlando Furioso* who journeyed to the Moon and found it a treasure-house of everything wasted on Earth: misspent time, ill-spent wealth, broken promises, unanswered prayers, fruitless tears, unfulfilled desires, failed quests, hopeless ambitions, aborted plans, and fruitless intentions. Each of these residues had its proper place: hung on hooks, stored in bellows, packed in trunks, and so on. Wasted talent was kept in vases, like the urns in which the ashes of the dead were sometimes stored in the Golden Age of Crematoria. It only takes a little leap of the imagination to think of a crater as a kind of vase.

The target picked out by the clandestine Project Astolpho was Endymion, named for the youth beloved of the Moon goddess Selene whose reward for her divine devotion was to live forever in dream-filled sleep.

Even in the days of Apollo—or shortly thereafter, at any rate—there had been people who liked the idea of burial in space. Even in the profligate twentieth, there had been dying men who did not want their ashes to be scattered upon the Earth, but wanted them blasted into space instead, where they would last *much* longer.

By 2080, when the Earth itself was dying, in critical condition at best, those who had tried hardest to save it—at least in their own estimation—became determined to save some tiny fraction of themselves from perishing with it. They did not want the relics of their flesh to be recycled into bacterial goo that would have to wait for millions of years before it essayed a new ascent toward complexity and intellect. They did not want their ashes to be consumed and recycled by the cockroaches which were every bookmaker's favorite to be the most sophisticated survivors of the eco-holocaust.

They knew, of course, that Project Astolpho was a colossal waste of money, but they also knew that *all* money would become worthless if it were not spent soon, and there was no salvation to be bought. Who could blame them for spending what might well have proved to be the last money in the world on ashes and tombstones?

Were they wrong? Would they have regretted what they had done, if they had known that the human race would survive its self-inflicted wounds? I don't know. Not one member of the aristocracy of wealth that I could put a name to came through the worst. Perhaps their servants and their mistresses came through, and perhaps not—but they themselves went down with the Ship of Fools they had commissioned, captained, and navigated. All that remains of them now is their legacies, among which the payloads deposited by illicit

Theseus launches in Endymion might easily be reckoned the least—and perhaps not the worst.

Dennis Mountjoy was right to describe me as a very small cog in the Engine of Fate. I did not plan Astolpho and I did not carry it out, but I did distribute the bribes. I was the bagman, the calculator, the fixer. Mathematics is a versatile art; it can be applied to widely different purposes. Math has no morality; it does not care what it counts or what it proves. Somewhere on Astolpho's moon, although Ariosto did not record that he ever found it, there must have been a hall of failed proofs, mistaken sums, illicit theorems, and follies of infinity, all neatly bound in webs of tenuous logic.

Had I not had the modest wealth I took as my commission on the extra Theseus shots, of course, I could not have been one of the survivors of the Crash. Had it not been for my brokerage of Project Astolpho, I could not have been, by the time that Dennis Mountjoy came to call, one of the oldest men in the world: the founder of a prolific dynasty. I, too, would have been nothing but ash, without even a tombstone, when the New Apollonians decided that it was time to reassert the glory and the godhood of the human race by duplicating its most magnificent folly: the Great Adventure.

I had never had any part in the first Adventure, and I wanted no part in the second. I had worked alongside men who had launched rockets into outer space, but the only things I ever helped to land on the Moon were the cargoes provided by the Pharaohs of Capitalism: the twenty-first century's answer to Pyramids.

I was companion to Astolpho, not Apollo: whenever I raised my eyes to the night sky, I saw nothing in the face of the Moon but the wastes of Earthly dreams and Earthly dreamers.

"None of that is relevant," Dennis Mountjoy told me, when I had explained it to him—or had tried to (the account just now set down has, of course, taken full advantage of *l'espirt de l'escalier*). He sat in an armchair waving his hands in the air. I had almost begun to wish that I'd offered him a cup of tea and a slice of cake, so that at least a few of his gestures would have been stifled.

"It's relevant to me," I told him, although I was fully cognizant by then of the fact that he had not the least interest in what was relevant to me.

"None of it's ever going to come out," he assured me. "You can forget it. You may be two-hundred-and-some years old, but that doesn't mean that you have to live in the past. We have to think of the future now. You should try to forget. That's what a good memory is, when all's said and done: one that can forget all the things it doesn't need to retain. There's no need for you to be hung up on the differences between Apollo and Astolpho in a world which can no longer tell them apart. As you said yourself, ninety percent of the people alive today are under forty. To them, it's all ancient history, and the names are just sounds. Apollo, Ariane, Theseus—it's all merged into a single mythical mishmash, including all the sidelines, official and unofficial. From the point of view of the people who believe in the New Adventure, and the people who *will* believe, once we've captured their imagination, it's all part of the same story, the one we're starting over. Your presence at the launch will confirm that. All that anyone will see when they look at you is a miracle: the last survivor of Project Theseus; the envoy of the First Space Age, extending his blessing to the Second."

"Do you know why Project Theseus was called by that name?" I asked him.

"Of course I do," he replied. "I know my history, even though I refuse to be bogged down by it. Ariane was the rocket used in the first European Space Program, named for the French version of Ariadne,

48 *Brian Stableford*

daughter of Minos of Crete. Theseus was one of seven
young men delivered to Minos as a tribute by the
Athenians, along with seven young women; they were
to be sacrificed to the minotaur—a monster that lived
in the heart of a maze called the labyrinth. Ariadne
fell in love with Theseus and gave him a thread which
allowed him to keep track of his route through the
maze. When he had killed the minotaur, he was able
to find his way out again. Theseus was the name given
to Ariane's successor in order to signify that it was
the heroic project which would secure humankind's
escape from the minotaur in the maze: the killer asteroid that might one day wipe out civilization."

"That's the official decoding," I admitted. "But
Theseus was also the betrayer of Ariane. He abandoned her. According to some sources, she committed
suicide or died of grief—but others suggested that she
was saved by Dionysus, the antithesis of Apollo."

"So what?" said Mountjoy, making yet another ex-
pansive gesture. "Whatever you and your crazy pals
might have read into that back in 2080, it doesn't matter *now*."

"Crazy pals?" I queried, remembering his earlier
reference to the Astolpho launches as "crazy shots."
Now I was beginning to wish that I had a cup of tea;
my own hands were beginning to stir as if in answer
to his.

"The guys who gave you the money to shoot their
ashes to the Moon," the young man said. "The Syndi-
cate. The Captains of Industry. The Hardinist Cartel.
Pick your cliché. They *were* crazy, weren't they? Paying you to drop those payloads in Endymion was only
the tip of the iceberg. I mean, they were the people
with the power—the people who had steered the
world straight into the Crash. That has to be reckoned
as causing death by dangerous driving—manslaughter
on a massive scale. Mad, bad, and dangerous to know,
wouldn't you say?"

"They didn't see it that way themselves," I pointed out mildly.

"They certainly didn't," he agreed. "But you're older and wiser, and you have the aid of hindsight, too. So give me your considered judgment, Professor Neal. Were they or were they not prime candidates for the straitjacket?"

I granted him a small laugh, but kept my hands still. "Maybe so," I said. "Maybe so. Can I get you a drink, by the way?"

He beamed, thinking that he'd won. One crack in the facade was all it needed to convince him.

"No thanks. We know how bad things were back then, and we don't blame you at all for what you did. The world is new again, and its newness is something for us all to celebrate. I understand why you've tried so hard to hide yourself away, and why you've built a maze of misinformation around your past. I understand how the thought of coming out of your shell after all these years must terrify you—but we *will* look after you. We *need* you, Professor Neal, to play Theseus in our own heroic drama. We need you to play the part of the man who slew the minotaur of despair and found the way out of the maze of human misery. I understand that you don't see yourself that way, that you don't *feel* like that kind of a hero, but in our eyes, that's what you are. In our eyes, and in the eyes of the world, you're the last living representative of early humanity's greatest adventure—the Adventure we're now taking up. We need you at the launch. We really can't do without you. Anything you want, just ask—but I'm here to make a deal, and I have to make it. No threats, of course, just honest persuasion—but I really do have to persuade you. You'll be in the news whether you like it or not—why not let us doctor the spin for you? If you're aboard, you have input; if not . . . you might end up with all the shit and none of the roses."

No threats, he'd said. Funnily enough, he meant it. He wouldn't breathe a word to a living soul—but if he'd found out about Astolpho, others could, and once the Great Adventure was all over the news, the incentive to dig would be there. Expert webwalkers researching Theseus would be bound to stumble over Astolpho eventually. The only smoke screen I could put up now was the smoke screen he was offering to lend me. If I didn't take it, I hadn't a hope of keeping the secret within the secret.

"Are you *sure* you wouldn't like something to drink?" I asked tiredly. His semaphoring arms and had begun to make my newly-reconditioned eyes feel dizzy.

He beamed again and almost said "Perhaps I will," but then his eyes narrowed slightly. "What *kind* of drink?" he said.

"I make it myself," I told him teasingly.

"That's what I'm afraid of," he said. "I've nothing against happy juice, but this isn't the time or the place—not for me. And to be perfectly honest, I'm not sure I could trust the homegrown stuff. You said yourself that it's been subject to generations of mutation and selection, and you know how delicate hybrid gentemplates are. Meaning no offense, but that garden is *infested*—and not everything that came out of Cade Maclaine's souped-up Trojan Cockroaches was a pretty pollen-carrier."

"Why should I help out in your Adventure," I asked him lightly, "if you won't help out in mine?"

He looked at me long and hard. It didn't need a trained mathematician to see the calculating clicking over in his mind. Whatever it took, he'd said. Anything I wanted, just ask.

"Well," he said finally, "I take your point. Are we talking about a deal here, or what? Are we talking about coming to an understanding? Sealing a compact?"

"Just the launch," I said. "One day only. You can make as much noise as you like—the more the merrier—but I only come out for one day. And everything you put out is Theseus, Theseus, and more Theseus. What's lost stays lost, from here to eternity."

"If that's what you want," he said. "One day only— and we'll give them so much Theseus they'll drown in it. Astolpho stays under wraps—*nobody* says a word about it. Not now, not ever. The records are ours, and we have no interest in letting the cat escape the bag. If we thought anyone would blow the whistle, we wouldn't want you waving us off. This is the Adventure, after all: the greatest moment so far in the history of the new human race. So far as we're concerned, the ashes of Endymion can stay buried for another two hundred years—or another two million. It doesn't matter; come the day when somebody stumbles over the tombstones, they'll just be an archaeological find: a nine day wonder. By then, we'll be out among the stars. Earth will be just our cradle."

I had thought when he first confronted me that he didn't have anything I wanted, just something he could threaten me with. I realized now that he had both— but he didn't know it. He and his crazy pals thought that they needed me at their launch, to give the blessing of the old human race to the new, and I needed them to be perfectly content with what they thought they had, to dig just so far and no farther. It had been foolish of me to refuse to return his calls, without even knowing what he had to say, and exactly how much he might have discovered.

"All right," I said, with all the fake weariness that a 40 percent synthetic man of two hundred and eighteen can muster. "You've worn me down. I give in. I do the launch, and the rest is silence. I appear, smile, disappear. Remembered for one brief moment, forgotten forever. Once I'm out of the way, your guys are the only heroes. Okay?"

"There *might* be other inquiries from TV," he said guardedly, "but as far as we're concerned, it's just the one symbolic gesture. That's all we need. I can't imagine that there'll be anything else that you can't reasonably turn down. You're two hundred and eighteen yeas old, after all. Nobody will get suspicious if you plead exhaustion."

"If you're so utterly convinced that you need it," I said, "who am I to deny you? And you're right— whatever other calls come in, I can be forgiven for refusing to answer on the grounds of creeping senility. I'll program my answerphone to imply that I really couldn't be trusted not to wet myself if I were face-to-face with a famous chat show host. *Now* do you want a drink? Nothing homemade, if you insist—for you I'll make an exception. I'll even break the seal in front of you, if you like."

"There's no need," he said, with an airy wave of his right hand. His voice was redolent with relief and triumph. "I trust you."

Theseus betrayed Ariadne; of that much the voice of myth is as certain as the voice of myth can ever be. If she did not die, she was thrust into the arms of Dionysus, the god of intoxication. If grief did not kill her, she gave herself over to the mind-blowing passion of the Bacchae.

"Ashes and tombstones" were the names that the Pharaohs of Capitalism gave to the payloads which they paid my associates to deposit in Endymion, near the north pole of the Moon. Ashes to ashes, dust to dust . . . but the remnants of their flesh that they sent to Endymion, actual vases to be placed within a symbolic vase, were not the remains of their dead. The "ashes" were actually frozen embryos: not their dead, but their multitudinous unborn children.

The "tombstones" carried aloft by valiant Astolpho were not inscribed with their epitaphs but with instructions for the resurrection of the human species, so deeply and so cleverly ingrained that they might still be deciphered after a million or a billion years, even by members of a species which had evolved a million or a billion light-years away and had formulated a very different language.

Like the Pharaohs of old, the Pharaohs of the End Time fully intended to rise again; their pyramids were not built as futile monuments but as fortresses to secure themselves against disaster.

Against *all* disaster, that is.

My "crazy pals" had believed that the world was doomed, and humankind with it. There was nothing remotely crazy in that belief, in 2080. The Earth was dying, and nothing short of a concatenation of miracles could have saved it. Perhaps the Pharaohs of Capitalism had been crazy to have let the world get into such a state, but they were not miracle workers themselves; they were only men. They thought that the only hope for humankind was to slumber for a million or a billion years in the bosom of the Moon, until someone might come who would recognize the Earth for the grave it was, and would search for relics of the race whose grave it was in the one place where such relics might have survived the ravages of decay: hard vacuum.

The disaster they had feared so much had not, in the end, been absolute. The human race had come through the crisis. Cade Maclaine's cockroach-borne omnispores and the underground Arks had enabled them to resuscitate the ecosphere and massage the fluttering rhythm of its heart back to steadiness.

By now, of course, the game had changed. The Repopulation was almost complete, and the Adventure had begun again. The New Human Race believed that its future was secure, and that the tricentennial launch of the mission to the Era of Tranquillity would help to make it secure.

Well, perhaps.

And perhaps not.

I knew that if the new Adventurers found the vases of Endymion, they would be reckoned merely one more Ark: one more seed-deposit, to be drawn on as and when convenient. The children of the Pharaohs would be disembArked at the whim and convenience of men like Dennis Mountjoy, who believed with all his heart that the minotaur at the heart of the labyrinth of fate was dead and gone, and every ancient nightmare with him.

That, to the crazy men who had paid my prices in order to deposit their heritage in Endymion, would almost certainly have seemed to be a disaster as great as the one that had been avoided. The Pharaohs had not handed down fortunes so that their offspring could be reabsorbed into the teeming millions of the New Human race, but in order that they should become *the* human race: a unique marvel in their own right.

Perhaps they were crazy to want that, but that is what they wanted. "Ashes and tombstones" was a smoke screen, intended to conceal a bid for resurrection, immortality, and the privilege of uniqueness in a universe where humankind was utterly forgotten—and nothing less.

My motives were somewhat different, of course, but I wanted the same result.

At two hundred and eighteen years of age, and having lived through the Crash, I could never convince myself that it could not happen again—but even if it never did, I wanted the vases of Endymion to rest in peace, not for a hundred years or a thousand, but for a million or a billion, as their deliverers had intended.

I did not want the "ashes and tombstones" to become an archaeological find and a nine day wonder. I wanted them to remain where they were until they were found by those who had been intended to find them: nonhuman beings, for whom the task of disembArkation would be an act of reCreation. It did not matter to me whether they were the spawn of another star or the remotest descendants of the ecosphere of Earth, remade by countless generations of mutation and selection into something far stranger than the New Human race—but I, too, wanted to leave my mark on the face of eternity. I, too, wanted to have gouged out a scratch on the infinite wall of the future, to have played a part in making something that would last, not for seventy years or two hundred, or even two thousand—which is as long as any man might reasonably expect to live, aided by our superbly clever and monstrously chimerical technologies of self-repair—but for two million or two billion.

All I had done was to calculate the price, but without me, none of it would have happened. The Moon would have been *exactly* as Astolpho found it: a treasury of the lost and the wasted, the futile and the functionless.

Thanks to me, it is more than that. In a million or a billion years, the time will come for the resurrection, and the new life. I do not want it to be soon: the longer, the better.

I thoroughly enjoyed the launch. I enjoyed it so tremendously, in fact, that I was glad I had allowed myself to be persuaded to take my place among its architects, to give their bold endeavor the blessing of all the billions of people who had died while I was young.

I was unworthy, of course. Who among us is not? Nor can I believe, even now, that Dennis Mountjoy was correct in thinking that his heroes needed me to set the seal of history on their endeavor—but the sight of that rocket riding its pillar of fire into the deep blue of the sky brought back so many memories, so many echoes of a self long-buried and half-forgotten, that I almost broke down and wept.

"I had forgotten what a sight it was," I admitted to the young man, "and I thought that I had lost the capacity to feel such deep emotions, along with the fleshy tables of my first heart."

He did not recognize the quotation, which came from Paul's second epistle to the Corinthians: an epistle, according to the text, "written not with ink but with the Spirit of the living God; not in tables of stone, but in fleshy tables of the heart." All he had to say in reply was: "I told you that you'd want to be here. This is Apollo reborn, Theseus reborn. This is what all the heroes of the race were made to accomplish. This time, we'll go all the way to the stars, whatever it costs."

Astolpho, your creator had not the least idea what truth he served when he sent you to the Moon, to discern its real nature and its real purpose.

THE WAY TO NORWICH

by Colin Greenland

1959

The Man in the Moon
Came down too soon
To ask the way to Norwich.
He went to the south
And burned his mouth
By eating cold pease porridge.

Tommy knew who the Man in the Moon was. His house was on the other side of the road.

The Man in the Moon's house was bigger than theirs. It was white, with thick black crooked lines all across the front of it. The lines made the house look like a jigsaw puzzle, Tommy thought; a really easy one, for babies.

Outside the Man in the Moon's house there was a picture of him. It was painted on a board that hung out over the door, on a sort of pole. It was the same picture on both sides of the board. If he went into Mummy's and Daddy's room, Tommy could see it out of their window.

In the picture, the Man in the Moon was sitting in the black night sky with little white stars all around him. He had a little skinny body and a big round shining yellow head. He was laughing. Under the picture, in black letters, was written his name: *The Man in the Moon.*

The Man in the Moon sat with his feet up, hugging his knees. He was wearing dark blue pajamas, with big yellow stars. The stars on the Man in the Moon's pajamas had five points, the way they did in pictures, that was so hard when you tried to draw them yourself.

On his feet the Man in the Moon had blue shoes with curly toes, and on his head a long skinny blue hat that hung all the way down his back. Mummy told Tommy the hat was a nightcap. In the olden days, she said, people used to wear hats like that in bed, to keep their heads warm.

Tommy was sorry for the Man in the Moon. He didn't think that hat could keep his head very warm. His head was so huge, and the hat was tiny. Tommy was sure it would fall off in the night. He tried to look into the Man in the Moon's bedroom, but the windows were made of round bits of glass like the bottoms of bottles, and you couldn't see in.

Tommy thought it would be a good idea if they had a picture of them outside their house; a picture of Mummy and Daddy and Tommy, with their names underneath. He asked Mummy if they could. She laughed and said it was a very good idea, so Tommy got a piece of paper and painted Mummy and Daddy with himself in the middle, holding their hands. He climbed on a chair and put the picture in the window, for everyone to see when they came along the street.

Daddy said the Man in the Moon's house was a public house. That Tommy didn't understand, though Daddy had tried to explain it to him. "Public" meant belonging to people. The public was everybody, everybody in the whole world. A public house was one everybody could go in, not just the people who lived there.

"Can we go in, Mummy?" Tommy asked one day, on the way home from school. He had run ahead of her so that he could linger outside the Man in the

Moon's house and try to look through the funny windows.

"It's not for little boys," Mummy said firmly. She took hold of his hand to cross the road.

"Why not?" asked Tommy.

"It's for people who drink," she told him. She didn't sound as if she approved of those people.

Tommy was more confused than ever. "I drink," he told her, as she turned the key in their front door. Tommy's favorite drink was milk. He didn't like fizzy drinks, because the bubbles went up his nose. "You drink, too," he said, sitting on the stairs to undo his shoelaces. "And Daddy does." Mummy's and Daddy's favorite drink was a cup of tea. Tommy didn't like that either. It was hot and tasted nasty. He started to ask Mummy why she and Daddy never went into the Man in the Moon's house, but she told him to stop asking so many questions and hurry up and wash his hands and face before tea.

They read the rhyme about the Man in the Moon on Children's Hour, on the wireless. Norwich was a town, a real one, Tommy knew. He didn't know where it was. He supposed it must be in the north, because the thing about the Man in the Moon rhyme was that it was nonsense. It didn't mean what it said. How could you burn your mouth by eating cold porridge? And whoever heard of putting peas in porridge anyway? So if the Man in the Moon went south, Norwich must be in the north. Anyway, its name started with *Nor,* and that sounded like *north.*

Before he got into bed that night, Tommy went to look at the picture of the Man in the Moon. It was dark, but there was a light that shone on the sign. The Man in the Moon looked happy. His eyes were closed, and he was laughing very hard, as if he knew a brilliant joke. He didn't look much like the *real* Man in the Moon.

The real Man in the Moon wasn't yellow. He was

cold gray and black and white, the colors of the ashes
Daddy cleaned out of the fireplace every morning. The
real Man in the Moon didn't look happy at all.

Tommy remembered Granddad telling him about
the real Man in the Moon. He was a poor old man,
and he'd been sent to live in the Moon, a long long
time ago, as a punishment for gathering firewood on
a Sunday. Tommy knew what firewood was. It was the
sticks that Daddy laid on top of the crumpled-up
paper in the fireplace, with the dirty black coal on top.
When the flames found them, the sticks went *pop*! and
crack! Tommy didn't know why you weren't supposed
to gather firewood on a Sunday, but Granddad said a
lot of things he didn't understand, and he wasn't sure
if he should ask.

Granddad smelled of shoe polish and tobacco. His
hands had brown spots on the backs of them. He had
held Tommy up to show him the full moon rising over
the hill. "There's the old man, Tommy," said Granddad, pointing. "There's his lantern, look. And the bundle of firewood, over his shoulder. And there's his
dog. Eh? See?"

But Tommy couldn't see a dog or a lantern, or any
firewood. All Tommy could see was the face. It was
the face of the real Man in the Moon. And he wasn't
laughing. He was screaming.

1969

*"The Moon belonged to the poets as long as it was out
of reach."*

"And this is what crowns you," said Melissa, as she
leaned down and turned over Trump XVIII: La Lune.

On the floor, Thomas was trying to concentrate. He
was more aware of Melissa than of the cards. Melissa
had wonderful long blonde hair that smelled of patch-
ouli, and big soulful eyes that were easy to get lost in.

"Terror, deception, occult powers, error," said Melissa, reading from her battered brown book. For an instant, Thomas felt all those forces, each as she named it. It was only the third time Melissa had come home with him, and this time they had had a joint together in the cemetery on the way. Thomas was awash with sensations. It was as if the floodgates of his senses had been opened to the universe in general, and Melissa in particular.

Melissa was two years older than him, nearly, and full of strange passions and ideals. She inspired him. Whatever she said was true, and not only true but profoundly revealing. She was sitting on his bed, though, and when she moved about, as she constantly did, Thomas could sometimes see up her miniskirt, which made it hard to think. He was desperate to show her he was a spiritual being, as she was, and not like the oafs in her year, who treated girls like plastic dolls, created for their pleasure, and boasted about it afterward.

On Thomas' bedside cabinet, the flames of the candles dipped and soared. On the record player his Jefferson Airplane album circled, the volume turned low so as not to disturb his parents downstairs. The lyrics kept getting muddled up with the drone of the TV, canned sitcom laughter floating among proclamations of the youth revolution.

"The hero is at a critical stage." Melissa's voice as she read was slow and solemn. "His existence lies in the balance."

Thomas caught his breath. He nodded gravely. He could practically feel that balance, tipping back and forth beneath him like a seesaw. Life, whatever it was, couldn't be just A levels and *Dr. Who* on Saturday afternoons. There was Poetry, and Justice, and the Cosmos, and, and, and Melissa's bare thighs, oh, God—

"If he allows himself to be entranced by the glamour of the Moon, his quest is at an end."

The cards lay on the carpet, a pattern of gaudy images, primitive and secret. They were telling him something important, if only he could see it. There was the Moon, a big pink circle with a face like a Victorian doll, and a yellow crescent under her chin. Below the Moon, a young man in a floppy hat was sitting by a tree, serenading an oversized woman who gestured to him from a miniature balcony. Beside the man lay a dog. Thomas supposed it was a dog, though it looked more like a sheep that had just been sheared. Beneath the man and the dog, drawn from a completely different angle as if it was actually part of another picture, there seemed to be a wall with a lobster crawling up it.

Melissa reached down and put her hand on his.

"You're on a quest, Thomas, aren't you?" she said. Her touch was warm, shockingly real. "You're a seeker. Yes . . ." She lifted her chin, satisfied with her diagnosis, sweeping her hair out of her face with the tip of her middle finger. "It's in your aura."

Thomas gazed at her until his eyes started to water. Blinking, ashamed, he looked back at the cards. *La Lune,* the Moon. The Americans had landed on the Moon, this summer. Thomas had seen them on TV, blobby white humans trampling that clean virgin world, exporting their imperialistic havoc. The BBC had played "Space Oddity" by David Bowie, not realizing it was actually a song of alienation and despair. It was ironic. It was true. The pub across the road had immediately changed its name, from The Man in the Moon to The Man *on* the Moon, and put up a new sign, of a figure in a space suit standing on a bleak gray plain with the Earth floating over his shoulder like a big blue-and-white marble. Thomas had sat in the library during break and written a poem about it all, about the rape of Diana by Apollo. He was quite pleased with that one. He wanted to get it now and show it to Melissa, but he was spellbound. His legs wouldn't move.

"The trump is number eighteen in the sequence," read Melissa, "which in Arabic numerals reduces to nine."

Thomas was wondering whether he should tell her about the Man in the Moon, that he had used to believe that the pub was the home of the man on the sign, the laughing man in the suit of stars. Thomas had never set foot in that pub. He never would, now that the Man in the Moon was gone.

Melissa had put aside her book. She was sitting back against the wall with her feet drawn up, hugging her knees. Dreamily she said:

"Habib the Wise commanded Mohammed to prove he was the Prophet by cutting the Moon in two. So Mohammed called the Moon, and she came down out of the sky for him. She flew seven times around the roof of the temple, and then she flew up the sleeve of Mohammed's garment. She flew up the right sleeve, and down the left. Then she went down inside the neck of his garment, and came out of the bottom. Then she split in two, like two strands of wool. One strand rose up in the eastern sky, and the other rose up in the west. And then the two halves joined themselves together again, and became whole."

What had she been saying? What had they been talking about? The sound of her words dinned in his head. The candlelight danced, and the moment swirled away from him like water.

1999

"The dirt adheres in fine layers, like powdered charcoal."

The days were getting shorter. The light was almost gone, though Dad was still out in the garden. Tom

could see him from the window of the spare room, in
his old mac and his wellingtons. Since Mum had died,
he spent most of this time out there, weeding, water-
ing, tending his beetroot and his runner beans.

Eventually he'd get too old to look after himself,
and then Tom and Sandra would have to have him.
The prospect didn't fill Tom with joy. Not that there
was anything wrong with the old man, really. It was
just what came with him: the past, his childhood; this
place. The thought of still owing it anything de-
pressed him.

There was any amount of junk in here, waiting to be
cleared out. That would be up to him, too, obviously.
Ancient books no one could possibly want to read; ancient lamps with parchment shades and fabric-covered
flexes; an ancient carpet, rolled up and propped between
the wall and the wardrobe. That he recognized, that
had been down in here when this had been his room.
What on earth had they been keeping that for? Irrita-
bly, Tom reached into the gap and pulled at it, reminding himself of its feel and smell, its hideous
pattern. Dislodged from somewhere, something flut-
tered down, striking his hand as it fell.

Tom crouched down to look for it. It was on the
floor under the wardrobe. He pulled it out.

It was a piece of stiff card, a rectangle with the
corners rounded off, printed with a pattern of diamond shapes. It looked like a playing card, but longer.

Memory began to stir in him. Candlelight, a musky
perfume. He turned the card over.

It certainly wasn't a card from any normal pack. It
had bold black Roman numerals at the top, XVIII,
and at the bottom, in capital letters, a title: LA LUNE.

The picture showed a young man with a dog and a
mandolin serenading a woman by moonlight. The
Moon had a calm, childish face. It was vast, fifty times
too big for the sky. There was a tree, mountains in
the distance, a castle on a hill.

Beneath that quaint scene, dividing the card in two, the artist had drawn a sort of ledge, like the eaves of a building. Beneath that was a strange stripy wall with two doorways and, climbing up between them, three unpleasant-looking creatures. At least the middle one was a creature, a bright red lobster sort of thing. The ones on either side looked more like a cross between weevils and radishes. It was all really quite grotesque.

A tarot card. He remembered now, perfectly. Well, rather hazily, to tell the truth. She must have dropped it. The girl. Big dopey eyes, very pretty. Fifteen he had been, sixteen. Utterly bewitched by her. What on earth was her name?

He looked at Dad out there, grubbing in the earth. For a moment he had the urge to throw up the window and call out to him, to ask him if he remembered. A sense of prudence, of potential embarrassment, dissuaded him.

Tarot cards. The I Ching, signs of the Zodiac. Mystical messages concealed on record sleeves. *La Lune,* yes, absolutely. Lunacy.

Tom shook his head and stood up, brushing fluff and dust from his hands. Not certain what he was doing in here anyway, he went next door, into Dad's room.

In there it was much tidier. The bed was made, the curtains gathered neatly in their retaining loops. Across the road, above the roofs, the Moon was rising.

A few short months ago, he had held a piece of the Moon in his hand.

"The surface is fine and powdery," Armstrong had told the listening world. (Or had it been Aldrin?) *"I can pick it up loosely with my tool."*

He had held it in his hand, but he hadn't been able to touch it.

It had arrived by Securicor, under lock and key in its own special carrying case, just like the case Mum and Dad bought him for his LP's when he went to university. Inside the case was a block of lucite; and inside that, a small portion of grit. It looked like something you might find in the bottom of a Hoover bag.

Moon rock. The head had applied for it, months before. This year was the anniversary of the first landing, he had reminded the staff. Everybody would be after Moon rock this summer, every school in the world.

Tom had passed the lucite block round the class. They had all wanted to see it. He had been struck by the way they had rubbed the surface of the block with their fingers while they peered into it, as if they hoped to pick up something from inside, some sensation, some *manna*.

"This sample is particularly interesting because it's igneous, which means what, anyone?" Blank faces. He wrote the word on the board and asked which of them was studying Latin, at which point someone, one of the bright ones, had volunteered that *ignis* was Latin for fire. Once upon a time, back before history began, the Taurus Mountains had been volcanoes, belching up molten rock. Fire on the Moon, what would the astrologers have made of that? This spoonful of pinkish ash, the most precious dirt in the world, had been brought back in 1972, Tom told them, by Harrison H. Schmitt, the first geologist on the Moon. Blank faces again. Who remembered Harrison H. Schmitt now, or Mission Commander Eugene A. Cernan? 1972, a dozen years before they were born, any of them. That was prehistory, too, now.

Melissa. That was her name. Someone had told him she had gone off and joined one of those cults. The Unification church, was it? Paper flowers and mantras, some Southeast Asian millionaire creaming off the profits.

The bedroom smelled stale, smelled of old man. Tom worked the sticking window down and let in three inches of damp autumn twilight.

The pub had been remodeled, plain plate glass windows put in at last, and the ludicrous half-timbering plastered over with some smooth inoffensive beige compound. They had changed its name again. Now it was The Office. The sign showed a man in a bowler hat. His face was blank, expressionless, like the men's in those Magritte paintings. He was raising a foaming tankard.

Behind the pub the Moon climbed slowly up the murky sky, farther away than ever.

"The word *moon* comes from an old word meaning *measure*," Tom had told his class, "because the Moon is the measurer of time. The Moon orbits the Earth every 27.32 days at a mean distance of 384,400 kilometers, always keeping the same face turned toward the Earth." The same face, the same screaming face. "It is 3,476 kilometers in diameter, and has a very thin atmosphere. As a consequence the temperature varies from 110 degrees Centigrade all the way down to minus 180."

Tom hadn't known any of these facts and figures himself. He had looked them up the night before on a CD-ROM in the library.

"Sorry I'm late, dear, I had to go into the Office . . ."

Something else he'd found in the library, that he hadn't told them:

In 1532, in his epic poem *Orlando Furioso*, Ludovico Ariosto described how the English knight, Astolpho, was taken to the Moon in a chariot, the same chariot that carried Elijah up to Heaven. The Moon, Astolpho found, was a "rich champain, with a valley where everything that is lost on Earth is collected and prized as treasure: wasted time, wasted money, unanswered prayers, idle tears, vain attempts, lost reputations, broken promises."

Tom checked his watch. He'd promised Sandra he'd be home by ten. He pushed the window up a couple of inches. Before he left, he'd have to make sure Dad knew it was open. They didn't want him sleeping in a draft and catching a chill.

Reaching to close the curtains, Tom felt something in his hip pocket, something stiff. He took it out. It was the tarot card, La Lune. He hadn't even known he'd put it in there. He stood there, looking at it. He didn't want it, but he couldn't just throw it in the bin.

He looked across at the pub again. The upstairs windows were dark, but as he looked, Tom was sure he could see something shining behind one of them, something big and round and yellow. It was someone with a huge round yellow head. Tom could see him quite distinctly through the glass. He had a long skinny blue nightcap perched on top that hung all the way down behind. His face was comically contorted, the eyes screwed up tight and the mouth open wide with mirth.

The Man in the Moon was still there; still laughing.

STEPS ALONG THE WAY

by *Eric Brown*

On the eve of my five hundredth rebirthday, as I strolled the gardens of my manse, a messenger appeared and informed me that I had a visitor.

"Severnius wishes to consult you on a matter of urgency," said the ball of the light. "Shall I make an appointment?"

"Severnius? How long has it been? No—I'll see him now."

The light disappeared.

It was the end of a long autumn afternoon, and a low sun was filling the garden with a rich and hazy light. I had been contemplating my immediate future, quite how I should approach the next century. I am a man methodical and naturally circumspect: not for me the grand announcements of intent detailing how I might spend my *next* five hundred years. I prefer to plan ahead one hundred years at a time, ever hopeful of the possibility of change, within myself and without. For the past week I had considered many avenues of inquiry and pursuit; but none had appealed to me. I had awoken early that morning, struck with an idea like a revelation: Quietus.

I composed myself on a marble bench beneath an arbor entwined with fragrant roses. The swollen sun sank amid bright tangerine strata, and on the other side of the sky the moon rose, full yet insubstantial, above the manse.

Severnius stepped from the converter and crossed

the glade. He always wore his primary soma-form when we met, as a gesture of respect: that of a wise man of yore, with flowing silver-gray hair and beard. He was a Fellow some two thousand years old, garbed in the magenta robes of the Academy.

We embraced in silence, a short communion in which I reacquainted myself with his humanity.

"Fifty years?" I asked.

He smiled. "More like eighty," he said, and then gave the customary greeting of these times: "To your knowledge."

"Your knowledge," I responded.

We sat and I gestured, and wine and glasses appeared upon the bench between us.

"Let me see, the last time we met you were still researching the Consensus of Rao."

"I concluded that it was an unworkable proposition, superseded by the latest theories." I smiled. "But worth the investigation."

Severnius sipped his wine. "And now?"

"I wound down my investigations ten years ago, and since then I've been exploring the Out-there. Seeking the new . . ."

He smiled, something almost condescending in his expression. He was my patron and teacher; he was disdainful of the concept of the new.

"Where are you now?" he asked. "What have you found?"

"Much as ever, permutations of what has been and what is known . . ." I closed my eyes, and made contact. "I^2 is on Pharia, in the Nilakantha Stardrift, taking in the ways of the natives there; I^3 is in love with a quasi-human on a nameless moon half a galaxy away; I^4 is climbing Selerious Mons on Titan."

"It appears that you are . . . *waiting?*" he said. "Biding your time with meaningless pursuits. Considering your options for the next century."

I hesitated. It occurred to me then how propitious

was his arrival. I would never have gone ahead with Quietus without consulting him.

"A thought came to me this morning, Severnius. Five hundred years is a long time. With your tutelage and my inquiries . . ." I gestured, "I have learned much, dare I say everything? I was contemplating a period of Quietus."

He nodded, considering my words. "A possibility," he agreed. "Might I inquire as to the duration?"

'It really only occurred to me at dawn. I don't know—perhaps a thousand years."

"I once enjoyed Quietus for five hundred," said Severnius. "I was reinvigorated upon awakening—the thrill of change, the knowledge of the learning to be caught up with."

"Precisely my thoughts."

"There is an alternative, of course."

I stared at him. "There is?"

He hesitated, marshaling his words. "My Fellows at the Academy last week Enstated and Enabled an Early," he said. "The process, though wholly success-ful physiologically, was far from psychologically ful-filled. We had to wipe his memories of the initial awakening and instruction. We are ready to try again."

I stared at him. The Enstating and Enabling of an Early was a rare occurrence indeed. I said as much.

"You," Severnius said, "were the last."

Even though I had been considered a success, my rehabilitation had required his prolonged patronage. I thought through what he had told me so far, the "ur-gency" of his presence here.

He was smiling. "I have been watching your progress closely these past eighty years," he said. "I submitted your name to the Academy. We agreed that you should be made a Fellow, subject to the successful completion of a certain test."

"And that is?" I asked, aware of my heartbeat. All

thought of Quietus fled at the prospect of becoming a Fellow.

"The patronage and stewardship of the Early we Enstated and Enabled last week," Severnius said.

It was a while before I could bring myself to reply. Awareness of the great honor of being considered by the Academy was offset by my understanding of the difficulty of patronage. "But you said that the subject was psychologically damaged."

Severnius gestured. "You studied advanced psychohealing in your second century. We have confidence in your abilities."

"It will be a considerable undertaking. A hundred years, more?"

"When we Enstated and Enabled you, I was your steward for almost fifty years. We think that perhaps a hundred years might suffice in this case."

"Perhaps," I said, "before I make a decision, might I meet the subject?"

Severnius nodded. "By all means," he replied, and while he gave me the details of the Early, his history, I closed my eyes and made contact. I recalled I^2 from his studies on Pharia, and I^4 from Titan. I^3 I gave a little time to conclude his affair with the alien. I would need to be augmented if I was to be successful with the Early.

Minutes later I^2 and I^4 followed each other from the converter and stepped across the glade, calling greetings to Severnius. They appeared as younger, more carefree versions of myself, before age and wisdom had cured me of vanity. I stood and reached out, and we merged.

Their thoughts, their respective experiences on Pharia and Titan, became mine—and while I^2 and I^4 had reveled in their experiences, to me they were the antics of children, and I learned nothing new. I resolved to edit the memories when an opportune moment arose.

Severnius, with the etiquette of the time, had averted his gaze during the process of merging. Now he looked up and smiled. "You are ready?"

I stood. We crossed to the converter, and then, before stepping upon the plate, both paused to look up at our destination.

The Moon, riding higher now, and more substantial against the darker sky, gazed down on us with a face altered little since time immemorial. The fact of its immutability, in an age passé with the boundless possibilities of change, filled me with awe.

We converted.

The Halls of the Fellowship of the Academy occupied the Sea of Tranquillity, an agglomeration of domes scintillating in the sunlight against the absolute black of the Luna night.

We stepped from the converter and crossed the regolith toward the Academy. Severnius led me into the cool, hushed shade of the domes and through the hallowed halls. He explained that if I agreed to steward the Early, then the ceremony of acceptance to the Fellowship would follow immediately. I glanced at him. He clearly assumed that I would accept without question.

The idea of ministering to the psychological well-being of an Early, for an indefinite duration, filled me with apprehension.

We came to the interior dome. The sight of the subject within the silver hemisphere, trapped like some insect for inspection, brought forth in me a rush of memories and emotions. Five hundred years ago, I, too, had awoken to find myself within a similar dome. Five hundred years ago, I presume, I had looked just as frightened and bewildered as this Early.

A gathering of Fellows—Academics, Scientists, Philosophers—stood in a semicircle around the dome, watching with interest and occasionally addressing comments to their colleagues. Upon the arrival of Severnius and myself, they made discreet gestures of acknowledgment and departed, some vanishing within their own converters, others choosing to walk.

I approached the skin of the dome and stared.

The Early was seated upon the edge of a low foamform, his elbows lodged upon his knees, his head in his hands. From time to time he looked up and stared about him, his clasped hands a knotted symbol of the fear in his eyes.

I felt an immediate empathy, a kinship.

Severnius had told me that he had died at the age of ninety, but they had restored him to a soma-type approximately half that age. His physique was lean and well-muscled, but his most striking attribute was his eyes, piercingly blue and intelligent.

I glanced at Severnius, who nodded. I walked around the dome, so that I would be before the Early when I entered, and stepped through the skin of the hemisphere. Even then, my sudden arrival startled him. He looked up, his hands gripping his knees, and the fear in his eyes intensified.

He spoke, but in an accented English so primitive that it was some seconds before I could understand his words.

"Who the hell are you?" he said. "What's happening to me?"

I held up a reassuring hand and emitted pheromones to calm his nerves. In his own tongue I said, "Please, do not be afraid. I am a friend."

Despite the pheromones and my reassurances, he was still nervous. He stood quickly and stared at me. "What the hell's happening here?"

His agitation brought back memories. I recalled my own awakening, my first meeting with Severnius. He had seemed a hostile figure, then. Humankind had changed over the course of thirty thousand years, become taller and more considerate in the expenditure of motion. He had appeared to me like some impossibly calm, otherworldly creature.

As I must have appeared to this Early.

"Please," I said, "sit down."

He did so, and I sat beside him, a hand on his arm. The touch eased him slightly.

"I'd like to know what's happening," he said, fixing me with his intense, sapphire stare. "I know this sounds crazy, but the last I remember . . . I was dying. I know I was dying. I'd been ill for a while, and then the hospitalization . . ."

He shook his head, tears appearing in his eyes as he gazed at his hand—the hand of a man half the age of the person he had been. I reached out and touched his arm, calming him.

"And then I woke up here, in this body. Christ, you don't know what it's like, to inhabit the body of a crippled ninety-year-old, and then to wake up suddenly . . . suddenly *young* again."

I smiled. I said nothing, but I could well recall the feeling, the wonder, the disbelief; the doubt and then the joy of apprehending the reality of renewal.

He looked up at me, quickly, something very much like terror in his eyes. "I'm alive, aren't I? This isn't some dream?"

"I assure you that what you are experiencing is no dream."

"So this is . . . Afterlife?"

"You could say that," I ventured. "Certainly, for you, this is an Afterlife." I emitted pheromones strong enough to forestall his disbelief.

He merely shook his head. "Where am I?" he asked in little more than a whisper.

"The time is more than thirty thousand years after the century of your birth."

"Thirty thousand years?" He enunciated each word separately, slowly.

"To you it might seem like a miracle beyond comprehension," I said, "but the very fact that you are here implies that the science of this age can accomplish what in your time would be considered magic. Imagine the reaction of a Stone Age man, say, to the wonders of twentieth-century space flight."

He looked at me. "So . . . to you I'm nothing more than a primitive—"

"Not at all," I said. "We deem you capable of understanding the concepts behind our world, though it might take a little time." This was a lie—there were many things that would be beyond his grasp for many years, even decades.

Severnius had told me that the subject had evinced signs of mental distress upon learning the disparity between his ability to understand and the facts as they were presented. I would have to be very careful with this subject—if, that was, I accepted the Fellowship.

"So," he said, staring at me. "Answer my question. How did you bring me here?"

I nodded. "Very well . . ." I proceeded to explain, in terms he might understand, the scientific miracle of Enstating and Enabling. It was a ludicrously simplistic description of the complex process, of course, but it would suffice.

His eyes bored into me. His left cheek had developed a quick, nervous tic. "I don't believe it . . ."

I touched his arm, the contact calming him. "Please . . . why would I lie?"

"But how could you possibly recover my memories, my feelings?"

"Think of your childhood," I said, "your earliest memories. Think of your greatest joy, your greatest fear. Tell me, have we succeeded?"

His expression was anguished. "Christ," he whispered. "I can remember everything . . . everything. My childhood, college." He shook his head in slow amazement. "But . . . but my understanding of the way the universe works . . . it tells me this can't be happening."

I laughed at this. "Come! You are a man of science, a rationalist. Things change: what was taken as written in stone is overturned; theory gives way to established fact, which in turn evolves yet more fundamental theory, which is then verified . . . and so proceeds the advance of scientific enlightenment."

"I understand what you're saying," he said. "It's just that I'm finding it hard to believe."

"In time," I said, "you will come to accept the miracles of this age."

Without warning he stood and strode toward the concave skin of the dome. He stared at his reflection, and then turned to face me.

"In time, you say? Just how long have I got?" He lifted his hand and stared at it. "Am I some laboratory animal you'll get rid of once your experiment's through?" He stopped and considered something. "If you built this body, then you must be able to keep it indefinitely—"

He stopped again, this time at something in my expression. I nodded. "You are immortal," I said.

I could see that he was shaken. The tight skin of his face colored as he nodded, trying to come to terms with my casual pronouncement of his new status.

"Thirty thousand years in the future," he whispered to himself, "the world is inhabited by immortals . . ."

"The galaxy," I corrected him. "Humankind has spread throughout the stars, inhabiting those planets amenable to life, adapting others, sharing worlds with intelligent beings."

Tears welled in his eyes. He fought not to let them spill, typical masculine product of the twentieth century that he was.

"If you did this for me," he said, "then it's within your capability to bring back to life the people I loved, my wife and family—"

"And where would we stop?" I asked. "Would we Enstate and Enable the loved ones of everyone we brought forward?" I smiled. "Where would it end? Soon, everyone who had ever lived would live again."

He failed to see the humor of my words. "You don't know how cruel that is," he said.

"I understand how cruel it seems," I said. "But it is the cruelty of necessity." I paused. I judged that the time was right to share my secret. "You see, I, too, was once like you, plucked from my deathbed, brought froward to this strange and wondrous age, fearful and little comprehending the miracles around me. I stand before you as testament to the fact that you will survive this ordeal, and come to understand."

He stared at me, suspicious. At last he said, "But why . . . ? Why you and me?"

"They, the people of this age, considered us men of importance in our time—men whose contributions to history were steps along the way to the position of preeminence that humankind now occupies. Ours is not to wonder, but to accept."

"So that's all I am—a curiosity? A specimen in some damned museum?"

"Not at all! They will be curious, of course; they'll want to know all about your time . . . but you are free to learn, to explore, to do with your limitless future what you will—with the guidance and stewardship of a patron, as I, too, was once guided."

The Early walked around the periphery of the dome. He completed a circuit, and then halted and stared at me. "Explore," he said at last, tasting the word. "You said explore? I want to explore the worlds beyond Earth! No—not only the worlds beyond Earth, the worlds *beyond* the worlds you've already explored. I want to break new ground, discover new worlds . . ." He stopped and looked at me. "I take it that you haven't charted *all* the universe?"

I hesitated. "There are places still beyond the known expanses of space," I said.

"Then I want to go there!"

I smiled, taken by his naïve enthusiasm. "There will be time enough for exploration," I said. "First, you must be copied, so that you can send your other selves out to explore the unexplored. There are dangers—"

He was staring at me in disbelief, but his disbelief was not for what I thought. "Dangers?" he almost scoffed. "What's the merit of exploration if there's no risk?"

I opened my mouth, but this time I had no answer. Something of his primitivism, his heedless, reckless thirst for life which discounted peril and hardship, reminded me of the person I had once been, an age ago.

I considered the next one hundred years, and beyond. I had reached that time of my life when all experience seemed jejune and passé; I had come to the point, after all, where I had even considered Quietus.

To go beyond the uncharted, to endanger oneself in the quest for knowledge, to think the unthinkable . . .

It was ridiculous—but why, then, did the notion bring tears to my eyes?

I hurried across the dome and took his arm. "Come," I said, leading him toward the skin of the hemisphere.

"Where—?" he began.

But we were already outside the dome, and then through the skin of another, and walking across the silver-gray regolith of the lunar surface.

He stopped and gazed about in wonder. "Christ," he whispered. "Oh, Christ, I never thought . . ."

"Over here," I said, leading him.

We crossed the plain toward the display, unchanged in thirty thousand years. He stared at the lunar module, stark beneath the unremitting light of the Sun. We stood on the platform encircling the display and

stared down at the footprints the first astronauts had
laid upon the surface of another world.

He looked at me, his expression beatific. "I often
dreamed," he said, "but I never thought I'd ever
return."

I smiled. I shared the emotions he experienced then.
I knew what it was to return. I recalled the time, not
long after my rebirth in this miraculous age, when I
had made the pilgrimage to Earth and looked again
upon the cell where over thirty thousand years ago I,
Galileo Galilei, had been imprisoned for my beliefs.

Haltingly, I told Armstrong who I was. We stared
up into the dark sky, past the earth and the brilliant
Sun, to the wonders awaiting us in the uncharted universe beyond.

We embraced for a long minute, and then turned
and retraced our steps across the surface of the Moon
toward the domes of the Academy, where Severnius
would be awaiting my decision.

THE MOON TREE

by Jerry Oltion

The Moon Tree lost its top last December. Six feet of perfect Douglas fir, callously hacked off by some selfish idiot out for a Christmas tree. The branches left behind look like the fingers of an open hand, reaching up to cradle a crown that's no longer there.

So said the newspaper reporter who covered the story. According to him, whoever did it probably had no idea that he'd vandalized a national treasure. The campus gardeners hadn't put a plaque or anything special around the tree, probably because they were afraid that somebody would vandalize it on purpose if they knew what it was. Not everybody loves the space program, after all, and Eugene, Oregon, where the tree resides, is a hotbed of political unrest.

No, the reporter figured that the person who topped it was probably just some cheap, selfish bastard who didn't want to pay twenty-five dollars for one of the local farm-grown trees. I'm glad that's the official explanation. It would be a shame if people thought it was done in protest, or worse, in anger.

Especially since we did it to save the world.

I knew it was special the moment I saw it. I don't spend much time on the University of Oregon campus, but I needed to find a magazine the public library didn't have, and it was a sunny autumn day, so I'd decided to take the long way past the flower gardens.

Stop and smell the last of the roses before winter set
in, and all that. I'd forgotten that sunny weather brings
out the coeds, too. I wound up watching them more
than the flowers, and wishing I were two decades
younger so they might look back at me with interest
instead of curiosity. One dark-haired, pale-skinned
young woman with a tight black T-shirt and long bare
legs was sitting on the grass and staring at me with
such puzzlement that I felt like walking up to her and
saying, "No, your eyes aren't deceiving you. I'm a
genuine relic of the sixties. This shirt is indeed tie-
dyed, my vest does indeed bear fringe, and these are
real beads around my neck. Get used to it; a lot of
people still dress this way in Eugene." But then my
eyes focused beyond her, and I instantly forgot her.

The tree was about twenty-five feet high, but its
aura rose twice that; a great, billowing silvery-blue
cloud of light, dancing and twisting in the ethereal
breeze. I thought at first I was witnessing some sort
of lightning discharge, but when it went on and on
without dissipating I realized I was seeing a true aura,
the strongest one I'd seen since 1972, when a Moon
rock had come to SWOMSI—our local science museum—as part of a traveling exhibit.

The lawn had been heavily landscaped, with con-
toured ridges four or five feet high in places. I stumbled
through the miniature hills and valleys toward the tree,
not caring where I placed my feet. I must have brushed
right past the dark-haired girl, but I felt nothing until
I reached the tree and touched a branch, running my
fingers over the soft, flat needles. The last three inches
or so of each tuft was a lighter shade of green from
this summer's growth. The aura seemed brighter at
the edges, too.

"Hey, you kicked me!"

I turned away from the tree. The girl had followed
me. I noticed now that she had a pierced eyebrow,
the silver ring standing out as she glared at me with

her brown eyes. Normally I don't like piercings, nor the butch, tattooed, and booted look she affected to go with it, but the tree's aura was already working on her, softening some of her features, enhancing others. It was entirely subjective, I'm sure, but that's the nature of physical attraction.

She smelled nice, too. Lilac, I guessed.

"Are you all right?" she asked, and from her expression I could tell she hadn't expected those words to come out of her mouth.

"I'm fine," I answered. I smiled, wondering if the tree would make her see the character in crooked teeth. Hoping so.

Its influence might have made her look beautiful, but she didn't look convinced. "You brushed right past me," she said. "Like you were in a trance."

"I'm sorry. I saw something that startled me, and I guess I kind of spaced out."

She looked at the tree, then back at me. "What did you see?"

"You don't see anything?" I reached out to touch a branch again.

"I see a tree. A fir tree." She seemed proud of knowing what kind it was.

"No aura around it?"

"No what?"

"Aura. Like a big glowing halo."

"No." Her frown just drew my attention to her lips. Naturally pink against her pale skin.

"How about me? Do you see anything . . . unusual about me? Besides the clothes?"

She made a big show of squinting and looking me up and down. "You still look kind of spacey, if that's what you mean. Are you on something?"

She was starting to glow herself, now. I had to look away in order to concentrate. "I think this tree was planted under a full Moon," I said. "Or maybe some of the soil it's growing in has Moondust in it. Something about it has a lunar influence, anyway."

She looked beautiful when exasperated, too. "You mean like astrology? You don't really believe that stuff, do you?"

"Well, yes, I do actually." Before she could run away, I added, "In an intellectual sort of way."

Only a student—someone trained to ask questions—would have stuck around to argue the philosophy of astrology, but she was game. She crossed her arms beneath her breasts (making their allure even stronger as my attention was drawn to them) and said, "An intellectual belief in astrology is an oxymoron, isn't it?"

I laughed. She was perfect. "Where have you been all my life?" I asked. "Yes, it's an oxymoron. It also happens to be true, to a limited extent. The Moon, at least, has a definite influence on our lives."

"Sure it does," she said, ignoring my compliment. "Tides. Light when it's full. Menstrual cycles."

"Ah, yes. Menses. Doesn't it seem a little too much coincidence that the cycle governing birth is tied so closely to the celestial symbol of love?"

She smiled a *gotcha!* sort of smile. "I thought Venus was the symbol of love."

That took me by surprise. It took me a moment to think through the implications before I answered. She waited, clearly enjoying my dilemma. At last I said, "You're right, but the Moon is a symbol of love, too, and it's a lot closer to us. It probably has more chance to shape our lives than Venus does."

"Probably?" she asked, still grinning. "I never heard of an astrologer saying 'probably' before."

"That's why my interest in it is more intellectual than most. I'm willing to admit it's mostly conjecture."

The tree was definitely doing its thing for her, now, too. She looked me over again, gave me a genuine smile, and said, "You know, I was starting to think all the old hippies around here were kind of pathetic, but you aren't. Different, that's for sure, but I think I kind of like that." She nodded toward the yellow backpack on the grass where she had been sitting when I first saw her. "Let's go sit down and you can tell me what the Moon and astrology have to do with this tree."

I looked beyond the tree toward the library. I'd been planning to spend the afternoon reading up on Oregon politics, trying to find a chink in the armor of Don Ravon, our Fundamentalist senator from Portland whose intolerance for anything other than his own lifestyle was making life hard for people like me, but the prospect of an afternoon in the grass with an interested college girl—even if that interest was brought on by external forces—seemed much more attractive. Ravon could wait.

So we walked back to her spot on a high berm in the heavily landscaped lawn and got comfortable, she lying long and sinuous on her left side, me sitting cross-legged before her.

"The connection between the Moon and the tree," I told her, "is that the Moon influences lovers, and the tree is making us fall for each other." I held up my hand to stop her embarrassed protest. "No, I mean it. Would you normally talk to a complete stranger the way you've been talking to me?"

"Maybe," she said. "If he was interesting."

"But you thought I was pathetic at first. Spaced out."

"And I asked if you were okay. Then I found out you were interesting."

"But if that tree weren't here, you wouldn't have done anything, would you?"

"I don't see what the tree has to do with it. I wasn't thinking about it when I saw you."

"You still don't see the aura?" I asked. "To me it's like a big silver-blue flame all around it. And some of it has spread to you, too."

"What?"

"You've got an aura now, too."

She looked down at her body, then held out the arm that wasn't propping her up so she could sight along it. "I can't see anything."

"Most people can't," I said with a sigh.

"But you can." If we'd been anywhere else but next to the tree, her tone of voice would have left no doubt that she thought I was insane, and that our conversation was over. But it didn't come out that way, quite.

I weighed my words, then realized what I was doing and tossed away the scale. I gave that up years ago. "Yeah," I said. "I think it was some bad acid I had back in '68. I was barely a teenager at the time, but I wanted to see what it as like. After that I was seeing auras around practically everything. Most of 'em went away after a year or so, but some stayed, and I started to notice things about them. Like, when the Moon is out, they seem to make people fall in love. Or maybe people falling in love under the Moon make auras, I don't know. It's hard to tell."

She was quiet for a long time before she said, "You really believe this, don't you?"

"I really do. And I notice you're not denying anything either."

She blushed. "Look, I like you well enough, but I'm not falling in love with you, okay?"

"Give it time," I said. "Or not. I'm at least twenty years older than you; it could be kind of inconvenient. For you, I mean. You may not want to have an old throwback to the flower days following you around. I don't think we're so far into it we couldn't get out if we wanted to. If you want, I'll go on over to the library and let you get on with whatever you were doing." I felt a real pang of regret at those words. We weren't head-over-heels yet, but we were definitely bonding.

She didn't look all that happy either. "You mean that, too, don't you?"

I nodded. "But if I go, you'd better move a little farther from that tree or you'll just fall for the next guy who comes along."

She glanced back over at the fir, warily, as if it might be sneaking up on her. "You make it sound like I don't have any choice in the matter."

"You don't. Not much, anyway. The longer we're together under its influence, the less choice either one of us will have."

"You don't seem too upset by the idea."

I shrugged. "I thought you were pretty even before I got within range of the tree. You're intelligent and curious as well. I could easily fall for someone like you without help."

"Thanks." She sat up and hugged her knees to herself. "Look, no offense, but this is getting a little too strange. Maybe you're used to this sort of thing, being from the sixties and all, but I don't even know your name."

"Arthur," I told her. "But my friends call me 'Jade.' Because I have green eyes."

"I noticed. All right, Jade. I'm Megan. And I'm a little confused right now, okay? I need a little time to myself to think about this. But I don't want you to just go away. Could we meet again in a couple of hours or something?"

"Sure." I didn't know if the lightness I was feeling came from me or the tree, but at that point I didn't particularly care. We were making a date.

"Right here?" she asked.

"Okay," I said, but a glance at the still-glowing tree made me say, "No, wait a minute. Let's make sure it's really our idea if we decide to see more of each other. How about we meet over in the student union? Neutral ground."

"All right. The student union in two hours."

"Shall we synchronize our watches?"

She looked down at her wrist before she realized

I'd been joking, then looked back up at me and grinned. "Get out of here."

I got. But I was whistling the whole way.

I spent the two hours in the library, but not looking up dirt on Don Ravon. I dug through the computerized card catalog for information on the campus trees, and eventually came up with an identification guide for a botany class. It had a map of campus with all the trees and shrubs marked, and when I looked at the listing for the one with the aura I saw a (17) and an (18) beside the label: "Douglas fir, *Pseudotsuga taxifolia*." Endnote number 17 talked about how to tell a Douglas fir from other firs, and how it isn't a "true fir" because the cones hang down instead of point upward. Number 18 said, "This particular fir is often called the 'Moon Tree' because it was grown from a seed that rode to the Moon and back in the Apollo 14 space capsule."

Ha! I'd been right. I checked out the book and walked back past the tree (still glowing) to the student union, where I bought a paper cup full of coffee and took a table out in front. While I waited for Megan to show up, I amused myself by watching the flickering auras on some of the students sitting at tables around me. Three of them, all sporting the same silver-blue glow I'd seen on the Moon Tree, were sitting together. Two guys and a girl. A green Frisbee rested on the table between them, also glowing silver, and I guessed they had been tossing it back and forth near the Tree. I wondered how the triangle would work out, and bet myself one of the guys would be the other one's best man. Or maybe they would all move in together.

One aura farther back toward the wall was different. It was red instead of silver, and so faint I could hardly tell it was there. It hardly reached beyond the clothing and hair of the buzz cut neo-Nazi radiating it. He was sitting alone at a table in the corner, his back to the wall, and he kept glancing up nervously from the book he was reading. He kept catching my eye before I could look way, and after about the fourth time he got up and stalked toward me. I thought he was going to demand to know why I was staring at him, but I held his gaze as he came toward me, and he looked away first. He brushed past my table, nearly spilling my coffee, and I glanced at his book as he swept by. Between his fingers I could just see the title: *Wartide,* and a picture of an overmuscled guy with a gun in his hands and a bandolier full of bullets over each shoulder.

I'd seen red auras before, usually on people stuck in traffic or banging on stubborn vending machines. I'd never seen one on a person reading for pleasure. I wanted to catch up with him and ask him why he cultivated that mind-set on purpose, but I couldn't think of a good way to broach the subject. Besides, he was leaving the building, and I had to stay and meet Megan.

She stepped up beside me a couple of minutes later and set her backpack and a can of orange pop on the table. "Hi," she said.

"How're you feeling?" I stood up and pulled out a chair for her.

She looked as if she'd never had anyone do that before, but then she smiled and sat down. "Not bad, actually. I walked around and tried to think of all the reasons why I shouldn't get involved with you, and I couldn't come up with one. I've got to tell you right up front that I don't believe in auras or that some tree made me fall for you, but I do want to find out more about you."

"Look at this first," I said, showing her the footnote in the botany book.

Her eyes grew wide when she read it. I could actually see her beliefs shift. Just a subtle change in the colored glow that surrounded her, like heat lightning seen out of the corner of your eye, but it was there.

"Wow, it really *was* influenced by the Moon."

"And now it's influencing everybody who gets near it."

She giggled. "I always thought this was a friendly campus. Now I know why."

"Yeah."

"And—" She tilted her head sideways. "Do you suppose that's how the whole free-love thing in the '60s happened? All that attention the country was paying to the Moon?"

I looked down at my tie-dye and love beads. "I prefer to think it was a lifestyle choice we made out of respect for the Earth and the people we share it with, but if the Moon had some effect on us, I guess that's okay with me."

She got a dreamy look in her eyes. "And maybe that's why all the astronauts are such hotties, too."

I shrugged. "I'll have to take your word for it that they are, but sure, it makes sense. The ones who were youngest when they went are probably the best looking today. The Moon supposedly has its greatest influence on young things."

"Like seeds," Megan pointed out. "And babies." She frowned. "I suppose that's where astrology came from. Ancient people must have noticed a connection between what was in the sky when a child was born and the way the child grew up. Then people kept claiming more and more connections until it became the mass of contradictions we've got today."

"Most myths have at least a little basis in fact." I took a sip of my coffee. "If we ever make it back there with a permanent base, the kids born there are going to be stunning. They'll be like a whole new race compared to us."

"Think of the movie stars they'd make." Megan

leaned back in her chair and sighed. "Unfortunately, we're not headed back to the Moon anytime soon."

"No?" I asked. "Not even with the space station?"

She shook her head. "Nope. The government wants another spectacle to sell the public on space again, so they're planning a mission to—" she stopped. "Uh-oh."

"What?"

"They're planning a mission to Mars."

I thought of the red aura I'd seen around the angry student just a few minutes earlier. Mars' influence? I had no way of knowing for sure, but I knew what would happen if we actually brought back samples from the god of War.

We've got samples already, of course, in the form of meteorites, but they're thousands—maybe millions—of years old. Their influence has faded over the millennia, but even so, it was strong enough to set the scientific community at each other's throats when one group of researchers thought they'd found evidence of life in one. I imagined what fresh Martian samples would do; or worse, what something like a Mars Tree could do if it were planted in Washington, D.C.

"We've got to do something," I said.

Megan held out her hands. "What can we do? Blow up the rocket?"

I looked at her in alarm, saw that she was kidding, but still said, "No, no, we can't go around blowing things up, or we're as bad as what we're trying to prevent."

"Maybe we could show the president what the Moon Tree does to people. If he knew the danger of going to Mars, maybe he'd cancel the project."

I shook my head. "We could never get him to come here. And even if we *could* convince him, he would probably be even more eager to go than before. He might mellow out a little near the Tree, but once he got back to Washington, he'd go right back to being his old self. He'd probably want to drop Mars samples

all through the Middle East to push them over the
edge and end his troubles once and for all."

She narrowed her eyes and pursed her lips in
thought. "You're right, but there's got to be somebody
we could convince. The head of NASA, maybe?"

"I can't think of a good way to get him out here
either." Then I remembered why I'd come to campus
today in the first place, and laughed out loud.

"What?"

"I just thought of one person we *could* bring here,
and it might do us more good than the President
anyway."

"Who?"

"Don Ravon. Oregon's very own proponent of intolerance and hatred."

"Him? He's worse than the president."

"Precisely. But he's also the top runner for the Re-
publican nomination in the next election. If we could
get to him . . ."

Life is more complicated than that, of course. You
can't just invite a senator out for a picnic on campus,
especially in the fall. That late in the year it's cold
and rainy most of the time, and senators are busy in
Washington anyway, trying to finish up the last of their
wheeling and dealing before breaking for the holidays.
And Ravon was too busy gearing up for next year's
election campaign, thinking up the most efficient way
to slander his liberal opponent.

We researched them both before we made our
move. After all, we didn't want to help put someone
even worse than Ravon in office. Irene Moldoya had
her faults, but we were mostly concerned with her
stance on the space program, and that was just what
we'd hoped for. She proposed cautious advancement
with a space station, then a base on the Moon, using
the ice deposits on the south lunar pole to help set
up a permanent base there before we went onward to

Mars. Under her plan, the effect of the Moon on living things would be known long before we got to the other planets. That might not keep us from going, but we would at least know what to expect, and maybe we could prepare for the effect it would have on us.

Megan and I spent most of October and November making our plans. Every few days we took our umbrellas and a tarp and sat on the grass not far from the Moon Tree, watching as other people came under its influence, paused a moment in their hasty course across campus, and walked away a little slower, smiling. Often they walked away in pairs, which confirmed what we already knew.

In early December we made our move.

Like I say, someone topped the Moon Tree. A few days later, after the furor died down, two people representing themselves as a private timber baron and his young wife made a contribution to Senator Ravon's campaign fund. As a personal gift, they brought a Christmas Tree for campaign headquarters, where they knew Ravon and his all-volunteer staff—composed primarily of young church-going college girls—would be putting in a lot of long hours through the holidays and would appreciate some midnight cheer.

We didn't alert the media. There will be plenty of opportunities for scandal to get out, and Ravon has political enemies far more devious than us who can figure òut the maximum use of the indiscretions that must surely be playing out in his office over the holidays.

No, we used the time to atone for our own sin. I've got some property outside of town, the remains of a commune that didn't work out. I doubt if Senator Ravon will notice that his office Christmas tree is missing all its cones, but we saw no reason to waste them. Christmas trees are big business around here, and my acreage—now Megan's and mine—is prime tree growing land. It will take a few years for Moon Tree Farms to produce anything tall enough to stand in anyone's living room, but we figure the timing should be just about right. Even if Ravon's opponent can't stop America from going straight to Mars, people all over the country will be feeling exceptionally fond of one another just about the time the first mission comes back with samples. With any luck, the feeling will overpower anything a few red rocks can do to the national spirit.

As we used to say when I was younger, "Make love, not war."

THE LAST MAN ON THE MOON
by Scott Edelman

For Neil Armstrong, the Moon was at last a reality. The simulations, the tests, the long hours of play-acting to prove to the techs that he was the one with the rightest of the right stuff—all that was history.

And history was what he was creating.

As the Lunar Module brought him nearer to the surface of the Moon, what he could see through the double-paned window unwound a spring in his heart. The magnificent desolation, growing closer, turned from a distant dream into a concrete vision of stark beauty. Planet Earth itself was what had now become the dream, jiggling far above him as the thrusters rocked their fragile cocoon down through the thin atmosphere.

Strapped into the Lunar Module beside Buzz Aldrin, Armstrong was distracted by the sudden sensation that he was being watched. At the same time, though he was unsure how, he somehow knew immediately that Aldrin, packed in tightly beside him intent on the computer controls during their descent, was not the cause of his unease. Armstrong was a reasonable man, always had been, not given to odd fancies—unless choosing the life of a test pilot was in itself odd—and the strange feeling baffled him. Which was uncomfortable, for he was also the sort of man who did not take easily to being baffled. He was not entirely occupying his own body, it seemed; he was both audience and participant for his own every breath.

He forced the mood away. More urgent issues were present to deal with than mere vaguely defined spiritual discomforts. He was no Ivy League college boy mesmerized by his own navel, he was the Commander of *Apollo 11*, and the mission's success depended on his focused concentration. Besides, with the whole world watching, who *wouldn't* feel an overwhelming sense of sitting in a department store window on the last shopping day before Christmas?

They were fast approaching a large crater, its bowl the size of a football field. A scattering of boulders confronted him, any one of which could cause irreparable damage to the Lunar Module and prevent their return to the Command Module. That, he knew, should be the only thought inhabiting his mind. Even a slight error could cause him to stub his toe during these final phases before a touchdown, he knew that, and so he shoved the invading feeling far from his mind.

The pockmarked landscape was rushing up to greet him like a fist. Armstrong took over manual control from the computer, quickly goosing the thrusters so that the Lunar Module would overshoot their initial target. He instead tried to have them come in long, aiming for a relatively smooth area a little farther on which contained only an array of smaller craters and rocks.

They thudded down hard. When the Contact Light blinked alive, showing that the probes hanging from each of the LM's three footpads had stroked the surface of the Moon, Armstrong allowed himself a deep breath in hopes of slowing his wildly beating heart. He tried not to think of what the boys back on Earth must be making of the thudding in his chest.

"Houston, Tranquility Base here," he said, smiling at Aldrin. "The Eagle has landed!"

The sun was low in the sky. Armstrong peered out at the almost colorless landscape that encircled them with a carpet of chalky gray ash. Their surroundings could be seen with sharp clarity, the shadows perfect and sudden. Nearby rocks bore newly formed fractures, damage from the harsh plume of their rocket engine.

His vision blurred momentarily, twinning the boulders before him. He felt yet again as if the eyes he was looking through were borrowed ones, the sights of victory not entirely his own. He frowned, and blinked the view back to normal. Or what passed for normal on the sterile Moon.

"Let's do it," he said to Aldrin. Armstrong shimmied into his Extravehicular Mobility Unit, squirming into the layers that would define his humanity, keeping the Moon outside and the Earth close to his skin. His training took over, and almost without thought he snapped his gloves into place, then locked on his helmet. It was time.

Aldrin, who had been going through the same motions, studied him quizzically.

"Ready?"

Armstrong's answer was a confident thumbs up. He dropped the signal to reach for the hatch with the same hand. After he swung the door inward, he rolled onto his knees to his left, readying himself to back out onto a new world. As he contorted and uncomfortably exited onto the platform, he did not see the Moon his destination, but only the fragile, awkward contraption that had brought him there. He slid out a foot and moved it from side to side, seeking the comfort of the ladder's top step. He could hear, as he slowly lowered himself down the struts, the voice of McCandless announce on Earth that their television screens were reflecting his steady descent. Armstrong stepped back, dropping off the ladder, repeating in his mind the words he had practiced for so long, and then, as his foot sank slightly into a top layer of fine powder, he began to speak.

"That's one small step for man," he said. "One giant leap for mankind."

As soon as the words had escaped his mouth, before Aldrin could reply from mere yards away, before Collins could wish him well from his orbit in the Command Module far above, before any cheers of jubilation could carry from terribly distant Houston, Armstrong grabbed his helmet roughly, tried to snap it free from around his fragile skull, and began a long, low scream.

Shrieking, Alexander Reece tore the VR skullcap from his temples and flung it across the small room. The heavy contraption beeped and chirped as it skittered end over end against the curved chrome floor of the chamber, and then slid back to settle beneath his central chair. He was embarrassed to see that his octogenarian's muscles were unable to hurl it as far as he wished, as far as his NASA-trained body once could. He studied the elongated face reflecting back at him off the silvery inner curved walls that closely surrounded him like the insides of a giant's egg, and remembered when his was the face of a man who had once tossed a football farther than any human ever had or ever would. Back when he'd been on the Moon for real.

Back before he knew he would be the last.

A rectangular seam blossomed in front of him, and as the thin cracks widened, he could hear frantic yelling outside that had only been muffled murmuring the instant before. A small door popped back, and Mel Lichtenstern and Leon Stober filled the sudden space, each trying to be the first one through the narrow entrance. Lichtenstern, narrow himself, pushed swiftly by the other man into the testing chamber.

"What went wrong?" Lichtenstern shouted.

"Are you all right?" asked Stober. The stocky man quickly loosened the straps that held Reece's snug bodysuit to the chair. Stober stumbled a bit on the slanted floor before gently taking one of Reece's thin wrists and checking his pulse.

"It's that damned helmet of yours, Leon," said Lichtenstern, kneeling to peer under Reece's chair. "It must have given the man a shock. You've got to be more careful. That's all DreamVert needs, to be known as the company that killed the last surviving man to walk on the Moon."

"Please, Mel," said Stober softly, still holding Reece's trembling arm. "As usual, your sense of humor falls flat. You're only being morbid."

"Don't worry, Mr. Reece," said Lichtenstern, smiling as he stood. "It was just a onetime computer error. Leon will make sure that it doesn't happen again."

"No, it won't happen again," said Reece in a choked voice, so enraged that he was almost weeping. "I'm fine, thank you very much. But your Virtual Reality program, it's wrong, all of it. What have you been doing the last three years? You don't need me as a consultant. You just need a garbageman. You'd be better off just throwing the whole thing out."

The two businessmen looked hurt, as if they were children on Halloween and Reece had just pulled back a handful of candy. After the blasphemy they'd put him through, though, those pained expressions gave Reece a jolt of malicious glee.

"Go back to making re-creations of skiing Mount Everest and skydiving without a parachute," continued Reece. "Putting a man on the Moon seems to be beyond you."

Lichtenstern seemed at a loss for a reply for the first time since Reece had met him days earlier. When he finally spoke, his words were slow and measured.

"You were hardly in there long enough to judge, Mr. Reece."

"I was in there more than long enough to be sickened," answered Reece. "You two, you say you're going to make a killing letting the world's lazy VR potatoes relive Neil Armstrong's trip to the Moon, and then you go ahead and make it all up! How did you imagine I'd react to that, that . . . monstrosity? You said you needed a man who'd really been to the Moon to help teach the world the way it really was. But you lied to me."

Reece was angry at them, but also angry at himself for the way his lower lip trembled as he spoke. He used to be able to take a stand without having to worry that he looked like an old fool.

"Mr. Reece," said Lichtenstern, "I know that you don't care for Virtual Reality, but please, you're making it sound as if we're some sort of criminals. We haven't lied to you."

"No? So then you really think you could get into your suit in a flash and step from the Lunar Module like out of an amusement park ride? There were *hours* of procedures and checklists between landing and stepping out onto the surface. And the descent from orbit was smooth, it wasn't like being in a damned cement mixer. And everything in there was too sharp—the real landing stirred up tons of dust. When you first get there, you see, it's like looking through a fog. It's only later, when the dust settles, that everything becomes clear. And—"

"I'm sorry, Mr. Reece, if we gave you the wrong impression, but this is a business first," said Lichtenstern. His cheeks flushed red as he spoke. "And business isn't necessarily about giving people the truth. Not our business, anyway. If we're going to be selling a product, we have to give people what they think they want. And they don't want a smooth landing. Where's the excitement in that? We don't get paid for smooth landings. And when they do land, they'll want to be able to see what they came for. So what if we tweak it a little? You could still help us by making sure we manage to nail down the heart of it."

"But you've put a stake right through the god-damned heart of it, can't you see? Those words you made him say! That was the worst part of all. You might as well go to Arlington National Cemetery and piss on Armstrong's grave. How could you make them come out of his mouth that way? You know he didn't say them like that. You *know* it."

Lichtenstern turned to look sheepishly at Stober, who was still struggling to unhook the system's many delicate sensors as Reece squirmed angrily in the chair. Stober would not meet Reece's gaze either, lost in the pretense that it was science, and not embarrassment, that kept him looking down.

"It was one small step for *a* man, you fools." Reece pulled himself free from the two men and angrily detached the final straps and wires on his own. Stober winced to hear the sudden ripping sounds. Reece stood, legs shaking, his heart racing. The enclosure was so cramped as to leave no room for him to get past the two of them to the door. So much for dramatic gestures. "Let me by."

They backed away, each trying to exit through the doorway first. Reece followed them into the cavernous laboratory that housed the VR mechanism and all the accompanying hardware and assistants DreamVert claimed they needed for testing. He stumbled down a short set of stairs, barely keeping to his feet as he reached the warehouse floor. Cursing, Reece went to the nearby alcove changing room. He began stripping off the suit that only hours before had comforted him by reminding him of the old days, but now just seemed vile. His body as it was revealed was thin and stringy, not what it once was, and nothing like the one he had a few short moments ago felt himself occupying.

"You have to understand, Alex," said Stober, stepping up carefully beside him. Lichtenstern hung back, making a show of eyeing the control console. "We're not villains. We didn't make up Armstrong's words.

That's the way they taped it back then, that's the way it appeared on all the transcripts. People will expect to hear those as the words that will come out of their mouths when they're being Armstrong. Anything else would be wrong. It would only confuse them."

"So what?" said Reece, the suit around his ankles. He kicked the collapsed skin toward Lichtenstern. This time, unlike with the helmet, he was satisfied by how far he made something fly. "The truth is meant to be confusing. Going to the Moon *was* confusing."

"This is ridiculous," said Lichtenstern, shouting from where he stood. "Look, you think we didn't have reasons for what we did? Even Buzz Aldrin says he heard it that way, and he was only few feet away."

"But he didn't hear Armstrong's words through the air," said Reece, waving a fist. "He heard the transmission the same way everyone else on Earth did, masked with all that crackle of static. You can't pay attention to what anyone else claimed. This isn't about what the world mistakenly thinks. This isn't about anyone else. This is about Armstrong. Just Armstrong. He said that he said it. You're going to have to take him at his word."

"This isn't why we asked you here," said Lichtenstern, stepping closer. "You were the last man on the Moon. You're the *last* last man on the Moon, the only one left. We're not concerned about words. We need you to tell us how it *feels.*"

"I'll tell you how it feels. It feels like I was an idiot for ever agreeing to fly up from Florida to try to explain to a couple of businessmen what it was like to land on the Moon."

A sudden weakness overcame Reece, and he sat down hard on a nearby wooden bench. Gladstone would kill him for putting himself through this strain, Reece thought, if the doctor ever found out about it, if the strain itself didn't kill him first. He was a ridiculous sight sitting there in his shorts, he knew. For the first time in his long life, he felt himself to be a pathetic sight. He dropped his head to his hands, drained.

"That didn't look like the Moon," he said wearily. "That didn't look like the Moon at all."

"Then help us," said Stober, sitting down beside him on the bench. "You can help it be the Moon, or at least the best Moon reality lets us have these days. It will happen with you or without you. You know that, Alex, don't you?"

"I can't believe it's come down to this," said Reece, hugging his gaunt arms as he trembled. "I'm the last of them. That should count for more than this, don't you think?"

"I'm sorry you feel that way," said Lichtenstern. His face was void of expression, his voice barely under control. "I hope you choose to continue with us on the project. We've offered to pay you well. If you feel you're not up to it, well, Leon is right. We'll just have to make do."

For a moment, Lichtenstern studied the silvery egg that towered on struts beside them, then nodded at Stober and walked away. Reece and Stober sat in silence as the footsteps echoed across the cavernous room, and then vanished. Stober clasped and unclasped his hands again and again. Reece could tell that the man was struggling unsuccessfully to find something to say.

"You know," Reece said quietly, "it seemed as if he knew that I was there."

"Who?" said Stober. "Lichtenstern?"

"No," said Reece, pausing, wondering how much he should admit. "Armstrong. When I was in there, in your testing contraption, being him instead of being me, letting him take over, he somehow knew that I was there. I was Armstrong, all right, your program sure did that fine, but at times it was an Armstrong who knew that someone else was riding his back. He *knew* that I was watching him. And I don't think he liked it."

"No one else has ever reported anything like that before," Stober said in a slow and reasoned tone, as if talking to a child. "The personas you don in VRs aren't aware. They can't be. They're just computer programs, and I certainly didn't input an ability like that. Are you sure you weren't just sensing Armstrong's nerves? You know, one thing I don't know whether you realize we got right was that his heart rate went through the roof when they were landing. It shot higher than any other mission commander's."

"No, it wasn't that," said Reece, recalling the curiosity of Armstrong's mind, remembering that though the Moon did not feel real, Armstrong himself did. "Forget about it. Forget I said anything."

Stober licked his lips nervously, and placed a hand lightly on Reece's shoulder.

"Alex, you're the closest thing we've got, that the whole *world's* got, to Neil Armstrong. Don't you think you owe this to him, to the memory of the space program? Wouldn't he have wanted you to hang in there to make it right for him?"

No, thought Reece. *He'd have laughed at this. He'd have wanted you to go back to the goddamned Moon for real.*

Sitting there, starting to shiver in his shorts, he thought of his Boca Raton condo full of medals that no one ever saw, and the newsmen who had him trot out the damned things on anniversaries for nostalgic stories on what it was like when men and women still stepped off this planet. Thinking of days full of working on memoirs he was not sure anyone would ever want to read, he got control of his pride and knew, just knew, what his answer would have to be.

"Okay, Stober," he said, the strength back in his voice. "Someone's got to stop you bastards from screwing this up royally. Let's do it. Let's go back to the Moon."

Reece, struggling with the staff meant to hold an American flag upright, grew tired of being Armstrong. Luckily, unlike Armstrong, frustrated by the stubborn mechanism, Reece had a choice about it.

Reece had by now spent many long repetitive days returning again and again to the surface of the Moon, troubleshooting the flawed program, watching Lichtenstern and Stober mostly ignore the feedback he'd give them on where they'd gone astray. Only a few of the suggestions did they actually bother to implement. Even that much surprised him, based on how he'd sized them up.

He scuffed the ground with a heavy boot, smiling as he watched the raised surface particles go out in a perfect ring. No swirl of dust, no roiling cloud like there would be on Earth, like there'd been in the VR simulation days before; just a clear and perfect fan against the terrain.

He did get a small amount of pleasure from being useful in that way, but it fell far short of what he knew he'd feel if they really paid attention to him. To some degree he was but a publicity gimmick for Dreamvert, he knew that. Whether they heeded his advice or not, they would make the best of it by allowing the world to think they had. He'd already almost quit many times. Neither Lichtenstern nor Stober had the power to make him stay.

Only Armstrong had that.

Neil Armstrong was magnetic. Perhaps not as strongly so as the real Armstrong had been, but as far as making the first man on the Moon seem real, Lichtenstern and Stober had done their jobs. Perhaps Stober should get most of the credit; Lichtenstern seemed to worry mainly about PR and money. Reece knew his kind. He was the sort who was a politician,

not the sort who made the rockets fly. But though
Reece got along with Stober, he still could not get the
man to accept all that the astronaut was telling him.

Armstrong's unease still remained, regardless of
what the two men kept insisting to Reece. That feeling
was still out there from time to time. Reece could not
avoid picking up the irritated signals from Armstrong,
as if the first man on the Moon was definitely made
uncomfortable by Reece's presence. There was no per-
sonhood present to *feel* discomfort, or so they kept
insisting, and so he'd stopped talking to them about
his sensations. But that didn't make the experience
any less wearying.

Having definitely had quite enough of being Armstrong today, Reece blinked his eyes in that special
way they'd taught him, and was abruptly shifted into
observer mode, his stomach jolted by the sudden dis-
connection. He wasn't up for this, he truly wasn't. Gri-
macing, he sat on a boulder and watched Armstrong
nearby.

Armstrong, ungainly in his space suit, moved clum-
sily in an attempt to set up the American flag, which
Reece knew would crumple and fall to the surface of
the Moon during takeoff. Reece wondered whether
Lichtenstern and Stober would be willing to show that
in their re-creation, or whether that would be one
more truth that would fall by the wayside so that the
VR potatoes who would shell out the big bucks for a
chance to pretend to be Armstrong wouldn't be
offended.

Aldrin, fated to be known forever as the second
man on the Moon—which Reece imagined was probably better than being known as the last man on the
Moon—was close beside Armstrong. It took the two
men working together to force the rod's hinge to snap
into position. When they finally had the staff jammed
as deeply as they could get it into the ground, the
weight of the flag spun the pole so that the stars and

stripes faced away from the ever-present camera. Armstrong and Aldrin swiveled the flag to the lens and posed. Reece smiled, remembering a time when people back on Earth actually bothered to look at such pictures.

The photo opportunity over, Aldrin turned his back to Reece and wandered back to the base of the Lunar Module, leaving Armstrong behind. Armstrong studied the flag while Reece studied Armstrong. To Reece, as the moments passed, Armstrong seemed lost in thought far too long for a man whose time on the surface of the Moon was to be so short.

Armstrong turned his head and looked toward Reece. Reece could feel his heart pounding, even though he knew it could only be some sort of coincidence. He hoped that the worrying Stober did not make note of it and deem it a reason to pull him out of the environment for his own safety. But when Armstrong began walking toward him, Reece feared that the thudding in his chest would have to be unignorable. Calm down, he told himself. Surely Armstrong had been programmed to sight some geological marvel in the distance, and was about to walk right *through* him to examine something that had existed millions of years before either of them had been born. When Armstrong stopped directly before him and looked down into Reece's eyes, down where he could *feel* it, the truth could no longer be denied.

"So you were the watcher I felt," said Armstrong, seemingly unperturbed to find a third man wandering the Moon. Reece's mouth was dry, and he wondered how they could manage to do that with VR. Reece had avoided the entire industry as much as possible; perhaps it wasn't that difficult after all. "Imagine meeting the last man on the Moon."

"Imagine *being* the last man on the Moon."

"I never thought that there'd be such a thing."

Armstrong's face hardened. Reece knew it wasn't

at him, but at them. And not just at Lichtenstern and
Stober, but at all the thems out there.

"There are a lot of things that didn't go the way
they should have," said Reece. "You wouldn't want
to know about them."

"That's the problem, Alex. You're here, so I already
do. It's a small, sad world out there."

"Some people don't seem to mind."

"Since when have we been 'some people?' "

"But you weren't even supposed to register that I
was here. And you certainly weren't supposed to be
interactive enough for us to have this conversation."
Reece pointed off at Aldrin, puttering with a bag of
tools. "He doesn't seem to notice me."

"Poor Buzz didn't get the care and attention that I
did. He's a good man, but I'm afraid that he isn't the
one they think is the star attraction here. They've
spent most of their time and most of the computer's
memory the past few years on me." Armstrong kicked
the boulder on which Reece sat, grunting at the unde-
niable solidity of it. "I guess those guys are better
scientists than they know. Do you mind if I sit down?"

Reece slid over to make room. As Armstrong sat,
the space suits of the astronauts disappeared. Their
cocoons blinked away, and they were suddenly in
street clothes, as comfortable sitting on a rock in the
airlessness of space as they would have been chatting
on a park bench. Startled, Reece looked at the back
of one hand, where the big-knuckled fingers he'd expected to see were gone, replaced by a young hand
he had not known in decades, the prominent veins
and spots that were brought to him by age faded to
but a memory.

"Virtual Reality can take you back to far more than
just the Moon," said Armstrong. "VR can take you
back."

They sat that way in space for a while, enjoying
what Lichtenstern and Stober and the countless

DreamVert technicians had created. They looked off across the varied craters that stretched off seemingly forever before them. They watched the American flag, quiet and still on the windless Moon. The Earth hung glowing above them.

"We weren't supposed to dip our toe in the water and then walk away from the ocean," said Armstrong. "We were supposed to keep going. You were supposed to continue the line, Reece, not be the one to end it. There were supposed to be colonies out here by now. Think of it. My great-grandchildren were supposed to be living here. There was supposed to be a city."

"People don't care anymore," said Reece. "I won't apologize for them. I guess I should. People have given up. All they have time to think about up there anymore is getting through the day. Finding a place to sleep, getting enough to eat, figuring out a way to stay safe. For all their technological toys, inside they're still cavemen. They think that what we did was very nice, but really, just get over it. They forget that someday the sun will flare, and take the Earth with it, and if we haven't moved on to a new home by then, that's it for the human race. We might as well have never existed."

"But they've got to know that. Surely they've been paying attention."

"On some level I'm sure they know. But on the level that counts? The level that gets things done? It sickens me to say this, but I think that they're more interested in playing video games than actually going anywhere for real. Neil, I'm afraid that mankind didn't seem to really want your small step."

"So you're saying that this may be as close as man ever gets to the Moon again."

Reece shook his head. Armstrong stared at him hard.

"I think you're a little jealous of me," said Armstrong.

"No," said Reece, confidently. "I'm not jealous of you, Neil. I'm jealous of the next guy. The one who gets to go back."

"Do you really think that there'll be someone like that? After all you just said about them?"

"There must be. Or else no one will ever have a chance to sit like this again for real."

The first and last men fell silent, and sat quietly together, waiting for the planet Earth to set.

"What was going on in there, Reece?"

The aged astronaut blinked and saw Stober hunched over him, the VR helmet cradled delicately in his hands. All Reece could do was stare uncomprehendingly. A moment before, he'd been on the Moon. As far as he was concerned, he never should have left. He slowly held up one hand that seemed impossibly bound by gravity, and gestured for Stober to have patience while he collected his wits.

"You seem okay now," Stober continued, "but your stats were screwy there for a while; it's as if we lost contact with you. I almost pulled you out of there. You had me worried."

"Why didn't you pull me out?" Reece said in a low voice. Even if he'd wanted to, he didn't know whether he had the energy to speak more loudly.

"It was Lichtenstern," Stober said in dull tone. "He wouldn't let me. Come. Let me help you out of here."

Reece, who usually ignored offers of aid, allowed Stober to help him. All each hour of testing taught Reece was that a man of his age wasn't up to a trip to the Moon, virtual or otherwise. Even as simple an act as standing after being seated for so long wasn't easy.

"You've managed not to answer my question, Alex. What was different in there?"

"Nothing. Nothing was different. I think your machines are acting up again, Leon."

They staggered out into the control room and sat quietly side by side. When Stober started to strip Reece out of his suit, and before he could pursue the issue any further, Lichtenstern scurried over.

"See, I told you that he was fine, Leon. You worry too much. Aren't you fine, Mr. Reece?"

"I've been to the Moon, Lichtenstern. Why wouldn't I be fine?"

"See, Leon? We won't have any surprises out of Mr. Reece. He's in amazing condition for a man his age."

Stober made as if to speak. Lichtenstern went back to his controls before a word could be uttered. Reece ignored them both and began to dress.

"You have to forgive him," said Stober, his hands shoved deep in his pockets.

"No, I don't have to forgive him," said Reece. "You're the one who has to forgive him each day, because you have to work with him. I don't need to make any such accommodation with my conscience. I'll be going home soon. If I had to remain behind like you, I'd probably have to come up with excuses for him, too."

"Understand that we've been at this project for a long time," said Stober, circling Reece in an attempt to plant himself in the man's field of vision. "Too long. And to find out as he did when he thought he was nearly done that there's so much longer still to go, well . . ."

"So then why didn't you bring me in earlier?" Reece asked, looking up from buckling his belt. Stober avoided his gaze.

"To be honest, we, um, we didn't know you were still alive. We thought the last of you was already long gone."

"Great. You sure know how to make a person feel special."

Reece finished buttoning up his shirt, and seemed ready for the street.

"You didn't answer my question," said Stober. "I'll ask it again. What happened in there? Today's readouts seemed completely different."

"Nothing out of the ordinary. But you still have to work on that perceived distance problem. Because of the atmosphere, you know, objects seem closer than they really are. Things don't fuzz off as they get farther away as they do here on Earth. I'll tell you all the details during the debriefing. But I'm sure you'll be able to take care of it easily enough."

"Why do I find I don't believe you? Listen to me, Alex. Level with me. If you're not feeling well, we can always stop for a while, start up again later. You're too important a man to risk on this project. Maybe Mel and I will just have to be content that we've gotten all the usable information out of you that you can afford to give."

"It's awfully nice of you to show such concern."

"I'd appreciate that more if you were able to leave out that subtle trace of sarcasm."

Reece was about to close his locker for the day when he paused to stare into it deeply as if gazing off at a distant crater.

"You're a smart man, Stober," said Reece, his voice soft and far away. "You're not Lichtenstern. You still have some passion left in you. Why do you keep working on projects like this? It's like churning out fake Rembrandts when you could be a Rembrandt all on your own. You have the ability. Why play let's pretend when you could use your smarts to get us back to the Moon for real?"

"There's probably no more than a handful of souls on this planet other than yourself willing to pay to go to the Moon for real. On the other hand, we could easily sell ten million units of this Moon program, and that's not even counting the schools. I don't have any choice in this, Reece. We're not in charge. The government isn't even in charge. It's the marketplace that's in charge, chaotic, random, and unforgiving."

"Have you ever thought of trying to use those smarts to change the marketplace? I could go on tour, remind them of what the Moon was really like, get them charged up for going back, and you, you could get them up there . . . for real."

"I'm not that kind of guy. I'm not the same kind of risk taker you are. I'm perfectly happy doing this."

"If you say so."

Reece slammed the locker door. Stober winced.

"Don't hate the world for letting you down, Alex."

"I don't hate what's here, Stober. I just love what's out there even more."

Reece hurried to the exit. Stober called after him.

"If it means anything to you, I'm sorry."

"Don't apologize to me," Reece replied as he walked through the door. "Apologize to Neil Armstrong."

Armstrong's final farewells to Tranquility Base could no longer be avoided. He'd come to visit, not to stay. The safety checklists having been negotiated and survived, and Collins' location in the orbiting Command Module pinned down with as much accuracy as their primitive computers could sustain, Armstrong reattached his waist restraint. Knowing what he knew now, though, knowing what Reece had told him, knowing even what Reece had been unable to tell him but which he'd been able to pick out of his mind, he'd just as soon toss the controls to one side and remain behind, letting Buzz go back home alone.

Unlike back at the initial landing, whenever Armstrong now felt an odd sense of doubling, a feeling that someone, something, was riding his shoulder, he knew what it was. He was no longer mystified. It was Reece, the Moon's last man, watching, listening, judging, touching him with the only bit of the present future that would ever bleed through.

Let him look, too, thought Armstrong, with what passed for thoughts. *Reece, too, had the right to say good-bye to the Moon in his own way.*

Armstrong heard Aldrin announce to the world that Eagle was now number one on the runway, and he knew that their time was almost up.

Armstrong peered out at the Moon's surface for one last look. He caught a glimpse of himself reflected back at him in the glass that separated them, and realized that the face he saw was not entirely his own. In the faceplate of his suit, the features of Alex Reece were superimposed over his own.

"This is it," said Reece. "It's time to go home."

"You're right," said Armstrong. The first man on the Moon smiled. "Later on, I'll have a billion chances at this. So why don't you take over the controls this time?"

Armstrong could feel the internal shifting of the bipartite beast of which he was now a part. Knowing that he would be here doing this again and again forever, Armstrong let Reece have the joy of controlling the ascent. He felt no need to jealously guard this first attempt. Let the man who'd been last be the first for once, Armstrong felt. He'd earned it as much from his works as from the status of his position itself. Armstrong slipped away to now become the secret sharer, riding on the shoulder of another.

Reece, not Armstrong, gave the final command. With an alien explosion, the ship began its swift ascent, seeking to mate with the machinery above them. He quickly glanced outside, where he saw the silent force of the rockets tossing the American flag this way and that, lifted by a wind at last, albeit a man-made one. The flag did not fall, holding firm under the assault.

"They'll never learn," muttered Reece. "Not even

Stober. Those bastards will sell whatever they think anyone will buy."

He choked at the thought of the mockery into which they would turn this place. Lichtenstern and Stober were building an amusement park on a hallowed battle-ground. As he grimaced, Reece's anger gripped him so unexpectedly that it took him a long moment to register the sudden palpitations of his heart.

"This is ridiculous," he said, shocked. Buzz Aldrin took no notice. "Hear me, Armstrong, you agree, isn't this ridiculous? I'm only virtual here. How can I have a heart attack?"

There was no answer, at least not a verbal one. The answer that came was that the one who'd been looking over his shoulder was gone. He felt totally, eternally, alone. The weight on his chest increased, and as con-sciousness bled away, the words that filtered through his mind were not his own. They were Armstrong's.

"That's one small step for a man," Reece whispered.

Aldrin turned to him, registering Reece's words at last.

"What was that again, Neil?" Aldrin asked.

"One giant leap," Reece continued. His voice trailed off, the famous quote never to be finished.

"Neil?" Aldrin shouted. "*Neil!* What's wrong?"

"Alex!" Stober shouted. "*Alex!* What's wrong?"

Stober, hunched over the swaddled Reece within the testing unit, received no reply.

"Damn."

He dropped the headset he'd removed to reveal Reece's still features, and called outside to Lichtenst-ern, who was slow to follow.

"I knew this would happen," said Stober, hurriedly peeling back Reece's bodysuit.

"He was an old man," said Lichtenstern, poking his head hesitantly through the doorway. "He's probably better off."

"We should have paid more attention when the signals went bad. He trusted us. We shouldn't have let him deal with the strain. We should have known better."

"What else would his life have been?" said Lichtenstern, frowning as he looked at the body. "Sitting in a room, waiting for the phone to ring? Spitting up speeches that he'd given a thousand times before to reporters who'd rather be elsewhere? Was the alternative really more attractive?"

"You're cold, Mel."

"No, I'm realistic. Wouldn't you have wanted to go this way? You knew him better than I did, but even I could tell that he'd have chosen this."

"We should get a doctor in here," said Stober, shaken.

"It's too late. A doctor wouldn't do him any good. He's moved beyond that, Leon."

"So what do we do now?" asked Stober. He held one of Reece's limp hands in his own.

"Let's not talk about this here," said Lichtenstern, averting his eyes from the body. "Not in front of him."

Stober let himself be led out through the small doorway and down the short ladder. Lichtenstern placed him in a chair from which he could not see back through the door. Lichtenstern stood between Stober and the door anyway.

"I asked you to tell me, Mel, now what? Don't play games with me. Moving me out here won't cause me to forget what's in there."

"What do you think we do? We go on as before."

"I don't think that's possible."

"Don't be ridiculous, Leon. If canning this program would bring him back to life, I'd shut it down myself."

"I'd like to think you would."

"What's with you lately? I've never seen you like this. Reece has gotten to you in some strange way I don't understand."

Stober looked off toward Reece's locker, which the last man on the Moon would never open again.

"You didn't talk to him much. You interfaced with him as little as you could get away with, I recall. To you he was just a resource to be used, not a human being with a life all his own. What's gotten into me? Maybe Alex has made me realize that I've been spending my life building fakes, all the while knowing that when he went out into space he did something for real. Maybe if I work at it hard enough, I can still go out and do something for real myself."

Lichtenstern shook his head as he sighed at his business partner.

"Maybe you're right," he said. "But there's something you're forgetting. Perhaps that's all that some of us are good for. Building fakes. Programming dreams. If we walk away from that, we might discover that we have nothing left. We should leave the heroism for the heroes, don't you think?"

"I think I'd feel better about this if you had it in you to sound a bit doubtful. You sound a little too sure of yourself."

"That's always been my job in this partnership, hasn't it? I'm just trying to keep my end up."

"So nothing's changed? We just push it out there?"

"As soon as possible."

"Won't that seem morbid?"

"No more morbid than sending a man to the Moon in the first place. Do you think everyone who paid attention to Neil Armstrong watched to see a safe landing? That's what they all told each other and themselves afterward, but no, I don't buy it—they all wanted to be able to tell their friends where they were when he went up in a fireball."

"It wasn't that bad," said Stober, angry at Lichtenstern for the first time in a long while. It felt good. "It was a different time. I think I liked that time."

"Yes, I agree, it was a different time. But still—we

shouldn't beat ourselves up for taking advantage of this, for being of *our* time. Reece was a man who liked taking risks. That's what allowed him to get to the Moon in the first place. We shouldn't bury the product he gave his life to perfect. He wouldn't want us to waste this. That wouldn't be fair to him."

"You're right. You're always right about these things."

"Again, I'm just—"

"Yes, I know. Keeping your end up. So whom do we tell? Remember, he had no surviving family."

"I think we need to announce his death to the world as quickly as possible. We should call a press conference."

"Only if you promise to keep your mouth shut," said Stober, standing up suddenly. "I won't have you turning what should be a eulogy into a commercial."

"Now, Leon—"

"No," said Stober, planting a finger on Lichtenstern's chest. "You stay out of this. This one's on me alone. Think of it as me keeping *my* end up."

Stober stalked away from his partner and went back to sit quietly with Reece, where he tried to think of what he would tell the world.

The new *DelusionX Disaster* game was what Jamey would rather be playing, but since his last Net grades had lined in low, his parents insisted that the only new software they'd be buying would be educational. He kept telling them, who needed an education when you wore the Web on your wrist, but they were unmoved. So he wasn't expecting much when he plugged in to his family's VR console, just a dull scenario that wouldn't even be distracting enough to take his mind off homework.

Why would anyone want to pretend to be the first man on the Moon anyway? What was the point?

Nothing was up there but rocks. Nothing worth shooting at at all.

The package had made big promises, but being Neil Armstrong didn't seem quite as exciting as the manufacturers—or at least their PR firm—had hoped it would be. Endless waiting for launch. Days of travel from the Earth to the Moon. Jamey's finger seemed to rest perpetually on the fast forward key, and he imagined that any of his peers stuck in this world would have done the same. Who would put up with such unexciting things for real, when in VR, you could skip the boring parts? What was VR supposed to be anyway, but life with the boring bits cut out?

Skipping randomly ahead, he found himself bounding on the surface of the Moon. The long leaps were fun, sort of like being on an enormous trampoline. The desolation that surrounded him mirrored his heart, and he liked the feeling of solitude. Though he knew that in the real world, his parents could cause him to disconnect anytime, it seemed as if no one could reach him here. Not his teachers. Not his parents. Not his friends who for the most part themselves bored him. They were all far overhead, back on an Earth that no longer felt as if it was crushing him. He looked back from his home to the surface of the Moon, which he hated to admit didn't seem so bad after all.

A figure approached him from off in the distance.

Jamey stood there, the Lunar Module behind him, feeling betrayed as he watched the tiny form become a man. If Jamey was supposed to be the first man in the Moon, why did they program some old guy here first? The invader looked as if he could have been his father. And worse than that, there had to have been some kind of error, for he was not even wearing a space suit. He was just some geezer in a flannel shirt who could have been out shopping.

"Do I get a refund?" asked Jamey. "This really blows the illusion."

"I'm not into illusions," said Alexander Reece, the last man on the Moon, as he stopped beside the boy who was wearing Neil Armstrong. "Personally, I find reality a lot more interesting."

"Reality sucks. Who are you?"

"I was the last. I shouldn't have been. Neither should you."

"What's up with the program? How did you get here?"

"I died," said Reece, smiling.

"Cool."

"No program put me here. This, I guess, is heaven."

"If you believe in heaven."

"Heaven's as real as you make it, Jamey. Have you ever thought about dying?"

"Sometimes. But I'm fourteen."

"The Universe doesn't care how old you are, I'm afraid. Someday, everything is going to die. You. Your family. Your great-great-great grandkids. Even the Earth itself. Even the Moon."

"That could never happen. Those things have been here forever."

"Forever doesn't last forever anymore. Look."

Reece pointed at the sun, which pulsed and swelled and leaped out like an angry wave to smother the Earth, and then for a fierce fiery moment, even the Moon itself on which they stood. Jamey gasped as the surge overcame him and passed on to the planets beyond. Before he could detach from the VR console, all was as before. He found himself standing in stillness beside a man who claimed to be dead, a man who asserted he had been the last man on the Moon.

"We've got to go back there, Jamey," said Reece, his voice choked with the passion of his belief. "Or else someday there won't be an out there, neither fake nor real, at least not with people on it. And there'll

be no more in here either, for there won't even be
VR chambers to dream in if someone doesn't start
making some dreams real. I need you to help make
some dreams real again, Jamey. Look. Look up."

Jamey tilted his head back and looked up with an
unaccustomed awe. And then, not only in his mind,
but in the hearts and minds of millions of other
plugged-in people around the world, overhead, without any fuss, the stars were going on, one by one.

CARRY THE MOON IN MY POCKET

by *James Lovegrove*

When, during break one morning, Luke Weatherby spied Barry Griffin striding purposefully across the school playground toward the low wall where he was sitting, he immediately did what any sane person familiar with Barry Griffin's reputation would have done. Hastily folding up the *National Geographic* he had been reading, he leaped to his feet and set off in the direction of the science block with the air of someone who has just remembered he is late for an urgent appointment.

The first time Barry called out his surname, Luke pretended not to hear and carried on walking. The second "Weatherby!" was bellowed with such vocative authority, however, that Luke had no choice but to stop dead in his tracks. Slowly, with a mouth gone suddenly dry and his heartbeat thumping in his ears, he turned around. He had no idea what he might have done to attract Barry's attention, but whatever it was, he was already regretting it.

Usually when Barry Griffin was about to beat someone up, his pudgy, pugnacious features would clench into a purple scowl of disapproval, a thundercloud that presaged a storm of physical violence. On this occasion, however, the expression Luke saw on his face was less overtly intimidating and, consequently, far more unnerving.

Barry was smiling.

"Yeah, Weatherby," he said, as he halted in front of Luke. "I been looking for you."

"Ohhhh?" said Luke. It came out more like a groan than anything.

"Yeah." Barry's breath wisped in the cold November air. "I got something for you."

"Something?" Luke imagined a smack in the mouth, a dead arm, a Chinese burn, a wedgie.

"An offer. I got something I think you might like. You're into the Moon and them spacemen and that, aren't you?"

This was something of an understatement. At that time, November of 1972, there couldn't have been many eleven-year-old boys who didn't have at least a passing interest in the Apollo missions. Luke, though, was not just a keen follower of the lunar landings. For him, the unfolding adventure of the American astronauts' voyages to and from the Moon was nothing short of a grand passion. An all-consuming obsession.

In response to Barry's inquiry, he gave a numb nod.

"So how would you like to own a piece of it?" Barry asked.

Luke blinked. "I'm sorry?"

Patiently Barry elaborated. "How would you like to own a genuine and absolutely real chunk of Moon rock?"

"You're serious? You have a chunk of Moon rock?"

"Yeah. Genuine and absolutely real."

"Well, I mean, how? I mean, where is it? Can I have a look? Now?"

"It's not here. I wouldn't bring it in to school, would I? Someone might try 'n nick it off me."

Given that Barry was taller and stockier than almost anyone else in the entire school, and noted for his violent tendencies, Luke didn't think that this was very likely, but he said nothing.

"Meet me at the gates after last bell and I'll take you to see it. All right?"

"Um, yeah," said Luke. "All right. Fine."

"Good," said Barry. He about-faced and walked away, leaving Luke standing bewildered, scarcely able to believe that the foregoing exchange had taken place and, moreover, that not one portion of his body was now either bruised or bleeding.

At lunch, over a plateful of suety steak-and-kidney pie, diced mixed vegetables, and two hard scoops of mashed potato, Luke regaled his best friend and confidante Mandy Briggs with an account of the brief breaktime encounter with Barry.

"I don't know what's harder to believe," Mandy said. "Barry saying he's got a bit of Moon rock, or you having a pleasant conversation with him."

"You think he's lying?"

"Well, it does sound a bit far-fetched. Like something he made up to appeal specially to you."

"To me? What for?"

Mandy spelled it out for him. "To get you on your own so he can do you in."

"But why? I've done nothing wrong."

"Makes no difference. Barry doesn't need a reason to beat somebody up."

"So why didn't he just do it there and then?" Luke argued. "It doesn't make sense. You know, Mandy," he added, unconsciously emulating the tolerant, liberal tones of Mr. Clement, their bearded, sandal-wearing RI teacher, "maybe Barry's not as bad as everyone makes out. Maybe it's time somebody gave him the benefit of the doubt."

At this, Mandy snorted so hard that morsels of half-masticated mashed potato shot out of her nose and into her bowl of spotted dick and custard. "Luke— Barry Griffin! You don't give Barry Griffin the benefit of the doubt. You steer clear of him."

"Even so," said Luke. "If there's a chance he's not lying and it's not a trick and he does have that Moon rock, then I have to meet him. I've got no choice."

"Well, if you have to, you have to," Mandy said with a grim grin. "Just tell me this. What music would you like played at your funeral?"

The sarcastic laugh with which Luke responded to Mandy's remark returned to haunt him as he stood outside the school gates three hours later. Back in the crowded, rowdy confines of the school canteen, he had found it easy to sneer at his friend's skepticism. Now, waiting for Barry to appear, he felt considerably less secure in his faith in Barry's better nature. Mandy might be right. This might just be an elaborate scheme on Barry's part to get Luke alone so that he could give him the kind of prolonged, uninterrupted duffing-up that could not easily be carried out on the school premises without the risk of teacher intervention. It did not matter that Luke still could not think of anything he had done to offend Barry. Did you have to offend the lightning bolt that struck you? The rabid dog that bit your hand?

Several times he nearly lost his nerve and fled. Only the thought of that lump of Moon rock, the possibility of being able to touch, to hold an actual fragment of the Moon, kept him there.

Eventually Barry emerged from the school building, accompanied by one of his lieutenants, Kevin Holroyd. Kevin, like Barry, was not the brightest of sparks, but unlike Barry he did not have brute physicality to compensate for his lack of academic prowess. Gangly, stoop-shouldered, and shuffling, with a drooping jaw, sluggish lips, and a maternally-inflicted haircut so atrocious that sometimes complete strangers would stop and point at him in the street, Kevin was patently one of life's losers. Perhaps the only shrewd decision he ever made—and many would argue that it was dumb luck rather than shrewdness—was to fall in with Barry. Association with such a notorious and dreaded figure afforded Kevin immunity from the insults and injuries that would otherwise, in the normal course of events, have been heaped upon him.

At the sight of Kevin, Luke's spirits sank. All at once his worst fears (not to mention Mandy's suspicions) were confirmed. Barry was bringing Kevin along as an accomplice, someone to pin Luke down on the ground while Barry delivered the blows.

Praying that Barry had not yet spotted him, Luke started to creep furtively away from the gates.

"Hoy! Weatherby!"

Luke froze.

"Where *you* off to?" Barry demanded.

"N–nowhere," Luke stammered. "I was just . . ." He fumbled for an excuse. "Thought I saw a five-pee on the ground. I was just going to pick it up." He mimed scrutinizing the pavement. "Only I think I made a mistake. Well anyway." He let out a somewhat too chirpy laugh. "Here we all are. Hello, Kevin."

"Wuh," said Kevin.

"This way," said Barry, pointing along the road. He and Kevin started walking, and Luke reluctantly fell in step behind.

In the misty, darkening light of the late-autumn afternoon the three boys wove their way through town. Barry and Kevin set a brisk pace, which Luke did his best to match, but it was an effort to keep his feet from lapsing into a condemned man's trudge. Where were they taking him? Some remote, secluded spot, no doubt. Somewhere where his cries would not be heard.

Several times he contemplated making a bid for freedom, only to reject the idea. If he ran and Barry and Kevin caught up with him, wouldn't the pummeling he received then be twice as severe? Slowly, resignation set in. He had never been beaten up before. Perhaps it wouldn't be as bad as he thought. One thing was certain: he wasn't going to offer any resistance when the time came. He would take his punishment like a coward.

They had gone about half a mile in silence when, abruptly, Kevin said, "S'yuh," to Barry and veered off down a terraced side street. Luke watched him go with a mixture of puzzlement and relief. So Kevin hadn't come along as an accomplice after all. And if that was the case, then maybe Luke had misread the situation and maybe—just maybe—Barry's Moon rock *did* exist.

Feeling considerably happier, though still not yet completely at ease, Luke continued walking alongside Barry, while one by one the streetlamps flickered on overhead, the dull red gleam of their bulbs quickening to orange.

The Sussex country town Luke called home was spread over several interleaving humps of the South Downs, and its social strata were roughly demarcated by altitude. The older, smarter, and costlier properties were situated on top of the hills and benefited from good views and spacious gardens. The further downslope you went, the closer-quartered and less venerable the houses became. Deep in the folds of the valleys was where the council estates huddled, honeycomb warrens of pebbledashed post-War semis.

It was to one of these estates that Barry led Luke, who, hailing as he did from a detached, four-bedroom Edwardian residence near one of the hilltops, seldom had cause to venture into the nether reaches of town and, doing so now, felt like a cross between Theseus and Dr. Livingstone.

A cockeyed garden gate provided access to a concrete pathway that crossed a square of overgrown lawn to the front door of what Luke correctly assumed to be the Griffin homestead. Outside the house an old, partially dismantled Triumph motorcycle leaned on its kickstand, removed components lying around it like body parts around a blown-up soldier. Inside, a dog

was barking, a baby was screaming, a TV set was jab-
bering, and music—the Rolling Stones, Luke
thought—was blaring.

Barry entered and, without announcing his arrival
to his family, headed straight upstairs. Luke followed
him in. Odors of cigarette smoke, dog urine, and
boiled cabbage stunned him. Through one doorway he
glimpsed a harried-looking woman pacing up and
down the linoleum of a kitchen floor, trying to quiet
a squalling infant. Through another doorway a pair of
sock-clad feet were visible, perched on the arm of a
sofa and tapping together in time to the theme tune
of *Screen Test.* From behind a third door, this one
firmly shut, came the sound of canine claws scratching
and scrabbling, along with that angry barking which,
to judge by its deepness and gruffness, emanated from
the throat of a hound the size of a shire-horse.

Having absorbed all these impressions of life *chez*
Griffin in the space of a few head-spinning seconds,
Luke decided he was safer off sticking close to
Barry—better the devil you know and all that—and
pursued him up the uncarpeted staircase and into his
bedroom.

The room was small, with just enough floor space
for a single bed, a wonky G-Plan wardrobe, and a low
armchair upholstered in a coarse, lime-green fabric.
The view from the window, through a grubby net cur-
tain, was of the side of the adjacent house. A pinup
of the current Brighton and Hove Albion squad,
pulled from the center of *Shoot!* magazine, was the
room's only decoration.

Barry was on his knees, groping under the bed.
Hearing Luke enter, he told him to close the door.
Luke did as commanded. The door somewhat muffled
the downstairs domestic racket, although the music,
which was coming from the adjacent bedroom, continued to pound through the intervening wall unabated.

From beneath the bed Barry produced a small steel

money box, which he unlocked and opened with a tiny key. Saying, "Here," he handed the box to Luke.

Inside, lying in a nest of crumpled toilet paper, was a lump of dark, brown-gray mineral approximately the size of a golf ball. It was rough-textured and porous like a sponge, pitted and knobbly and near-spherical, with here and there a twinkling glint of something crystalline in its composition.

Luke stared at it, conscious of not breathing, of not *daring* to breathe.

Was it . . . ?

Could it really be . . . ?

It certainly *looked* as though it came from the Moon. It looked, in fact, like a miniature Moon it- self—like a tiny, scale-model replica of the Earth's cosmic traveling companion, small enough to pick up, to hold in one's hand, to lift up and just block the real Moon from sight.

He didn't want to believe that it was Moon rock. He didn't want to believe that it had been gathered up from the Moon's surface by one of the Apollo astronauts (which one?) and taken aboard a lunar module to be ferried a quarter of a million miles back to Earth. He didn't want to believe this because, ratio- nally, he knew that there was no way a young boy in a small, unremarkable English country town—a young boy, moreover, like Barry Griffin—could have ob- tained something so fantastically valuable and rare. It was impossible. Inconceivable.

Yet—oh, God—in his heart of hearts Luke *knew*. He *knew* what he was looking at. He *knew*—from the sonorous, reverberant chime of recognition that was thrilling through him—that the rock was the genuine article.

And he knew that he had to possess it.

"So, um, Barry," he said, when he had regained sufficient composure to speak again, "where did you get it from?" It seemed wise to investigate the rock's provenance and give an impression of circumspection before the negotiations began.

"Me mum's brother give it to me," came the reply. "He's an engineer, and he was working over in—where's that place where them rockets take off?"

"Houston, Texas."

"Yeah, there. There was a lump going spare, so they said he could have it."

That wounded plausible to Luke. Or at any rate, it didn't sound *im*plausible. Hundreds of rock samples had been brought back from the Moon by the five successful Apollo missions to date. Surely the NASA geologists didn't need *all* of them.

"And, er, how much are you asking for it? I mean, if we're talking cash, then the best I could offer is, oh, say, fifty pence?" In fact Luke was prepared to go as high as one pound, but he knew it was a good idea to start with a low bid. Perhaps Barry was too stupid to realize the true value of his uncle's gift.

"A tenner," said Barry, simply.

"What!"

"Ten quid," Barry reiterated.

"Ten quid? But that's—that's a fortune!"

"Take it or leave it," Barry said, relieving Luke of the box and closing the lid.

And so it was that Luke learned one of the hard lessons of commerce: that which the buyer desires the most, he must expect to pay a high premium for.

He had no alternative but to agree to Barry's price.

He knew his parents would not give him the money, but he asked them anyway and, as expected, was turned down. He then asked if they would *lend* him the money, which they also refused to do, his mother referring to that sage maxim, "Neither a borrower nor a lender be."

"What do you want ten pounds for anyway, Lunatic Luke?" his father inquired.

He couldn't tell them. They would think it was ridiculous. They would say he was wasting his money.

"Nothing," he said.

"Awful lot of lolly to spend on nothing," said his father, with a genial twitch of his eyebrows.

Christmas was coming soon, and with it the customary annual windfall of checks and postal orders from uncles, aunts, godparents, and grandparents. But Luke didn't think he could wait that long to buy the Moon rock; and besides, before he had left Barry's house, Barry had intimated to him that the Moon rock was not going to be available for long. Several other buyers were interested, Barry had said, so if Luke wanted it for himself he was going to have to move fast.

There was nothing else for it. He would have to earn the money.

Over the ensuing fortnight Luke washed cars, weeded neighbors' flower beds, ran errands for elderly Miss Warburton, polished all the brass fixtures and silverware at the Fraylings' house, and served as a bow-tied and thoroughly *charming* butler at one of Mrs. Stoughton-Hadley's Saturday coffee-mornings.

The result of all this activity, which took up every minute of his spare time for those two weeks, was a net haul of a little over six pounds. That sum, added to the modest savings that had accumulated in his post office account, took him to a total of seven pounds and fifty-three pence. Still not enough, and Barry was making it clear to him that the window of opportunity was closing fast. If Luke didn't come up with the cash soon, one of the other buyers was going to nip in and snatch the Moon rock out from under his nose.

Drastic action was called for. In order to make up the shortfall, Luke began selling off treasured possessions. Justin Watkins had long had his eye on Luke's impeccably assembled Airfix Saturn V booster and didn't need much persuasion to part with thirty pence

for it, while Stefan Meyer generously agreed to take
Luke's revolving Moon-globe off his hands for the
princely sum of forty-five pence and Tom Greenough
brought Luke's Dinky Toy lunar rover for a figure not
much higher. None of the items Luke sold fetched
anything close to what he considered to be its true
market value, but that was just another hard lesson of
commerce to be learned: a desperate vendor is always
at a disadvantage.

Eventually, by the beginning of December, Luke
was in possession of ten pounds' worth of gleaming,
newly-decimalized change in assorted denominations.
At the bank on the high street he exchanged the coins
for a pair of crisp blue five-pound notes.

The long-awaited transaction took place, by prear-
rangement, in the school playground shortly before
morning assembly. Barry Griffin strolled away with
the two fivers folded tidily in his trouser pocket, while
Luke was left clutching the chunk of Moon rock,
scarcely able to believe that this moment had finally
arrived. For over two weeks he had been on tenter-
hooks, not knowing for sure if he was going to be able
to scrape the money together in time or if someone
else was going to get the rock that he so earnestly
desired and so eminently deserved to own. Now, with
the coveted object in his hands, he was excited, certainly, but he was also suffused with a sense of utter
rightness and calm. The agony of uncertainty was
over. An inner tumult had subsided. He had passed
from an ocean of storms to a sea of tranquillity. The
rock was his.

Luke could not remember a time when the Apollo
program had not been a fundamental part of his life.
His father liked to claim that Luke had been born the
very day in May 1961 on which President Kennedy
made his speech to the U.S. Congress vowing that
America would put a man on the Moon before the

decade was out, and although this was untrue—Luke had been born two days later—it did, with its suggestion of a synchronicitous and quasimystical source for Luke's Moon-landing mania, make for a good story.

The truth was, Luke had loved the Moon from a very early age. He loved its quiet radiance; the way on clear nights, when full, it illuminated the scene outside his bedroom window, picking out every detail—every leaf, every roof tile, every blade of grass—in delicate silvery filigree. He pitied its solitude, surrounded by cold blackness and the inferior stars. He admired its modesty (so unlike its brash daytime counterpart the sun). And when his father told him that it was not merely a glimmering, facelike disk in the sky but an arid, airless, orbiting planetoid, Earth's lesser twin, his compassion for it only intensified. He longed for it to be happy, and wished there was some way for it to know that it was not alone.

Then one day he learned in school that over in America, at a place called Houston, plans were afoot to send men to the Moon in a rocket. And suddenly it seemed that his wish had been granted. The Apollo missions would be a slender bridge between the Earth and its satellite, a lifeline across the void. The Moon would be lonely no more.

He began pestering his parents for further information about the Apollo program. They, only too keen to encourage their son in the pursuit of knowledge, bought him a Ladybird book about space exploration. He devoured it and begged for more. More books followed, and then for his fifth birthday his parents presented him with a large wall chart consisting of detailed maps of the Moon. Immediately Luke set about learning the name of every feature of lunar topography, every mountain range, crater, and sea. Daily he pored over the wall chart, until its monochrome patterns were etched in his mind and its gray contours were virtually a map of his own brain.

Thereafter, further lunar-related gifts came in from
relatives who were delighted not only that serious-
minded young Luke had developed such a passionate
and mature interest in so grown-up a subject, but also
that this made choosing birthday and Christmas pres-
ents for him considerably simpler. By the age of eight
Luke had amassed an enviable collection of parapher-
nalia directly and tangentially related to the Moon
landings. If, before the purchase of the Moon rock, he
had had to single out one item that he prized above
all the others, it would have been the telescope from
his great-aunt Georgina, for its lenses brought the
Moon into such close proximity and such sharp relief
that sometimes its Earthward-directed face appeared
to be little more than an arm's length away, almost
within reach of his fingertips.

His relatives also began sending him articles, clipped
from newspapers and magazines, on the subject of the
Apollo program. These he pasted neatly and methodi-
cally into a series of scrapbooks, and read and reread
until he had grasped most of what the journalists were
trying to convey. A certain amount of the technical
jargon remained beyond him, but the gist of the articles was quite clear, and the narrative they were cumulatively telling was an encouraging one. Step by step,
month by month the people at NASA were steadily
drawing closer to their goal.

The first three lunar-orbiting missions, Apollos 8 to
10, occurred while Luke was nine and ten. He followed their progress via the newspapers and television, but did not allow himself to become too excited.
Not yet. He knew that these missions were merely
appetite-whetters for the main course, the overture
before the opera began.

The moment Apollo 11 took off from the launchpad
and tore into the sky, Luke was transfixed and trans-
figured. Teachers noted a decline in his attentiveness
in class; friends found him more than usually aloof

and prone to bouts of dreamy, faraway staring. It was as if he was no longer completely there. And he wasn't. His body was on Earth, but his mind was with Armstrong and Aldrin and Collins in their spacecraft as they hurtled toward the Moon at the unimaginable speed of over two thousand miles per hour.

By special parental dispensation he was allowed to stay up late on the evening of July 19, 1969 for the live broadcast of the lunar module *Eagle*'s touchdown. (In truth, his mother and father knew that, had they denied Luke permission to do so, he would probably have never spoken to them again. Besides, it was the school holidays and a Saturday.)

Cross-legged on the living-room floor in his pajamas, dressing gown, and slippers, Luke watched the blurry black-and-white images relayed by the BBC with rapt fascination, adding his own commentary to that of the onscreen reporters, pundits, and experts, and on a couple of occasions hotly and indignantly correcting them when they got their facts wrong.

When *Eagle* finally set foot in the lunar dust, it was a moment of epiphany for Luke. He cried. He chortled. He hugged his legs and yelled with glee. And when, around midnight, he received his last warning to go to bed *or else*, he made sure before crawling beneath the covers that the curtains in his room were wide open so that, lying in the dark, he could see the Moon through the window.

"We're here," he whispered to the shining, lopsided face in the heavens as he sank exhaustedly into slumber. "We're *here*."

The next day there was further joy for Luke, as the footage of the first-ever Moon walk, which had taken place while he slept, was played and replayed on TV. It was one small step for Neil Armstrong, one giant leap for Luke Weatherby's soul.

After the wonder and majesty of that July weekend, everything else could only be an anticlimax. Nevertheless, Luke devotedly followed each of the subsequent Moon missions, even as the media decided that the Apollo program was of diminishing public interest and accorded it increasingly less coverage. He made sure he was clear on the scientific objectives of each mission, and assiduously and with painstaking exactitude marked the site of each landing on his wall chart with a fluorescent orange sticker-dot and traced the route of each Moon walk with a dotted line drawn in red fiber-tip pen. While the crew of Apollo 13 were struggling for their lives in the vacuum gulfs of space, Luke was with them in their spacecraft every inch of the way, sharing, as acutely as if it were his own, their anxiety, their fear and, in the end, their relief when they splashed down safe and sound in the Pacific.

Throughout 1970 and 1971 Luke kept his faith in the continuing validity of the Apollo program even while others more important than him were losing theirs. By 1972, however, it was clear even to him that the adventure was coming to an end. NASA's funding had been cut, Apollo 18 had been canceled, and it was commonly held that Apollo 17, scheduled for liftoff on December 7th, would be the last manned mission to the Moon for the foreseeable future, and possibly forever.

Autumn of that year, therefore, was a time of hollowness for Luke, a long, protracted period of mourning and decline. The days cooled, the nights drew in, and within Luke a deep-seated ache of loss yawned ever wider.

The Moon rock—sought at such risk, bought at such expense—offered some consolation. With the help of his woodwork teacher, Mr. Eden, Luke fashioned a display container for it, a plywood box eight inches square with a sliding perspex lid and a raised inlay of navy-blue card with a circular hole cut in it for the rock to rest in. The box was accorded a place on a shelf all its own in his bedroom, just below his library of space-exploration literature and Apollo-article scrapbooks, and at least once a day he would fetch it down, take out the rock, and turn it over and over in his hands, committing every detail of its surface to memory, every minuscule cleft and declivity. He would hold it up to his nose and inhale its peppery, alien scent, then would rub the tip of his index finger over its rough surface until the whorls of his fingerprint were grimed with ashy Moon dust. He wondered if, hammered open, the Moon rock might reveal an interior of white anorthosite, or maybe green olivine. But of course he would not dream of damaging it, not even in the interests of science.

He felt, when all was said and done, that he had gotten the better end of the bargain with Barry. In retrospect, ten pounds didn't seem too high a price to pay for such a beautiful and cherishable artefact. Ten pounds to own a part of the Moon? If necessary, he would have paid twenty, fifty, a *hundred* pounds for it.

On Monday, December 11, 1972, as scheduled, Gene Cernan and Jack Schmitt landed in the lunar module *Challenger* at Littrow Crater near the Taurus Mountains.

On Tuesday, December 12th, Luke learned how cruelly he had been deceived.

It was the last day of the term. The classrooms and corridors of the school were bedecked with paperchains, tinsel, and handmade foil stars, and throughout the building there was an atmosphere of hilarity, of barely restrained anarchy. Voices were loud. Every now and then someone would break out spontaneously and raucously into a Christmas carol. Teachers smiled and indulged a certain level of misbehavior.

It would have been pointless trying to cram any last few crumbs of knowledge into the minds of boys and girls already filled to bursting with thoughts of the imminent holidays and freedom, so lessons that day were unscripted and extracurricular. In science, Miss Barker put on a "fireworks display" of pyrotechnical chemical reactions, which included dropping tiny fragments of pure sodium into a bowl of water so that they raced about like fizzing water-boatmen, and igniting a small pile of orangey-red powder so that it erupted like a volcano, spewing itself into a conical heap of dark green ashes; while in RI, Mr. Clement led the class in an improvised retelling of the Nativity story, giving the events a contemporary setting—an inner-city high-rise block—and recasting Mary as a single mother, the shepherds as Hell's Angels, and the Three Wise Men as a group of peace-loving flower children; and in English, Mrs. Lloyd had each member of the class come up to the front of the room in turn and give an impromptu one-minute talk on any subject he or she wanted, as an exercise in off-the-cuff public speaking.

Luke, naturally, took the Moon landings as his topic, and delivered a ferocious harangue against the Nixon administration, criticizing its shortsightedness and its criminal irresponsibility in halting the Apollo program. A reusable space shuttle was not, he admitted, an idea entirely without merit, but in his opinion NASA ought to be concentrating its efforts on establishing a manned lunar base. The Moon, he argued, was mankind's stepping stone to Mars, our gateway to exploring and colonizing the entire universe. And, he said by way of conclusion, one day mankind would return to its senses and send rockets there again.

This last claim was not just bravado. It was, as far as Luke was concerned, a promise.

The speech earned a sustained ripple of applause from his classmates and commendation from Mrs. Lloyd, who said it had been an impressively fiery and eloquent piece of rhetoric.

After the lesson, Luke bumped into Mandy in a

corridor. He was eager to brag about his speech, but she had news that took precedence.

"I should have told you this yesterday, Luke," she said, "but I wasn't sure how to go about breaking it."

"Breaking what?" Luke replied breezily. At that moment he was feeling invulnerable. Invincible. Mrs. Lloyd's praise had kindled a fire of pride in him that was still blazing strongly.

"Look, it's just something I overheard, so it may not be true. He could just have been boasting."

"Who could?"

Mandy hesitated. "Barry Griffin."

"Go on," said Luke.

"Well, you know how in the downstairs girls' bogs you can hear everything that goes on in the downstairs boys' bogs?"

"It works the other way, too. The sound all sort of echoes through the ventilation system."

"I know. Anyway, I was in the girls' yesterday afternoon, and I heard Barry and someone else talking in the boys'. Whoever he was talking to just went kind of 'duh' and 'uh' so it must have been Kevin Holroyd. Anyway, I wasn't really paying much attention until I heard Barry mention *your* name."

All of a sudden Luke felt a chill, as though a cold draft had blown in through a chink somewhere. He had had his first, vague presentiment of the bad news that was coming.

"Of course he could just have been saying what he said in order to impress Kevin," Mandy went on.

Luke's voice was hoarse and hollow. "Tell me what he said."

"It was about the Moon rock."

"What about it?"

But he knew. He knew what Mandy was going to say. Perhaps he had known the truth all along, but in wanting to believe that the Moon rock was genuine, in wanting so much to obtain some small, tangible

memento of the magnificent era that was shortly coming to a close, he had deliberately not listened to his
instincts; had deliberately ignored common sense and
handed over a large sum of money for a fabulous
illusion.

The rock, it transpired, *had* been a gift from Barry's
uncle, but thereafter everything Barry had told Luke
about it had been false. Barry's uncle was not a part-
time rocket engineer, he was a coal miner from
Swansea. Last November he had come down to stay
with Barry's family for a weekend and brought the
rock with him as a present for his nephew. He had
thought Barry might be amused by it because it
looked like something from the Moon, even though it
actually had come from nowhere more unearthly than
a slag heap near Merthyr Tydfil. According to Mandy,
Barry had then gone on to inform Kevin that his uncle
was coming down to stay again over Christmas and
that Barry had asked him to bring a few more "Moon
rocks," which he could then flog to that stupid sucker
Weatherby. And at that, Barry had started a gleeful
chortling which Kevin, after taking a second to work
out what the joke was, had joined in.

"I'm sorry, Luke," Mandy said, laying a hand on
his arm. "I didn't want to tell you but I really thought
you ought to know, and I thought it would be better
coming from me than anybody else."

"That's okay," said Luke. His eyes felt hot, and
there seemed to be an excess of saliva at the back of
his throat. "I mean, actually I'd pretty much worked
it out for myself."

"Really?" said Mandy, dubiously.

"Yeah. By examining the rock. The mineral content
was all wrong. As a matter of fact, I've been meaning
to have a word with Barry about it for some time."

"Right," said Mandy. "Yes. Of course."

He was grateful to her for granting him, for his
dignity's sake, that small fig leaf of a lie.

He didn't confront Barry about the rock. Of course he didn't. Walk up to the biggest bully in the school and accuse him of swindling? Not likely. Not unless he was keen to lose a few teeth.

Instead, at home that evening, he took the rock from its display box and rolled it from hand to hand while he debated whether to pound it to smithereens with a hammer or merely toss it into the bin like the piece of worthless rubbish it was.

In the end, after much pondering, he decided against either course of action. He simply put the rock back into the box and returned the box to its shelf.

Thirty-one years later, Professor Lucas Weatherby, head of the geology faculty at Oxford University, became the first civilian British astronaut to set foot on the Moon.

The first thing the professor did, after stepping out of the air lock of Selene Base in the Aristarchus Crater on his maiden Moon walk, was bend down and plant something in the dust at his feet. It was an object he had brought with him aboard the Euro-Russian lunar shuttle *General Lebed* all the way from the launch site at Baikonur—a small, round, unremarkable-looking lump of rock.

Then, straightening up awkwardly in his space suit, the professor spoke the following words, so softly that the comms mike in his helmet did not pick them up.

"We're here. I said we'd come back, didn't I? And we're *here*."

MOON HUNTERS

by Kathleen M. Massie-Ferch

"He wants to buy the Moon? I didn't know it was for sale."

"It's not!"

"That's like trying to buy America."

"Buying America would be easier, only one government to bribe."

"Dale went along with it?"

"Of course the bitch did. It's now our job to get him one first-class Moon."

"How long do we have?"

"She wants it for a present!"

"Birthday? Which year?"

"Dr. Packard, what's our distance now?" Dale Morgan's soft voice carried through the ship's flight deck and over the soft whirl of the circulation fans.

I tensed automatically, and pushed at my bangs; a wayward strand of hair still tickled my nose. I liked Dale, some of the time, but when her voice had that soft-yet-intense quality, she was usually about to lose her temper. I rechecked my calculations.

"Dr. Packard?" Her voice held even less warmth now.

"Just a second, Dale. This object is very irregular. My signal is bouncing all over the solar system. Very little is coming back to me."

I took a quick breath. The numbers ranged from three thousand to forty-five hundred kilometers—the most steady values I had seen in the last twenty min-

utes. I recorded the readings for a very long ten seconds and asked for an average. The computer gave
me a range of values.

I didn't need this!

Take a guess!

Any guess, Lizbeth.

"Dr. Morgan, it looks like we are thirty-five hundred kilometers away," I said.

"Right on target! Good job, Lizbeth," Conrad
Davis added. He winked at me before turning back
to his own control screens.

Dale looked as if she wanted to question the figure,
but instead said, "Deceleration burn for ninety seconds on my mark."

"On your mark," Conrad answered her.

"Mark." The engines engaged and the distant power
vibrated through the ship's decks. "We hold this path
until we confirm this rock's viability," Dale added.

"Aye, aye, Captain," Conrad said.

I glared at him, trying not to smile. Dale studied
him only a moment. He flashed his half smile. He
could be so charming, even when he only half tried.
Dale refused to comment and instead engaged the
ship's communications link.

"Crew, this is Dr. Morgan," Dale began. As if the
two men and three women down one deck didn't
know her composed voice by now. It felt as if someone
had lowered the temperature on the flight deck. Did
they feel it, too? We had been on this ship together
for five months and two unsuccessful rendezvous. I
held my tongue and turned back to my computer. All
too soon Dale would want to know if this was an accept-
able rock. I had to find the right answers for her.

"Deceleration completed," Dale spoke into the
com-link again. "We're on a matching orbit with asteroid 10 740GP. Resume your standard duties."

"Dr. Morgan, how long before we know if this is
finally the right one?" Don Gradey's voice rumbled

over the headset. He was our construction crew boss and the only one of us who didn't flinch when Dale turned her pale eyes our way.

"Are you anxious to go home, Mr. Gradey?"

"No, ma'am. I want to put my new toys through their tests."

"I'd like that, too. Two days at most," Dale answered. She turned to Conrad. I'm going downshift for my exercise period." She moved through the small space easily in the zero-g. Dale never bumped instrument bays or wayward computer pads as I seemed to do continuously. If her muscles were sore from so many months in weightlessness, you'd never know by the way she moved.

The hours passed as I collected data. It would have been easier if we were closer, but Dale was always cautious about disturbing any asteroid's orbit with our ship's engine exhaust—even a rock out in the Kuiper Belt. I understood her reasoning, but I didn't have to like the extra work it caused me.

As if on cue, Dale entered the flight deck and floated over to where I worked.

"Well?" Her voice was quiet; she almost purred. Her pale cheeks had a slight flush to them. Her hair smelled faintly of flowers. Didn't she even sweat? If she did, she'd probably still smell like flowers! Good workouts always left her calm and rested. They always left me wrecked and sore.

"Dr. Morgan, we need to move closer to this asteroid," I said, being as diplomatic as possible.

"Why?"

I felt myself tense up, yet it was a reasonable question, and I wiped my hands against my coveralls. "It's dark and irregularly shaped. I'm having a rough time getting signals back for assessment."

"Could it be spinning faster than most rocks?" Conrad asked. His freckled face was nearly unreadable at the moment.

"Yeah. Could be. Can't tell for sure what the problem is. Every time I think I've got a value for the rotation the numbers change."

"Visuals?" she asked.

"Useless. We're coming in from the dark side."

"Is it worth getting closer?" Dale asked. "Are we just wasting any time we spend if it's too irregular?"

A shiver ran through me. What was the right answer? I had to give her an answer. "I—I need more information before deciding that. Can we cut our distance in half?"

Dale raised her left eyebrow over that. "Are you sure?" It was a simple question. There was nothing suspicious in her voice.

"Yes," I answered with only the slightest hesitation. Maybe she didn't notice because she stopped asking questions and went to work. I stayed on the flight deck for the next few hours and watched her and Conrad work while pretending to clean the area again.

What pretending? Our last encounter had seen us on the surface of an asteroid. No matter how we tried to keep the regolith outside our ship, an annoying amount returned with every excursion to the surface. We could never let the dust get out of hand, or it would devastate our computers. We had backup equipment, but that would mean an end to the current mission, and we would be homeward bound soon after.

Watching Dale pilot the ship was almost like watching a magician. She softly touched the controls as if they might bruise or they were her children, and the ship moved. Her pale eyes held a warmth I seldom saw. Her black hair was the longest it had been since our mission began, and it lifted away from her head in the weightlessness, softening the angular lines of her thin face. Her features looked tranquil, less withdrawn. For a second, I wondered what could frighten her? My guess was nothing.

The ship responded to her sure touch with ease and grace. Power moved through the ship's surfaces and into me. I felt more alive. In the end Dale got us within five hundred klics; she was that good a pilot. Close enough for my work, though we weren't in the same orbit. We chased the asteroid. Our exhaust gas aimed away from the rock. Safe. Asteroid 10 740GP should have looked impressive, but we were both still heading toward our distant Sun and most of the unlit side of the rock was facing us. We saw only a sliver of reflecting light.

I tried to suppress a yawn. I should have slept while Dale and Conrad moved our ship this last time. It had been foolish to watch them work; however, having a much cleaner ship was a nice bonus. Even the air smelled fresher. Maybe one of the crew had changed the air filters again. A few minutes back at my computer, and I knew why this was such a hard rock to view.

"The little—"

"Doctor," Dale began as a warning. She hated any foul language, which cut my working vocabulary in half, at least.

"The little monster," I started again, "is tumbling! And it's not just about one axis. It must be in at least two pieces moving close together."

Conrad was looking over my shoulder at the image. "And I'd say both pieces are not in sync, but slightly out of phase."

"Yeah, that's my read, too."

"A sandbox?" Conrad asked.

"No, it has too much mass for that."

"Pieces are not a good sign," Dale said. "A wasted trip, after all."

"Maybe not." Conrad said.

"She doesn't need your protection," Dale said. Her soft voice carried the weight of her command.

I didn't answer. I could feel my ears burning as I looked away and concentrated on the data coming in.

"I need a sleep shift before we move again," Dale said. "So do you, Dr. Packard."

"No, I'd rather work and get what data we can." I had to prove this wasn't a wasted visit.

"Your choice. You've got just six hours to collect your data and decide if we stay or not."

"Six hours?" My stomach knotted up. "I need more time!"

"If it's in pieces, we can't move it and it's useless to me."

"I want at least another day," I tried again.

"Six hours and then we move, or you prove to me we can keep this one." Dale was all business again. The softness her face had acquired while moving the ship was gone. She then glided down the ladder to the lower decks and her sleeping cube.

Conrad helped me silently and efficiently for about half an hour, then he moved over to Dale's work-station. His fingers glided over her pads.

"What are you doing?"

He gave me that impish grin. "Dale's too tired to move this ship again anytime soon. I turned off her alarm. She will wake naturally in ten or twelve hours."

"Thanks, but she'll have your head."

"Yeah, so what? She needs me, and we need her awake and alert."

Six hours later the puzzle was at least taking on a form and I didn't like it one bit. After another three hours the pieces, though still not together, were enough for me to see the full picture.

I started as all of a sudden Conrad was massaging my shoulders. I tried to pull away. "What are you doing?"

"Relax. You're so tense you'll be up half your next sleep shift with neck cramps."

"That does really feel good." He was close enough so I could smell his musk aftershave. He was the only man on board who shaved every day, or nearly so. His hair was red-blond, but his beard was carrot red. If I were him, I'd shave it off, too. I tried to just enjoy the rare moment.

After five minutes Conrad said, "You're not relaxing. This isn't a test. There is no one right answer. If you're wrong, Dale's not going to eat you. You try too hard to please her."

"I don't care what she thinks."

"Whatever you say. What's the data show?"

"It's an Arjuna subclass."

His hands stopped their soothing motions, and he pulled himself forward to look at my computer screen. "It's an Apollo? Not Kuiper Belt?"

"Yeah. My guess is these Twins are recent crossovers."

"It's big. What's its eccentricity?"

"Yeah, it's big. Both pieces together are fifteen kilometers by twenty. Inclination eccentricity is about point zero-seven."

He whistled. "Almost in Earth's orbital plane! Did you do a rough orbit?"

I nodded. "Just finished another model. In five years it'll come by Earth. I think whatever object knocked it out of the Kuiper Belt also broke it apart."

"How close?" I didn't answer him. "Lizbeth, how close?"

My stomach twisted into a knot, again. "Right on, plus or minus twenty-five thousand kilometers."

His eyes got wide, the deep brown irises standing out against the whites and his freckled skin. "How wide of an event window is that?"

"Five to seven hours." My voice seemed unnaturally steady to me.

"But we need at least two more weeks of plotting the orbit to be sure." He sounded as if he were trying to reassure us both.

"That would be nice, but we've been plotting it for ten days. I didn't bother to run the parameters before because I thought we were far enough out not to see this class of orbit. I should have checked it sooner."

"Who would have guessed? Besides, if it were in one piece, we'd want to keep it."

"I've checked the orbital numbers through the model at least ten times. I get the same value."

"What value?" Dale Morgan asked as she pulled herself up the ladder from the lower crew deck. She looked rested but slightly pissed as she moved to her station and checked her panel. "Who turned off my wake-up call?"

"I did," Conrad answered. "You needed more rest."

"You haven't that right—"

"Yes, I do. I'm senior med-tech. You gave me that power."

"We've a timetable to follow."

"Three hours won't make that big a difference to your timetable."

Dale stared at him for several moments and then she turned her pale, almost ice-blue eyes to me. "What values were you two talking about? You look ashen. What's up?"

I hooked a wayward lock of hair back behind my ear. "This is an Arjuna rock."

She immediately pushed herself over to my station. She smelled shower-fresh: lilac and summer breezes.

"Show me." She watched the display of my saved computations, a frown creasing her creamy brow. "Four point seven years," she murmured. "A five-hour-wide event window! How could Spacewatch have missed this one?"

"It's very dark," I offered, defending my former

coworkers. "The surface is almost pure carbon. I think it just recently spun down into this orbit."

"We could move it into a less threatening orbit and give Earth more time to respond," Conrad said.

I nodded. "Delayed Doppler shows at least one piece is predominantly stony under the regolith, with more than enough raw materials to fuel the tug. A little push would make a big difference."

She looked at the stream of data again. "Yes, and having only twenty-five thousand kilometers with which to play, we could send it right down on Paris or Chicago. Although, at this size it wouldn't matter where it hit. Whereas, on its own, it might miss Earth on this pass."

"It wouldn't take much time or energy to move it now, and guarantee a better orbital path," Conrad said.

"We could insure a safer orbit with a little time," I added.

"Are you still recording data?" Dale asked.

"Continuously."

"We need more information before any decision can be made. You both have been up too long. Go get some food and then sleep." She pushed off and moved toward her station. "In your own quarters."

I could feel my face heating. Conrad nudged me down to the lower deck first. He was shaking his head and smiling by the time we reached the galley.

"I wasn't going to say a thing to her," I said as he threw a ration-pack at me.

"Yeah, right. You should see how red your face is."

I tossed the ration back. "I'm not hungry."

He pushed toward me and placed the ration back in my hands. "Eat it anyway." He gave me a quick hug before pulling himself past me toward his quarters.

We had never been a couple. A few sleep cycles spent together now and then. His attention didn't make me feel special. I think he slept with every other crew member on this ship, except Dale. She was the one he wanted, but she kept to herself. Still I could use his arms, or anyone's, around me now for a day or two to warm me up. Instead I swallowed some meat-flavored, high-calorie goo and went to bed, only to awaken much later to Conrad shaking me.

"We're under thrust. Come on!"

I followed him up to the flight deck against the tug of a slight g-force. It was enough of a force to say we had been under power for at least an hour, maybe two.

I scanned for 10 740GP out the port window. It was an even dimmer target now. "Morgan, why the hell are we moving? We need more data. That rock is a real threat to Earth!"

"Don't you believe Lizbeth?" Conrad asked.

"I know I don't have much data to support my claim, but I know I'm right." I tried to keep the pain of frustration out of my voice.

"I know you're right, too, Dr. Packard."

"What?" I asked, my voice hardly more than a whisper.

"The reason you're on this ship is because you can extrapolate on a small amount of astrophysical data better than anyone else I know."

"Then why leave?" I demanded.

"Because we're not equipped for moving that rock," Morgan answered.

"The hell we aren't!" I answered. "That's exactly what we're here for, moving asteroids."

"It's in two pieces now. We need a minimum of two tugs, three would be better if one of those pieces breaks again. Or the third could gather and remove the smaller fragments."

"But?" I stammered. "What if we don't make it back to warn Earth? As dark as this sucker is they'll never see it in time."

"I sent all of your data on your Wayward Twins,

with your conclusions, down to JPL. Their reply stated they got the info and it was intact. Ten minutes later Dr. Sumi himself sent a message stating that because it's your work, he's putting his best people on the problem."

"Sumi said that?" I couldn't keep the awe out of my voice. If he had trusted me that much when I worked for JPL, I wouldn't have left. Who am I kidding? I had run just ahead of the pink slip. If I had been able to make decisions, I'd have survived the budget cuts.

Dale nodded. "He even liked your name for them, Wayward Twins."

"NASA doesn't have three tugs anymore," Conrad said. He was always so practical. "They have only one after the collision last year. MSpace is the only one with enough tugs."

"And we're using the biggest one now," I added. "Outside a planetary gravity well, we could move a good size moon."

"I think Mr. Gates-Pendelton will be generous in aiding the world in this crisis." Dale looked really pleased with herself. "He is one of the foremost conservationists. He's reforested very large tracts of land, bigger than some countries."

"Yeah, this will be the biggest public relations coup in history," Conrad interrupted.

"He doesn't need it!" Dale insisted. "He's as brilliant as his grandfather, and as loved!"

Conrad shrugged. "Even nice, rich people have enemies. And your boyfriend has his share."

"I don't get it. This asteroid is rich in minerals," I murmured. "The platinum and gold alone in these rocks are worth a fortune. Why just leave?"

Conrad swatted my arm. "The payback, silly. Gates-Pendelton gives NASA the use of his tugs and our expertise. We did, after all, find this object. NASA foots the bill and he keeps the mineral resources."

"Small compensation," Dale said.

"So who did the message go to first? JPL or Gates-Pendelton?" Conrad asked.

"Does it matter?"

"Gates-Pendelton." Both Conrad and I said it together.

We moved our ship again. It took two additional tries to find a rock worthy of our attention. As soon as Dale saw 10 742GP, I knew she'd want it. Not only was it the most spherical of any of the asteroids we had ever surveyed, it was also the biggest at some 489 kilometers across. We all wanted to get closer.

But as much as Dale itched for this one, she asked the proper questions. The second most important of which was, could we move it? And the first, could we control it in Earth's gravity well? I hardly slept until I got the answers for her. It took me two days. She actually smiled when I told her.

Asteroids aren't pretty, and this one was much darker than most. Usually asteroids are heavily pitted and cratered. Not this one. A few circular features resembled flooded craters. Overall this asteroid was almost smooth, the smoothest rock I'd ever seen. I wanted to know why. What volcanic processes flooded its surface? The geophysical data said it was a solid, with a cold center, no major fractures. Solid is good, but I needed more info on the composition than I could get by delayed Doppler or spectral analysis, and for that I needed deep core samples. But that wasn't something I'd be getting anytime soon. So I waited at my station aboard the orbital portion of the tug, studying the influx of data as I continued bouncing signals off the rock's surface while everyone else was intent on setting up the tug.

I started as hands slid around my waist. "Conrad! You scared me. I didn't know you were back." I pushed his hands away. "Not now. I'm busy." He moved away, not hurt at all. He put up with my shit better than most people.

"You missed your last exercise period and skipped supper."

"I'm not hungry. Go bother someone else."

"Overworking yourself will not get Dale's attention."

"What?"

"Neither will finding her the perfect asteroid. We deliver this rock to Gates-Pendelton, and she hands him the perfect wedding gift. She won't remember you or any of the rest of us."

I stared at him in confusion. "What are you talking about?"

"Your obsessive need to please her. You're attracted to her."

"No, I'm not. You're just jealous!"

"Of course I am. You deserve better. You're pretty and smart."

"I'm not in the mood, all right?"

He laughed. "That's not what I'm after. Still, it would help you relax. I outrank you on this ship."

I glared at him. He laughed again.

"And I'm the med-tech. You're going off-shift until you eat and complete your regular exercise routine."

I shook my head to clear it. "Later. Come and look at this." I pointed to my screen.

"So," he said after looking. "We know it has a slightly lower density already. Having a high water content is great. It'll make this hunk of rock more valuable to inhabit later."

"Yeah, but where is the ice? Why is the surface so smooth?"

"It's young?"

"I don't think so. Not from the cosmic ray age profile of the regolith samples we've gotten so far. Plus the samples are unusually high in carbon. Would you help me get a deep core of it? Now."

"Not now. Too dangerous. The tug's almost in place. Once we're on our way and this rock is in stable motion, no problem. Until then, no unnecessary excursions. That means you. Now get down below and eat and then exercise. I'll watch your data from here."

Just then my stomach betrayed me and let out a loud growl. I had no choice and went for some food, but I wasn't happy.

It took nearly a week to get the tug secure and the asteroid moving along a stable trajectory. We quickly built up speed. Dale was in a hurry to get home.

The rock shifted. I saw it on our scans, both infrared and real-time Doppler. I thought I noticed a groan or two through our monitors on the surface. One small piece of rock flew off, but overall the asteroid held together. The tug's engines flared on every cue and we moved in-system. Days passed, and I finally convinced Conrad to go exploring with me on the rock.

We had eight core samples. The number Conrad and I had agreed upon, or rather what he had bullied me into accepting, before we started this EVA. But I wasn't happy. We stood staring out across the gray landscape. A smooth, marelike plain stretched beyond the small ridge under my feet.

"I want one more core, Conrad."

"Don't think so."

I stepped off the ridge and slowly moved one small step by one small step. This ground didn't feel any less solid, but there was a difference. I remembered all the rock outcrops I had walked and climbed over as an undergrad in college. Granite never felt the same as sandstone and both were different than lunar regolith, and this land felt even more different. The ground shifted slightly beneath my feet, and I knew Conrad had stepped off the ridge and onto the plain. With each step he took toward me, I felt less certain of the ground beneath my feet. We had to quickly get a core from here, then we'd go to Dale.

"Doctors, this is ridiculous," Dale started. "Why the constant probing? It's a wasted effort. You won't find anything new."

"I know this is a precious cargo."

She stared at me as if I had sprouted antennae. Tact. I needed to be more tactful. Usually at this point Mr. Tact, Conrad, stepped in. Today he was strangely quiet as he continued working at his computer. I knew he trusted our data, so why was he quiet?

"Dale." Not the best way to be tactful. If I were smarter, I wouldn't irritate her. But I was tired of the formalities. "We're—I'm not trying to stop this mission."

"I should hope not! If you want to ever get back to your Wayward Twins, we have to first get this rock into Earth orbit."

"That's the fifth time you've said that in four days!" I regretted the words as I spoke them.

Conrad cleared his throat as he continued trying to appear as if he were working at his station. I took a deep breath and went on.

"I'm not trying to shut down this mission, but rather keep it moving. Just look at this data, Dale."

She looked at me sharply, again, then at the computer screen. "What am I looking at?"

"Rock cores of the first nine meters of material in ten different spots."

"Will this tell me why a chunk of material broke off, even though we can't find any fractures to account for the breakage?"

"I think so. Nine of the cores show solid rock after the first section of soft regolith. The soil is thinnest here on the south limb at twenty-five centimeters. These were all taken in the small hills we've seen. But this core—taken from those smooth, dark plains—shows a thin layer of almost pure carbon over ice."

"So?" she asked. Then her eyes got slightly wider. "Carbon as in what we've found on dead comets?"

"Yeah, pretty much."

"Is this asteroid related to the Wayward Twins?"

"Maybe."

"Tell her your theory," Conrad urged.

I shrugged. "The Twins are what's left of a comet which hit this asteroid, 10 742GP. That's why this one is so smooth and why a piece broke off. The craters filled with ice, both water and carbon dioxide, and then were coated with regolith. My guess is a comet hit it recently. The impact melted the ice, and flooded the craters. We heated one section too much and off flew a hunk of asteroid."

"You're basing this all on one anomalous point? Why didn't you take other cores to prove your case?"

"Not enough time, and it's too dangerous."

"She swears she heard the ground shift," Conrad said, "as we walked the Rock."

"Through your EVA suit? A good trick," Dale said.

"It was more *felt*. The craters are filled with ice, and it's shifting. Small ice quakes. The ground is too dangerous to be on. However, the tug is on firm ground."

Dale nodded. "I agree, we took soundings near there. Although we were looking for rubble pockets to avoid, not ice. But if this were ice, wouldn't we see some of the ridges and rafting features as on Europa?"

"Only if the lower reaches of the lakes are liquid. This is a cold-core body. No tidal stresses ever warmed this object, but the ice is now warming."

"And as we near the sun, bigger chunks will break off," she finished for me. "Good work, Doctor. Any suggestion on how we can save this mission?" She looked from me to Conrad. "You're our engineer."

"The simplest way is to keep moving it toward the Sun and encourage its spinning."

"Spinning?" Dale asked. "We just stopped its rotation, remember? How will this save the mission if we have to remove the tug and abandon this rock?"

"We do have to disengage the tug." He held up his hand, stopping her. "Spinning doesn't mean we abandon it. We travel ahead of it and let the Sun heat it, as we move toward Earth. The surface ice melts and dislodges any really loose chunks. It will take longer to complete our journey, but it will be safer."

"If what you say is true, what if some of those chunks are rather big? We'd be sending a gravel pile toward Earth. Not something I care to be responsible for doing. Once the scope of this mission is fully realized, there'll be enough protests that we don't know what we're doing, that we'll mismanage the project and crash this rock on their heads. If we have boulders beating us there and lighting up the sky as a warning of worse things to come—"

"True, we don't have the maneuverability to catch them," Conrad said. "So we have to keep them as small as possible. Lots of space debris lands on Earth every day. If it's small, it'll do no damage."

"If we don't follow your plan?"

"The tug could get caught by an escaping iceberg, either expelled off or damaged. Either way doesn't appeal to me."

"And the mission is lost. You're not leaving me a great deal of options here, Doctor."

"We're not yet on a direct trajectory to Earth," I interjected. "We could use explosive charges to break up some of the frozen lakes before we reach our final path. The pieces won't be on their way to Earth for a long time, if ever."

"Even dirty ice will eventually melt. In any case, ice is less of a problem for Earth. Orbiting spacecraft is another matter." She pushed over to her workstation. "I want hard values, and I want them before either of you go downshift."

* * *

We set our asteroid on a precise course, inbound toward the sun and eventually Earth, and then removed the tug. Dale opted for the use of explosives in the base of some of the larger craters. Once the majority of ice was removed, we replaced the tug and started the asteroid rotating again. I watched from the orbiter section as 10 742GP spun slowly below me.

"Conrad."

"Hum?"

"It's pretty."

"What is? Space or da' rock?"

"Well, both. But the rock is prettier now. The blasting left lighter colored rock exposed. Once more of the ice burns off, I suspect it will make a much brighter spot in the night sky. Kind of like the difference between the bright ejecta rays coming from Tycho Crater on the Moon."

"As opposed to the dark mare?"

"Yeah."

Conrad had moved over to look out the window beside me. "What should we call it? We can't keep calling it the Rock."

"Isn't the right to name it Gates-Pendelton's? He paid for this excursion."

"Yeah, right. He'll call it something mundane like Moon 2, or Luna Also. No, we have to name it."

I drifted over to the communications panel. Dale was still on the surface of the asteroid with some of the construction crew. No one was chatting at the moment.

"Packard to Morgan," I said.

"Doctor Morgan here. Go ahead, Doctor."

"I was just thinking. Dale, what do you want to name this rock?"

"I don't think it is our right."

"Yes, it is. We captured it. I named the last one. Name this one, Dale. Gates-Pendelton will go along with whatever you say. It'll be better than anything he'll choose."

She paused for so long I didn't think she remembered me. Then she sighed. Her voice was soft. "I always thought Selena would be beautiful."

"I like that. Selena it is."

"Or whatever Mr. Gates-Pendelton wants." She suddenly sounded embarrassed.

"No, I think that's a good name, Dale," Don chimed in. "It's a right pretty rock now and getting prettier every day. It deserves a good name."

"Yeah, that's better than 'Da Rock,' which is what I've been calling it," Conrad began. "Or the 'Pain-in-the-ass,' which is what Lizbeth has been calling it."

We heard Dale's faint chuckle. "Selena it is."

"What will it look like?" Don asked from the surface. "I've been so busy trying to catch it I forgot to ask."

"From Earth?" I asked back.

"Yeah. Will we be able to see it?"

"Oh, yes. At its brightest, it'll be almost as wide as the lit portion of our Moon when it's about a day and a half past new moon. We'll see a disk, and it will be brighter than Venus at its brightest. I don't think you'll be able to see any craters with your naked eye. It'll rise four hours before Luna and shepherd her across the night sky with a sixty-degree separation. We'll be able to sit on her and bask in the light of Luna and Earth in our sky." Everyone was quiet as we thought about the scene we'd soon be seeing.

"We're on our way back up," Dale said, breaking my dreaming. "We should see you in about three hours. We'll be expecting dinner."

"Yeah, didn't someone say they'd have dinner ready?" Don added.

"Conrad said that," I said. "I heard him."

"I heard him say so, too," Don said.

"Only if you monkeys clean yourselves up," Conrad

began. "Lizbeth cleaned this ship again real good while you were gone, and we like it that way."

I reached over and turned off the communication speakers. The constant noise was giving me a headache. Who cared what the news media said? I had enough doubts of my own.

"They're really worried we can't handle this," Conrad started.

"Yeah, yeah, and this is the end of the world. It's too late now to turn back. We're deep in the Earth-Moon gravity well. Selena is never leaving this system now. Besides, I know what I'm doing." If that were true, why did I have a knot the size of Jupiter in my stomach?

"That's my girl!" Conrad said, and even Dale smiled.

"Why do you think I picked this time in the lunar cycle to do this?"

"What do you mean?" Dale asked.

"It's before new moon. There are only about two hours when we can be easily seen, and then it's a rather bright sky, in the wee hours of morning. Most people are asleep. If the scientists would just keep their mouths shut, most people won't notice anything different."

"How could they not notice?" Conrad asked.

"Every few years some lost soul mistakes Venus for a UFO, just because they never bothered looking up before. Furthermore, we're already in a safe orbit. Even if I didn't do anything else, it would take years for this orbit to decay to the point where it'll spiral down into Earth. A slight nudge, and it'd hit the Moon instead. Selena is not the rock they should be worrying about. She might even help catch some other wayward objects that wander by. The Moon is one of the best celestial catcher's mitts of all times. I suspect Selena will do her part, too."

*   *   *

Selena was bright over our heads and the growing Luna was close behind. We were on the edge of a mountainside, looking out over the valley. The night sky filled our view. There were no artificial lights anywhere, for tens and tens of miles. By the light of the two moons, the Milky Way, and the summer constellations, Dr. Dale Morgan and Mr. Robert Gates-Pendelton exchanged wedding vows.

"What do you think he got her for a present?" Conrad asked in a very soft whisper. Not soft enough as I elbowed him in the ribs to quiet him. He had made me come to this and had even bought me a dress.

Dress! If you could call it that. By the time I had bothered to look at the object of my disgust, it was too late to get another one. This one was strapless, tightly fitted and the long skirt was slit almost to mid thigh. All of this in a black, satin-like material. I rolled my shoulders again and tugged, trying to keep the top at a decent level of exposure. Conrad insisted I had all the right equipment to wear it. Maybe when I was in college, but that was five years ago. Now?

Now, I wanted to push him over the cliff. Of course if I waited till we got back to Tycho Base, I could push him off a crater limb, perhaps more than once before he'd get seriously hurt. If he weren't such a good engineer, I'd . . .

I sipped my champagne and stood at the cliff's edge. I saw only the stars and the two moons, one new and one old. I felt as if I were floating in space all alone. The cool breeze smelled of pine trees and blossoms. The beauty took my breath away and gave me goose bumps.

We did it!

"It is the most beautiful sight I've ever seen," Dale said from beside me. She looked stunning in her white dress. She had woven flowers in her dark, shoulder-length hair. Conrad moved to stand beside her, too.

"You'll both come with us, won't you?" she asked.

"Us?" I asked.

"Robert and me. To find the Twins, of course."

"Of course," I said. I wasn't certain if that was a yes or not. I could decide tomorrow. I just wanted to stare up at the sky and the moons for a while longer. Maybe forever.

THE LITTLE BITS THAT COUNT

by Alan Dean Foster

"**M**orning, Hank. Anything to declare?"
Beneath his shiny, chromed helmet the guard looked bored, sounded bored, was bored. And why not? Henry Deavers thought. His was a boring job. Not nearly as exciting as Henry's. Nevertheless, he smiled pleasantly, his expression neutral as he replied in the negative. Mechanical in his movements, the guard waved him through and turned his semi-soporific attention to the next worker in line.

Henry passed through the primary metal detector, the shape-and-form detector, the chemical sniffer, the secondary metal detector, waited while his weight was checked and his retina scanned, and repeated the nothing-to-declare routine at the last guarded checkpoint before emerging into the hallway that led to the parking lot. Waving good-bye to coworkers Steve Hernandez and Laura Patrick, he made his way to his four-year-old car, thumbed the compact remote on his key chain to unlock it, and slipped inside. The guard at the gate let him pass and left the barrier up so Steve and Laura could follow, Laura in her Taurus and Steve on his presumptuous, growling Harley. Once on the access road they headed in different directions: Steve and Laura north along the coast, Henry inland. Behind them, the stark sentinels of the Cape's launching platforms stood silent and waiting against the tepid, pastel Florida sky.

Maneuvering the steering wheel languidly with the

heel of one hand, the pungent smells of sea and space receding rapidly aft, Henry Deavers relaxed. He'd gotten away with it again.

How many times was it now? More than several thousand, at least. He should know exactly, but after the first five years he had grown tired of keeping the count in his head. It was enough to have it at home, buried innocuously on his computer in the midst of a list of household items. A file inoculated with innocuousness, he mused contentedly. No one could imagine that next to the mundane columns that listed books and recordings and insurance numbers was one that kept careful track of pieces of the Moon.

Because Henry "Hank" Deavers was a thief. Had been a thief for a little more than ten years now. Had been thieving nearly every day of those ten years, without once getting caught. He chuckled at his foresight, smiled grimly at his patience. It had not been easy. The temptation to steal much more each day was always great. But greed, he knew, could trip up even the cleverest thief. So he had begun modestly and remained so, knowing that time was on his side. Today was yet another confirmation of the efficacy of caution.

It was just as well that he was nearly sated. They were going to move the entire facility next week, shift it to Houston. His opportunities for thievery would transfer with it, but he did not care. Ten years of stealing was enough. His retirement was in the bank, as it were, safely stored in plain sight at home. No one had ever suspected, even though several friends and neighbors had passed right by his hoard. A few had even gazed directly at it, suspecting nothing.

His most recent pilferage reposed, as it always did, in his shoe, under the conveniently high arch of his left foot. Two fragments of stone smaller than his little fingernail. Dull grayish-white in appearance, they would automatically have been ignored and dismissed by anyone not knowing what they were or where they had come from. Chips of rock rendered immensely valuable because they had not come from the beach, had not been picked up in a supermarket parking lot, had not cracked loose from a friend's decorative garden wall. Their origin was to be found in the sliver of silver that was just now becoming visible above the horizon behind him. They had come from a shallow valley called a mare that lay two hundred thousand plus miles away.

Tiny pieces of Moon rock.

Working in the lab, slaving long, tedious hours for an unchanging salary, garnering none of the glory or recognition of scientists or astronauts, Henry Deavers had hit upon the idea of stealing pieces of Moon some twelve years ago. With the resumption of the lunar landing program and its regularly scheduled flights from orbit, Moon rock had once again become available, but only for study and exhibition in the world's great museums. The public clamored to see it, photograph it, touch it. They had to content themselves with small samples locked away in secured glass cases, because the great bulk of material the astronauts brought back vanished into laboratories and institutions of higher learning and advanced study around the world. A few billionaires managed to acquire tiny pieces; the ultimate collector's trophy. One Saudi prince had a fragment the size of a pencil eraser set in a platinum ring. Among common, everyday millionaires the demand for the material was there. It was the supply that was lacking, strictly controlled as it was by NASA and its associated agencies. This state of affairs was about to change.

He, Henry Deavers, senior lab technician, was going to change it.

Ten years he had been smuggling tiny chips of Moon rock out of the preparation lab, using a system of hide-and-seek he had laboriously perfected. Involved as he was in the initial stages of preparing specimens for transshipment to laboratories and universities around the world, he quickly discovered it was possible to adjust the records ever so slightly without drawing attention to the manipulation. No one missed the tiny slivers he slipped into his shoes, between sock and leather. Only one trip to the bathroom was necessary to make the transfer. The key was to take only minuscule fragments, no more than two at a time, sometimes only one.

His largest prize to date was not big enough to set in a ring surrounded by diamonds, but sealed in a presentation case of polished lucite, it would bring a fine price. Multiplied by thousands, even less the seller's commission, it would make him rich.

Over the years he had watched everything settle neatly into place: the shadowy network of brokers who would shield his privacy when in a few months the fragments of Moon began to come onto the market, the secret bank accounts in the Cayman and Cook Islands where his share of the profits would be deposited, the falsified identity papers that would attest to the death of the rich cousin in Austria who upon passing had willed his entire fortune to Henry J. Deavers, thereby explaining the lab technician's sudden wealth, and much more. He was quite confident. After all, he had been preparing for the culmination of his scheme for more than a decade.

He was whistling happily by the time he pulled into the driveway of his unassuming suburban home. Billie was waiting for him, persevering and unsuspecting as always. Kind, good-natured, unimaginative Billie. They had been married a long time. When the money began to roll in, he had no intention of divorcing her. For one thing, he was used to having her around. For another, it might draw suspicion to him. Easy enough to keep his wife and add a decorative mistress should the desire strike him. Or two.

Reaching down, he paused to stroke Galileo and Copernicus, their two mature tabbies. Billie had recently adopted a third stray, whom she promptly named Aristarchus. Ari for short. Theirs was a lunar household, in more ways than his wife suspected. She was proud of his work at the Cape, even if he dismissed it as the repetitive and deadly dull routine he knew it to be. "My Hank," she would tell new acquaintances, "he works in the space program!" She was happy in central Florida, happy with their life together, and content in its predictability.

Prepare yourself for a change, Billie-my-girl. Get ready for early retirement and an extended vacation. Cousin Badenhofer is going to die on the 24th of next month, right on schedule. Following a quick, preprepared probate, your easygoin', easy-lovin' Hank is going to take you to Europe and points east.

Hurriedly running through the day's requisite catch-up small talk, he left her to finish making dinner and headed, as always, for his workshop. Only rarely did she tempt the confusion of tools, lumber, and accumulated supplies, just as he spent little time poking through the incomprehensible depths of the kitchen cabinets. The cats followed him, rubbing up against his legs and meowing for attention. Absently, he would bend to scratch one or the other behind the ears, or smooth out a fluffy tail.

The heavy-duty paper sack was not hidden. There was no reason to hide it. He kept it near the back of the workshop, propped up between some salvaged one-by-six planks and splattered cans of paint. It was almost three-quarters full, containing between nine and ten pounds of Moon rock in the form of tiny, inconspicuous, patiently smuggled shards, taken one or two at a time from the preparation lab at the Cape. To this hoard he would now add the two riding in his shoe.

Like escorting fighters leaving a slow-moving carrier, the cats peeled off to inspect a possible mouse hole. Henry started to reach down to remove his right shoe, feeling the shards shift against his foot. His eyes flicked in the direction of the bag—and he paused, half bent over, and stared. Stared without moving.

The bag was not there.

He did not have to pinch himself. His wakefulness was an unequivocal, crushing, inescapable reality. The bag was gone.

Frantically, he searched the immediate area, then started on the rest of the workshop, making no more noise than was necessary. Curious, newcomer Ari helped him look, without having a cat-clue what her master was so desperately hunting. Her presence brought him no luck. The sack, the fruit of ten years' careful brigandage, was missing. It was not leaning up against the cans of old paint, it had not risen up on unsuspected pseudopodia and walked to the other side of the workroom, it was not there.

Stunned beyond measure, he sat down heavily in the capacious old easy chair Billie had bought for him six years ago at a garage sale in Daytona Beach. His heart was racing as he strove to settle himself. Think, goddamn it! Who could have known about what he had been doing? Who might have observed him on his regular visits to the restroom?

That was it! No fools worked in the lab. Someone had seen and taken note of his surreptitious activities, had figured out what he was doing, and had decided to bide their time, letting him do the dangerous work of thievery only to steal from him in their turn. His lips compressed tightly together and a muscle in his jaw twitched. They wouldn't get away with it. He had friends, he did. Knew people not involved in the space program, unsavory folk who had helped him with his grand design. One of his colleagues was going to be receiving a visit from the bearers of serious trouble. All he had to do was figure out who it was.

If he didn't recover the sack, that someone might be him, he knew. His "friends" were expecting a delivery of thousands of tiny fragments of Moon, had been preparing to receive it for some years now. If he did not produce it, they might very likely be inclined to express their disappointment in the most violent antisocial manner imaginable.

A bit bewildered by the uncharacteristic intensity he displayed at the dinner table, Billie avowed as how she could not remember anyone from the lab visiting since yesterday. Yes, she had been out shopping for a few hours this morning, but why should that be occasion for comment? What was the matter? His face was so red and . . .

Wordlessly, he pushed back from the table and fled from her concern. A careful check of the driveway produced no clues. No skid marks left behind by tires in a hurry to leave, no dropped evidence. He went across the street, then up and down it, querying neighbors. Had they seen anyone parked at his house this morning? Had any trucks made deliveries to the neighborhood? Most critically, had they seen anyone walking in the vicinity of his home carrying a large, nondescript reinforced paper sack?

Eyeing him askance, his neighbors replied regularly and depressingly in the negative. Disconsolate but not yet broken, he returned home and somehow forced himself to engage in halfway normal inconsequential chatter with his wife while they had dessert. That night, the usual evening of television and conversation was pure hell. Despite his exhaustion, he did not sleep at all.

It *had* to be someone at work, someone at the lab. Realizing that he could expose them, his contacts would not have taken the cache. Why should they risk that anyway, when there was plenty of looming profit to be had by all? No neighbor would enter his workshop without him present, even if Billie would have let them in. Thieving kids would have taken glue or chemicals, while addicts looking to support their habit would have stolen expensive tools. No, it was unarguable: no one would bother to steal a sack of splintered rock who was not cognizant of its true nature.

The next day he confronted one colleague after another, meeting their eyes and searching their faces, trying to single out the individual who had appropriated his birthright. Whoever it was did not crack. Darapa he suspected immediately. The man was too clever by half, too smart for his own good, and a foreigner besides. Noticing his stares, the smaller man turned away uneasily. *Yes, it could well be Darapa,* Henry thought. Or possibly Glenna, hiding behind her clean suit and thick glasses, striving to maintain an air of mousy insignificance. It did not matter who it was. He would find them out, and then he would contact his new friends, and someone would get hurt. He took perverse pleasure in the anticipation.

Nearly a week passed, however, without him arriving at a conviction. He knew time was running out. He would have to do something quickly. Having been assured of and promised delivery of the merchandise by a certain date, his "friends" would be having to deal with a long list of increasingly anxious and very important clients. They would be growing uneasy. So was Henry. They were not the sort of people he wanted to keep waiting.

Just before dinner, it struck him. His own mind-set was the source of the trouble. Having engaged for so long in illegal activity, he had automatically assumed that his loss must be due to the same. All week he had been tearing himself apart and unnerving his fellow workers for no reason.

It was Billie. It had to be. For reasons unknown she had moved the bag. She never bothered anything in his workshop, hardly ever went in there, in fact. But such a scenario was not unprecedented. Once, she had decided to reseal the back deck, and had helped herself to the big can of spar varnish he kept in the back. Another time, he recalled her borrowing a screwdriver when the one she kept in her kitchen work drawer proved too big for the task at hand.

No reason to panic, he told himself. Even if she had used some of the fine "gravel" to line the bottom of a pot for a new houseplant or something, it would still be available for recovery. And if, for some horrid reason, it was not, surely she would not have used all of it for some such purpose without his permission.

She was standing by the sink scrubbing a skillet when he came out of the workshop, smiling as warmly as badly jangled nerves would allow him.

"Hon, there was a sack of small rocks, really small rocks, in the workroom. Back by where I keep the paint and some of the lumber. By any chance, have you seen it?"

Glancing back at him without stopping work, she looked thoughtful for a moment, then smiled. "Oh, that?" she nodded, and the terrible tension that had gripped his gut for days began to subside. "Sure, I found it."

He swallowed hard but kept smiling. "Where did you put it, hon?"

Her expression fell. "Oh, did you need it? I'm sorry, Hank. I didn't think it was anything important. What was it for—making cement or something?"

"No," he told her, more tightly than he intended. "It was not for making cement. What did you do with it?"

"Threw it out. About a week ago." She was openly apologetic. "I'm really sorry. Whatever it was for, I'll buy you a new bag."

His legs started to go and he just did make it to one of the kitchen chairs. "You—threw it out." His tone was hollow, echoing inside his head. It sounded very much like the voice of a dead man. Which he would be when his business associates came looking for their promised merchandise. Unless he raced to the Cape and confessed everything to Security, and had himself remanded to protective custody.

No, wait! There was still a chance, a possibility. Maybe she had "thrown it out" outside the house, in the yard. Even if the birds had been at it, even after she had watered down the grass and plants, he still might be able to recover the bulk of the priceless, irreplaceable lunar material.

"Where—is it now?" He was amazed at how calm he was, how steady his voice and comprehensible his words. "What the he—what on Earth did you use it for?" On "Earth," he thought. How droll. How very amusing. In his mind's eye he saw his disappointed friends removing his appendages, one by one, without anesthetic. Or maybe just a quick, clean free flight out over the Atlantic, only—watch that first step. His blood chilled.

"I'm really sorry, Hank." Despite his strenuous attempts to hide his feelings, she could sense how upset he was. "I didn't have any choice. I mean, we were all out, that was the day my car was being worked on, and the box was really stinking. I remembered seeing that bag the last time I was in the shop and I thought it would work. I'll replace it, I promise. Please don't be angry with me." Her nose wrinkled up. "Believe me, if you had been stuck in the house with that smell, you would have done the same thing."

"Sure I would," he mumbled, utterly distraught. Blinking, he looked up. "Smell? What smell?"

"You know." Her pleasant, matronly smile returned. "I was right about the stuff in the sack, anyway. It worked just fine." Relieved, she returned to her dirty dishes.

Ohmigod, he thought. Omigod, omigod. This past week, when he had been searching frantically, had been interrogating his neighbors, had been trying to stare down suspected coworkers, it had been *in the house all the time.* Right under his nose, so to speak. Hysteria built within him, and he fought to keep from being overwhelmed by it. A dozen times, a hundred, he had walked right past his precious stolen lunar hoard; without suspecting, without thinking, perhaps even glancing in its direction. Never realizing. Smelling, but never realizing.

Billie put the now gleaming, freshly scoured skillet in the dish drainer and started on the dirty forks and knives. "I can tell you that the cats were crazy for it. Acted like it was the best stuff they'd ever used. Naturally, when they were finished with it, I had to throw it out." Once again, for a last time, her nose wrinkled in disgust. "What would anyone want with used kitty litter?"

PEOPLE CAME FROM EARTH

by *Stephen Baxter*

At Dawn I stepped out of my house. The air frosted white from my nose, and the deep Moon chill cut through papery flesh to my spindly bones. The silver-gray light came from Earth and Mirror in the sky: twin spheres, the one milky cloud, the other a hard image of the sun. But the sun itself was already shouldering above the horizon. Beads of light like trapped stars marked rim mountain summits, and a deep bloody crimson was working its way high into our tall sky. I imagined I could see the lid of that sky, the millennial leaking of our air into space.

I walked down the path that leads to the circular sea. There was frost everywhere, of course, but the path's lunar dirt, patiently raked in my youth, is friendly and gripped my sandals. The water at the sea's rim was black and oily, lapping softly. I could see the gray sheen of ice farther out, and the hard glint of pack ice beyond that, though the close horizon hid the bulk of the sea from me. Fingers of sunlight stretched across the ice, and gray-gold smoke shimmered above open water.

I listened to the ice for a while. There is a constant tumult of groans and cracks as the ice rises and falls on the sea's mighty shoulders. The water never freezes at Tycho's rim; conversely, it never thaws at the center, so that there is a fat torus of ice floating out there around the central mountains. It is as if the rim of this artificial ocean is striving to emulate the unfrozen seas of Earth which bore its makers, while its remote heart is straining to grow back the cold carapace it enjoyed when our water—and air—still orbited remote Jupiter.

I thought I heard a barking out on the pack ice. Perhaps it was a seal. A bell clanked: an early fishing boat leaving port, a fat, comforting sound that carried through the still dense air. I sought the boat's lights, but my eyes, rheumy, stinging with cold, failed me.

I paid attention to my creaking body: the aches in my too-thin, too-long, calcium-starved bones, the obscure spurts of pain in my urethral system, the strange itches that afflict my liver-spotted flesh. I was already growing too cold. Mirror returns enough heat to the Moon's long Night to keep our seas and air from snowing out around us, but I would welcome a little more comfort.

I turned and began to labor back up my regolith path to my house.

And when I got there, Berge, my nephew, was waiting for me. I did not know then, of course, that he would not survive the new Day.

He was eager to talk about Leonardo da Vinci.

He had taken off his wings and stacked them up against the concrete wall of my house. I could see how the wings were thick with frost, so dense the paper feathers could surely have had little play.

I scolded him even as I brought him into the warmth, and prepared hot soup and tea for him in my pressure kettles. "You're a fool as your father was," I said. "I was with him when he fell from the sky, leaving you orphaned. You know how dangerous it is in the pre-Dawn turbulence."

"Ah, but the power of those great thermals, Uncle," he said, as he accepted the soup. "I can fly miles high without the slightest effort."

I would have berated him further, which is the prerogative of old age. But I didn't have the heart. He stood before me, eager, heartbreakingly thin. Berge always was slender, even compared to the rest of us skinny lunar folk; but now he was clearly frail. Even these long minutes after landing, he was still panting, and his smooth fashionably-shaven scalp (so bare it showed the great bubble profile of his lunar-born skull) was dotted with beads of grimy sweat.

And, most ominous of all, a waxy, golden sheen seemed to linger about his skin. I had no desire to raise that—not here, not now, not until I was sure what it meant, that it wasn't some trickery of my own age-yellowed eyes.

So I kept my counsel. We made our ritual obeisance—murmurs about dedicating our bones and flesh to the salvation of the world—and finished up our soup.

And then, with his youthful eagerness, Berge launched into the seminar he was evidently itching to deliver on Leonardo da Vinci, long-dead citizen of a long-dead planet. Brusquely displacing the empty soup bowls to the floor, he produced papers from his jacket and spread them out before me. The sheets, yellowed and stained with age, were covered in a crabby, indecipherable handwriting, broken with sketches of gadgets or flowing water or geometric figures. I picked out a luminously beautiful sketch of the crescent Earth—

"No," said Berge patiently. "Think about it. It must have been the crescent *Moon.*" Of course he was right. "You see, Leonardo understood the phenomenon he called the ashen Moon—like our ashen Earth, the old Earth visible in the arms of the new. He was a hundred years ahead of his time with *that* one. . . ."

This document had been called many things in its long history, but most familiarly the Codex Leicester. Berge's copy had been printed off in haste during The Failing, those frantic hours when our dying libraries had disgorged their great snowfalls of paper. It was a treatise centering on what Leonardo called the "body of the Earth," but with diversions to consider such matters as water engineering, the geometry of Earth and Moon, and the origins of fossils.

The issue of the fossils particularly excited Berge. Leonardo had been much agitated by the presence of the fossils of marine animals, fishes and oysters and corals, high in the mountains of Italy. Lacking any knowledge of tectonic processes, he had struggled to explain how the fossils might have been deposited by a series of great global floods.

It made me remember how, when he was a boy, I once had to explain to Berge what a "fossil" was. There are no fossils on the Moon: no bones in the ground, of course, save those we put there. Now he was much more interested in the words of long-dead Leonardo than his uncle's.

"You have to think about the world Leonardo inhabited," he said. "The ancient paradigms still persisted: the stationary Earth, a sky laden with spheres, crude Aristotelian proto-physics. But Leonardo's instinct was to proceed from observation to theory—and he observed many things in the world which didn't fit with the prevailing world view—"

"Like mountaintop fossils."

"Yes. Working alone, he struggled to come up with explanations. And some of his reasoning was, well, eerie."

"Eerie?"

"Prescient." Gold-flecked eyes gleamed. "Leonardo talks about the Moon in several places." The boy flicked back and forth through the Codex, pointing out spidery pictures of Earth and Moon and sun, neat circles connected by spidery light ray traces. "Remember, the Moon was thought to be a transparent crystal sphere. What intrigued Leonardo was why the Moon wasn't much brighter in Earth's sky, as bright as the

sun, in fact. It should have been brighter if it was
perfectly reflective—"

"Like Mirror."

"Yes. So Leonardo argued the Moon must be covered in oceans." He found a diagram showing a Moon,
bathed in spidery sunlight rays, coated with great out-
of-scale choppy waves. "Leonardo said waves on the
Moon's oceans must deflect much of the reflected sunlight away from Earth. He thought the darker patches
visible on the Moon's surface must mark great standing waves, or even storms, on the Moon."

"He was wrong," I said. "In Leonardo's time, the
Moon was a ball of rock. The dark areas were just
lava sheets."

"But now," Berge said eagerly, "the Moon *is* mostly
covered by water. You see? And there *are* great
storms, wave crests hundreds of kilometers long,
which are visible from Earth—or would be, if anybody
was left to see."

"What exactly are you suggesting?"

"Ah," he said, and he smiled and tapped his thin
nose. "I'm like Leonardo. I observe, *then* deduce. And
I don't have my conclusions just yet. Patience,
Uncle . . ."

We talked for hours.

When he left, the Day was little advanced, the rake
of sunlight still sparse on the ice. And Mirror still rode
bright in the sky. Here was another strange forward
echo of Leonardo's, it struck me, though I preferred
not to mention it to my already overexcited nephew:
in my time, there *are* crystal spheres in orbit around
the Earth. The difference is, we put them there.

Such musing failed to distract me from thoughts of
Berge's frailness, and his disturbing golden pallor. I
bade him farewell, hiding my concern.

As I closed the door, I heard the honking of geese,
a great flock of them fleeing the excessive brightness
of full Day.

*   *   *

Each Morning, as the sun labors into the sky, there are storms. Thick fat clouds race across the sky, and water gushes down, carving new rivulets and craters in the ancient soil, and turning the ice at the rim of the Tycho pack into a thin, fragile layer of gray slush.

Most people choose to shelter from the rain, but to me it is a pleasure. I like to think of myself standing in the band of storms that circles the whole of the slow-turning Moon. Raindrops are fat glimmering spheres the size of my thumb. They float from the sky, gently flattened by the resistance of our thick air, and they fall on my head and back with soft, almost caressing impacts. So long and slow has been their fall from the high clouds, the drops are often warm, and the air thick and humid and muggy, and the water clings to my flesh in great sheets and globes I must scrape off with my fingers.

It was in such a storm that, as Noon approached on that last Day, I traveled with Berge to the phytomine celebration to be held on the lower slopes of Maginus.

We made our way past sprawling fields tilled by human and animal muscle, thin crops straining toward the sky, frost shelters laid open to the muggy heat. And as we traveled, we joined streams of more traffic, all heading for Maginus: battered carts, spindly adults, and their skinny, hollow-eyed children; the Moon soil is thin and cannot nourish us well, and we are all, of course, slowly poisoned besides, even the cattle and horses and mules.

Maginus is an old, eroded crater complex some kilometers southeast of Tycho. Its ancient walls glimmer with crescent lakes and glaciers. Sheltered from the winds of Morning and Evening, Maginus is a center of life, and as the rain cleared I saw the tops of the giant trees looming over the horizon long before we reached the foothills. I thought I saw creatures leaping between the tree branches. They may have been lemurs, or even bats; or perhaps they were kites wielded by ambitious children.

Berge took delight as we crossed the many water courses, pointing out engineering features which had been anticipated by Leonardo, dams and bridges and canal diversions and so forth, some of them even constructed since the Failing.

But I took little comfort, oppressed as I was by the evidence of our fall. For example, we journeyed along a road made of lunar glass, flat as ice and utterly impervious to erosion, carved long ago into the regolith. But our cart was wooden, and drawn by a spavined, thin-legged mule. Such contrasts are unendingly startling. All our technology would have been more than familiar to Leonardo. We make gadgets of levers and pulleys and gears, their wooden teeth constantly stripped; we have turnbuckles, devices to help us erect our cathedrals of Moon concrete; we even fight our pathetic wars with catapults and crossbows, throwing lumps of rock a few kilometers.

But once we hurled ice moons across the solar system. We know this is so, else we could not exist here.

As we neared the phytomine, the streams of traffic converged to a great confluence of people and animals. There was a swam of reunions of friends and family, and a rich human noise carried on the thick air.

When the crowds grew too dense, we abandoned our wagon and walked. Berge, with unconscious generosity, supported me with a hand clasped about my arm, guiding me through this human maelstrom. All Berge wanted to talk about was Leonardo da Vinci. "Leonardo was trying to figure out the cycles of the Earth. For instance, how water could be restored to the mountaintops. Listen to this." He fumbled, one-handed, with his dog-eared manuscript. "*We may say that the Earth has a spirit of growth, and that its flesh is the soil; its bones are the successive strata of the rocks which form the mountains, its cartilage is the tufa*

stone; its blood the veins of its waters. . . . And the
vital heat of the world is fire which is spread throughout
the Earth; and the dwelling place of the spirit of growth
is in the fires, which in divers parts of the Earth are
breathed out in baths and sulfur mines. . . . You understand what he's saying? He was trying to explain the
Earth's cycles by analogy with the systems of the
human body."

"He was wrong."

"But he was more right than wrong, Uncle! Don't
you see? This was centuries before geology was for-
malized, even longer before matter and energy cycles
would be understood. Leonardo had gotten the right
idea, from somewhere. He just didn't have the intellectual infrastructure to express it. . . ."

And so on. None of it was of much interest to me.
As we walked, it seemed to me that *his* weight was
the heavier, as if I, the old fool, was constrained to
support him, the young buck. It was evident his sick-
liness was advancing fast—and it seemed that others
around us noticed it, too, and separated around us, a
sea of unwilling sympathy.

Children darted around my feet, so fast I found it
impossible to believe *I* could ever have been so young,
so rapid, so compact, and I felt a mask of old-man
irritability settle on me. But many of the children
were, at age seven or eight or nine, already taller than
me, girls with languid eyes and the delicate posture of
giraffes. The one constant of human evolution on the
Moon is how our children stretch out, ever more lan-
guorous, in the gentle Moon gravity. But they pay a
heavy price in later life in brittle, calcium-depleted
bones.

At last we reached the plantation itself. We had to
join queues, more or less orderly. There was noise,
chatter, a sense of excitement. For many people, such
visits are the peak of each slow lunar Day.

Separated from us by a row of wooden stakes and

a few meters of bare soil was a sea of green, predominantly mustard plants. Chosen for their bulk and fast growth, all of these plants had grown from seed or shoots since the last lunar Dawn. The plants themselves grew thick, their feathery leaves bright. But many of the leaves were sickly, already yellowing. The fence was supervised by an unsmiling attendant, who wore—to show the people their sacrifice had a genuine goal—artifacts of unimaginable value, ear rings and brooches and bracelets of pure copper and nickel and bronze.

The Maginus mine is the most famous and exotic of all the phytomines: for here gold is mined, still the most compelling of all metals. Sullenly, the attendant told us that the mustard plants grow in soil in which gold, dissolved out of the base rock by ammonium thiocyanate, can be found at a concentration of four parts per million. But when the plants are harvested and burned, their ash contains four *hundred* parts per million of gold, drawn out of the soil by the plants during their brief lives.

The phytomines are perhaps our planet's most important industry.

It took just a handful of dust, a nanoweapon from the last war that ravaged Earth, to remove every scrap of worked metal from the surface of the Moon. It was the Failing. The cities crumbled. Aircraft fell from the sky. Ships on the great circular seas disintegrated, tipping their hapless passengers into freezing waters. Striving for independence from Earth, caught in this crosscurrent of war, our Moon nation was soon reduced to a rabble, scraping for survival.

But our lunar soil is sparse and ungenerous. If Leonardo was right—that Earth with its great cycles of rock and water is like a living thing—then the poor Moon, its reluctant daughter, is surely dead. The Moon, ripped from the outer layers of parent Earth by a massive primordial impact, lacks the rich iron

which populates much of Earth's bulk. It is much too
small to have retained the inner heat which fuels
Earth's great tectonic cycles, and so died rapidly; and
without the water baked out by the violence of its
formation, the Moon is deprived of the great ore lodes
peppered through Earth's interior.

Moon rock is mostly olivine, pyroxene, and plagio-
clase feldspar. These are silicates of iron, magnesium,
and aluminum. There is a trace of native iron, and
thinner scrapings of metals like copper, tin, and gold,
much of it implanted by meteorite impacts. An Earth
miner would have cast aside the richest rocks of our
poor Moon as worthless slag.

And yet the Moon is all we have.

We have neither the means nor the will to rip up
the top hundred meters of our world to find the precious metals we need. Drained of strength and tools,
we must be more subtle.

Hence the phytomines. The technology is old—
older than the human Moon, older than spaceflight
itself. The Vikings, marauders of Earth's darkest age
(before this, the darkest of all) would mine their iron
from "bog ore," iron-rich stony nodules deposited
near the surface of bogs by bacteria which had flour-
ished there: miniature miners, not even visible to the
Vikings who burned their little corpses to make their
nails and swords and pans and cauldrons.

And so it goes, across our battered, parched little
planet, a hierarchy of bacteria and plants and insects
and animals and birds, collecting gold and silver and
nickel and copper and bronze, their evanescent bodies
comprising a slow merging trickle of scattered molecules, stored in leaves and flesh and bones, all for
the benefit of that future generation who must save
the Moon.

Berge and I, solemnly, took ritual scraps of mustard-
plant leaf on our tongues, swallowed ceremonially.
With my age-furred tongue I could barely taste the

mustard's sharpness. There were no drawn-back frost covers here because these poor mustard plants would not survive to the Sunset: they die within a lunar Day, from poisoning by the cyanide.

Berge met friends and melted into the crowds.

I returned home alone, brooding.

I found my family of seals had lumbered out of the ocean and onto the shore. These are constant visitors. During the warmth of Noon they will bask for hours, males and females and children draped over each other in casual, sexless abandon, so long that the patch of regolith they inhabit becomes sodden and stinking with their droppings. The seals, uniquely among the creatures from Earth, have not adapted in any apparent way to the lunar conditions. In the flimsy gravity they could surely perform somersaults with those flippers of theirs. But they choose not to; instead they bask, as their ancestors did on remote Arctic beaches. I don't know why this is so. Perhaps they are, simply, wiser than we struggling, dreaming humans.

The long Afternoon sank into its mellow warmth. The low sunlight diffused, yellow-red, to the very top of our tall sky, and I would sit on my stoop imagining I could see our precious oxygen evaporating away from the top of that sky, molecule by molecule, escaping back to the space from which we had dragged it, as if hoping in some mute chemical way to reform the ice moon we had destroyed.

Berge's illness advanced without pity. I was touched when he chose to come stay with me, to "see it out," as he put it.

My fondness for Berge is not hard to understand. My wife died in her only attempt at childbirth. This is not uncommon, as pelvises evolved in heavy Earth gravity struggle to release the great fragile skulls of Moon-born children. So I had rejoiced when Berge was born; at least some of my genes, I consoled myself, which had emanated from primeval oceans now lost in the sky, would travel on to the farthest future. But now, it seemed, I would lose even that.

Berge spent his dwindling energies in feverish activities. Still his obsession with Leonardo clung about him. He showed me pictures of impossible machines, far beyond the technology of Leonardo's time (and, incidentally, of ours); shafts and cogwheels for generating enormous heat, a diving apparatus, an "easy-moving wagon" capable of independent locomotion. The famous helicopter intrigued Berge particularly. He built many spiral-shaped models of bamboo and paper; they soared into the thick air, easily defying the Moon's gravity, catching the reddening light.

I have never been sure if he knew he was dying. If he knew, he did not mention it, nor did I press him.

In my gloomier hours—when I sat with my nephew as he struggled to sleep, or as I lay listening to the ominous, mysterious rumbles of my own failing body, cumulatively poisoned, wracked by the strange distortions of lunar gravity—I wondered how much farther we must descend.

The heavy molecules of our thick atmosphere are too fast-moving to be contained by the Moon's gravity. The air will be thinned in a few thousand years: a long time, but not beyond comprehension. Long before then we must have reconquered this world we built, or we will die.

So we gather metals. And, besides that, we will need knowledge.

We have become a world of patient monks, endlessly transcribing the great texts of the past, pounding into the brains of our wretched young the wisdom of the millennia. It seems essential we do not lose our concentration as a people, our memory. But I fear it is impossible. We are Stone Age farmers, the young broken by toil even as they learn. I have lived long enough to realize that we are, fragment by fragment, losing what we once knew.

If I had one simple message to transmit to the future generations, one thing they should remember lest they descend into savagery, it would be this: *People came from Earth.* There: cosmology and the history of the species and the promise of the future, wrapped up in one baffling, enigmatic, heroic sentence. I repeat it to everyone I meet. Perhaps those future thinkers will decode its meaning, and will understand what they must do.

Berge's decline quickened, even as the sun slid down the sky, the clockwork of our little universe mirroring his condition with a clumsy, if mindless, irony. In the last hours I sat with him, quietly reading and talking, responding to his near-adolescent philosophizing with my customary brusqueness, which I was careful not to modify in this last hour.

". . . But have you ever wondered why we are *here* and *now?*" He was whispering, the sickly gold of his face picked out by the dwindling sun. "What are we, a few million, scattered in our towns and farms around the Moon? What do we compare to the *billions* who swarmed over Earth in the final years? Why do I find myself *here* and *now* rather than *then?* It is so unlikely . . ." He turned his great lunar head to me. "Do you ever feel you have been born out of your time, as if you are stranded in the wrong era, an *unconscious* time traveler?"

I had to confess I never did, but he whispered on.

"Suppose a modern human—or someone of the great ages of Earth—was stranded in the sixteenth century, Leonardo's time. Suppose he forgot everything of his culture, all its science and learning—"

"Why? How?"

"*I* don't know. . . . But if it were true—and if his unconscious mind retained the slightest trace of the

learning he had discarded—wouldn't he do exactly
what Leonardo did? Study obsessively, try to fit awkward facts into the prevailing, unsatisfactory paradigms, grope for the deeper truths he had lost?"

"Like Earth's systems being analogous to the
human body."

"Exactly." A wisp of excitement stirred him. "Don't
you see? Leonardo behaved *exactly* as a stranded time
traveler would."

"Ah." I thought I understood; of course, I didn't.
"You think *you're* out of time. And your Leonardo,
too!" I laughed, but he didn't rise to my gentle mockery. And in my unthinking way I launched into a long
and pompous discourse on feelings of dislocation: on
how every adolescent felt stranded in a body, an adult
culture, unprepared . . .

But Berge wasn't listening. He turned away, to look
again at the bloated sun. "All this will pass," he said.
"The sun will die. The universe may collapse on itself,
or spread to a cold infinity. In either case it may be
possible to build a giant machine that will recreate this
universe—everything, every detail of this moment—so
that we will all live again. But how can we know if
this is the first time? Perhaps the universe has already
died, many times, to be born again. Perhaps Leonardo
was no traveler. Perhaps he was simply *remembering*."
He looked up, challenging me to argue; but the challenge was distressingly feeble.

"I think," I said, "you should drink more soup."

But he had no more need of soup, and he turned
to look at the sun once more.

It seemed too soon when the cold started to settle
on the land once more, with great pancakes of new
ice clustering around the rim of the Tycho Sea.

I summoned his friends, teachers, those who had
loved him.

I clung to the greater goal: that the atoms of gold

and nickel and zinc which had coursed in Berge's blood and bones, killing him like the mustard plants of Maginus—killing us all, in fact, at one rate or another—would now gather in even greater concentrations in the bodies of those who would follow us. Perhaps the pathetic scrap of gold or nickel which had cost poor Berge his life would at last, mined, close the circuit which would lift the first of our ceramic-hulled ships beyond the thick, deadening atmosphere of the Moon.

Perhaps. But it was cold comfort.

We ate the soup, of his dissolved bones and flesh, in solemn silence. We took his life's sole gift, further concentrating the metal traces to the far future, shortening our lives as he had.

I have never been a skillful host. As soon as they could, the young people dispersed. I talked with Berge's teachers, but we had little to say to each other; I was merely his uncle, after all, a genetic tributary, not a parent. I wasn't sorry to be left alone.

Before I slept again, even before the sun's bloated hull had slid below the toothed horizon, the winds had turned. The warm air that had cradled me was treacherously fleeing after the sinking sun. Soon the first flurries of snow came pattering on the black, swelling surface of the Tycho Sea. My seals slid back into the water, to seek out whatever riches or dangers awaited them under Callisto ice.

VISIONS OF THE GREEN MOON

by *Robert Sheckley*

Avery drove up New York State Highway 41 on a
dark day with low clouds and rain already splat-
tering his windshield. He almost missed McDougald's
place. The little sign tacked to a tree was modest to
the point of invisibility. And the house itself was
smaller than he'd expected, tucked under the crest of
a hill and almost lost in a fringe of trees. He had to
back up to get into the long dirt driveway that snaked
up to the house. When he got there, he stopped and
looked it over. It was definitely on the small side for
a farmhouse, but nicely cared for, with a mowed lawn
bordered by birches. It looked like it had been a long
time since it had been a working farm. The place
might have been a city man's retreat of fifty years ago
when the Adirondacks were a popular holiday
destination.

Avery stopped his rental car just past McDougald's
house. He was in his early thirties, a large, soft-looking
man, going bald, with a fringe of curly black hair
around his round head. He was of average height and
a little overweight. He had a pleasant, round, studious
face. His hands, tapping nervously on the steering
wheel, were small and well cared for. A graduate of
Julliard, he had produced his first professional musical
in his early twenties at the Paper Mill Playhouse in
New Jersey—the critically acclaimed *An Evening with
Erik Satie*.

A Manhattanite most of his life, Avery rented a car

when he needed one, which was rarely. This was one of those occasions. He was off on what he considered a wild goose chase. Or rather, a wild dream chase. It would waste a couple of days that he couldn't really spare. But he had to do something.

McDougald's house looked pleasant enough, but hardly luxurious. Not the sort of place Avery would ordinarily spend an afternoon, much less overnight.

He sat in his car for a few minutes, just looking at the house, tempted to turn around and go back to New York City. He'd had his doubts ever since Alex had told him about it. Alex was his manager, and had handled all the arrangements for Avery's two previous shows. Avery's new one, *Moon Follies*, was due to open off-Broadway in less than a month. The cast was all in Manhattan, doing final rehearsals. Everything was ready except for one thing. The lead song, which was both the opener and the finale number. Alex still didn't have it.

Finally, he got out of his car and went to the front door. McDougald was there to greet him. He was a tall man, white-haired, perhaps in his sixties. He had faded blue eyes beneath tufted eyebrows. They went with his craggy face and work-toughened hands. He wore a red-checked lumberjack shirt, ironed blue jeans, and black lace-up work boots.

Avery introduced himself, and McDougald offered his hand, saying, "I was expecting you." His speech was the curiously inflected speech of upper New York State, a mixture of Midwestern and New England.

"I'm not sure I made myself clear over the phone," Avery said. "It's not a prophetic dream I'm after. It's an artistic one."

"The two can be much the same," McDougald said. "Anyhow, I don't make any claim for the ones you get here. If you get any at all."

"I'm still not sure of this," Avery said. "I don't

think I understand exactly what it is you're peddling.
No insult intended . . ."

McDougald was amused. He sat Avery down in a
wooden chair in his kitchen. Poured him a cup of coffee without asking first if he wanted it. Then he lit a
battered brown pipe, and when it was drawing nicely,
addressed himself to Avery's question.

"I don't know myself what it is I do," McDougald
said. "Or if I do anything. My wife and I used to farm
here, back when she was alive. But the climate is too
bitter most of the year to compete with southern agri-
culture. I quit while I was ahead, sold most of my land
to a resort chain. They went bust, too, but I got my
money before they folded. My wife and I always loved
this spot. Indians used to live here, Mr. Avery. Iro-
quois. Claimed it was a power spot. We turned our
farmhouse into a small hotel, and when that didn't go,
made it into a bed and breakfast place for folks on
their way to Lake Placid and Ausable Chasm."

"But what about the dreams?" Avery asked.

McDougald shrugged. "Everyone told us about
what great nights of sleep they got, and what wonderful dreams they had."

"So it's the place that's magical, not you in particular," Avery said. "Please understand—"

"I know, no insult intended," McDougald said.

"It's just that I didn't come here for a refreshing
night's sleep, though God knows I could use one. I'm
looking for—let's call it inspiration. And my manager,
Alex Zibirsky, thought I ought to come here. Said
he'd had some amazing insights from dreams he'd had
in this place. Never told me what they were, though."

"I remember Mr. Zibirsky," McDougald said. "Nice
man. Excitable, but nice. He complimented me on his
dreams. As if I had anything to do with them!"

"Didn't you?"

McDougald shook his head and put his pipe into a
dark glass ashtray. "How in the hell should I know?

I'm a farmer—an ex-farmer—not a dream expert. All I know is, people seem to have dreams here, and they seem happy to get them. If that's inspiration, I guess that's what I'm peddling."

Avery was disappointed. He had been expecting a pitch, although he had steeled himself against buying into it. "Well, I'm here, so I guess I'll try it out."

"Suit yourself," McDougald said.

"What do you charge, Mr. McDougald?"

"The room's eighty-nine dollars a night," McDougald said.

"That seems reasonable enough."

"It's what the Mountain Inn two miles up the road charges. I'm not as fancy as them. But I make better coffee, the sheets are clean, and you get eggs and home fries in the morning."

"Fair enough. And what do you charge for the dream?"

"I have nothing to do with the dream," McDougald said. "Consequently, you get that for nothing."

Avery stared at the man for a moment, then lowered his eyes. He hadn't been expecting this. After a moment, he said, "I was expecting something more."

"I can't help that," McDougald said.

"Do I talk to you first about what I want to dream?"

"It isn't customary," McDougald said. "That's your business. And it wouldn't help anyway." He stood up. "Let me show you your room."

The guest bedroom on the second floor was small but pleasant, with familiar farm smells and a view across the valley. The bed seemed firm and there were plenty of blankets. Avery unpacked his overnight bag, then drove to the North Woods Inn and had dinner. The North Woods Inn served a pretty fair streak. The atmosphere was low-key, and the lighting was subdued. Avery had two drinks with dinner. While he ate,

he looked over his notes, reading them over again
for the millionth time, chain-smoking cigarette after
.cigarette. No ideas came, no happy inspiration. He
hoped the dream would do something for him, because he was dead in the water.

Avery needed a dream about the Moon.

What he had in mind was a loving evocation of
the Moon throughout the ages—the Moon of lovers,
dreamers, visionaries, little children. The song would
be tender, loving, and a little wry. It was to be per-
formed by Ernst Carson doing his Maurice Chevalier
imitation—strolling around the darkened stage in a
straw hat and swinging a bamboo cane, while groups
of children and lovers were spotlighted around the
stage. It had to be a delicious song, a catchy song.
Avery had the rest of the numbers nailed. But somehow he had missed on this one, even though it should
have been the simplest of the lot.

Maybe the trouble was it was too simple, too direct,
too clichéd. It should have been a simple problem, but
unaccountably, his mind had seized up. Moon, June,
spoon, that's all he'd been able to think. Alex had
told him not to worry, it would come. How could the
man heralded as the new Gershwin fail? How could
a man whose cleverness and originality was something
you could take to the bank not come up with what
he needed?

Avery had tried. He'd locked himself in his brown-
stone apartment near Grammercy Park. A nearby
diner delivered food to his door. As often as not it
congealed into an unsavory mess while he sat at the
piano, in his shirtsleeves, his hair wild, unshaven,
banging out one tune after another, one concept after
another, and hating them all.

He'd gone a little crazy in those last weeks. He'd
ignored his friends, paid no attention to the news.
What did the world have to do with him or he with
it? Crop failures in the Midwest—so what? He had

his own crop failures to contend with. He'd been un-moved by the report that a big chunk of Antarctica that had been threatening to shelve off and raise the ocean levels had refrozen. Great, more power to it. Science talks on television by learned and affable scientists on the new cooling phenomenon hadn't interested him. He had his own cooling phenomenon to contend with. It had to do with his own brain. To hell with the world, his own brain was cooling down, seizing up, grinding to a stop. The inspiration that had seemed never to fail, the happy and useful thoughts that came to him as sure as clockwork, all seemed to have deserted him. Moon, June, spoon, doom. He had his own personal catastrophe to contend with, and the world would just have to take care of itself.

When he returned to the farmhouse near midnight, the lights were out except for one over the front door. Avery let himself in with the key that McDougald had given him. The house was quiet. By the light of a forty-watt bulb he found his way upstairs to his room. He undressed, put on his bathrobe, went down the hall to the bathroom and brushed his teeth, and returned to his room. Although it was early July, there was a chill in the air, and a light sheen of frost on the window. The house was very quiet. Just the soft creak of a board as he crossed to his bed. He got in and propped himself up with a couple of pillows. He had brought pencils, a pad, an electronic keyboard, and several books, just in case he couldn't sleep. He always had trouble sleeping in unfamiliar surroundings. But tonight he dozed off almost immediately, tired out by the long drive from the city. He slept, and he dreamed.

He was standing on a road somewhere. The details were hazy. He didn't know where he was. Just a long blacktop road winding between low hills. He was alone, but someone was coming down the road. First it was no more than a tiny dot, but as it got closer, he saw a huge hairy man driving up in a vehicle that looked for all the world like a Batmobile. The person behind the wheel was very large and covered with yellowish-white hair. He looked somehow familiar. In a moment, Avery identified him from artists' conceptions. It was an abominable snowman!

In his dream, Avery was not surprised. When the vehicle stopped, he asked, "What are you doing here? And why are you in that?"

The abominable snowman stretched, and eased a kink in his neck. He got out of the Batmobile, stretched, then said, "Hey, have you got a smoke?"

Avery just stared at him. He wasn't surprised or frightened. In the uncanny way of dreams, this seemed to be business as usual.

"What do you want?" Avery asked.

"Hey," the snowman said, "I just want something to smoke. It's difficult to keep any cigarettes on you when you don't have clothes. Now, come on, be a sport. Do I have to ask again?"

Avery found one last cigarette in his pack and handed it to the snowman.

"Light it for me, would you? I don't want to set my fur on fire."

Avery found his lighter and did so. He told himself, *This isn't happening.* It was just beginning to occur to him that something very strange was going on.

"Where are you going?" Avery asked.

"To the Moon," the snowman said.

"In that?" Avery asked, jerking his thumb at the sleek black Batmobile.

"Of course, in this."

"But how will you be able to breathe?"

"I'll close the canopy," the snowman said.

"But you'll freeze out there."

"Naw. Got a pretty good heater in this contraption."

There were other things Avery wanted to know, but the snowman gave an impatient grimace, got back in the Batmobile, put it into gear, and took off, the cigarette clenched in his long yellow teeth. Avery watched the vehicle pick up speed as it moved down the road. Then it extended bat wings and soared into the air. Was a Batmobile supposed to be able to do that?

Avery wasn't sure. Anyhow, it was only a dream.

The next thing he saw was someone on a bicycle coming down the road. Only it wasn't just anyone, it was a tall man, his skin a dark reddish-brown, naked to the waist, and his head was the head of some animal. A dog? No, Avery recognized the creature as a jackal. So this had to be Anubis, the jackal-headed Egyptian god, whom Avery remembered from the statue in the Egyptian wing of the Metropolitan Museum of Art.

"Where are you going?" Avery asked.

Anubis stopped and got off the bicycle. He mopped his muzzle with a clawed hand.

"Mighty hot work, this," Anubis said.

Avery wanted to tell Anubis that he shouldn't be riding a bicycle. Everyone knew that Egyptians gods didn't ride bicycles. But he decided to keep that to himself.

"I asked where you're going," Avery said.

"It's no secret," Anubis said. "I'm on my way to the Moon."

"On that?"

"As you see."

"But it's going to take a very long time."

"There's no rush," Anubis said.

"You'd have done better in the Batmobile," Avery said.

"That's someone else's territory," Anubis said. "You wouldn't happen to have a cigarette, would you?"

Avery thought he was out, but when he checked his pack there was still one remaining. He shook it out and lighted it for the creature or deity or whatever it was.

"So what's on the Moon?" Avery asked.

"Don't know. Haven't been there yet."

"Then how come you're going?"

Anubis shrugged. "The directive came down. 'All imaginary creatures report to the Moon.' Mine not to reason why."

"Who puts out such directives?"

"How the hell should I know? I just follow orders. Nice talking to you, fellow."

He got back on his bicycle and pedaled off.

The next person or whatever it was that Avery met in his dream was a beautiful young girl dressed all in white, riding in a coach pulled by four giant frogs. The coach came to a stop beside Avery. The young girl unrolled the window and leaned out.

"Hi," she said.

"Who're you?" Avery asked.

"I'm Cinderella."

"And who are these guys pulling your coach?"

"They're frogs."

"Big ones," Avery commented.

"This coach is heavier than it looks," she told him.

Avery didn't remember any version of the Cinderella story in which she went anywhere in a coach pulled by giant frogs. He wanted to tell her so, but she interrupted him.

"You wouldn't happen to have a cigarette, would you?"

"I think I'm fresh out," Avery said. But when he looked at his pack, there was one cigarette left, bent but still usable. He lit it and handed it to her.

"Thanks a lot," Cinderella said. "They told me you'd be here."

"Me?"

"Well, someone like you. Someone who would hand out the last artifact of dear old Earth."

"A cigarette? That's the last artifact?"

"Sure. There'll be no smoking where I'm going."

"I suppose you're going to the Moon?"

"You suppose correctly."

"I may be along myself one of these days."

"I doubt that."

"Why?"

"Because your job is to stand here and hand out cigarettes."

She made a clucking sound, and the frogs leaned into the harness. The coach mounted into the air. In a little while she was gone.

"I wish I knew what was going on," Avery said to himself.

Someone must have been listening, because a voice behind him said, "That's the problem with you Earth people. You always want to know what's going on, and that prevents you from ever knowing anything important."

Avery turned and saw a man in a cutaway coat and tight trousers with a tall hat on his head. He had a turnip-shaped watch in his hand and was peering at it nervously. Avery recognized him at once from the famous drawings by—was it Tenniel? The Mad Hatter was muttering, "Oh, my, I'll be late."

"Where are you off to?" Avery asked.

The Mad Hatter stopped, blinked, looked at Avery with a puzzled gaze, then his expression brightened and he said, "I know who you are!"

"Who am I?" Avery asked.

"You're the Cigarette Guy, that's who! Got one for me?"

"Just ran out," Avery said.

"Check and see," the Mad Hatter suggested.

Avery looked in his pack and found a cigarette where he had been sure there'd been none before.

"That's impossible," he said. "In fact, this whole thing is impossible. What's happening?"

"Where?" the Mad Hatter said.

"What's happening to me?" Avery said.

"You've been selected," the Mad Hatter said.

"To do what?"

"To hand out the party favors."

"You mean these?" Avery said, holding up his crumpled pack.

"Of course. You're supposed to give one of them to each of us as we leave Earth. It's going to be a long time between smokes."

"Are you going to the Moon, too?"

"Where else?"

"Can't you get any cigarettes there?"

"Afraid not. No atmosphere, you know."

Avery nodded as if that was the most reasonable statement in the world.

"But why am I here?"

"Hey," the Hatter said, "somebody's got to do it."

"I don't see why."

"It's a little nicety. A sort of farewell gesture. The powers that be arranged it. Nice of them, don't you think? The last cigarette is a sort of souvenir. Something to remember Earth by. It's the perfect symbol of man's greatest invention."

"And what would that be?"

"Something desirable that's not good for you."

Avery lighted the cigarette for the Mad Hatter and waited until the top-hatted figure was puffing contentedly.

Then he said, "Are there a lot more of you?"

"Oh, quite a few," the Hatter said.

"You realize, of course, that you're purely imaginary."

"Of course. And you realize, I hope, that only the imaginary counts."

Avery looked, and he saw a great line of creatures extending along the road beyond his vision. He could make out a few of them. There was the Cowardly

Lion, and he was talking with someone who was probably Hercules, to judge by his lion skin and club.

Behind him was Little Bo Peep, and behind her was a young boy in lederhosen who might have been Hansel, followed closely by a dirndled girl who was probably Gretel. The line stretched away into the unfathomable distance.

Avery wrenched his gaze away. "What's going on here?"

"We're leaving."

"All of you?"

The Mad Hatter nodded. "All of us imaginary constructs who are mankind's only reality."

"Where are you going?"

"To the Moon!"

"But why are you leaving the Earth?"

"There's no place for us here anymore."

"But how could that be? People will always want imaginary creatures."

"There won't be people here much longer to want us. When the people have to leave a place, their dreams leave first."

"I don't understand what's going on. And anyhow, what makes you think the Moon will be any better?"

"That's too many questions," the Mad Hatter said. "You'll have to find the answers yourself. I suggest you consult the spirit of Christmas to Come."

And the Mad Hatter hurried off, puffing his cigarette and skipping lightly into the air, where he continued climbing until he could no longer be seen.

The next person was a young boy. He had no distinguishing characteristics, but Avery thought he knew who he was anyway.

"You're the spirit of Christmas to Come?"

"You got it!" the boy said. "Could I have a cigarette, please?"

"You're too young to smoke."

"It's just symbolic smoking," the boy said. "I don't really inhale."

Avery was used now to finding a final cigarette in his pack. He lighted it and gave it to the boy.

"Thanks," the boy said. "I needed that."

"Glad to oblige," Avery said. "But what I want from you in return is an idea of what Christmas to come will look like."

"You won't like it," the boy said.

"Show it to me anyhow."

The boy made a gesture in the air, and Avery found himself in space looking down at the Earth. At least, he assumed it was the Earth. It looked nothing like the pictures he had seen of his home planet. This Earth was not green or blue. It was the silvery color of the Moon, white, bare, and it glittered. There was a narrow wavering band around its middle. That band was colored black.

"That's really the Earth?" Avery asked.

"That's it," the boy said.

"What happened to it?"

"It turned into what you see."

"That white stuff. Is that ice?"

"Yes, and snow."

"And that black line around it?"

"That's the equator. The ice hasn't reached quite that far. Not that that helps. No one lives in the place any more."

"What about the human race?"

"They had to abandon the planet, move to the Moon. Those who were able. That's why all of us imaginary beings left. With the people gone, there were no imaginations left to conceive of us. Mankind had no more use for imagination when the ice came. It came very rapidly, you know."

Avery stared dumbly at the frozen snowball Earth. A great sorrow came up in him, a sorrow at the lost hopes, the lost chances, the end of it all, and the pity of it all.

"So it's all over," Avery mumbled. "And I alone remain."

"No, you silly man, you don't remain either. Here in your dream you hand out the cigarettes, but in actual fact you won't be here."

"Where will I be?"

"Up there, if you're one of the lucky few." The boy pointed. Avery looked, and he saw the Moon. But it was not the Moon remembered. It was the Moon of time to come. It was green, and it shimmered with a nimbus of atmosphere.

"That's where we all are now," the boys said. "On the Moon, our refuge from the frozen Earth."

"Thank God we made it!" Avery said.

"Only a few of you," the boy said. "Only a few people, that is. Scientists were able to give it an atmosphere. You'll have to ask them how they did it. What really counts is that we constructs of the imagination are all alive and well."

Avery stared dumbly at the Moon, then at the frozen Earth. In his dream, he could take in both of them at a glance.

"So it's all gone," he said. "All the nations."

"Oh, the nations are all right," the boy said.

"How can that be?"

"One of the last things the survivors did before leaving was to draw up maps. There are accurate maps now of exactly where all the countries were. The survivors will be able to go back, repopulate the planet again."

"Again?"

"In a couple of hundred million years, or whenever the ice melts. You don't think this is the first time this has happened, do you?"

"It has happened before?"

"Oh, yes. But this is the first time they have the

maps. They'll be able to put it all back together.
America. Namibia. Albania. They're all there under
the ice."

Somehow, Avery didn't find that a consoling
thought.

The boy took a final drag on his cigarette and threw
it down. "Well, it's been nice talking to you. See you
on the other side." And then he left, too, the last of
the imaginary creatures of Earth, fleeing a place where
ice had taken the place of imagination.

Late in the morning, when Avery came downstairs,
McDougald asked him, "What happened? Did you
have a dream?"

Avery nodded cheerfully. He had awakened early
in the morning and started working on his electronic
keyboard. The song was complete, just a few touches
to change when he got to a real piano. But he had it.
At last he had his lead song, the show opener and
closer. "The Moon is Green." It would be a sensation.
That was really all that counted.

HOW WE LOST THE MOON, A TRUE STORY BY FRANK W. ALLEN

by *Paul J. McAuley*

You probably think that you know everything about it. After all, here we are, barely into the second quarter of the first century of the Third Millennium, and it's being touted as the biggest event in the history of humanity. Yeah, right. But tossing aside such impossibly grandiose claims, it was and still is a hell of a story. It's generated millions of bytes of Web journalism (two years after, there are still more than two hundred official Web sites, not to mention the tens of thousands of unofficial newsgroups devoted to proving that it was really caused by God, or aliens, or St. Elvis), tens of thousands of hours of TV and a hundred schlocky movies (and I do include James Cameron's seven-hour blockbuster), thousands of scientific papers and dozens of thick technical reports, including the ten-million-page Congressional report, and the ghostwritten biographies of scientists Who Should Have Known Better.

Now you might think that I'm sending out my version because I was either misrepresented or completely ignored in all the above. Not at all. I'll be the first to admit that my part in the whole thing was pretty insignificant, but nevertheless I *was* there, right at the beginning. So consider this shareware text a footnote or even a tall tale, and if you like it, do feel free to pass it on, but don't change the text or drop the byline, if you please.

                              *   *   *

It began in the middle of a routine calibration run in the Exawatt Fusion facility. All the alarms went off and the AI in charge shut everything down, but there was no obvious problem. The robots could find no evidence of physical damage, yet the integrity and radiation alarms kept ringing, and analysis of experimental data showed that there had been a tremendous fluctuation in energy levels just *after* the fusion pulse. So the scientists sent the two of us, Mike Doherty and me, over the horizon to eyeball the place.

You've probably seen a zillion pictures. It was a low, square concrete block half-buried in the smooth floor of Mendeleev Crater on the Moon's far side, surrounded by bulldozed roadways and cable trenches, the two nuclear reactors which powered it just at the level horizon to the south. At peak, the Exawatt used a thousand million times more power than the entire U.S. electrical grid to fire up, for less than a millisecond, six pulsed lasers focused on a target barely ten micrometers across, producing conditions which simulated those in the first picoseconds of the Big Bang, before symmetry was broken. Like the atom bomb a century before, it pushed the envelopes of engineering and physics. The scientists responsible for firing off that first thermonuclear device believed that there was a slight but definite chance that it would set fire to the Earth's atmosphere; the scientists running the Exawatt thought that there was a possibility that it might burst its containment and vaporize several hundred square kilometers around it. That was why they had built it on the Moon's far side, inside a deep crater. That's why it was run by robots, with the actual labs in a bunker buried over the horizon.

That's why, when it went wrong, they sent in a couple of GLPs to take a look.

We went in an open rover, straight down the service road. We were wearing bright orange radiation-proof shrouds over our Moon suits, and camera rigs on our shoulders so that the scientists could see what we saw. The plant looked intact, burning salt-white in the glare of a lunar afternoon, throwing a long black shadow toward us. The red-and-green perimeter lights were on; the cooling sink, a borehole three kilometers deep, wasn't venting. I drove the rover all the way around it, and then we went in.

The plant was essentially one big hall filled with the laser-pumping assemblies, huge frames of parallel color-coded pipes each as big as one of those old Saturn rockets and threaded through with bundles of heavy cables and trackways for the robots which serviced them. We crept along the tiled floor in their shadows like a pair of orange mice, directing our camera rigs here and there at the request of the scientists. The emergency lights were still strobing, and I asked someone to switch them off, which they did after only five minutes' discussion about whether it was a good idea to disturb anything.

The six laser-focusing pipes, two meters in diameter, converged on the bus-sized experimental chamber. Containment was a big problem; that chamber was crammed with powerful magnetic tori which generated the fields in which the target, a pellet of ultra-compressed metallic hydrogen, was heated by chirped pulse amplification to ten billion degrees Centigrade. It was surrounded by catwalks and hidden by the flared ends of the focusing pipes, the capillary grid of the liquid sodium cooling system, and a hundred different kinds of monitor. We checked the system diagnostics of the monitors, which told us only that several detectors on the underside had ceased to function, and then, harangued by scientists, crawled all around the chamber as best we could, sweating heavily in our suits and chafing our elbows and knees.

Mike found a clue to what had happened when he managed to wriggle into the crawl space beneath the chamber, quite a feat in a pressurized suit. He had taken off his camera rig to do it, and it took quite a bit of prompting before he started to describe what he saw.

"There's a severed cable here, and something has punched a hole in the box above it. Let me shift around. . . . Okay, I can see a hole in the floor, too. About two centimeters across. I'm poking my screwdriver into it. Well, it must go all the way through the tiles, I can't see how deep. Hey, Frank, get me some of that wire, will you?"

There was a spool of copper cable nearby. I cut off a length and passed it in.

"You two get on out of there now," one of the scientists advised.

"This won't take but a minute," Mike said, and started humming tunelessly, which meant that he was thinking hard about something.

I asked, because I knew he wouldn't say anything otherwise, "What is it?"

"Looks like someone took a shot at this old thing," Mike said. "Shit. How deep does the foundation go?"

"The concrete was poured to three meters," someone said over the radio link, and the scientist who'd spoken before said, "It really isn't a good idea to mess around there, fellows."

"It goes all the way through," Mike said. "I wiggled the wire around and it came back up with dust on the end."

"This is Ridpath," someone else said. Ridpath, you may remember, was the chief of the science team. Although he wasn't exactly responsible for what happened, he made millions from selling the rights to his story, and then hanged himself six months after it was all over. He said, "You boys get on out of there. We'll take it from here."

Five rolligons passed us on our way back, big fat pressurized vehicles making speed. "You put a hair up someone's ass," I told Mike, who'd been real quiet after he crawled out from beneath the chamber.

"I think something escaped," he said.

"Maybe some of the laser energy was deflected."

"There weren't any traces of melting," Mike said, with a preoccupied air. "And just a bit of all that energy would make a hell of a mess, not leave a neat little hole. Hmm. Kind of an interesting problem."

But he didn't say any more about it until a week later, about an hour before the president went on the air to explain what had happened.

The Moon was a good place to be working then. It was more-or-less run by scientists, the way Antarctica had been before the drillers and miners got to it. There were about two thousand people living there at any one time, either working on projects like the Exawatt or the Big Array or the ongoing resource mapping surveys, or doing their own little thing. Mike and I were both part of the General Labor Pool, ready to help anyone. We'd earned our chops doing Ph.D.s, but we didn't have the drive or desire to work our way up the ladder of promotion. We didn't want responsibility, didn't want to be burdened with administration and hustling for funds, which was the lot of career researchers. We liked to get our hands dirty. Mike has a double Ph.D. in pure physics and cybernetics and is a whiz at electronics; I'm a run-of-the-mill geologist who is also a fair pilot. We made a pretty good team back then and generally worked together whenever we could, and we'd worked just about every place on the Moon.

When the president made the announcement, we'd moved on from the Exawatt and were taking a few days R&R. I'd found out about a gig supervising the construction of a railway from the South Pole to the permanent base at Clavius, but Mike wouldn't sign up and wouldn't say why, except that it was to do with what had happened at the Exawatt.

We'd been exposed to a small amount of radiation when we'd gone into the plant—Mike a little more than me—and had spent a day being checked out before getting back on the job. The scientists were all over the plant by then. The reaction chamber had been dismantled by robots, and we brought in all kinds of monitoring equipment. Not only radiation counters, but a gravity measuring device and a neutrino detector. We helped bore a shaft five hundred meters deep parallel to the hole punched through the floor, and probes and motion sensors and cameras were lowered into it.

Mike claimed to have worked out what had happened as soon as he stuck the wire in the hole through the foundation, but he wouldn't tell me. "You should be able to guess from what they were trying to measure," he said, the one time I asked, and smiled when I called him a son of a bitch. He's very smart, but sort of fucked up in the head, antisocial, careless of his appearance and untidy as hell, and proud that he has four of the five symptoms of Asperger's Syndrome. But he was my partner, and I trusted him; when he said it wasn't a good idea to take up a new contract, I nagged him for a straight hour to explain why, and went along with him even though he wouldn't. He was spending all his spare time making calculations on his slate, and was still working on them at the South Pole facility.

I raised the subject again when news of the special presidential announcement broke. "You'd better tell me what you think happened," I told Mike, "because I'll hear the truth in less than an hour, and after that I won't believe you."

We were in an arbor in the dome of the South Pole facility. Real plants, cycads and banana plants and ferns, growing in real dirt around us, sunlight pouring in at a low angle through the diamond panes high above. The dome capped a small crater some three hundred meters across, on a high ridge near the edge of the South Pole-Aitken Basin and in permanent sunlight, the sun circling around the horizon once every twenty-eight days. It was hot and humid, and the people splashing in the lake below our arbor were making a lot of noise. The lake and its scattering of atolls took up most of the crater's floor, with arbors and cafés and cabins on the bench terrace around it. The water was billion-year-old comet water, mined from the regolith in permanently shadowed craters. A rail gun used to lob shaped loads of ice to supply the Clavius base in the early days, but Clavius had grown, and its administration was uncomfortable with the idea of being bombarded with ice meteors, which was why they wanted to build a railway. In the low gravity, the waves out on the lake were five or six meters high, and big droplets flew a long way, changing shape like amoebas, before falling back. People were body surfing the waves; a game of water polo had been going on for several days in one of the bays.

I'd just been playing for a few hours, and I was in a good mood, which was why I didn't strangle Mike when, after I asked him to tell me what he knew, he flashed his goofy smile at me and went back to scratching figures on his slate. Instead, I snatched the slate from his hands and held it over the edge of the arbor and said, "You tell me right now, or the slate gets it."

Mike scratched the swirl of black hair on his bare chest and said, "You know you won't do it."

I made to skim it through the air and said, "How many times do you think it would bounce before it sank?"

"I thought I'd give you a chance to work it out. And it isn't as if there's anything we can do. Didn't you enjoy the rest?"

"What's this got to do with not taking up that contract?"

"There's no point building anything anymore. You still haven't guessed, have you?"

I tossed the slate to him. "Maybe I should pick *you* up and throw you in the lake."

I meant it, and I'm a lot bigger than him.

"It's a black hole," he said.

"A black hole."

"Sure. My guess is that the experiment caused a runaway quantum fluctuation that created a black hole. It had to be bigger than the Planck size, and most probably was a bit bigger than a hydrogen atom, because it obviously has been taking up other atoms easily enough. Say around ten to the power twenty-three kilograms. The mass of a big mountain, like Everest. The magnetic containment fields couldn't hold it, of course, and it dropped straight out of the reaction chamber and went through the plant's floor."

I said, "The hole we saw was a lot bigger than the width of a hydrogen atom."

"Sure. The black hole disrupted stuff by tidal force over a far greater distance than its Swartzschild radius, and sucked some of it right in. That's why there was no trace of melting, even though it was pretty hot, and spitting out X-rays and probably accelerated protons, too—cosmic rays."

I didn't believe him, of course, but it was an interesting intellectual exercise. I said, "So where did the mass come from? Not from the combustion chamber fuel."

"Of course not. It was a quantum fluctuation, just like the Universe, which also came out of nothing. And the Universe weighs a lot more than ten to the power twenty-three kilograms. Something like, let's see—"

"Okay," I said quickly, before Mike lost himself in esoteric calculations. "But where is it now?"

"Well, it went all the way through," Mike said.

"Through the Moon? Then it came out, let's see—" I tried to visualize the Moon's globe, "—somewhere in Mare Fecunditas."

"Not exactly. It accelerated in free fall toward the core, went past, and started to fall back again. It's sweeping back and forth, gaining mass and losing amplitude with each pass. That's what the president is going to tell everyone."

I thought about it. Something just bigger than an atom but massing as much as a mountain, plunging through the twenty-five-kilometer-thick outer layer of gardened regolith, smashing a centimeter-wide tunnel through the basalt crust and the mantle, passing through the tiny iron core, gathering mass and slowing, so that it did not quite emerge at the far side before falling back.

"You were lucky it didn't come right back at you," I said.

"The amplitude diminishes with each pass. Eventually it'll settle at the Moon's gravitational center. And that's why I didn't want to sign the contract. After the president tells everyone what I've just told you, all the construction contracts will be put on hold. What you should do is make sure we're first on the list for evacuation work."

"Evacuation?"

"There's no way to capture the black hole. The Moon, Frank, is fucked. But we'll get plenty of work before it's over."

He was half-right, because the next day, after the president had admitted that an experiment had somehow dropped a black hole inside the Moon, a serious problem that would require an international team to monitor, we were both issued with summonses to appear at the hastily set up Congressional inquiry.

It was a bunch of bullshit, of course. We went down to Washington, D.C. and spent a week locked up in

the Watergate hotel watching bad cable movies and
endless talk shows, with NASA lawyers showing up
every now and then to rehearse our Q&As, and in
the end we had no more than half an hour of easy
questions before the committee let us go. Our lawyers
shook our hands on the steps of the Congress building,
in front of a bored video crew, and we went back to
Canaveral and then to the Moon. Why not? By then
Mike had convinced me about what was going to happen. There would be plenty of work for us.

We signed up as part of a roving seismology team,
placing remote stations at various points around the
Moon's equator. The Exawatt plant had been dismantled and a monitoring station built on its site to try
and track the period of the black hole, which someone
had labeled Mendeleev X-1. Mike was as happy as I
had ever seen him; he was getting some of the raw
data and doing his own calculations on the black
hole's accretion rate and orbital path within the Moon.
He stayed up long after our workday was over,
hunched over his slate in the driving chair of our rolligon, with sunlight pouring in through the bubble canopy while I tried to sleep in the hammock stretched
across the cabin, my skin itching with the Moon dust
which got everywhere, and our Moon suits propped
in back like two silent witnesses to our squabbling.
His latest best estimate was that the Moon had between two hundred and five thousand days.

"But things will start to get exciting before then."

"Excitement is something I can do without. What
do you mean?"

"Oh, it'll be a lot of fun."

"You're doing it again, you son of a bitch."

"You're the geologist, Frank," Mike said. "It's easy
enough to work out. It's just—"

"Basic physics. Yeah. Well, you tell me if it's going
to put us in danger. Okay?"

"Oh, it won't. Not yet, anyhow."

We were already picking up regular moonquakes on the seismometer network. With a big point mass swinging back and forth through it, the Moon's solid iron core was ringing like a bell. There were some odd subsidiary traces, too, smooshy echoes as if spaces were opening in the mantle—hard to believe, because pressure should have annealed any voids. I was pretty sure that Mike had a theory about these anomalies, too, but I kept quiet. After all, I was the geologist. I should have been able to work it out.

Meanwhile, we toured west across the Mare Insularium, with its lava floods overlaid by ejecta from Copernicus, and on across the Oceanus Procellarum, dropping seismometers every two hundred kilometers. We made good time, speeding across rolling, lightly cratered landscape, detouring only for the largest wrinkle ridges, driving through the long day and the Earth-lit night into brilliant dawn, the sun slowly moving across the sky toward noon once more. The Moon had its own harsh yet serene beauty, shaped mainly by vulcanism and impacts. Without weather, erosion took place on geological timescales, but because almost every feature was more than three billion years old, gravity and ceaseless micrometeorite bombardment had smoothed or leveled every hill or crater ridge. With the sun at the right angle, it was like riding across an infinite plain gentled by a deep blanket of snow. We rested up twice at unmanned shelters, and had a two-day layover at a roving Swedish selenology station which had squatted down on the mare like a collection of tin cans. A week later, just after we had picked up fresh supplies from a rocket lofted from Clavius, we felt our first moonquake.

It was as if the rolligon had dropped over a curb, but there was no curb. I was in the driving chair; Mike was asleep in the hammock. I told the AI to stop, and looked out through the canopy at the 180-degree panorama. The horizon was drawn closely all around.

An ancient crater eroded by three billion years of micrometeorite bombardment dished it to the north and a few pockmarked boulders were sprinkled here and there, including a fractured block as big as a house. Something skittered in the corner of my eye—a little rock rolling down the gentle five degree slope we were climbing, plowing a meandering track in the dust. It ran out quite a way. The rolligon swayed gently, from side to side. I found I was gripping the padded arms of the chair so tightly my knuckles had turned white. Behind me, Mike stirred in his hammock and sleepily asked what was up; at the same moment, I saw the gas plume.

It was very faint, visible only because the dust it lofted caught the sunlight. Gas plumes were not uncommon on the Moon, caused by pockets of radon and other products of fission decay of unstable isotopes overpressuring the crevices where they collected. Earth-based astronomers sometimes glimpsed them when they temporarily obscured surface features while dissipating into vacuum. This, though, was different, more like a heat-driven geyser, venting steadily from a source below the horizon.

I told the AI to drive toward it. Mike leaned beside me, scratching himself through his suit of thermal underwear. He smelled strongly of old sweat; we hadn't bathed properly since the interlude with the Swedes. I had a sudden insight and said, "How hot is the black hole?"

"Oh, the smaller the black hole, the more fiercely it radiates. It's a simple inverse relationship. It was pretty hot to begin with, but it's been getting cooler as it accretes mass. Hmm."

"Is it still hot enough to melt rock?"

Mike's eyes refocused. "You know, I think it must have been much bigger than I first thought. Anyway, anything that gets close enough to it to melt is already falling toward the event horizon. That's why there was no trace of melting or burning when it dropped out of the reaction chamber. But there's also the heat generated by friction as stuff pours toward its gravity well."

"Then it's remelting the interior. Those anomalies in the seismology signals are melt caverns full of lava."

Mike said thoughtfully, "I'm sure we'll start picking up a weak magnetic field soon, when the iron core liquifies and starts circulating. Of course, the end will be pretty close by then. Wow. That thing out there is really big."

The rolligon was climbing a long gentle slope toward the top of a curved ridge more than a kilometer high, the remnants of the rim of a crater which had been mostly buried by the fluid lava flow which had formed the Oceanus Procellarum. I told the AI to stop when I spotted the source of the plume. It was a huge fresh-looking crevice that ran out from a volcanic dome; gas was jetting out of the slumped side of the dome like steam from a boiling kettle. Dust fell straight down in sheets kilometers long. Already, an appreciable ray of brighter material was forming on the regolith beneath the plume.

"We should get closer," Mike said. He was rocking back and forth in his chair like a delighted child.

"I don't think so. There will be plenty of rocks lofted along with the gas and dust."

We transmitted some pictures, then suited up and went outside to set up a seismology package. The sun was in the east, painting long shadows on the ground, which shook, ever so gently, under my boots. With no atmosphere to scatter the light, shadows were razor sharp, and color changed as I moved about. The dusty regolith was deep brown in my shadow, but a bright blinding white when I looked toward the sun, turning ashy gray to either side. The gas plume glittered and flashed against the black sky. I told Mike that it was probably from a source deep in the megaregolith;

pressure increased in gas pockets with depth. A quake, probably at the interface between the megaregolith and the rigid crust, must have opened a path to the surface.

"There'll be a lot more of these," Mike said.

"It'll blow itself out soon enough."

But it was still venting strongly when we had finished our work, and we drove a long way north to skirt around it, with Mike scratching away on his slate, factoring this new evidence into his calculations.

We were out for another two weeks, ending our run in lunar night at the Big Array Station at Korolev. It was one of the biggest craters on the far side, with slumped terraced walls and hummocky rim deposits like ranges of low hills. Its floor was spattered with newer craters, including a dark-floored lava-flooded crater on its southern edge which was now the focus of a series of quakes of steadily increasing amplitude. Korolev Station, up on the rim, was being evacuated; the radio telescopes of the Big Array, scattered across the far side in a regular pattern, were to be kept running by remote link. Most of the personnel had already departed by shuttle, and although there were still large amounts of equipment to be taken out, the railway which linked Korolev with Clavius had been cut by a rockslide. After a couple of spooky days' rest in the almost deserted yet fully functional station, Mike and I went out with a couple of other GLPs to supervise the robots which were clearing the slide and relaying track.

It was a nice ride: the pressurized railcar had a big observational bubble, and I spent a lot of time up there, watching the heavily cratered highland plains flow past at two hundred kilometers an hour. The Orientale Basin dominated the west side of the Moon: a fissured basin of fractured blocks partly flooded with impact melt lava and ringed round with three immense

scarps and an inner bench like ripples frozen in rock.
The engineers had cut the railway through the rings
of the Rook and Cordillera Mountains; the landslide
had blocked the track where it passed close to one of
the tall knobs of the Montes Rook Formation, a ten-
kilometer-high piece of ejecta which had smashed
down onto the surrounding plain—the impact really
was very big.

A slide had run out from one of its steeply graded
faces, covering more than a kilometer of track, and
we were more than a week out there, helping the robots fix everything up. When we finally arrived at the
station in Clavius, it was a day ahead of the Mendeleev eruption and the beginning of the evacuation of
the Moon.

The whole floor of the Mendeleev Crater had fractured into blocks in the biggest quake ever recorded
on the Moon, and lava had flooded up through dykes
emplaced between the blocks. Lava vented from dykes
beyond the crater rim, too, and flowed a long way,
forming a new mare. Other vents appeared, setting
off secondary quakes and long rock slides. The Moon
shivered and shook uneasily, as if awakening from a
long sleep.

Small teams were sent out to collect the old Rang-
ers, Lunas, Surveyors, Lunokhods, and descent stages
of Apollo LEMs from the first wave of Moon exploration. Mike and I went out for a last time, to Mare
Tranquillitatis, to the site of the first manned lunar
landing.

When a permanent scientific presence had first been
established on the Moon, there was considerable de-
bate about what to do with the sites of the Apollo
landings and the various old robot probes and other
debris scattered across the surface. There had been a
serious proposal to dome the Apollo 11 site to protect
it from damage by micrometeorites and to stop people

from swiping souvenirs, but even without protection it
would last for millions of years, and everyone on the
Moon was tagged with a continuously monitored
global positioning sensor so no one could go anywhere
without it being logged, and in the end the site had
been left open.

We arrived a few hours after dawn. It was a lonely
place, not much visited despite its historic importance.
A big squat carrier rocket had gone ahead, landing
two kilometers to the north, and the robots were already waiting. There were four of us: a historian from
the Museum of Air and Space in Washington, a pho-
tographer, and Mike and me. The site was ringed
around with laser sensors. As we loped through the
perimeter, an automatic beacon on the common band
warned us that we were trespassing on a U.N. heritage
site and started to recite the relevant penalties until
the historian found it and turned it off. The angular
platform of the lunar module's descent stage had been
scorched by the rocket of the ascent stage; the gold
foil which had wrapped it was torn and tattered, white
paint beneath turned tan by exposure to the sun's raw
ultraviolet. One of its spidery legs had collapsed after
a recent quake focused near new volcanic cones to
the southeast. We lifted everything, working inward
toward the ascent stage: the Passive Seismometer and
the Laser Ranging Retroreflector; the flag, its ordinary
fabric, stiffened by wires, faded and fragile; an assort-
ment of discarded geology tools; human waste and
food containers and wipes and other litter in crum-
bling jettison bags; the plaque with a message from a
long-dead president. Before the descent stage was
lifted away, a robot sawed away a chunk of dirt beside
its ladder, the spot where the first human footprint
had been made on the Moon. There was some dispute
about which print was actually the first, so two square
meters were carefully lifted. And at last the descent
stage was carried off to the cargo rocket, and there

was only a litter of cleated footprints left, our own overlaying Armstrong's and Aldrin's.

It was time to go.

As the eruptions grew more frequent, even the skeleton crews of the various stations were evacuated, leaving a host of robot surveyors in close orbit or crawling about the troubled surface to monitor the unfolding disaster. Mike and I went on one of the last shuttles, everyone crowding to the ports as it made a single low orbital pass before lighting out for Earth.

It was six months after the Mendeleev X-1 incident. The heat generated by the black hole's accretion process and tidal forces had remelted the iron core; pockets of molten basalt in the mantle had swollen and conjoined. A vast rift opened in the Oceanus Procellarum, splitting the nearside down its northwestern quadrant and raising new scarps as high and jagged as those in an old Chesley Bonestell painting. The Orientale Basin flooded with lava and the fractured blocks of the Maunder formation sank like foundering ships as new lava flows began to well up. Volcanic activity was less on the far side, where the crust was thicker, but the Mare Ingenii collapsed and reflooded, forming a vast new basin which swallowed the Jules Verne and Gagarin Craters.

It took two more months.

As the end neared, the Moon's surface split into short-lived plates afloat on a wholly molten mantle, with lava-filled rifts opening and scabbing over and reopening along their edges. There were frantic attempts to insure that the population of the Earth's southern hemisphere would all have some kind of shelter, for the Moon would be in the sky above the Pacific in its final hour. Those unlucky or stubborn enough to remain outside saw the Moon rise for the last time, half-full, the dark part of her disk riven with glowing cracks which spread as the black hole sucked in exponentially increasing amounts of matter. And then there was a terrific flare of light, brighter than a thousand suns. Those witnesses who had not been blinded saw that the Moon was gone, leaving expanding shells of luminous gas around a fading image trapped at the edge of the black hole's event horizon, and a short-lived accretion disk as ejected material spiraled back into the black hole, which, although it massed the same as the Moon it had devoured, had an event horizon circumference of less than a millimeter.

The radiation pulse was mostly absorbed by the Earth's atmosphere; the orbit of the space station had been altered so that it was in opposition when the Moon vanished. I was aboard it at the time, and spent the next six months helping repair satellites whose circuits had been fried.

There are still tides, of course, for the same amount of mass still orbits the Earth. Marine organisms which synchronized their reproduction by the Moon's phases, such as horseshoe crabs, corals, and palolo worms, were in danger of extinction, but a cooperative mission by NASA and the Russian and European space agencies lofted a space mirror which reflects the same amount of light as the Moon, and even goes through the same phases. There'll be a big problem in 5×10^{43} years, when by loss of mass through Hawking radiation the black hole finally becomes small enough to begin its runaway evaporation. But long before then the sun will have evolved into a white dwarf and guttered out; even its very protons will have decayed. The black hole will be the last remnant of the solar system in a cooling and vastly expanded universe.

There are various proposals to make use of the black hole—as the ultimate garbage disposal device (I want to be well away from the solar system when they try that), or as an interstellar signaling device, for if it can be made to bob in its orbit (perhaps by putting another black hole in orbit around it), it will produce sharply focused gravity waves of tremendous amplitude. Meanwhile, it will keep the physicists busy for a thousand years. Mike is working at one of the stations which orbit beyond its event horizon. I keep in touch with him by e-mail, but the correspondence is becoming more and more infrequent as he vanishes into his own personal event horizon.

As for me, I'm heading out. The space program has realigned its goals, and it turns out that the black hole retained the Moon's rotational energy, so it provides a useful slingshot for free acceleration. After all, there are plenty of other moons in the solar system, and most are far more interesting than the one we lost.

(For Stephen Baxter)

THE MAN WHO STOLE THE MOON
by Paul Di Filippo

Hawthorne "Horty" Lopenbloke missed many fine
things once extant during his glory days as a quar-
terback for the multi-Superbowl-winning Sausalito
Satellites. He missed the adulation of fans and the
media. He missed hearing his teammates protect him
by crunching the bones of his opponents. He missed
rifling the pigskin ovoid many yards farther than any
of his peers. He missed the parties, the copious free
drugs, and the constant travel. But most critically, he
missed the endless stream of beautiful women eager
to consummate sexual relations with a famous sports
star. In veritable droves, assorted gorgeous women of
every age, race, creed, and educational status had once
lined up on a nightly basis for a chance to perform—
alone, in tandem, or in packs exhibiting the astounding
coordination of trapeze artists—enthusiastic deviltries
upon his iconic body, asking nothing more in return
than an autographed football, a wax impression of his
victory ring, or a simple plaster casting of the object
of their lusts.

But cruel fate in the form of a severely busted-up
shoulder (experienced ignominiously not on the playing field but while horsing around poolside) had unexpectedly put an end to this easy carnal cavorting. Once
mustered out of the ranks of professional Monday
Night warriors, Lopenbloke had found the glamorous
women no longer quite so accessible. It appeared that
the magnitude of ex-sports stars diminished more

quickly than that of a nova. And like a nova, retired athletes, having violently blown off everything that sustained them in a short extravagant display, frequently were reduced to mere pitiful cinders.

None of this sat well with Horty Lopenbloke, resettled now in California. Still fairly well off monetarily, thanks to the forceful advice of his financial adviser, Horty had not immediately felt compelled to find a real job after his retirement. But this fiscal cushion was not as beneficial as one might think, for leisure gave Horty too much time to ponder what he termed "the injustice of it all." By this phrase, Horty basically meant "the fact that I can't instantly have everything I want anymore." And, as mentioned, the area of his life where he felt this sting most potently was sexual relations.

Professional sports had unfitted Horty Lopenbloke for more than the mundane workplace. The ex-quarterback had completely forgotten how to conduct himself with a woman whom he desired. The unnatural ease with which he had plucked feminine fruit from the vine of life had destroyed any previous skills he might have had along those lines (skills that had already begun to atrophy, it should be duly noted, in college). Moreover, Horty had lost patience for the ritual maneuvers of the mating dance. He wanted what he wanted immediately and without niceties. As for monogamy, finding the perfect soulmate and marrying her—why, Horty would have laughed in the face of anyone who dared to suggest such a limiting proposition.

Which is why Horty Lopenbloke became a serial date-rapist.

Oh, nothing violent. Horty always maintained complete control of his bulky muscled frame, no matter how impulsive his urges. Not for him the assault by a stranger in a darkened alley or even the threat of physical violence face-to-face with a victim. No, Horty was not a crude fellow, despite his former mindless

avocation. He prided himself on a certain level of sub-
tlety and discretion. That and some seriously illicit and
devastating pharmaceuticals pretty much always did
the trick.

In the Sausalito night sky above the disco called
Cory Thalia's Hunt Club, the new Moon reigned. Its
blank, black face could be just faintly discerned
rimmed with the most minute ring of diffuse amber,
offering implicit promise of tomorrow's rebirth as a
threadlike sickle. This mysterious and awe-inspiring
sight was lost, however, on Horty as he emerged from
his sporty two-seater BMW Z3 and strode across the
club's parking lot. Horty had no attention to spare for
astronomical phenomena: he was on the prowl for sex.

Recalling the days when clubs infinitely classier than
this one would have paid *him* to enter, Horty forked
over the cover charge disdainfully. Inside the crowded,
noisy disco, oblivious to the techno music and faddish
moves of the dancers, Horty immediately applied the
same quick perceptions that had once allowed him to
spot holes in the opposition's defense to zero in on
unattached females. Grading and cataloging the available talent, Horty began his circuit at the bar. Drink in
hand, he moved swiftly toward his number one choice.

Instinctively, like an experienced safari guide testing
the trigger of his elephant gun, he fingered the vial of
roofies in the breast pocket of his 44L sports jacket.
All set to dissolve in the drink of his chosen "date."
(After one or two bad experiences with animal tran-
quilizers, Horty had switched to Rohypnol. The drug
left his victims pliable yet somewhat aware, and had
wonderful memory-erasing properties. Of course, the
active participation and delightful initiative Horty had
once enjoyed from his partners was nowadays utterly
lacking, causing him further to lament "the injustice
of it all," but a philosophical fellow took what he
could get.)

The first woman Horty approached, despite a killer body, proved on closer inspection to be treacherously concealing very blotchy facial skin beneath a surplus of makeup. Horty was mildly outraged at the deception. Didn't people have any standards of honesty these days? After some *pro forma* banter, he moved on to choice number two.

The woman sat alone at a round-topped table the diameter of an extra-large pizza. Slimmer than Horty generally approved of, yet not without the requisite curves, she was dressed entirely in white: sleeveless silk blouse and billowy linen pants tucked into the tops of ivory boots of soft leather. Her skin exhibited an opalescent purity, a milky depth. Most startling, cascades of platinum hair broke on her shoulders. As the colored lights of the club played over her, she seemed to fill with the various tints of the gels: orange to rose to green. Only in the occasional moments when a brilliant colorless spotlight lanced the mirror-ball could Horty be sure of her real complexion.

Horty snagged an empty chair from a neighboring table and carried it over to the woman, ostentatiously employing a single finger to balance the chair's not insignificant weight. He spoke loudly enough to be heard above the music. "Mind if I sit down?"

The woman had been focused intently on the dance floor scene, absorbing the unexceptional antics of the dancers as if she had seldom witnessed such a relatively common sight. Her right hand rested on the stem of the glass holding her drink, and Horty noticed that her nails were painted silver, to match her eye shadow. For a moment, the woman's uniformity of skin, clothes, and makeup sent a queer shiver through him. Was she some kind of freak or psycho? Horty put the suspicion aside. What practical difference would it make if she were? He wasn't planning to have any kind of *relationship* with her.

The woman looked up at Horty and blinked, and

Horty observed that her eyelashes were white, too. Was she an albino? No, for her irises gleamed not pink, but—silver. Some kind of contacts, of course.

The woman smiled—her teeth, it went without saying, were practically radiant—and spoke. Horty heard elfin bells in her voice, but disregarded their charm. A dulcet voice meant little, for this gal wouldn't be doing much talking tonight. "Mind if you sit? Not at all," she said. "Especially since you were thoughtful enough to bring your own chair."

Horty arranged himself close beside her. "What's with your getup?" he bluntly asked. Rohypnol afforded a suitor the rare luxury of offering deliberate social offense, as all transgressions would be wiped clean chemically. "Are you like one of those Goth types? I thought they dressed all in black. Or maybe you're into vampires."

The woman continued to smile. "Neither. I've just always dressed this way. You could say it's who I am."

"What's your name?"

"Selena. What's yours?"

"Troy. Troy Stag. No last name, Selena?"

"None that I care to use."

"Kinda like your pop star namesake, huh?"

"You could say that—Troy." Selena resumed her study of the dance floor, her silver eyes assuming a hundred-yard stare.

The woman's cool imperturbability irked Horty, and his remarkably scant silo of patience leaked further grains. He had been planning to waste as much as an hour dancing with this broad and chatting her up, but her failure immediately to fall all over him made him say screw it. He'd move right into Mickey Finn territory.

"Whatcha drinking, Selena?"

Selena returned her attention to her tablemate. "White zinfandel. It's from a Sonoma winery named—"

"Yeah, yeah, all those fancy-pants rip-off artists share the same grapes. They just mix it all up in a big vat and drain it off into bottles with their own labels. Knock that one back, and I'll get you a glass of the house brand."

"How generous of you, Troy."

"That's just the kinda guy I am, babe."

At the bar, Horty slyly decanted the knockout drug into Selena's new drink while the bartender's focus was elsewhere. He returned to the white-clad woman and was somewhat surprised to see she had obligingly finished her first drink. Usually he had to cajole his victims to some degree, as most women tended to meter their liquor intake to avoid getting smashed and the risks that condition entailed. This pigeon was making things almost too easy. A vague foreboding peeped up in Horty's backbrain, but he squelched it. With nonexistent savoir faire he set the glass down before Selena. Lifting his own, he proposed a sentimental toast: "Down the ol' pie-hole, kid."

Selena sipped her wine. "Not bad, but the bouquet—"

"You want a bouquet, visit a florist. The kick's the thing."

"That's one way of looking at oenology, I suppose." A curious smile graced Selena's face. "Where are you from, Troy?"

"Oh, I've kicked around some."

"No roots? Where were your parents from?" Selena swallowed more wine, and Horty answered her truthfully just to keep her drinking. Telling the truth was easier than making stuff up, and what could it hurt?

"My folks raised me up in Jersey, small town named Luna Park."

"Did your family always live there? Previous generations, I mean."

" 'Course not. Who has roots like that these days?"

"You'd be surprised. Some people seem to stay in one place forever."

"Well, that sure don't describe my situation. Like practically everybody else in this goddamn great country, we were pretty recent immigrants. My great-grandparents came here from England through Ellis Island."

"And before that?"

"Jesus, what is this, Genealogy 101? If you gotta know, the family line goes way back to France. The ones that moved to England even changed their last name. But enough of this crap, let's get stewed."

Selena obediently finished her drink. Was this chick simpleminded or what? Within minutes, her eyes seemed to be moving independently of each other, her speech grew slurred, and she was slumping ever lower in her seat. Horty gathered her up with a big arm wrapped around her waist and with one of her arms draped over his broad shoulders. He looked around for Selena's purse, but saw none. Weird, but the hell with it.

"Gotta get the missus home," Horty offered to the one or two onlookers curious enough to cast a speculative glance at him and his shuffling burden. "She just can't handle the ol' juice."

Outside, the new Moon cast its impassive negative light over the parking lot. Horty dumped his "date" into the passenger seat of the Z3, then climbed behind the wheel.

Horty owned a small but impressively situated pastel-colored house on the Headlands with a view of San Francisco Bay. He parked at a hasty angle near the front door, and soon had Selena's weight in his arms.

In the bedroom, undressing Selena took only minutes. Horty had become well acquainted with this fairly intricate procedure. He even insured that his victim's clothes would remain unwrinkled by carefully draping them over a chair. Naked, recumbent on the bed, his latest conquest mumbled and twitched. Horty, naked also, sized up her attractive form as he rummaged in a bureau drawer for a pack of condoms. No point taking any chances, Horty always felt.

You just couldn't safely assume anything about strangers these days.

Mornings after one of Horty's conquests generally progressed according to a fairly predictable pattern. Waking from her drug-induced sleep, the ravished woman of the moment would exhibit varying degrees of embarrassment, confusion, alarm, and anger. Imperturbable, Horty would emphasize three angles: her shameful inebriation that had left events muzzy in her mind, his trusting sensitivity, and their mutual consent. Matters of considerate venereal protection would be stressed. Horty would be dressed, the woman naked, and the balance of power would be skewed, especially since they occupied his house not hers. After a short period of either muted distress or feminine histrionics, the victim would in all likelihood accept Horty's invitation either to deliver her back to her parked car or to call a cab. And that would be that, until the next such postcoital parting. Ninety-nine percent of the time, Horty managed to hit the gym by noon.

This time belonged among the one-percent anomalies.

For one thing, Selena failed to awaken at a reasonable hour. Horty had tried everything to rouse her: subtle tactics such as brewing fragrant coffee, flushing the toilet, taking a loud shower, and whistling; followed by cruder measures like cranking up the radio, slamming doors, and even shaking her. But Selena slept deeply on, as if her constitution had reacted uniquely to the roofies. Unwilling to leave his guest alone in the house, Horty chafed and fretted, growing more irritated with Selena by the minute. What nerve this woman had!

Around 2:00 P.M., just when Horty was beginning to worry that administration of the Rohypnol had unaccountably plunged Selena into some kind of coma, she opened her silver eyes. Horty had placed the small bed table clock on her stomach while she slept on her back, and her gaze now fell naturally enough on its dial. The afternoon hour, verified by the sunlight pouring in through the bedroom window, had the predictable effect of causing a shocked look to materialize on Selena's pale face. She leaped out of the bed, casting covers and clock to the floor. But her first uncanny words bore no resemblance to any exclamation Horty had ever heard from any of his overnight guests.

"The Man in the Moon! He's locked me out by now!"

Horty held Selena's clothes, crumpled in one big hand, out toward her. "Listen, babe, whatever nickname you call your main squeeze, he's gotta take you home, cuz I sure ain't having you hanging around here any more. You've already put a crimp in my schedule. Get dressed now, and I'll bring you back to the club parking lot."

Selena ignored her clothes and sat despondently back down on the bed. Horty felt a stir of arousal as his look wandered over her splendid breasts—two generous scoops of French vanilla ice cream—and her creamy thighs. (Her nipples were the color of pewter, and her pubic bush—well, as Horty liked to phrase it, "the carpet matched the drapes.") Quickly, he repressed the lustful feelings. Violation of his one-night-stand policy was unthinkable. And Selena's next words just hardened his heart further, for they indicated that she was plainly a mental case.

"Oh, never in ten thousand years has such a thing happened! To betray my lunar office for a single night of mortal pleasure!" Selena looked up at Horty curiously. "We *did* have some pleasure last night, didn't we, Troy? Events are so hazy. . . ."

Horty didn't bother to offer his correct name.

"Yeah, yeah, you were superduper. Now cover your butt. We've got to get a move on before my favorite Nautilus machine is all sweated out."

Reassured about her prowess as a bed-partner, Selena resumed her mournful recriminations. "What could I have been thinking? Now who will light the Moon through all its phases? How will humanity fare without its immemorial, marmoreal shining beacon?"

Selena's elaborate phraseology made Horty's head hurt, and he lost patience. "Honey, you'll have a different kind of shiner to worry about if you don't hustle your pretty ass."

Selena reacted to the threat in an unexpected manner. She shot to her feet, quivering with rage. Her beautiful face assumed a bloodless wrathful look similar to what one might see on the tusked mask of a cornered warthog. Her expression actually made Horty stumble backward a step.

"Do you have any idea whom you're addressing in your impudent fashion, mortal? Do you?"

"Nuh–no. Who, uh, who do you think you are?"

"I am the Goddess of the Moon! And if I were back home at this moment, your arrogant carcass would be buried beneath the Mare Imbrium by now!"

At this exact moment Horty realized the true dimensions of his unwise choice of bed-partner. He had unintentionally saddled himself with a genuine psycho, a looney-tune who could not be brushed off as cavalierly as the majority of his used-up disposable women. Getting rid of this one was going to take some finesse.

"Uh, Selena, I'm totally behind all this kind of empowerment bullshit. You're a moon goddess, I'm a centaur, whatever pushes your buttons. Far be it from me to get between someone and their fantasies. But being in charge of the Moon must be like a full-time job, right? You certainly don't have any time to spend goofing off around here. So why not get dressed and I'll bring you wherever you want to go."

Horty offered Selena her clothes once more, and this time she snatched them away. Donning them with contained fury, she said, "Weren't you listening to me? Although I have a car, I have no place to go. I was only visiting Earth on my one free night of the month, and I overstayed my return. I'm sure the Man in the Moon has locked the door against me now. He's threatened to do it often enough. You don't know him, what he's like. He's insane!"

A sinking feeling growing in his gut, Horty sat down on a chair. The more Selena talked, the more complicated things became. He knew that responding to her nutty babbling was a mistake that would only drag him deeper into her psychosis, but he found he couldn't resist interrogating her.

"If you're the Moon Goddess, the babe in charge, then who's this other guy? What's he do?"

Clothed now and mellowed somewhat, Selena grabbed Horty's hairbrush from his dresser top and began pulling it through her long platinum tresses. "I control the machinery that lights the Moon. He controls the machinery that darkens it."

"Machinery?"

"Oh, yes, caverns upon caverns full of very ancient and intricate equipment."

Horty squeezed his brow with the same talented throwing hand that had brought victory out of defeat so many times in the past. He hoped for similar results now. Trying to recall basic astronomical facts gleaned from one of the few college lectures he had attended, he formulated another question. "Doesn't the Moon shine because of reflected sunlight?"

Selena laughed brightly. "What a foolish notion! Of course not. It's all my hard work that brings the Moon's light your way. Starting with today's new Moon, I'm supposed to be notching my controls forward a little bit each night, illuminating bigger and bigger pieces of the Moon's surface from the inside, while my coworker backs off on his darkness levels. Eventually we reach the full Moon. That's *his* night off-duty, of course, although he hasn't made use of the time to visit Earth for millennia, that antisocial *jerk!* Anyhow, the night after the full Moon he begins to bump his levels up while I diminish mine—in a symmetrical patterning, naturally, to create the waning shapes that differ from the waxing ones. Although the procedure's second nature to me now, it's all quite complex, and it took me a long time to learn. Why, when I recall the mistakes I made when I first began— I think I drove several species of hominids so crazy they went extinct!"

Horty's skull felt as if compressed under several linebackers. "Honey, you've got a major problem, and I don't mean how to fly back home. I really think you believe everything you've told me. And that makes you choice bait for the guys with the big butterfly nets."

For the moment, Selena seemed tolerant of Horty's criticism. "Oh, Troy, I know you don't place any faith in what I've told you. But I'll show you by tonight that it's all true."

Horty gained his feet in one convulsive motion. "Tonight! I can't have you around here tonight!"

Selena laid a lily-pale hand on Horty's arm. "Really, Troy, was I that disappointing?"

He shrugged her off. "Quit calling me Troy! My name's Horty, Horty Lopenbloke."

Selena giggled. "What an unlikely name. Are you entirely sure?"

"Of course I'm sure! I'll show you a dozen trophies if you don't believe me!"

"That won't be necessary—Horty. I'm certain that we'll practice complete honesty between us from now on. And in that vein, let me tell you that I'm famished. What's for breakfast? Or should I say lunch?"

Horty's indignation faded. He had experienced too

many emotions in too short a span to sustain any of
them. This intractable problem left him despairing.
"You're not leaving, then?"

Selena firmed her silver lips in a tight line and firmly
shook her head no.

"Uh, well, then, let's see— Um, in training camp I
learned from our chef how to make a mean batch of
chocolate-chip pancakes."

Selena's handclap expressed her delight vividly.
"That's perfect! We have no chocolate on the Moon.
It's one of the wonderful things I try to sample each
month on Earth. What brand?"

"Huh?"

"What brand of chocolate chips?"

"Ghiradelli?"

"Perfect!"

Much to Horty's surprise, the remainder of his un-
conventional day passed pleasantly enough. Selena
was not a chatterbox, the kind of loquacious broad
that got on Horty's nerves. During the meal of chip-
spotted, cocoa-tinted pancakes—round and dark as
the new Moon—she simply ate appreciatively, offering
only a few wordless exclamations of delight. Afterward, she even insisted on doing all the dishes, wash-
ing each plate and cup and utensil as if she were
handling the crown jewels.

"You don't know how much fun this is, Horty! I so
seldom get to do such simple chores. I have an entire
army of servants that won't let me lift a finger."

"Servants, huh? Like butlers and maids?"

"Well, not exactly. . . ."

Around four o'clock, Selena asked if they could
drive into the city. "With my visits to Earth limited
to twenty-four hours, I don't ever get a chance to
really explore San Francisco, which is about as far as
I dare venture anyway. Maybe you could show me a
few sights."

Horty ignored the insane portion of her speech. "Okay, I guess. You like strip clubs?"

"What are they?"

"Well, you see—oh, just forget about it. We'll go look at the stupid bridge or something."

In the city, they hit the standard tourist spots. Exhibiting a bored indifference he hoped would drive Selena away, Horty improvised implausible anecdotes and local history, all of which Selena received with naive expressions of delight. By seven, they were seated in the restaurant at Cliff House, looking west over the Pacific. As the horizon bit into the sun, Selena grew excited.

"If I had made it home, when the sun went down tonight, you would have seen the first small crescent after the new Moon, low in the sky. But with my lesser half at the controls, who knows what will happen?"

"Yeah, sure. Are you gonna eat that last shrimp or not?"

The sun drowned in an oceanic pool of blood, and the sky gradually assumed nocturnal hues, violet, teal, lilac. Selena's attention was riveted on the western reaches of the celestial dome. Finished with Selena's appetizer, Horty looked up as well. He was just in time to witness a startling display.

Like the round lens of a flashlight instantly powered on, the full Moon suddenly snapped into view. In the space of three seconds, it cycled through a number of colors: gold, blue, green, and cinnamon. Then the schizophrenic orb vanished, overwhelmed by darkness.

Horty's fork dropped to the floor with a melodious tinkle. His jaw seemed intent on popping its hinges. Several other diners who had noticed the brief spectacle were reacting likewise.

Selena was fuming. "That moron! He's tweaking me deliberately. If I ever get my hands on him—"

Horty found his voice hiding somewhere in the vicinity of his jockstrap. "Holy shit! You weren't kidding about any of this!"

"Why, of course not. Would a goddess ever stoop to lying?"

To say that the world went wild at the Moon's misbehavior would be to overstate the cumulative reactions of the average sensation-jaded citizen. First of all, only the nighted half of the globe played host to the capricious chromatic behavior of Earth's satellite. The bulk of the Oriental masses experienced nothing untoward until the next day, and their night brought only the Moon's forewarned absence. In Horty's hemisphere, the majority of potential observers failed to have their eyes on the sky during the critical seconds, and so were spared the paradigm-shattering vision. Astronomers, of course, went mad in herds. Coincidentally captured in amateur and professional photographs, the Moon's disturbing fan dance gained solidity, could not be written off as an episode of mass hypnosis. Disseminated to the media, these photographs engendered a twenty-four-hour crisis.

Truth to tell, the disappearance of the Moon meant little to the average late-twentieth-century urbanite, suburbanite, and edge-city resident. Most people never noticed the Moon in its nightly course anyway. Ask the mythical Man in the Street prior to this trouble what phase of the Moon was currently showing, and you'd receive a stony look of incomprehension. So in a short time, reassuring hypotheses for the Moon's altered albedo began to surface and gain uncritical acceptance: a cosmic dust cloud, alien intervention, an act of God. So long as the tides still rose and fell—the Moon's gravity being unperturbed—and so long as the artificial satellites on which the Earth's communications were so dependent remained unaffected by whatever had canceled out the Moon, people were content to do without a visible satellite. Save for the reminders of a couple of instant novelty songs and some topical jokes on late-night TV, within two days of the vanishing of Earth's old friend most people had thrust the anomaly from their minds.

Not so for Selena and Horty.

Heading north on Route 101 out of Sausalito, Horty sat back in the passenger seat of Selena's car, terrified. He tried to remember why he had ever consented to her doing the driving. Her mode of handling her car precisely characterized the type of motorist she represented herself to be: a self-taught driver who had gotten behind the wheel only one day every month ever since the invention of the automobile. Her style was a unique mix of enthusiasm, false confidence, and skittishness. As they narrowly avoided one titanic smashup after another, Horty prayed for deliverance to the only deity he knew, other than Selena: the Supreme Coach, a figure he always pictured as a skyscraper-sized Bear Bryant, complete with trademark fedora big as a blimp.

For thirty-six hours after the Moon's convulsive display, Selena had brooded in Horty's home. Bereft of her vocation, locked out of the Moon by her shadowy doppelganger, she seemed enervated and despairing. Horty refrained from questioning her about her future plans or from delving deeper into her past, tiptoeing quietly around her brooding form with exaggerated caution. He had never drugged and seduced a supernatural or nonhuman woman before, and felt somewhat appalled by the cosmic repercussions of his actions. Finally, though, Selena transcended her funk.

"Stop that pacing, Horty! We're going to pay a visit now to the door that brought me here. I've thought of a way I might be able to override the lock."

Horty felt a trifle irked by Selena's air of command and by her assumption that he'd be accompanying her. True, he supposed, he bore responsibility for her plight. But how much did a guy have to do in the way of payback? Hadn't sheltering and feeding her for a couple of days while neglecting all his own vital concerns been enough?

"And where the hell might this door be? I hope it's not too damn far away."

"Not at all. We just have to drive to the Valley of the Moon."

And so a mild, sunny Tuesday morning found Selena and Horty back in the parking lot of Cory Thalia's Hunt Club. Selena's car, a drab Jeep with federal plates, awaited them untouched.

"How come you're driving a government car?" asked Horty suspiciously. He suddenly imagined that all the confusing events of the past few days represented an elaborate setup to bag him for that extra-large cocaine purchase back in '93.

"This vehicle belongs to the Park Service. I bribed a Ranger to make me a set of keys and let me use it once a month."

"Bribe? What does a goddess use for folding money?"

Selena looked at Horty as if he had asked the result of two plus two. "Do you have any idea what the Exploratorium in San Francisco pays for genuine chunks of lunar rock?"

"Oh."

The Valley of the Moon, Horty knew, was a picturesque part of Sonoma County. It featured many wineries, resorts, and recreation areas. Other than that, he knew little about the region. So as Selena conducted them now at alarming speeds through such towns as San Rafael, Novato, and Petaluma—she had insisted on staying together and on using the Jeep, not Horty's BMW ("My Ranger friend could get in trouble if I don't return his car.")—Horty listened to Selena's history about the area with gratitude, as a means of diverting his attention from imminent accidents.

"Before Europeans arrived, the Miwok and Pomo Indians inhabited Sonoma, which in their language means 'Place of Many Moons.' I was their incarnate goddess, of course, appearing once a month on Earth in their midst. They were such a nice group of people, but limited in what they could offer a girl in the way of entertainment. Blackened salmon dinners and music heavy on the drumbeats get stale awfully fast—although when I encountered a similar mix just recently in a fancy restaurant, I became *so* nostalgic. Certainly I began to miss the Old World pleasures I had enjoyed for so many millennia in Greece and Rome, Avignon and Camelot, Ur and Babylon. But the portal had refocused itself here in what would one day become California, and I had no choice in the matter."

"What do you mean? You're the goddess who controls all these Moon gadgets you've told me about. Couldn't you make your doorway pop up anywhere you wanted?"

"Not really. You see, I didn't create all the Moon machinery, and a lot of it is beyond my understanding. I'm just a caretaker established by those known as Almost the Oldest Ones."

"And who're they?"

"A race of incredibly antique—but not ultimately ancient—beings from somewhere else in our galaxy. They're the ones who decided mankind needed a luminescent satellite to help in their development. They plucked me from my home world while humanity was still dragging their knuckles and put me in charge of the Moon. They brought the Man in the Moon from elsewhere, as well as our servants."

"So your badass partner up there's not as human as you?"

"Not in certain respects, no."

Horty pondered this information, while Selena continued her story and the intermittent horns of angry drivers assailed them. "When Western civilization arrived, I became friends with various prospectors and settlers and farmers, showing up at my regular times. But only once since then have I revealed my true identity to a certain special man."

Horty felt irrational jealousy. "Who was this jerk?"

"Jack London."

Dim college memories surfaced in Horty. "The guy who wrote stories about wolves?"

"And much more. Jack owned a farm some eight hundred acres in extent in the Valley of the Moon. His land included my portal. It would hardly be polite to materialize in someone's parlor without introducing yourself now, would it?"

"So we're heading for his house now. Is this London guy still alive?"

Selena sighed. "Alas, Jack died in 1916. And his house stands now in ruins."

Selena's incredible talk of visiting savage Indians had affected Horty less than the suddenly vivid picture of her consorting with some geezer dead nearly a century, whose very house unforgiving time had crumbled. He regarded her pale profile in silence for many miles thereafter.

In the town of Santa Rosa, they turned east on Highway 12. The Mayacamas Mountains loomed to the north, paralleled by Sonoma Mountain to the south. Vineyards stretched away on either side of the road. They traveled now through the extravagantly lush and splendid scenery of the Valley of the Moon.

A sign advertising Jack London State Historic Park advised them to turn off onto Arnold Drive some two miles outside the town of Glen Ellen. Selena drove this familiar road with more confidence, soon bringing them to a gravel parking lot. They left the Jeep, paid a small fee, and entered the grounds of the park. On this weekday, very few other people roamed Beauty Ranch, the former estate of the famous writer. For a time however, until they could be certain no witnesses

would observe them, Selena and Horty ambled inno-
cently among the ruins and restored structures: a cot-
tage, barns, stone silos, a winery. Selena paused by
London's grave for a moment of silence while Horty
fidgeted. Then, seemingly alone on the property, they
moved illicitly inside the posted ruins of Wolf House.
In the corner of one shattered room, Selena approached an innocuous fragment of wall and began
fooling with unseen features on its surface.

Horty nervously looked back over his shoulder, concerned some Ranger would intrude. "Are you sure—"
he began to ask, turning back to Selena. And then he
saw what the goddess had wrought.

A person-sized oval of silver mist had replaced a
portion of the wall. And out of the fog stuck the head
and shoulders of an alien abomination.

Comic books were Horty's favorite reading material. He preferred either violent ones involving ill-
mannered and heavily armed vigilantes or risque ones
featuring big-bosomed and immoral teenagers. But
once Horty had accidentally purchased a black-and-
white reprint of some space cartoons by Basil Wolverton. What goggled at him now from the doorway to
the Moon recalled a Wolverton drawing. From scaly
shoulders broad as any found in the NFL emerged a
plucked-looking, scabby neck as long as Horty's arm.
The neck supported a disproportionate blocky head
topped with a shaggy mat of orange hair partially ob-
scuring saucerlike eyes. A nose like a warty cucumber
protruded out four inches. The creature's lower jaw
hung open, revealing rows of squarish teeth looped
with green saliva.

"Jesus!" shouted Horty. Instinctively, he stepped
forward and swung his fist at the creature. Hitting the
alien felt like punching a rotten moss-covered plank.
He connected at the same moment that Selena managed to shut the door to the Moon. The closing of the

portal severed the monster at the neck, and its head thumped to the floor amidst a gout of green blood.

Selena regarded the remnant of the alien somberly. "Poor Pretzel," she said.

"You *recognize* this hideous thing?"

"Of course. Pretzel was the Man in the Moon's chief servant. He must have been set to guard the door against my possible return. Pretzel had no choice but to obey, but he never would have hurt me. And now he's dead."

Horty sized up the repulsive features of "poor Pretzel," then asked, "Are *your* servants this ugly?"

"Oh, no," Selena replied. "Much less handsome."

In the early part of the twentieth century, a traveling salesman for the Chattanooga Bakery in Tennessee, a man named Earl Mitchell, continually sought new ways to please his customers, mostly rough-and-ready coal miners in his home state and the bordering ones of Kentucky and West Virginia. The brawny, grimy workers frequently expressed a desire for a snack that would withstand the rigors of the miner's life, something filling, sturdy, and tasty. Earl was stymied by their demands, and sought clarification at least on size. "How big this here snack's gotta be?" he asked a miner one day. Seeing the full Moon rise over the company store, the anonymous hillbilly kobold framed the orb with his hands and said, "Jest like thet." Back at the bakery, Mitchell, like some confectionary Edison, experimented with graham crackers, marshmallow, and chocolate in the appropriate dimensions. And eventually at one Eureka moment, the enormously popular Moon Pie was born, that legendary Southern delicacy invariably washed down with an RC Cola.

The Moon Pie, of course, in its round chocolatey darkness, paradoxically ended up representing not the full Moon, but the new. And it was in the Moon Pie

Factory that the Man in the Moon had established or found *his* doorway to Earth.

"He doesn't believe I know the location of his door," Selena told Horty after the debacle at Jack London's house. "As I told you before, he hasn't used the portal in so long, I think he's almost forgotten about it himself. All his attention and all his guards will be focused on my door. He'll never expect us to enter through his."

Thus it was that Horty now drove himself and Selena in their rented car through the streets of mountain-girt Chattanooga, heading toward the premises where Moon Pies were created. His head still spun from the encounter a day ago with the nightmarish Pretzel, and he tried to trace the steps that had led him to this moment. How was it that his life had become so entangled with Selena's? What spell had she cast on him? Did she represent the only real excitement he had experienced since his NFL career ended? How far was he willing to go with this adventure? Possibilities and limits swirled in his fevered brain, and he could barely concentrate on the road.

They parked in the factory lot, and emerged to join a line for the visitors' tour. Sweet odors of chocolate and marshmallow and cracker flour wafted over them, and Horty began to salivate. The double stack of pancakes and the half pound of bacon he had consumed for breakfast—while Selena watched and sipped at her tea—hadn't stood by him as well as he might have wished.

As if sensing this hunger, Selena said, "We won't sneak away from the tour until after the free samples."

A guide assembled the group and led them inside. Horty paid little attention to his industrial surroundings. The scents of baking were driving him crazy. At last the pastry samples materialized. Selena took a Moon Pie and broke it open to reveal the dark cake's white interior. She fed a piece to Horty, and Horty gratefully devoured it as if it were a strange communion. A blissful satiation filled him, and he felt in control again. He congratulated himself on putting up with Selena so patiently; a much wiser strategy than storm and bluster. Soon now he'd be shut of her forever, thanks to his devilish slyness.

As they were being conducted out, Selena hung back. With a whispered, "Now!" she pulled Horty into an alcove.

Within minutes, they had worked their way unobserved to the basement level of the factory. Selena zeroed in knowingly on an unlocked storeroom door. And in that dimly lit bunker, amidst burlap sacks of flour, she unhesitatingly opened up the Man in the Moon's doorway.

The Moon Goddess paused at the silver oval. She blinked her mesmerizing eyes, and said, "Farewell, Horty, and accept my thanks! I go now to battle for my kingdom!"

Selena stepped into the matter-transmitter and was gone. The portal began to shrink uniformly from its edges inward. A feeling of loss and despair filled his guts, and Horty yelled, "No!" He dove through the dwindling gate as if between a narrow gap flanked by opposing tackles.

The breathable air below the surface of the Moon smelled faintly like moldering hay. And the dusty illumination in these enormous high-vaulted caverns of the Moon resembled moonlight itself as received by Earth. Everything from the rough-hewn floor to the distant walls and lofty ceiling, from the spectacle of an infinite corridor to the gargantuan towering masses and ranks of complex machinery seemed painted by some master of chiaroscuro. The stark palette of black, white, and grays made Horty remember an old film he had watched once called *Forbidden Planet*, especially the scene when the visiting Earthmen toured the relics of the Krel with that dame in the short skirt.

Awed, Horty regained his feet with the nimbleness conferred by one-sixth gravity, not even feeling the pain of his scuffed hands. Selena stood a few yards off. "So, my champion has decided to accompany me. Very well, let us confront our nemesis without delay."

Selena let Horty come up alongside her, and then she led the way down the long corridor.

Horty lost all track of time. It seemed they marched for weeks, past a plethora of strange sights. Huge lever-arms that ceaselessly rocked, bellows big as houses that inflated and shrank, monitors that showed terrestrial and intergalactic scenes, deep bubbling fume-wreathed pits filled with something like mercury and rimmed with catwalks along which Selena and Horty hurried. The marvels saturated him until he grew numb and moved in a fog. Once Selena had to pull him back with a shouted warning: "Don't fall over those klystron tubes!" Her voice reinvigorated Horty, and he moved with renewed mindfulness.

Eventually they reached their destination: a room big as several football stadiums. The space was half-filled with hordes of aliens like Pretzel, and half-filled with another race that Horty realized must be Selena's minions. Her servants resembled human-sized bipedal turtles with scorpion tails and beaked faces. They did indeed win the Wolverton Draw-alike Ugly Contest, thought Horty. On a control dais in the center of this assemblage sat a hunched figure whose features Horty could not discern at this distance.

Selena and Horty had entered the amphitheater at a point high up one of its curving walls, where a balcony turned into a flight of steps. Now Selena bellied up to the balcony's rail and vented a defiant rallying cry.

"Servants of the Goddess! Your mistress has returned!"

Chaos erupted immediately, as the two alien races began struggling in hand-to-hand combat in a scene that quirkily fused the pummeling of a Three Stooges fracas with the surreal inhabitants of a Bosch canvas. Selena grabbed Horty's hand and started down the stairs. "Quickly! We must stop the Man in the Moon before he escapes!"

On the floor, they wove their way through the tumult, Horty bulling through in the lead. None of the Man in the Moon's servants dared lay a hand on Selena, and the advancing pair simply had to avoid getting accidentally bowled over. Soon enough, they attained the edge of the control platform.

The Man in the Moon stood up from a bank of switches, and Horty staggered backward at his appearance.

From the neck down, Selena's dark partner was human enough. But his head destroyed any illusion of normality. Consider first that his head measured as long as his body. Second, that it was shaped like a pockmarked crescent and colored a waxy yellow. Third, that it was approximately two inches thick. Bulbous eyes occurred a third of the way down on either side, a needlelike nose at the halfway point, and a grinning split of a toothless mouth in the lower third. Horty was instantly reminded of the foam-rubber headgear worn by rabid football fans.

"Get him, Horty!"

At the sound of Selena's voice, Horty mastered his emotions. He leaped onto the low dais. The Man in the Moon raised his arms—in defense or attack, Horty could not be sure. So he launched a roundhouse swing.

Horty's fist went in one side of the Man in the Moon's thin head and out the other. The alien's whole lunar cranium crumbled into fragments then, like a hunk of bad cheese, and Selena's ex-partner collapsed to the floor.

Bringing up his fist to his nose, Horty sniffed. Cheese, indeed.

Upon the destruction of the Man in the Moon's

fragile head, the fighting among the servants stopped. Selena jumped up beside Horty.

"The battle is over! Welcome your new master, the White Rabbit!"

Horty was baffled. "What are you talking about, Selena? Who's this White Rabbit?"

"You are, of course. Your family's French name, Horty, was *Lapinblanc*. Your ancestors were my loyal devotees for generations. Many cultures see in the Moon's mottlings not a Man, but a White Rabbit, my preferred symbol. I chose you to replace my old consort. He grew wearisome to me some centuries ago, but none of your line appealed to me till now."

"*You* chose *me?* But, but—I drugged you and kept you from getting home!"

Selena laughed in an eerie peal, and Horty realized he had known nothing about her till this moment. "Your drugs had no effect on me, nor did the Man in the Moon truly lock me out. Poor Pretzel was only stationed at my door to welcome me home. No, the old cheesehead still loved me and wanted me back, provided I returned alone. Alas, Horty, I confess now, I played you like a helpless mooncalf! But don't be angry—not that it would do you any good. I've elevated you far above your kind, both literally and figuratively. In exchange for a few small mechanical responsibilities, you possess me and my charms, a vastly extended life—as long as you keep me amused—and dominion over half the Moon."

Horty could barely believe his fate. "But how will I stay busy up here?"

Selena snuggled up sinuously to her new consort. "That shouldn't be a problem. And don't forget, you get to visit Chattanooga once a month."

"But what about from day to day? What will I do with myself?" Horty looked out over the sea of grotesque yet obedient aliens waiting expectantly for his reaction like two rival teams—

Two rival teams. Suddenly inspired, Horty reached down for several hunks of the Man in the Moon's head. He wadded them up into a torpedo shape, then pitched the mock football into the audience. In the Moon's light gravity, several aliens soared high to catch it.

Smiling, Horty turned to Selena. "Call me Coach White Rabbit, and you've got a deal."

ELEGY

by Michelle West

Metal slices hair away from the stretched skin over his skull. He knows this experience. Although he has never undergone it, the whisper of memory is there: death, the preparation for death. He's seen it a hundred times. A thousand times. In person. On the visionscreens. On the cinatorium screens of his crowded youth.

That youth comes back to him in fragments, in fragrance; the smell of sweat and perfume, alcohol, urine, salt—bodies pressed thickly together in crowded rooms, crowded halls, crowded floors, lights dim by design and not by torrid necessity; that will follow; does follow.

"What are you watching, Hank?" Pretty girl. Blonde, again by design, roots already a touch too dark. A statement, not an accident: *I can look like whatever I want. Body's decor; mind's everything.* Shirt like a spiderweb, embedded with sequins that only look cheap when the light's on. Mouth wide, thick, sultry as a summer night. As any night, now.

He can't remember her name, but it doesn't matter; she's pressed into the crowd like another part of the wall, small and slender and destined for early age and anonymity. She wants his attention.

But floor to ceiling in the crowded mock warehouse, cut only by support beams and low-hanging light struts, flickering where negatives have been slicked or

251

scratched by poor handling, this week's offering: Moonlight.

Bright white, bright gray, bright black; larger across than anything he's ever seen, an expanse of perfect, cratered wilderness, clear night, Milky Way twisting like some torn veil behind it.

"Watcha watching, Hank?"

"Sky."

She looks at the wall; at its lowest remove, boys and girls are casting shadows that dip and bend and meld, or worse, they're wearing the image's edge, distorting it with the curve of bodies that won't stand still even when they don't have far to move. "Hey, shit, isn't that Marty and Lou?" She nods when he doesn't answer; the answer is irrelevant.

Things crowded and dirty fill the sky—used to be called clouds when they didn't go on forever. That's what his grandmother told him before she went. He wonders what she would have said, standing beside him at the cinatorium, her body just another wedge in a crowd of backgrounders.

Something slow and creaky and insectoid is landing on the surface of the moon. Some jerk is talking, talking, talking. He'd shut him up, if he could; he doesn't need the words. Words are everywhere.

But some guy, in a suit that's so obviously ancient it looks like a monstrous bulge of retro-armor, is moving in slo-mo across the theater, his giant, padded feet distorted where it passes over bodies. Crackling, his voice is electrifying where the other voices simply annoy.

He says *one small step for man one giant leap for mankind*.

They pause a moment, the dancers, the voyeurs, the watchers, as if bearing witness, as if forced to bear witness, to the words and the moment.

God, there's just so much *room*. So much *space*. It

hangs there, empty, the promise of such an expanse of land more potent than sex or drugs.

Then someone says, "Hey, I *know* that one—it's the Moon."

"It's not the Moon, buttass!"

"It's the Moon, I tell you—before it was civilized. It's the fuckin' *Moon.*"

"Yeah. Great," someone else says. "It's not even true anymore. What's the fuckin' point of watching this shit?"

Agreement changes the mood of the crowd, blending some convivial nodding, some convivial cursing into a mutual ground most people can stand on.

Hank watches. Watches in something like awe, in silence, in the huddle of the crowded 'torium. He wants to keep on watching in a silence informed by jerky motion and glaring white space.

The moment doesn't last. It's gone, as if it were written by a twig in water, in the puddles of an even farther youth.

"We'll have to leave soon," his grandmother says softly, as he stares into the puddle's still surface. Behind him, jostling for a glimpse of that puddle, an army of children (his mother's words), held back by their parents, their grandparents, their tired older siblings. Held back, that's all that matters.

"Why?"

"Because there are other children," she says softly. "The rain was mild, love. We don't see many like it. The sky is—the sky is open, just a bit. See there?" She points to his feet, not to the sky, and the stick in his hand stills. "Look, and then come away. Let other people see too."

"But why are there so many people?" Water beneath his branch; Moon in the puddle, dark eyes open and mouth full. Her reflection is a shadow, and his, a smaller shadow beside it. There are people in the streets, rushing to and from wherever it is that people rush. It's not like there's anything to rush to.

"There won't always be so many people," she says softly.

"But why are there so many now?"

She doesn't answer him. Instead, she puts her arms around him and pulls him up, stick and all, into a quiet hug. She says, "There's no one else in the universe anything like you. No matter how many children are born, there's only one of you."

Later, he'll find out—from his dad, mostly—about war and biology and radiation and chemical damage—about the fact that the arid, airless surface of the Moon is safer and easier to live on than most of the continent. Not, his father will add, that there are too many people—but that there are too many survivors and too little space.

Too little work.

But just then, her arms about him and the face of the bright, bright Moon in the gap between folds of sky, he doesn't care.

Head shaved, he waits. The branch is breaking the meniscus of the water; the knife is breaking the surface of the skin. Memory and fact blend, and he likes memory better. But that's the problem he's always had with this life: he likes memory better. The past is the land of glory and hope; the present the land of waiting. In the future there is only the dead, and how you die—

It's such a complicated procedure you have to stay awake for it. Neural damage being what it is.

He snarls; his head is in a vise, and good damn thing, or he'd yank it out, yank it away before they could finish what they've begun. And *that* would be a messy, wasted death.

*   *   *

There are teenagers, of course. They're everywhere. They're the brunt of the lost generation; the leftovers, the artifacts, the examples of the *waste*. Murder is still illegal, but there are so few laws enforced in the urbs, the packed, cramped quarters of the cities. You don't go out on your own if you're too young or too pretty—but then again, you don't go out on your own much anyway.

There used to be a problem with violence. Dad's generation, Mom's—they went trigger, they found old guns and things that could kill and they killed. Killing the leftovers didn't matter much, so they'd kill the ones who ran the country, tried to keep it all together.

That changed their lives, all right.

There is no school.

There is no education.

There is no way out.

Hank's family waits here, in the poorly kept buildings that are all the home they're allowed—unless they somehow manage to win the lotteries the government runs—and they pray and hope and weep. They go to the food depot on Wednesday—I-L day—and they trade in their brass tickets for whatever comes in the convoys the army guards.

Funny that, his mother says grimly. They always have enough money and food for the army.

His grandmother told him that they used to send people to the Moon. The Moon stories died with her, but he knows that people in the urbs went to Mars, for a while. He heard stories and watched the 'torium screens; he'd even broken two laws and forged a pass to get into the 'torium out of rotation just so he could cleave to the edges of the room and find out *more*. But the stories just stopped coming. And after the stories: Hope.

The Space Commission is looking for volunteers.

*   *   *

His arm is bandaged. His urine analysis sample is sitting on a jar on the wide, sterile desk. He knows it's his because it's got his name on it. He can read that much. His grandmother taught him, and she left him the books.

But the books have long since gone; sold. He remembers the words as clearly as he can, but age takes them, eating away at the edges until only the core remains.

"Hank Iverton?"

He blinks. "Ma'am."

The wide lady in green has him step up on something that clanks and clatters while she makes adjustments to the pieces of metal that run across the top of a crossbar, her eyes a little too dark, a little too wide. He smells something on her breath, not alcohol, not synth—but something—and she pushes buttons on the pad she carries before telling him to get down.

He gets down. He'd jerk off in public if she asked him to; she asks him to provide a sample in private. He does that. It's not hard. He's so excited he can hardly breathe. There's no first kiss, no first fuck, no first *anything* that's been as much of a rush and a shake as this: a chance to do something. A chance to be out in the breadth of space, with *room*.

He's pathetic, really, and he knows it. Tries not to be, because no one wants pathetic.

I'll do anything. He says it. Means it. Anything at all. He'd ship out as a sex toy, he'd lick the grease off the kitchen floor, he'd clean the toilets with his tongue. Anything.

She says, "Do you know how to read?"

Yes.

"Do you know how to write?"

Some.

"Did you learn any math?"

Where? Where could he have learned to play with

numbers? To force them to make sense, as if they were words in an abstract form?

Yes.

She says, "Continue."

He gathers his clothing and he leaves the room. They hand him a pad like the one she carries; they hand him a stylus. They lead him to someplace small and private—a place with no windows and a door that makes his home's door look narrow. They tell him to answer the questions that appear across the display to the best of his ability.

He starts to read the questions, but half the words don't make any sense. He rages at the words, as if the anger and anxiety will force them to conform to what he knows. He weeps.

They leave him alone in the cubicle with the pad for two whole hours; more privacy than he's had in a lifetime of memories, and all he can do is despair.

The lady in green opens the door at the end of the trial; takes that pad from hands that have curled into fists around its edges. He knows once he lets it go. He's gone; there are no more chances.

She flinches. Speaks to him in the quiet, quiet voice that his grandmother used to use. Almost against his will, he gives her back the pad. She murmurs something, not his name—she probably doesn't remember that—but something just beyond the edge of his hearing. Red-eyed, but not teary, she leads him back to the bunker, crowded with smells and people.

We're saving humanity, she says. *Try not to judge us too harshly.*

Hope is the ugliest thing of all.

They bring out the lists.

The names they speak mean nothing to him because none of them are his.

*   *   *

He works his way up the political ladder of the cinatorium. Gets added to the guest list, which means he
can show three days a week, as long as he takes care
not to wear the same colors—and not to use the same
name. The same name will match the list, and the list
will tell you to bugger off, more or less. If you don't,
the bouncers enforce its commands. It's sort of
funny—when he's junked—that a box the size of his
left foot, but sleeker and stronger somehow—can tell
four grown men what to do. But it can; they do. It
works.

The list *will* query voice if the voice is registered—
his is—but queries are handled by the guys behind the
bouncers, and they pass him through.

Rex—not his real name, but he likes it because he
says it has something to do with dinosaurs—is older
than his dad. He's special, here: he knows how to *do*
something. He mans the projectors that cause the
great wall of the 'torium to come to life with image
and vision. He doesn't have to be here, in the urbs.
It makes him almost magical.

He asks Rex about the projectors, about the
splashes. Rex snorts. "Outside," he says, "they have
things you couldn't even dream of."

"Like what?"

"Those pictures—those images?"

"Yeah?"

"Imagine," Rex says softly, "walking in them. Imagine that you could be part of whatever it is you see.
Imagine that it's so damn real you can't tell you aren't
there. You can taste the air. You can feel the sun.
You can see the clouds. You can—"

"Walk on the Moon?"

For a moment, Rex tenses, eyes narrowed and suspicious. But the expression loses shape and edge as
Hank waits, breath held, for his reply.

"Yeah, kid," he says, some bitterness layering the
words with an emotional sediment that he can't iden-

tify. "You can walk on the Moon." He turns back to the controls that look so ornate they might be from one vid or another. Touches them. Tweaks a knob or two. It's mostly for effect.

"But the Moon isn't what it used to be."

"What did it used to be?"

Rex shrugs. "Empty," he says, with a bitter laugh.

"Oh." He starts to turn away, and the old man catches his arm.

"Don't go there," he says.

"Where?"

But he doesn't answer the question.

"What about Mars?"

"What about it?"

"What happened?"

"Mars is Mars. What do you mean what happened?"

"They did all the recruiting—"

Rex's face, empty, deathlike. He's seen the dead often enough to know. "It's over," he says quietly.

"But—"

"It's over."

Three weeks later, they bring in the Machines.

They: Men in army coats, in army dress. They come with a food convoy, but they don't go to the food bunkers. They go to the cinatorium. They go to the youth.

Memory.

His grandmother, hand in his hand, face a mask as she pulls him out of their way.

But a friendly man in green stops her. "Ma'am," he says, his voice as patient as if he's talking to his own grandmother, "this is something even you'll find interesting. Here." He shoves something into her hand. Paper. Real paper. Words on it, like a story.

It's not how you live that matters, it's how you die! Join the Virtual Marines! Fight for your America!

Her expression—he remembers this clearly—if halfway between a smile and a word, lips parted to say hello to the friendly, earnest young man. But her eyes fall to paper that shakes although her hand seems steady enough and Lord knows there's no wind. Gran can read.

She drops it as if it burns to touch.

"Do you *know* what you're saying?" She says, her voice thin and high and terrible because it's suddenly lost all strength. Oh, it's loud enough, but it's not her voice, not anymore.

He steps back at the force of it, as if he can't hear the weakness. "I just follow orders, Ma'am," he says.

"Have you even *read* this?"

"Yes, Ma'am."

"How can you distribute this to—"

"Does it matter?" He snaps back, losing the suit he's shrouded in. "More than half of you can't even *read* it!"

"Corporal!"

He turns; a man's voice. Older, deeper, resonant with command. Not anger, though. His face is lined and old the way Rex's is.

"Can I help you?" he says.

Hank's grandmother stares at him. "Do you know what it is you're offering?"

He starts to say something; happy-speak, cheerful. But you don't happy speak Gran. You can't. It's the way his face twists up, like Rex's, that makes Hank look down at the paper that has landed between his grandmother's feet.

He picks it up.

God, he hates that part of the memory more than he hates *anything*. He picks it up.

"Yes, Ma'am," he says quietly. "I know what it is we're offering."

His gentleness stops her a moment; stops her the way a fist might. Or a knife, if it hit something vital, but not badly enough to kill. She is gasping for breath.

He says, "For better or worse, Ma'am. History will judge us. But we can't continue like this. We don't have the resources."

She turns away. There was faith in her until the moment those words were spoken; it's gone.

"We can't save everyone. We've come to accept that." His gaze is intent. Hank's seen it before; he's asking for something. "This way, *this* way, they can at least have a normal life."

She laughs. "Is that what you call it?"

"Yes. Come to the site. Try it for yourself. We're equipped for testing, and we'll give everyone who comes the operation required free of charge."

They give him air. At least it tastes like air: tinny and stale as it comes down the tube and into the mask that's fitted over his face. Tinny and stale is better than what it replaces: Antiseptic not strong enough to cover the trace smell of urine and vomit. They tell him to lie back; he can't even say whether or not their voices are male or female, they come echoing down like thunder from a greater and greater distance.

But he feels it, air and distance or no: the hard, cold plate at his back; the stiffening of his body. The needle.

The funny thing is this: Neil Armstrong had the most important line in human history—at least in the human history that Hank knows—and he *flubbed* it. He left out a word. Think about it—does it make any sense? *One small step for man, one giant leap for mankind.*

Rex tells him, laughing, his face as animated as the characters lighting the wall in a splash against the darkness. "He was so damn nervous; he knew it was such a momentous—I mean, a big moment. Big thing. He knew it. He'd thought about what to say. He'd figured it out. He'd rehearsed it.

"But he got out there, and it was—the end of all dreams. It was just too much to take in and spit back out for the rest of us."

"The end? But he got what he wanted!"

"Yeah." Rex's smile was thin enough it turned sidewise and vanished. "He did. End of all dreams is when you get what you want, kid. After that, what is there?"

What was there? He had no idea how to find out what had happened after the Moon Landing. It grew in his mind; it filled the whole of his mental landscape until he managed to coax a bit more information out of Rex. Neil Armstrong didn't die, not immediately. He went on to do other things. But nothing as glorious as that, seen from the outside.

"History swallowed him," Rex added, staring at the panels. Staring.

"Yeah, well," he says. "History must be pretty hungry these days."

He takes the piece of paper out of his pocket three days after they'd handed it out.

"What's that?" his father asks.

"It's nothing," he says, because his grandmother's face has gone ash-gray with something that might be anger. Funny, how she's the only person who has enough anger that she can actually hurt him with it, because she's the only one who never tries. When it happens, it happens.

Like now.

Their hands—father and son—intersect over the edges of the paper.

"It's paper?" his father says. At that moment, his grip is the stronger of the two. Hank doesn't want the paper to rip or to shred. Years of inculcation against waste loose his fingers.

His father reads the whole thing. When he finishes, he says to his mother—to Hank's grandmother—"Can they do this?"

But it doesn't mean to Hank what his grandmother's question meant.

"Do what, Dad?"

"Why don't you go to the cinatorium, Hank?"

It's at the cinatorium that he gets his answers. Not on paper, of course, because he can't really read much of it. He gets his answers in the splash. Tonight's epic of choice is about: Doing the right thing for your country.

It shows his whole life—the life they're all familiar with: crowded streets. Crowded rooms. Clothing that might as well not be clothing, it fits so poorly most of the time. There's face paint, though; the sections of town reflected in silvered foreheads and cheeks. Glitter. Dust. Youth. That's what they have.

Get a whole new life!

The images shift, flickering so fast you'd have to be junked just to catch 'em all. Luckily, he is. Those same kids, those same streets, but emptier, cleaner, wider. Clothing that looks like it comes off the 'torium screen; babies held in the arms of young parents, not parents as old and worn-out as his are. Flash to people sitting at desks, people working in fields, sun on their backs and sky the weirdest sky color he's ever seen. Mountains, people on ropes—but they look *happy* to be there, so it can't be a bad thing—water, as far as the eye can see.

Then the images shift again, the panorama of wonder shoved sideways into the spill of the worst of the familiar: Death. He knows it because he's seen it so often. In the rooms next door, Mr. Glover hacked his family to bits with an old ax. They screamed and screamed and screamed, but the emergency locks had gone up; no one could leave their quarters to help, even if they wanted to.

Dad was on the phone for half an hour. Dad was on the phone until the screaming stopped.

Mr. Glover had a quicker death; he jumped.

But his broken body, their bloodied corpse bits, are only there and gone in an instant. There are those who starve to death in the streets; they forget where they are 'cause they're junked. There are the gang victims, the old and the infirm, the young, the bored and stupid—they all look the same in the end: a little bit of blood and a complete absence of movement.

Get a brand new death!

And there it is, at last, quiet, sleeping people in large beds with smiles on their faces. They're surrounded by doctors, by nurses, by caring people—and by so much room you could fit four families into the space people don't occupy.

Take your whole family with you and you can live the life you *should* have lived!

Flash: there are four beds. A man, a woman, two children. They lie down, and the beds are so close together they can make a human chain by grabbing hands. The doctors are still there as they slide into sleep, hands clasped, faces easing from worry and fear into joy and peace.

Then they wake. They wake and the doctors are gone, and they have this *whole house* to themselves. They hug, they cry, they run off to explore the rooms and rooms full of space. They find beds, they find *toys,* they find something in the backyard that's blue and full of water. They find this four-legged creature that seems happy enough to see them. And they find the door.

Fulfill the dreams you've always had!

The door opens into a street full of houses bigger than the houses in city North where Rex lives. Another door opens; a man steps out and smiles. "Good thing it's a weekend," he says, in that happy-speak voice that's so irritating, "or we'd be late for work!"

And as he laughs heartily, the sky is transformed from a shade of turquoise to a shade of ebony, broken only by the crisp flicker of starlight and the face of the full Moon.

"Does it work?" he asks Rex, the Moon still full and perfect in the artificial sky.

"Yeah."

"For how long?"

"No one's certain. You get—ah, there it is. See that? It's a 'net plug of sorts. It manipulates your brain directly. People use 'em now all the time."

There's a lie there, but he's not sure what it is.

"Scientists have determined that the sense of passing time is greatly decelerated during REM sleep, and they've created a special plug that can stimulate REM while a person is dying."

"You mean it—"

"Don't you understand it even when it's spelled out?"

"No."

"You volunteer to die. We don't have to feed you, clothe you, clean up your corpse when you commit suicide or someone else decides to kill you because human beings weren't meant to be cramped in spaces this tiny for more than an hour at a time." The sentence breaks for his breath, but the breath is fast, ragged; he tumbles back into the words. "In return, we fit you with those tiny little plugs and you plug into a great big network and we stimulate a REMlike state in which you process a great amount of sensory input at speeds no normal person could handle for more than five minutes at a time.

"You live a normal life. Our research indicates—" He shakes his head. "Our research shows us that from *your* perspective, sixty to eighty years can pass before you die. Sixty to eighty years of life."

"And we only have to die for it."

"We're all walking dead, one way or the other. Once you're plugged in, you're the type of dead that has total control of every other element of your life. If you can figure out the gateway ports, you've got an on and off to the most expensive arrays of information in the galaxy."

"What does that mean?"

"It means the answer to any question you've ever even thought of asking."

"I want to tell you a story," his grandmother says, her voice soft and low.

"Why?"

She flinches. She's never lied to him before. She doesn't now. "There once was a little girl," she says quietly, "who lived with her drunken father."

"What about her mother?"

"They were very, very poor. She was sent out to beg in the streets or to sell matches, and this is how her family survived. But the winter—"

"What's winter?"

"A very, very cold time," she says, drawing him into her arms the way she had when he was a child. "The winter was very, very cold. Her cheeks were red and her lips blue and her hair stiff with snow and frost. And she thought if she lit a bundle of matches, just one, she would be warm.

"She lit. She was warm. But not by fire; by vision: She saw a—" she stopped a moment, "a room, just like ours, people huddled together and singing the dark-away songs.

"She reached out to touch them, and the matches went out, and she was left in the cold and the dark. So she struggled on. She tried to do her best by her family. She tried to sell her matches. But it was a busy time of year. . . ."

"Gran?"

"I'm sorry, Hank. It was a busy time of year, and no one had time for a poor girl. She grew cold again, and this time, she promised herself just one last bundle. She lit the matches, and as she did, she was surrounded by—by food, so much food that she'd never have to stand in line by the bunkers again, not an I-L day, or A-D day, or any day. She thought, if she could just have some of that food, she'd be well—and she reached for it. Burned her hand, silly girl, for her trouble."

"Gran, why are you telling me this story?"

"But the night got colder, and she was deathly afraid to go home without money or food. Huddled in the snow—it's like rain, but it's frozen, darling—in rags just like yours, she lit one more bundle of matches."

"And what'd she see?"

"She saw her grandmother, her dead grandmother, the only person in her life who had loved her and made her happy." His grandmother turned away, and he saw it, saw it beneath the oddly combed strands of her hair: a jack.

"She lit all those matches in a terror of losing her, and her grandmother caught her in her arms and took her away some place where cold and hunger and pain couldn't touch her anymore."

He remembers what his mother said first: *Theresa, we'll lose a whole room if you leave us; you* know *the minimum for two rooms is five people.*

His father, voice much sharper and much less comfortable, said, *Madeleine*! And his mother—just as Hank would have—subsided, falling into her own anger, her expression sallow and frightening because it speaks to the boy of the future, and it's not a future he wants. Not one he has any control over. He'll get used to that, in time.

But then, just then, it's his grandmother's face he
sees, the lines of it twisting like the wire across the
fences of the Big Houses at city North—the ones you
can see from blocks away, but you can't *get* near. She
told him, once, that if he tried to climb fences like
that he'd regret it because the little bits of metal
would tear him up—and catch him up as well.

And he knows what she means, although he's never
tried climbing the fences, because her face does that,
her expression so terrible he has never once forgotten
it. His father says, *Mom*. And reaches out for her,
one-handed. She takes that hand and after a minute
his dad pulls back and stands up, almost yanking her
off the chair. He leaves the room.

Kit, she's too damn small to know what's going on.
Mom's angry but she won't speak. And Hank wants
to run into her arms, his grandmother's slightly open
arms, but he doesn't know how anymore, because the
lines of her face are like wire and she's behind them.

Grandma? He says, but she stands up, stands up to
go after his dad.

Later, they argue. They always argue when they
think the kids are asleep. His mom. His dad. His
grandmother's nowhere to be seen; she goes out for
walks at night. She'll be back.

"It's like a goddam nursing home. This," his father
says, "the whole damn thing. Worse."

"We're not in bed. We're not dependent on nurses
to change our diapers. We've got food. We've got each
other. Things are going to get better!"

He howls like wind in the scrapers. "When?"

"Phil—"

"No! Don't *Phil* me. We can't even educate our
kids. We go out, we come home, we sweep streets, we
do nothing. I wasn't trained for this. You weren't.
Even if things *get better*," and he makes the words an
ugly sneer, "what's in it for *them?*"

"They'll be alive. They've adapted."

"They won't be able to *do anything!*"

"They'll learn."

His laugher is awful.

"Do the math, Maddy—do it! They've already taken everything they can use. We're just a drain on their resources and their time."

"But she—"

"It *doesn't matter*. She's done everything she can; she's been a model citizen for her whole damn life. This *is* what she wants. God," he said, his voice changing, the thunder falling out of it in a minute, "this is what we all want, if we're not too damn scared to admit it."

The ringing sound of her hand striking the side of his face fills the room; there is no other reply.

They don't offer him a spacious bed. They don't have beds. They have closet-shaped storage bins, cubicles that serve two purposes. One: a container for a living, standing boy who's committed himself to a different life. Two: a coffin that can be carted straight to the crematorium once that life is over.

He understands now why his grandmother didn't wait. Why she went to her death alone. Actually, it wasn't exactly alone; the lifebanks—as they're called—don't operate with less than one hundred connections. They don't send people to death alone, and even as long as a minute in the array in isolation is considered an unspeakable act of cruelty. Like killing them all quickly isn't.

She leaves him a message, and it's in small enough words that he doesn't need her to read it for him. But he's not sure he understands it, so he takes it to the only person he's willing to ask questions like this of: Rex.

Rex doesn't want to read it, but he does; that's the

thing about Rex. He's the kind of guy you can make do things he doesn't want to do because he feels like he's failing somehow if he doesn't.

"You understand this?" He says, as he sets the pamphlet that offers this new life and new death on the table, exposing the words she wrote on the unused bits of margin.

"I don't know."

"It says she—it says she's not so certain what life is anymore. It says she—it says—she's perfectly happy to die as long as she doesn't have to bury any more of her children. Or grandchildren. She says she knows it's selfish." He flips the paper over so the words aren't visible anymore. "It says she loves you and she's—"

He lifts a hand. "I understood that part," he says, because he doesn't want to hear those words in any voice that isn't hers.

He wonders what her dream was.

More and more of his friends go for the quickie test run. They get their heads half-shaved—it's a look now—and they sit in these chairs while people carve away bits of their skull. It's ugly, but he feels compelled to watch and bear witness, just in case he chooses to follow.

They get clipped. They get plugged in. Their eyelids fall as if they're never going to open. But they don't die. They blink a few times. That's it. And then they stand up, in disoriented groups, some weeping with frustration and terror, and they voice-sig the list that will put them *back*. Forever. Suicide. Deep sleep. Death.

But while they're waiting—and they do wait, eyes drying as they realize they're not still trapped on this side of the divide—they tell everyone: We were gone for *months*. We did *so much*. We had *everything*. They turn to each other as if they're all old friends, as if nothing in the real world has any meaning or any value anymore. They hug. They even giggle.

Word and image is spread as if the lives of the urb dwellers is kindling and this, at last, the fire they've been waiting for.

He misses the stories.

He misses the songs, and that's stupid; his mother's the only person in the family who can sing at all. Dad's off-key so often you wish he'd lose his voice for keeps, and Kit's off-word, but Grandma doesn't care.

"She doesn't know what a cow is," is her reasoned response, "but she knows what coon is. Does it matter which one jumps over the moon?"

No—it *was* her reasoned response. She's gone now, and no one sings. No one tells stories. No one offers him any way out now, any way clear to the truths she always told. If he was a better liar, it wouldn't matter.

She never taught him how to lie; he learned it, bumbling and insecure, all on his own.

He wanders through the streets of the urbs closest to the 'torium, cause those are the streets he knows best. He lies to himself every step of the way. He doesn't understand why, but there is no light in the sky; it's all on the ground in the wells of grungy little lamps and neon warning signs.

Rex.

"Yeah," he says, the day that Hank makes his decision. "What's life anyway but one big race to death? You could create whole families in a reality that the living can only barely touch without burning out their cerebral cortexes."

"It burns out your—"

"Brain. Does it matter?"

Hank is silent for a long time. "Why do you know all this stuff?"

"Why do you think I know all this stuff?"

"Do you know what Neil Armstrong did when he got back to Earth?"

"I haven't a clue."

"But you could find out."

"Yes."

"Will you?"

Rex looks so old these days.

The cinatorium is half-packed, and it's getting less crowded by the day. The only difficulty the army seems to be having is getting rid of the bodies of the transits fast enough. Bodies are always a deterrent.

"No," he said quietly. "You can, if you want. There's one way."

"You told me—"

"I know." He shrugs. "I'm afraid."

"Of dying?"

"Sure. But dying is something we all have to face. I'm more afraid of watching everyone and everything I know die. That's something that's chance and bad luck. You know that old splash? The one with the Moon?"

He knows it as well as he knows how to walk; maybe less well than he knows how to breathe.

"You could do that, in there."

"*You* could."

"It's a one-way trip," Rex says. "And I'm not finished up here yet."

"What are you doing here anyway?" Hank says, because he's never really asked before.

"I'm trying to do what we're all trying to do. Save humanity. What about you?"

"I'm trying to make up for stupid mistakes."

"Lucky you don't have my life, kid. You'd need more time than God has."

There are only two things he wants.

He wants his mother to stop crying. And he wants to go back in time.

He can't make his mother stop crying. He offers her what she doesn't want: The opportunity to die at his side. "Look, Mom," he says, "you've seen—"

"I am *not* going to allow this!" She catches his younger sister in her arms, but his sister is old enough now that she pulls away. "This can't be legal. You aren't of age."

But it *is* legal. He wants her to stop crying, but in the end, it really doesn't matter if she does. He knows she's going to be lonely. Her and Dad, sitting it out while the urbs empty. Who knows? If they wait long enough, they might find a place in the new tomorrow that has no room for him.

He says, "Yeah, well, it sucks, but the only thing we can do for our country is die, and I don't want to die badly."

They open the box. It's like paper, but thicker, and it smells funny. He can't move; he's strapped to something hard. They crate him up, lever him in, make sure the wires attached to the top of his head aren't dislodged, and close the door. They don't really speak to him. They don't meet his eyes. They reek of death.

He's never pitied them before—the ones that get to live. But seeing them, he thinks about what it must be like to pull all the switches and throw out the dead. God, that'd send him trigger for sure. He'd thank them, but there's a tiny part of his mind that doesn't trust 'em, and by the time he knows whether or not he's being fair, it'll be way too late.

He wants to go back in time.

They turn out the lights.

It's dark without lights. He hears voices, like static, but he can't see a thing. Can't smell all that much either. His arms feel funny; his legs feel funny. He can think, though. That's something.

The lights flicker on, pale but bright in the cramped

cabin. Cramped even by his standards; another man in a suit at his side. Voices in his ear.

He wants to tell them all to shut up, but there's something he has to do first; doesn't want to waste his time shouting any words but the right ones. He can see out the window. Small window, for all that, but it doesn't matter. He calls for more light, and lo: There's a wild, crazy light in the distance that's bright enough to live by. No, not a light. A place.

As he gets used to the dark, he can see his hands; his hands encased in something retro and funky and hyper-real. He hears the words.

The Eagle has landed.

He thinks they're the right words; it's fuzzier than he thought it would be. Oh, it feels like he's here all right; no one lied about that. But there's something that isn't real *enough*.

He's going to die for this.

He's already made that choice.

Things he's never heard of rush in to take over his body; he sees doors open and close and he hears instructions and something lewd from another crewmate. Voices teaming with excitement, envy forgotten: they're here. This is the Moon.

God, it takes so long.

It takes so long in the strange airless silence, the microphone a static crackle that never quite dies into stillness.

He doesn't *know* what all these parts are.

(Oxygen. Air Lock.)

He doesn't know how they work.

He doesn't know how to take the small step.

But someone does, and he makes it out into the forlorn, empty corner of perfect space, the earthlight almost blinding in its perfect beauty. Frozen, he stops; they laugh in his ear, voices heavy with excitement. He wanted this. He won this.

·   He paid.

He lifts a foot, just like he's done so many, many times, but it goes higher than any step he's ever taken. Higher. He goes up. Comes down. He could be junked, it all seems so surreal.

The words leave his mouth in a rush, but he says them:

One small step for a man, one giant leap for mankind.

He says it right. It had to be said right. Even if history isn't watching, even if no one does.

And no one does. He hadn't thought it would be like this: he had thought there might be a moment of triumph, of excitement, of freedom. But that's the life lived from start to finish, not the single moment; the glory isn't in doing, but in achieving. He understands that now. He could never have had that moment because he could never have had that life.

Hank sits down in the dusty isolation that speaks of who he is; he sees craters, he sees stars; he sees things so empty of life they're almost a comfort.

This is the land where the dead go to sleep.

Grandma, he says, and she answers, and he weeps.

Come, Hank, she says, and she holds out her hand and her smile is so beatific.

The sun blazes as he grabs onto her, as he throws his arms round her waist and holds tight to all things that have glory: memory and love. When the light fades, he intends to go with her.

BREAKFAST ON THE MOON,
WITH GEORGES

by Ian McDonald

Present at the September meeting of the International Society of Extreme Geography at Montreuil are President for Life Barbenfouillis, Messrs. Alcofrisbas, Micromega, and Parafaragamus, Mr. William Crackford of England, his son John, M. Claude Ravel, M. Lucien Reulos, and M. Georges Melies. Minutes are kept by Hon. Secretary, M. Gaston Melies. Dinner is served at eight sharp, concluding at twelve-thirty after much cheese and fine dessert wine.

Afterward, the Members attend to matters of Extreme Geography. President Barbenfouillis stands and gives the speech. This 1904 is perhaps the greatest year of all history. Humanity pirouettes atop a confection of scientific achievement and technological progress. This City of Light is more than just the capital of France, it is the capital of the world, City of Man. This is an age of vision, of the unbounded imagination of visionary men. In such a golden time it is more important than ever that the International Society for Extreme Geography maintain its reputation for boldly going where no Frenchman (apologies to our English colleagues) has gone before. Not merely maintain. *Extend.*

He sits down to much applause and the finest wines available to humanity. Stirred, the members then present their schemes. From Alcofrisbas, a bathysphere voyage to the bottom of the sea. From M. Micromega, a journey beneath the northern ice pole in a submarine powered by the mysterious properties of radium. From M. Parafaragamus, antipodeanly minded, a proposal to trip to the South Pole by a fleet of airships. From Crackford father and son, an expedition through the mouth of the Vattnajokul Volcano, to test the currently fashionable Hollow Earth theory and discover if there is indeed a counter-world, exact in every detail, cupped within our own.

Then stands M. Georges Melies. With a gleam in his eyes and a twirl in his waxed mustache, he announces his idea.

"Gentlemen, colleagues, honored pioneers," he says. "Our esteemed president has spoken the *mot juste*. This is a time of vision and imagination, of humanity triumphantly stepping over every bound set before it. In this spirit, I place before the Society an expedition that many before us have made in the imagination, but none, until now, in reality. We have the technology, we have the vision, and if—no, gentlemen, *when*—we succeed, it will be the crowning achievement of our age. Gentlemen, I propose a voyage to the Moon!"

Stupefaction, then rapturous applause led by M. Melies' brother, Gaston, and his supporters, M. Reulos and M. Ravel. Enter a troupe of leotarded demoiselles from the Paris Opera, at the march, drawing on silk ribbons a float in the shape of a throne supported by representations of the four winds. Behind troop women and children in celestial costumes—stars, comets, planets, goddesses, angels. M. Melies takes the throne and is borne around the room to a song specially composed by M. Ravel, *The Leader of the Starry Skies*. Streamers and confetti are thrown, horns blown, gifts strewn from papier mâchè cornucopia. Such is the excitement that proper business is forgotten and the members of the Society for Extreme

Geography fall to disport with the ladies of the Paris Opera, with wine, and cheese, and cigars.

At some point before the following dawn, the motion is passed unanimously.

Who is this M. Georges Melies? A small man, dapper, with elegant goatee and fine mustaches. Receding hairline. Well-dressed, manner restrained, despite his theatrical background. Well featured, eyes always lit by a glitter of humor. It is the eyes you notice most in photographs of him; they draw you into conspiracy. I know something you know, but no one else here knows, they say. A trick, a joke. A little magic.

But that is how he seems. That is artifice and he is, by his own proclamation, master of artifice. Who, what, is Georges Melies?

Third son of a fancy boot manufacturer enriched by the Second Empire. Lycee-educated, though an incessant classroom doodler, which almost cost him his baccalaureate. A lifelong rebel against the bourgeois values of his family—the family home at Montreuil—where the epochal meeting of the Society takes place—was commandeered by the Communards, its Second Empire furniture burned.

A family snapshot from 1892. The family of Jean-Louis-Stanislas Melies. A bright day. Against trees. Fat, smiling, happy women, two oppressed-looking children with croquet mallets, a frowning patriarch unaware that a birch tree is apparently growing out of his head. On the right of the group, three young men. Extreme right, a bearded, balding man in a gray suit, holding a croquet mallet as if playing a banjo in a minstrel show. The lone grinner.

A devotee of and initiate into the mysteries of Robert-Houdin, prestidigitator. A one time traveler in dry-goods who in London was seduced by Maskelyne and Cook's Egyptian Hall. In Paris, illusion, artifice, magic.

October, 1888. For forty thousand francs cash,

Georges Melies has bought and refurbished the Theatre Robert Houdin. Before the best of Paris, he performs his first original illusion. He calls it "The Persian Stroubaika." The audience oohs and claps as the plump, levitating houri floats around the stage, seemingly under the control of the magician's fingertips. After the interval, in which patrons may examine, and be amazed by, the Houdin mechanomats (are they man, are they machine?) and the fairy pantomime, the performance ends with a magic lantern slide show. Hannibal crosses the Alps. Blizzards buffet his army. Avalanches sweep elephants and regiments of infantry into terrible chasms. Such is the realism that the nervously disposed are quite upset. At the end, the short man with the neat goatee steps forward and bows and receives the applause of the people of Paris.

A prestidigitator. An illusionist. A trickster, a Mephistopheles—his favorite role. His second favorite is Faust.

It is 1895 now. In a small room at 14 Boulevard du Capucines are one hundred chairs and a screen. Among those who have paid the one franc admission this December night is Georges Melies. He watches a Lumiere-adapted Edison kinetoscope project moving pictures of a train draw up at a suburban railway station. His life is changed. When Antoine Lumiere refuses to sell him the projector because he believes fundamentally that the moving picture has absolutely no commercial future, Georges determines to do it himself. He has always been creator and orchestrator of his own illusions.

Within five years he is France's most famous filmmaker. His Star Film studio at Montreuil turns out eighty motion pictures a year. He is renowned for his cine-magic, his love of effect and illusion.

And now he proposes to go to the Moon. Recorded, of course, by Star Films.

*   *   *

In late May, 1905, the Members of the International Society for Extreme Geography meet at a health hydro at Sarcy in the foothills of the French Alps. They have gathered to observe the progress on the Lunar Railway. The customary members have been joined today by Nicolai Tesla, designer of the electromagnetic induction system that will launch the Star-Train toward the Moon. The gentlemen are arranged in an attractive tableau around the rail of the refreshment deck. President for Life Barbenfouillis gestures theatrically with his cane at the mountainside up which climbs a gleaming ribbon of fresh new iron track. His colleagues look on admiringly. Cameras, still and moving, record the scene with flashes of powder and puffs of smoke, impress it into a hundred newspapers. Far left, a lone grinner. Bottom right corner, a copyright board for Star Films, M. Melies' production company.

After lunch, the media harlequinade decamps to Mt. Sarcy herself, where construction workers are nearing completion of the ramp. Leering beneath welding masks, laborers wield cutting torches and arc guns. President Barbenfouillis can hardly make himself heard as whole cantilevered sections are swung into place by steam cranes and made fast by hammering armies of riveters. Flash-pans blaze, cameras crank. There is an opportunity for questions from the gentlemen of the press.

One of the criticisms is that electrostatic forces are too weak to lift even a kitten from its mother's teat, let alone a train of many carriages into space.

M. Tesla takes this one.

"Were we employing mere electrostatic forces, I would agree with you. But we are employing the power of electromagnetism, the fundamental force of all nature. At every second, our planet spins through lines of flux flowing between Earth and sun powerful enough to propel a Space-Train not merely to the

Moon, but to the stars themselves. While it is true that even the most powerful magnetos of our age cannot generate even a fraction of a fraction of this force, by the process of synchronization, by which the Space-Train will orbit on a circular track, it can gain sufficient acceleration with each circuit that, when released on to this ramp, it can easily escape Earth's gravitational pull. I have absolute confidence, we ride the power of the universe herself."

What about the comment of the English Royal Society that the electromagnetic forces strong enough to launch the Star-Train into the sky would tear the red corpuscles out of the lunanauts' bloodstreams?

"Perhaps it might tear the iron from the thin blood of the English," President Barbenfouillis adds. "But we are thick-blooded Frenchmen, and we have much more iron in us than *les rosbifs*." Much laughter, even from engineers Crackford and Son.

Would the Society care to comment on the news from Berlin that Germany has developed a monstrous space cannon, and intends to fire a shell-load of Teutons to the Moon within one month? Will the Anglo-French Space-Train be left at the platform?

"Typical of the Boche to ride to the stars by force of arms," M. Micromega says. "We ride by first-class carriage; the Germans must always march."

Dr. Crackford comments, in execrable French, "We long ago dismissed the notion of a space-cannon. The accelerations of firing would reduce its crew to the consistency of marmalade."

But it is a race now, and the gentlemen of the press are aware that a gun that can shoot the Moon can shell any place on Earth.

Crackford and Son Engineering Works, Sarcy Branch. Here the Space-Train itself gleams in the light pouring through the great glass roof of the locomotive shed. Crackford and Son's head of engineering, a peppery Scot named Dalrymple but known ubiquitously as "Ecossais," is introducing guests to the Space-Train. Among them is the German Ambassador and his military attaché, a barrel-chested military gentleman, with a ridiculous mustache. Georges Melies notes the changing *moues* of the mouth beneath the whiskers as Ecossais demonstrates the hermetically sealed carriages on their gimbal bogies: "to counteract the centripetal forces of the orbital railway." The Lunar Automobile carriage; curiosity. The crew compartment, upholstered in studded Morocco leather and trimmed with brass; mild disdain. The provisions wagon, containing the atmospheric generation plant which will sustain the lunanuats across the void, as well as necessary comestibles for the trip, including several vintage champagnes: outright contempt. These French and their creature comforts. The Germans' ballistonauts will travel on iron rations, strapped to the inside of their space-shell. It is more than a mere matter of mass; the national constitution will be publicly displayed. Space travel is a thing of stoicism.

The aeronautical car, containing the dirigible which will carry the explorers on longer forays across the lunar surface; slight respect. The Tesla locomotive, shedding crackling ribbons of electricity as its capacitors are charged: downright respect.

Yes, and these steel wheels and iron rods will soon take us to the stars, thinks M. Georges Melies. The press surge forward with shorthand books and questions. Presently, luncheon is served.

And now the day has come. Dignitaries and crowned heads are arrayed on the stands which line the ascent ramp. The hoi polloi of France and nations beyond throng the roped-off public areas between stands and line. Gendarmes and detachments of cavalry maintain a respectful distance; when the train goes, the rush of air will be strong enough to sweep a man into space in its wake. Half a kilometer is con-

sidered safe. Vendors of cardboard periscopes, ear-
plugs, and *Tricoleurs* are making their fortunes. In
France it is a National Holiday. A massed choir of
children from every school in France has been assembled to sing M. Ravel's commemorative composition,
From the Earth to the Moon.

Mr. Tesla's Space-Train stands on the track a half
kilometer from the start of the induction loop. It
crackles potently. Spooks and efreets of ball-lightning
race along its streamlined flanks. The people stand
back as Ecossais mounts the cab. Sky-tight doors are
sealed and dogged. A rising hum fills the air. Those
closest to the track feel their hair stand on end as
electricity from M. Tesla's twelve power plants is
poured into the line.

A collective *ooh*. The train is moving. Very slowly,
with a great smell of ozone and funfairs, it draws level
to the platform where the Members of the Society for
Extreme Geography are gathered in their fine leather
lunar suits. The Space-Train stops in a shower of
sparks. The President of France personally shakes the
hands of his nationals; the King of England dubs his
subjects with honorary titles. Military bands play the
national anthems of both nations. Speeches, songs, or-
atorios in praise of the peaceful exploration of space.
The German experiment failed in its first test; the cannon of the gun, named "Big Brenda," burst under a
full charge of explosives. The boom deafened some
three hundred nearby villagers, but no workers were
harmed, being safely sheltered in underground bunkers several miles from the test firing. Now all humanity's hope rides on the Anglo-French Space-Train.

With dignity and solemnity, the Members of the Society for Extreme Geography enter the crew carriage.
On either side, Moulin girls cancan and whoop, frills
and rounded thighs. Last to board is Georges Melies.
He smiles impishly and waves. The crowd erupts. The
carriage is sealed, lock wheels spun.

And the train is off. It slides onto the induction loop. The acceleration is impressive, the Space-Train leaps through ribbons of soft blue arc light as the fundamental force of the universe grabs it and hurls it around the frustrating track. A brief glimpse of the lunanauts waving from behind their crystal and brass portholes, then the Space-Train is moving too fast for the human eye to follow. Cavalrymen and gendarmes move the people back as complex hydraulics lift the outer edge of the track into a banked curve. The Space-Train is now a raging shriek of lightnings. A sudden boom. The people of France reel back, but still the Space-Train hurtles on its wall of death, so fast now it has sucked the alpine air into a twisting black vortex. The loading platform groans perturbingly. President and King are hastily evacuated; as the last bandsmen and burlesque girls flee, the timbers give way. They are sucked into the wake of the train, tossed high and shredded by the tornado. A rain of matchsticks falls on the heads of the people, who are fleeing for their lives, without order or patriotism. *Sauve qui peut,* the militaries sound on their bugles. *Sauve qui peut.*

There is nothing of the Anglo-French Space-Train now but a howling funnel of black cloud, riven by lightning. But the engineers in their stout blockhouse are faithful. *Escape 0.5,* reads the brass needle of the big speed dial. *Escape 0.6 Escape 0.7. Escape 0.85. Escape 0.95* Almost. Almost. Hands hover over the big points switch. Eyes on the needle. *Escape Velocity.* Five strong men throw the lever.

With a thunder like divine destruction, the Space-Train shrieks on to, up, and off the jump ramp. Reeling, the engineers rush to the slit windows to watch the column of glowing air that is the Space-Train's wake. Echoes die away among the mountain peaks. The engineers wave their caps and cheer raggedly.

Inside the riveted steel of the crew carriage, the

Members of the Society for Extreme Geography strapped into their swivel chairs find that their fingers can be unglued from the armrests, their backs from the studded leather.

"We are flying free!" The members rush to the portholes. There is no more Extreme Geography than seeing the physical world drop away in ever-increasing scales beneath you: the villages and towns of the *Haut Sarcy,* with the fleeing spectators like a black lace trim; then the Alps themselves, ridge upon ridge, ripple upon ripple; then the blue splash of the Mediterranean swims into view and beneath them is France, and even as they look, she recedes into the cloud-scabbed map of Europe, curving around the stretch of the world into the mysterious east. The blue sky outside the windows turns indigo. Stars kindle in the firmament. The shriek of rarified air against carriage drops to a keen, to a whisper, to silence.

"Gentlemen, we are floating in space," announces Georges Melies. And with those words, the Members find themselves floating weightless from their chairs. With whooping and boyish humor, *Belle Epoque* gentlemen swim like overdressed grampuses through the honey-thick air, turning somersaults, corkscrewing in midair, performing extraordinary flatulent demonstrations of Newton's Third Law beyond the dreams of even the Great Petomaine. Georges Melies wriggles through the hatch into the provisions carriage and fetches a Shalmanezer of champagne. The recoil as the bottle orgasms, foaming blobs of champagne, fires him the length of crew and comestibles carriages. Laughing uproariously, the gentlemen of the Society for Extreme Geography chase vagrant brut with glasses and jiggers and open mouths.

After an evening repast glued to the plates with Bearnaise sauce and Dijon mustard, the Members turn to stargazing. There are various sizes of telescopes in the observation car; some turn their lenses on the beauty of the Earth receding behind the Lunar Automobile carriage, others look forward, surveying the pock-marked face of the Moon for an eye in which to land. But Georges Melies looks outward, to the stars, as he has always done. He turns his telescope on the silvery tail of a passing comet. And is amazed.

In his eyepiece, he sees not a wisp of vapors and stardust, but a woman, well-endowed, dressed in an immodest silvery shift. She wears a headdress in the shape of a star from which long streamers of gossamer and gold trail and twine. As if feeling the touch of the lens upon her, she smiles and waves to him.

Georges Melies flies backward in astonishment across the carriage. When his powers of speech have recovered sufficiently to explain what he has seen, his fellow members train their lenses great and small on the comet. They look at the comet and see indeed a shooting-star-haired girl. She smiles and waves. They look at the sun and Moon and see a bright-faced girl surrounded by rays and a somber, Pierrot-faced boy painted sad silver. The girl in the sun is smiling at the boy in the Moon, but he pays no attention. They look at the planets and see chiton-clad women riding the war-arrows of Mars, swinging on the rings of Saturn, riding the mer-horses of Neptune. They look at the stars and see that the constellations are sororities of women, looped together by swatches of soft fabric, carrying blazing flambeaux.

Astounded, they call Ecossais in his cab on the gosport and order him to detour to the comet. M. Tesla has built some degree of freedom into the Space-Train, using the magnetic fields of planets, moons, and sun to warp momentum. Within minutes the comet has resolved into the star-woman—"Maisie-Sue," as Engineer Crackford Senior calls her rather disrespectfully. In space it is hard to tell how, but by the time it takes for the wonder-woman to fill and then dominate the glass roof of the observation car, and the size

of the shadow the Space-Train casts across her belly
as she rolls, laughing, onto her back, the learned gentlemen conclude she is many tens of kilometers long.
As the Space-Train passes over her head and through
the wispy ribbons of her hairpiece, she caresses it with
a loop of her comet-train. The passengers swear that
a veil of soft luminescence passes *through* the walls of
the crew carriage. Then Maisie-Sue is lost as Ecossais
resets course for the eye of the Moon.

The Members of the Society for Extreme Geography
roll disconsolately in the champagne-perfumed air.

"But how . . . ?" asks Micromega.

"Gentlemen, this is a serious pass," states Barbenfouillis.

"Everything we know is false," moans Alcofrisbas.

"All reason, science, and logic is so much
starshine," says Parafaragamus.

"Gentlemen, the universe is not as we thought it to
be," says Crackford *Pere,* ashen-faced.

"Exactly!" declares Georges Melies. The lone grinner. "Learned colleagues, I propose a modest theory.
That the universe is no less, no more, and no other
than exactly what we think it to be. Consider!" A
finger held to attention. "We pride ourselves on being
the scientific and moral pinnacle of history. We boast
that we have conquered the elements, tamed the natural world, bound all things to our service. It would be
no exaggeration to say that our twentieth-century
world is supremely the product of human thought and
human ingenuity. We live in human thought made
manifest, made solid. But, gentlemen, we have left
that world! We are outside the domain of human
thought and reason, we are in the place that existed
before logic and enlightenment. Gentlemen, we are in
the realm of the gods, by which I mean unbridled,
unconstrained human imagination. Here, everything is
no more and no less than we dream it to be."

"Melies, do you mean to say we have flown back

into the Golden Age?" demands President Barbenfouillis.

But whatever Georges Melies means to say goes unspoken, for suddenly there is a burst of frantic whistling from the gosport. Parafaragamus uncaps the tube; at the far end is Ecossais' tinny voice, most alarmed.

"Captain, there's a nightmare right in front of us, and I can't steer us away!"

The Members leap to the telescopes, though there is no need of magnification. Dead ahead of them, mighty and inexorable as an iceberg, is a tremendous dream-creature. A horse, seemingly spun from rags and drifts of clouds, gallops across the firmament. Starshine strikes from its hooves, mingled in its mane are starshine and the brief faces of every terrible thing that ever terrified a dreamer. It can be nothing else than Nightmare, and the Anglo-French Space-Train is headed right for it.

Though neither reason nor science informs them, the members all understand that to plunge into that cloudy form is to lose yourself forever in bad dreams.

"Hard aport!" yells President for Life Barbenfouillis.

"Evasive action!" shout Messrs. Alcofrisbas, Parafaragamus, and Micromega.

"Ecossais, get us away!" M. Ravel calls down the gosport.

"Away, avaunt!" declares Gaston Melies, greatly the worse for champagne.

"Wait!" cries Georges Melies, for he has sized up the peril even before Ecossais' frenzied reply that he doesn't have enough power, enough lateral momentum. "I have a devilish plan!"

Devilish indeed, and inspired in an instant by his brother's predicament.

The Members of the Society for Extreme Geography fit with poor ease into the comestibles carriage air lock.

"The last one here, please," Georges Melies says. As M. Micromega hands Melies the bottle of premier cru, he cannot resist a glance through the porthole. The roiling form of the Nightmare fills all his field of vision.

"For the devil's sake, get a move on, Melies," says Crackford, Senior. Melies, with many glances through the glass, arranges the last bottle into the rack, just so.

"Gentlemen, we should retire." As they tumble over each other in their efforts to all fit at once through the crew carriage door, Melies grasps the gosport and swings himself 'round. "M. Engineer, now, with all your might!" In the driving cab, Ecossais manhandles huge magnetic baffles. Down the train, George Melies throws the dog that blows open the comestibles air lock. The lock depressurizes. One hundred and twelve bottles of finest champagne blow their tops simultaneously in a broadside of corks and flash-frozen chardonnay. The sudden acceleration sends the lunanauts into a pile against the wall. From the bottom of the heap, Georges Melies sees the vaporous flank of the Nightmare roll away beneath him. The portholes fill with clear space and the puzzled expressions of the stellar maidens. The Anglo-French Space-Train fills with cheers and jubilation.

Parafaragamus and Micromega, mission astrogators, calculate that the detour around the Nightmare has done only small violence to their transit time to the Moon, which now fills their forward vision with its benign beam. However, it is now necessary to recalculate their landing site.

"Here," Micromega says, tapping his hastily hand-sketched maps of the transformed Moon. "By my reckoning, we will splash down in the Lake of Dreams in twenty-three hours, twelve minutes, shortly after dinner."

A fine dinner it is, for the last repast before moon-fall. There is quail, well-hung, and several cheeses, and the little cream cakes that translate as "nuns' farts," which offend the English contingent greatly. Behind the train streams a procession of star-women, vying gently for position to roll and stare at this strange steel intruder as it dives down across the sleeping face of the Moon. As the lunanauts uncork the last claret and unseal the humidor, unseen by any of them, the Moon opens an eye the size of a sea, and winks.

"Gentlemen, to your seats!" announces Professor Barbenfouillis. The gentlemen walrus to their chairs, aware of a vague tug of gravity, and more; a tremor, a whisper against the hull, as if the most attenuated of airs is passing over it.

"Impossible!" exclaims Doctor Alcofrisbas. "The Moon, as we know it, is quite airless!"

"But this is not the Moon as we know it," replies Georges Melies as the whisper rises to a shriek, and then all is lost in the roar and fire and thunder as the Space-Train plunges through the upper airs of the airless Moon. Through the judder and air-glare outside, Georges Melies thinks he glimpses fantastic cities all spires and filigree, vast landscapes of orreries and astrolabes and chronometric dials within dials, lakes seemingly made up of swarming silver insects, glass pyramids, crystal spheres the size of mountains, kilometer-high aeolian harps trembling to the touch of the stellar wind, dried-up ocean beds filled with monstrous stone faces, all different, all widemouthed in wonder and following the descent of the Space-Train with slow-rolling eyes.

Ecossais on the gosport: "I'm making final course adjustments, we're on course for the heart of the Lake of Dreams . . ." Then a tremendous impact that hurls the Members against their restraints. The Space-Train bucks, bounces, bounds in a great plume of silver dust. And down again. Brakes lock, steel wheels squeal as Ecossais wrestles to stop the great machine short of the looming crater wall. Less than a kilometer to go, the Anglo-French Space-Train comes to a steaming, creaking halt.

For a long time, nothing stirs. Curious Selenites, a crustaceanlike race, peer, alarmed, from their revetments among the crater walls. Steam billows, they reach for their crossbows. Then a hatch opens in the side of what seems, to them, a great silver star-snake. Memories of the first great star-snake, that devoured constellations and galaxy maidens like nuns' farts, are fresh among the Selenites. They cock their weapons, draw cautious beads. Steps unfold on to the lunar surface. They watch a strange figure swathed in improbable layers of patterned and styled fabric step cautiously on to the surface. They watch him turn to the star-snake, utter uncouth sounds with his mouth. Bemused, they watch the strange creature unfurl a huge piece of fabric, striped red, white, and blue in equal measures.

Satisfied that they will not be imminently devoured, the Selenites uncock their weapons and creep away into their sublunar metropolises.

"Fellow members of the Society for Extreme Geography!" declares President Barbenfouillis. "I claim this great new world of the imagination in the name of the President of France!"

"And His Majesty the King!" chime in Crackford father and son.

Georges Melies' logbook of the Anglo-French lunar expedition reads:

The surface of this part of the Moon we call the Lake of Dreams is exceeding strange. It would barely seem strong enough to support us, were it not for the fact that all of us have been abroad upon it, and none have come to peril. It has the appearance of layer upon layer of the clearest ice—and has much of the treacherous nature of ice, as the bruised posteriors of M. Ravel and my friend Reulos will testify. These layers are separated by piers, buttresses, and vaults of the most delicate spi-

derweb construction. How many layers there are is impossible to say, more than twenty I cannot see, for
though they are of the most marvelous clarity, they are
filled with strange, swirling images, like fragments of
half-formed dreams, and the occlusions of these mi-
rages obscure the deepest profundities. I am not de-
luded by the fact that it seems to be supporting the
weight of the Space-Train; Ecossais, after an inspection
of the rolling-stock, informs me that we are balanced
on a reef of lunar rock breaking the surface of the
Lake of Dreams.

Nonetheless, Barbenfouillis and Micromega are impatient to unstrap the Lunar Automobile and test its
mettle, for Micromega's preliminary surveys have dis-
closed an interesting formation on the farther shore of
the lake. It suggests no other than a ruined chateau
of classical design, though what a chateau! From the
dimensions of what appear to be the fallen caryatids
and cracked portico, it must have stood over five kilometers tall, a prodigious feat of engineering, even under
this world's low gravitational pull.

Of course, my curiosity is piqued, construction implies a constructor, but I am not so certain that I would
wish to meet the Olympian creature that would inhabit
such halls. Perhaps they are as vanished as the original
Olympians—possibly extinct for millions of years. Or
maybe it is that these strange autochthones, of which
we have caught glimpses moving among the crater rim-
rocks, careful not to expose themselves to our telescopes, are the fallen remnants of this once-mighty
breed. If so, it is a fall indeed, from highest nobility, to
fruits de mer. Yet I cannot rid myself of an impression,
brought on, doubtless, by the low pull, light airs, and
general suffusion of dreaminess from the substrate of
the lake in which we are embedded, that a spirit haunts
those ruins—even that they are no ruins at all, that their
dilapidation is a work of architecture more significant
than any triumphal arch or thrusting steel tower.

*   *   *

For breakfast on his first day on the Moon, this is
what Georges Melies eats at the table beneath the silk
parasol that shades him from the rays of the circling
stars: cantaloupe, English kippers, croissants—a little
stale—and a bowl of coffee fresh from the steaming
entrails of the Space-Train. Selenites observe his repast through strange ocular devices, and scurry much.
Were they capable of recognizing terrene expressions,
they would note the grave look on his face. Georges
Melies writes in his journal:

*Catastrophe! I warned them, but they would not lis-
ten. And now they are lost, irretrievably—none dare go
where they have gone to attempt a rescue. Such is the
price of overweening ambition.*

*Such was their curiosity that even before breakfast,
Alcofrisbas and Crackford Senior had prepared the
Lunar Automobile for an expedition to what we term
the Temple of Dreams. I advised them most strenuously
to test the surface, but they were adamant that if it could
withstand the weight of the assembled membership of
the Society, it could easily bear one alcohol-fueled automobile and crew. Thus they departed, with a jaunty
Tricoleur on one wing and a Union flag on the other,
fluttering in the early lunar breeze (of course, I note
that night here is actually fourteen days, give or take).
We waved them adieu and watched them drive away
across the frozen lake. Then,* quel horreur, *I heard
a loud crack and simultaneously saw the rear of the
automobile tip up, and the whole vanish into a pit that
had opened up beneath them.*

*As quickly as was commensurate with safety, we
rushed to the place of their disappearance with ropes,
pitons, and battery lanterns. We saw a chasm at our
feet, the weight of the car had torn open the thin integu-
ment of the lake surface and punched through to the
deepest levels. Of the vehicle there was no sign, but
at the uttermost limits of our light beams we saw our*

*colleagues clinging to the torn edges of the magical
glass, like survivors to the Raft of the Medusa. Their
cries for help were pitiful in the extreme, and became
frenzied as the swirling dream shapes that inhabited the
planes coalesced, as if disturbed, and gathered around
them. I threw a rope to Crackford, the nearer of the
two, but in vain. The vaporous forms, transmogrifying
from chimera of griffin to cotton-wool elephant to
flowers of vaguely obscene character, overwhelmed
them and they went down.*

*Both my esteemed colleagues foundered in their own
dreams. We must count them as lost to us.*

On the third day of the expedition to the Moon,
the Selenites observe the back of one of the segments
of the star-snake crank open, and an infant emerge.
This infant is cylindrical, pointed at each end, carrying
a pouch slung beneath it, and flying. Consternation.
Their worst nightmares have returned. The star-snake
is seeding young across Mother Moon. "To Arms!"
resounds from crystal-carapace horns through the sublunar hive-cities. Exoskeletal armies muster. The King
is in peril.

Astrogated by Micromega, with the indomitable
Reulos at the wheel, the Lighter-Than-Air *Hirondelle*
takes to the skies of the moon. Buoyancy is hard to
judge in the thin air and light gravity; *Hirondelle*
bounces stomach-turningly several times before Reulos—onetime aeronaut supreme of the Melies and
Houdin *Cirque Aerielle*—establishes even trim. Then
the members bend to their crossbars, push down on
their pedals. Cranks turn, gears mesh, propellers spin.
Bicycle-powered *Hirondelle* drifts gently over the
treacherous face of the Lake of Dreams.

Reports from the lookouts stationed at telescopes
around the gondola.

For'ard: *Steer two point west of nor'west for the*

Temple of Dream. Reulos brings the wheel about. *Hirondelle* responds with the liveliness of a girl skipping.

Port: *Dreams storm on the southern horizon, ranging twenty kilometers. Great cumuli of illusions.* Sweat beads brows as the Members flash concerned looks at each other and pedal harder.

Starboard: *Selenite movements on the Plain of Delusions. Whole shoals of them Cap'n!* "Whereaway?" demands Reulos.

"Due west," says Lookout Ravel.

"We'll be there long before them," Reulos says.

Aft: *They have the train! The Selenites are towing the train away!* The pedalers stop. The wheel goes slack in Reulos' hands. All rush to the aft telescope. *Hirondelle* sags, unbalanced in the air. Taking turns, they see the lobster-clawed Selenites attach ropes to the Tesla locomotive and, in their thousands and tens of thousands, haul it by heave and start toward a hellmouth that has opened in the crater wall. They see Crackford Junior, left behind to recuperate in his extremity after the loss of his father, and faithful Ecossais trussed up in line like spider-prey in silk, passed like fire buckets in a man-chain, from pincer to pincer to claw. They see them vanish into the dark maw, and the maw seal over.

"It is too late," President Barbenfouillis mourns. "They have the train."

"And Ecossais and Crackford!" says resolute Alcofrisbas.

"The devils!" announces Gaston Melies, with crack of fist in palm.

"We cannot get back!" wails despondent Parafaragamus.

"Our only hope is onward," says Georges Melies. His fellow Members stare at him. He says, "How else can it be? We know with surety what is behind us, and that there is no hope of return, so whatever lies before us cannot be any worse. And, gentlemen, we

are in the domain of dreaming now, and all wise men
know that our dreams point to the future, not to the
past."

Stirred, a little shaken, the remaining Members return to their posts. Pedals crank, propellers whir. The
drifting *Hirondelle* sets course for the heart of the
lost temple.

Suddenly, there is a cry from the taciturn Ravel.
"There, down there! In the name of Mary, there are
millions of them!" For arrayed on the farther shores
of the Lake of Dreams is the legion of the Selenites;
rank upon rank upon lobstery rank. And they have
bows drawn. And the bows are aimed into the sky,
and the smiling, chubby girl-face of Mama Earth.

"Evasive action!" thunders Barbenfouillis. Reulos
throws the wheel. *Hirondelle* heels. Too late. The
arrows are aflight. And they are no ordinary arrows,
no mere whistle and pierce. They arc high over the
veering dirigible, and burst, like fireworks. But they
drop not sparks, but dreams. A cloud-burst of illusions
rains down through the canopy and the gondola and
the brains of the Members. Dream-stormed, the crew
drop at their posts. Uncontrolled, *Hirondelle* goes into
a glide, loses altitude, and spirals down to a nudge
landing in the soft moondust of the farther shore of
the Lake of Dreams. The Selenites swarm aboard,
spinning dream-silk from their spinnerets. The crew
are trussed within instants. Five frail Selenites to one
Terrene, the Members of the Anglo-French Expedition to the Moon are borne into the heart of the Temple of Dreams. They are carried through cavernous
marble halls, beneath titanic eggshell vaults, cracked
and leaking vagrant earthlight, along endless corridors
lined with sleep-eyed caryatids, who every dozen steps
or so together emit a colossal, sad sigh that stirs the
moondust from the floor, along thousand-level galleries that peer down into pits sunk into the very dream
stuff of the Moon itself, down, always downward, in-

ward and downward, to the dream dungeons. All are oblivious of their fates, lolling and drooling in their private head-spaces. All, save one, the master dreamer himself, the one whose expertise on turning his dreams into reality has enabled him to resist the assault of the Selenites. Georges Melies, *auteur*. The lone grinner. Surreptitiously, he has worked free his many-bladed rigger's knife. Strand by strand, he cuts through the binding web. And as the captors hesitate a moment at the top of a seemingly endless staircase leading down into the misty depths of the undermoon, he flexes his muscles, and with one bound he is free.

Georges Melies runs. He does not know where. He does not care. He trusts the truth of his imagination. He runs through the cavernous marble halls and the titanic cracked-egg vaults and the endless caryatid-lined corridors and the galleries overlooking the bottomless pits. And in one of those places, he runs into a small, old man with a white face and a white beard, dressed in white, with a ruff the size of a carousel around his neck, who says, "And where are you running to, M. Georges Melies?"

The words blow the gale out of his spinnaker. Georges Melies stops in his tracks, and the weight of all he has done and seen hangs like lead around him.

"I don't know," he says. "Away."

"Away?" asks the little man, who has a curious bald head, curious in that a little pagoda of twisted white hair rises up straight from the middle of it.

"From the Selenites," says Georges Melies. "They have captured all my friends. I alone am escaped!"

"And where do you think you can escape to?" says the little man. Then it is that Georges Melies realizes where he is, and who this curious albino is. For the Moon has always been the repository of man's dreams and imagination, and every repository must have a resident assassin.

"I am the King of Dreams," the little man announces.

"I know," says Georges Melies.

"And I know who you are," says the King of Dreams. "But you have not answered my question. Where do you think you can escape to?"

"My world," says Georges Melies. "Home."

"Home," says *Roi des Reves*. "Home. Earth. France. Yes. Hah. Let me show you that."

"Why?" asks Georges Melies.

"Because I can," says the King of Dreams. "You ask me that?" And he grabs hold of his huge ruff and pulls it outward. It rushes toward Georges. He reels back, but the pleats are opening before him like tunnel mouths, and now the folds of the ruff are all the world and he is reduced to the size of a cow, then a vole, then a tiny thing, and he falls helpless into the folds of the pleat. Colors and patterns warp around him; he would be dazed and confused helplessly but for the presence of another, the *Roi des Reves,* flying alongside him. The ruff-tunnel narrows, the hypnagogic illusions become foreshortened, comprehensible: trains, planes, automobiles. Champagne and good times. Marching militaries and hoodlums with great hats and awful firepower. Focusing in on a place, a time. Georges Melies and the King of Dreams drop off dream-time into the Gare Montparnasse, to the left of the *Tabac,* on the cheap side of the tracks, not at all close to the ticket office. By a little stall selling toys and tricks and games and things to amuse children on long train journeys to not very exciting relatives in not very exciting places.

"Wh . . ." Georges Melies says.

". . ." says the King of Dreams, which is a finger touched to pursed lips, then pointed to the man behind the counter of the toy stall. A little man, in his early sixties. What little hair his head holds is white, but his neat goatee is still stiff with iron, and the twin-

kle in his eyes is bright and sharp and devilish and
joyful. It is the glint of the kind of man who puts his
dreams on screens. The kind of man who is the lone
grinner in the family snapshot. A prestidigitator. An
illusionist. A trickster, a Mephistopheles.

"Wh . . ." Georges Melies says again, but this time
the King of Dreams says, "If you escape, this is where
you will escape to."

"A toy stall in the Gare Montparnasse?" Georges
Melies asks, which is so self-answering a question that
the King of Dreams does not even grace it with a nod,
but merely pulls out another fold of his ruff collar and
sends himself and Georges through it. And the patterns in the fabric of this time tunnel are all the
dreams that a trickster called Georges Melies ever
dreamed, or ever will dream, that he sees consigned
to celluloid, to delight, and amaze, and amuse, and to
fail one day to all and any of those things, to be superseded and lost and piled up in shut-down studios and
cobwebby projection booths, and to be lost along with
the magic. He sees a time when the dreams will become jokes, crude as fart cushions, incomprehensible
to a people for whom the nature of the dream is how
much like reality it can be made to feel. He stands in
the time when the man who dreamed all these has
faded like old celluloid, to end his days selling *jouettes*
in a railway station kiosk.

"How?" Georges Melies asks, and in answer the
King of Dreams—whose face is becoming more and
more familiar to Georges Melies with every passing
moment, who seems to have lost weight, to have found
cheekbones, to have changed eye color, to maybe be
sporting the tiniest wisp of chin-beard—sends him
down another fold of his ruff, into another future. This
future of the future of a future imagined by another
great dreamer. In this future, the King of Dreams
shows Georges Melies great ships like nothing he ever
dreamed, that sail between stars as his once sailed

between Earth and Moon, magnificent starships, and
a universe of thousands of worlds friendly and hostile
and strange and familiar, and of great dreams for the
common lot of mankind, and visions of bold venturing
where no one had ever ventured before. He sees the
future of this future, when all the dreaming has become ash and bad sandwiches, sold cheap and free of
taste. He is taken to a time when the dream is called
"the franchise," when it is a thing that may be bought
into, and cut up and handed out like so much cheese,
but so much less than any cheese of France. He is
shown a time when the thing that draws people to this
dream is its utter familiarity and predictability. He is
shown a time when it becomes a uniform that people
wear to mark how different they are from everyone
else, which the more marks their sameness, like a
badge over your heart you touch, like a talisman. He
sees a time when the dreams cease to be dreams, caryatids in a temple of the fantastic, but become a ziggu-
rat of piled silver francs, reaching far beyond Earth
and Moon, Moon and sun, sun and worlds; that
reaches to the edge of the universe itself.

"But that is the end of all dreaming!" cries
Georges Melies.

"Yes," says the King of Dreams. "Dreams sold by
the kilo, not by taste; made to measure, not tailor-
crafted. Production line dreams for people afraid of
their imaginations."

"And I, a toy-vendor!" wails Georges Melies. "How
can I endure in such a world!"

"Who says you must?" says the King of Dreams
and in four words two things happen. The first is that
Georges Melies realizes he must have fallen through
the ruff without knowing it, for he is back among the
slow-falling silver dust of the Temple of Dreams, and
the second is that he now knows what it is that is so
maddeningly familiar about the face of the *Roi des
Reves.*

That prestidigitator flaunt. That illusionist's aura. That Faustian arrogance. That Mephistophelean delight. *L'auteur.* The lone grinner.

In that moment, there are two *Roi des Reves* in the ghost-vaulted great hall of the ruined Temple of Dreams.

Then it seems to Georges Melies, whoever he might consider himself to be, whatever he might conceive himself to be, whatever rolls he might shoot of the steam inside his brain, that the vaults and colonnades and arcades and porticos of the Temple of Dreams, of the whole Moon himself, become insubstantial, and he sees their true construction. He sees cogs; gears within gears, endlessly whirring and running, and cams connected to the cogs, and pistons on the ends of the cams, and vapors that condense and sigh and wisp from the cylinders that drive the cams. He sees levers, and heavy gear that must be thrown by hands protected from scalding energies by gloves and thick rags. He sees piles and mills and presses that work on the raw material of dreams. He sees armies of drilled Selenites at their positions in the great moon machine, well-mannered laborers who have never heard the name of Marx, for the way it works is that no one in the factory of dreams ever dreams himself.

Georges Melies sees himself as Master Engineer of the foundry of every precious dream and vision underneath the stars. He understands that the universe is the very mechanism of dreaming.

Georges Melies sees himself an old, sad, merry man, selling toys in the Gare Montparnasse.

He is back in the cracked dome of the Temple with his alter self.

"I understand," he says. "It is all magic and artifice. Mirrors and dancing girls."

"Yes," says the other *Roi des Reves*. "And the joy, the true joy, of it is that only you will ever know how the trick is done."

"And it will always be new."

"It will never be *la franchise*."

"It will never be commodity."

"The true dreams can never be sold by the kilo."

Now there is only one King of Dreams in the temple that is no longer ruinous as it recently was. This King surveys his domain. He sees the bound bodies of his colleagues being trooped down the spiral that leads into the oldest dreams in the world.

Seafood has never known anything important.

This King sees the Anglo-French Space-Train, moored down by webs of Selenite silk in a deep sublunar cavern, scaring overbold hatchlings with its wisps of steam and crackles of electricity.

With a beat of his will, he dreams it different.

Poised on the edge of the edge of the lower lip of a beaky-nosed crescent Moon, the Anglo-French Space-Train wavers over the abyss. Aboard are President for Life Barbenfouillis, Messrs. Alcofrisbas, Parafaragamus, Micromega—ach, sure you know all this. Suffice it to say that all who were thought lost are unlost, and that the champagne carriage is recharged, and that, on a word from the indomitable Ecossais, all the Members of the Society for Extreme Geography will run to the foremost carriage, thus unbalancing the penduluming train and sending it into the abyss.

Absent among the Members is M. Georges Melies. But in this dreaming, he never was a member of the Society for Extreme Geography. He never finessed the stage of Houdin-Melies. He never was seduced by the magic lantern light of the Brothers Lumiere, he never became the most famous film director in France, and therefore the world.

He never ended up selling toys in the Gare Montparnasse. He never saw his dreams derided. He never saw *imagination* become *franchise*.

But once, in a house bare and chair-free because the

Communards had burned all the bourgeois furniture for proletarian heat, there was a boy, who looked out of his window at the face of the Man in the Moon, and winked, and saw the Man in the Moon wink back at him.

For three days the Anglo-French Space-Train falls through the space between Earth and Moon, where the stars remain dots of light and have no coiffeurs or immodest shifts, and do not—ever—primp and preen. Then comes the first tug of atmosphere, and in the driver's cab Ecossais shouts staging warnings, and pulls the red-lacquered brass lever that separates the Space-Train out, blasts free the needless comestibles, car and dirigible compartment, and links loco and crew carriage into one tight, stubby reentryable aerobody.

As they did for its launch, the people of France turn out for the star-blazing return of the lunanauts. With *ooohs* and *aaahs* and bands playing and much consumption of snack food, they watch a blazing meteor descend the length of France, from the Midi, over Lyons, low enough over Paris to rattle the roof tiles with a sonic boom, finally to plummet into the Manche with a roar and hiss of steam.

Two hours later, the lunanauts are rescued by the maritime steam-crane *Patopan Massif*. The hatches are undogged. Crowned heads greet the achievement of the age.

"The future will never be the same," says the President of the Republic, bestowing medals on the lunanuats. Massed bands play the specially composed anthem *From the Moon to the Earth!* by M. Ravel. Children strew rose petals. The heroes are chaired through the streets. The triumph of human vision, imagination, and ingenuity is sealed for all perpetuity.

Elsewhere, a man with a mischievous grin pulls a lever. Gears whir. Hammers pound, workers labor. The evanescent stuff of dreams is forged into reality. The Moon moves in its course through the place that is outside rationality and reason. The people of Earth sleep. They toss. They groan. They see things. They understand, for an instant, just an instant, how the universe *really* works.

That night, everyone in France dreams the most *extraordinary* dream.

AUTHORS' BIOGRAPHIES

In the 1950s and '60s, Brian Aldiss regaled readers of the innovative *New Worlds* magazine with a different slant on science fiction. His novels *Hothouse, The Malacia Tapestry*, and the Helliconia trilogy, and the Hugo Award-winning overview of the Science Fiction genre, *The Trillion Year Spree*, remain beacons of achievement in the fields of fantasy and Science Fiction. Despite this, he has repeatedly returned to mainstream fiction, embracing the contemporary and the classical with the same consummate ease that he displays when writing of the far reaches of space. His autobiography, *The Twinkling of an Eye*, was published last year, and 1999 will see the publication of *When the Feast is Finished*, an autobiographical postscript which deals with the death of his beloved wife, Margaret.

Before becoming a full-time writer, Stephen Baxter worked as a teacher of math and physics and in information technology. His nine published science fiction novels (*Raft, Timelike Infinity, Anti-Ice, Flux, Ring, The Time Ships, Voyage, Titan*, and *Moonseed*) have won the Philip K. Dick Award, the John Campbell Memorial Award, the British Science Fiction Association Award, the Kurd Lasswitz Award (Germany), and the Seiun Award (Japan) as well as being nominated for several others, including the Arthur C. Clarke, the Hugo, and Locus Awards.

The author of more than ninety futuristic novels and nonfiction books, Ben Bova became involved in the U.S. space program two years before the creation of NASA. He was editor of *Analog* and *Omni* magazines, has written teaching films with Nobel laureate scientists, and is President Emeritus of the National Space Society. He lectures on topics such as the impact of science on politics (and vice versa), the craft of writing fiction, and the biomedical discoveries that will reverse aging and allow people to live for centuries. His book *The Beauty of Light* was voted one of the best science books of 1988 by the American Librarians' Association. His novel *Moonrise* was hailed by the ALA as the best science-fiction novel of 1996.

Eric Brown was born in the tiny English village of Haworth in 1960, and has since lived in Australia, India, and Greece. His first book was the collection *The Time-Lapsed Man and other Stories,* which appeared in 1990. His first novel, *Meridian Days,* followed in 1992. He has published more than fifty stories in various science fiction anthologies and magazines. His next novel, *Penumbra,* is due out in 1999, around the same time as the children's Web book *Walkabout.*

Formerly working in IT, music journalism, advertising, and corporate communications before turning to full-time writing and editing in 1995, Englishman Peter Crowther has made his literary mark through his prolific output of short stories—most of which, covering a variety of genres, are set and first published in the U.S.—a string of original anthologies (of which *Moon Shots*, his second collaborative project with Martin H. Greenberg, is the tenth to be published), columns and interviews on both sides of the Atlantic, two chapbooks, and the novel *Escardy Gap*, written in collaboration with James Lovegrove. His first short story collection, *The Longest Single Note (And Other*

Strange Compositions), was published in 1999. For the record, while most people can (allegedly) remember where they were when they heard the news that President John F. Kennedy had been shot, Crowther can recall exactly where he was when that famous first lunar step was televised live to a waiting world in 1969: he was in a bowling alley in or near the town of Cuyahoga Falls, Ohio, coming to terms with a 7–10 pin split. This anthology is a late "Thank you" to the crew of Apollo 11 for taking attention away from his feeble (and unsuccessful) attempt at making a spare.

There's currently no law against reading Paul Di Filippo's work but it can only be a matter of time before something that's so enjoyable has to be rendered illegal. Di Filippo was born in 1954, the year Elvis Presley first entered Sun Studios, and one of his first memories is of lying on the floor and scribbling in a coloring book while "Hound Dog" played over a big console radio. He is the author of one uncategorizable novel (*Ciphers*) and many short stories—most of them wacky and concerning some reference to music—which have been gathered into four (so far) collections, the third of which (*Fractal Paisleys*) was nominated for the World Fantasy Award. The world is clearly beginning to catch up with where Di Filippo's at . . . but be warned: he won't be there for long!

Scott Edelman is the editor of *Science Fiction Age,* editor of *Sci-Fi Entertainment* (the official magazine of the Sci-Fi Channel), and editor of *Sci-Fi Universe*. He has been a Hugo Award finalist for Best Editor on three separate occasions . . . though he tries not to think about that. In the 1970s, Edelman worked as an assistant editor for Marvel Comics, before freelancing for both Marvel and DC. His first novel, *The Gift*, was a finalist for a Lambda Literary Award. His short stories have appeared in numerous anthologies and magazines; his writing for television includes work for Hanna-Barbera and treatments for the syndicated TV show *Tales From the Darkside;* and his book reviews have appeared in *The Washington Post, The New York Review of Science Fiction,* and *Science Fiction and Fantasy Book Review.* His five-act play that crosses *Night of the Living Dead* with *Romeo and Juliet* was a Stoker Award finalist.

Alan Dean Foster's writing career began when, in 1968, August Derleth bought his long Lovecraftian letter and published it as a short story. Sales of short fiction to other magazines followed and then, in 1972, his first novel appeared. Foster's sometimes humorous, occasionally poignant but always entertaining short fiction has appeared in all the major science fiction magazines as well as in original anthologies and *Year's Best* volumes. Five collections of his stories have been published and Foster has written the novelizations of many films (including *Star Wars*, the first three *Alien* movies and *Alien Nation*). His novel *Cyber Way* won the Southwest Book Award for Fiction in 1990, the first science fiction work to do so. As well as having lectured at universities around the country and in Europe, Foster has taught screenwriting, literature, and film history at UCLA and Los Angeles City College.

Colin Greenland's first book was about a fire engine that laid an egg. He was five years old. Since then, Greenland has become one of Britain's most distinctive science fiction authors, building on his doctorate study of "New Wave" Science Fictoin (entitled *The Entropy Exhibition*, published in 1983) and moving through a string of wonderful novels to produce the recent and much-loved Tabitha Jute trilogy, a bizarre and colorful space opera whose first volume, *Take Back Plenty*, was the first book to win all three of the British Science Fiction awards. *Mother of Plenty*, the final volume (following *Seasons of Plenty*), was published in 1998. Greenland's short stories were collected in 1997, under the title *The Plenty Principle*.

James Lovegrove is the author of *The Hope* and *Days,* which was short-listed for the Arthur C. Clarke Award, as well as coauthor (with some bloke named Peter Crowther) of the American Gothic epic *Escardy Gap*. He has contributed a novel, *Computopia,* to the highly successful children's science fiction series *The Web,* and, under the somewhat penetrable pseudonym of J.M.H. Lovegrove, is writing the *Guardians* series, the second novel of which, *Berserker,* has just been published. He currently resides in the county of East Sussex, where the sight of the Moon gleaming—perfect and penny-round—over the South Downs still has the capacity to make him stop and stand and stare in awe.

Paul McAuley has worked as a researcher in biology in various universities, including Oxford, England and UCLA. His first novel, *Four Hundred Billion Stars*, won the Philip K. Dick Memorial Award; his fifth, *Fairyland*, won the Arthur C. Clarke Award and the John W. Campbell Award. As well as short stories and novels, he writes a regular review column for the British science fiction magazine Interzone. He has just completed a very long novel, *Confluence*, set ten million years in the future. The first part, *Child of the River*, was published in the U.S. in 1998. The second, *Ancients of Days*, will be published in 1999, and the last part, *Shrine of Stars*, in 2000. His short stories have been collected in two volumes—*The King of the Hill* and *The Invisible Country*, the latter containing the widely anthologized story "Gene Wars" which has been used as a teaching aid in at least two university courses . . . one biology and the other law.

Ian McDonald was born in Manchester, England but moved to Northern Ireland as a child. He found his literary feet with his first novel—the masterful Arthur C. Clarke Award runner-up, *Desolation Road*—and has since gone on to even greater things with the sublime triptych-novel *King of Morning, Queen of Day* (winner of the Philip K. Dick Award), *Hearts, Hands, and Voices* (another Clarke Award runner-up), and *Chaga*, a science fiction novel set in twenty-first century Africa. His short stories have appeared in various magazines and anthologies, and many of these have been collected into *Empire Dreams* and *Speaking in Tongues*.

Kathleen Massie-Ferch was born and raised in Wisconsin. She's there still, with a wonderful husband, two Scottie dogs, several telescopes, numerous rocks, and more books than she cares to count. She worked her way through college, earning degrees in astronomy, physics, and geology-geophysics. For the past twenty years she has worked for the University of Wisconsin as a research geologist. Massie-Ferch has made short fiction sales to a variety of places, such as Marion Zimmer Bradley's Fantasy magazine, *Sword and Sorceress, Warrior Princesses, New Amazons*, and *New Altars*. She has coedited two historical fantasy anthologies for DAW Books, *Ancient Enchantresses* and *Warrior Enchantresses*.

Jerry Oltion has been a gardener, stone mason, carpenter, oilfield worker, forester, land surveyor, rock 'n' roll deejay, printer, proofreader, editor, publisher, computer consultant, movie extra, corporate secretary, and garbage truck driver. For the last seventeen years, he has also been a writer. He is the author of over eighty published stories in *Analog, F&SF,* and various other magazines and anthologies. He has written nine novels, the most recent of which is *Where Sea Meets Sky*, a *Star Trek* novel. His work has won the Nebula

Award and been nominated for the Hugo Award. He
has also won the *Analog* Readers' Choice Award. He
lives in Eugene, Oregon, with his wife, Kathy, and the
obligatory writer's cat, Ginger.

Robert Sheckley vaulted to the front ranks of science
fiction writers in the 1950s with his prodigious output
of short, witty stories that explored the human condition in a variety of earthly and unearthly settings. His
best tales have been collected in *Untouched by Human
Hands, Pilgrimage to Earth,* and the comprehensive
Collected Short Stories of Robert Sheckley. His novels
include the futuristic tales *The Status Civilization,
Mindswap,* and *Immortality Delivered,* which was
filmed as *Freejack.* He has also written the crime novels *Calibre .50* and *Time Limit.* Elio Petri's cult film
The Tenth Victim is based on Sheckley's story "The
Seventh Victim."

Brian Stableford was born in 1948 in the Yorkshire
(England) town of Shipley. He was awarded a BA in
Biology and a D.Phil. in Sociology by the University
of York before teaching Sociology for twelve years at
the University of Reading. He has been a full-time
writer since 1988. He is the author of forty-five novels,
more than nineteen hundred short stories, and fifteen
nonfiction books, most recently *Inherit the Earth* and
The Dictionary of Science Fiction Places. He is also a
contributor to many reference books, most recently
The Ultimate Encyclopedia of Fantasy and *Science Fiction Writers.*

Michelle West is the author of the *Sacred Hunt* duol-
ogy, as well as *The Broken Crown, The Uncrowned
King,* and the forthcoming *The Shining Court.* She reviews books—a job she loves because it gives her not
only an excuse but also an obligation to read—for *The
Magazine of Fantasy and Science Fiction.* She managed

to survive losing the Campbell award twice and, as that wasn't enough to discourage her, she's likely to continue to write stories like the one you're just read.

Gene Wolfe is sixty-seven years old and, he says, dumber than he looks. As a small boy he used to hide behind the candy case in the Richmond Pharmacy to read the pulps—and in a sense, he says, he has never come out. Because it's easier, he tells people he's retired . . . but in dark and lonely moments he schemes to write something better than anything he's written up to now. A tall order by any measurement. His wife, Rosemary, tries to keep him out of mischief . . . still unaware—they've been together for more than forty years—that he is it. He's written "No Planets Strike," which was nominated for a Hugo, plus a couple of hundred other stories. Also some books, he says with grand understatement, including *Operation Ares, The Fifth Head of Cerberus,* and *Shadow & Claw*. The most recent is *Exodus From the Long Sun* . . . part of *The Book Of The Long Sun,* a tetralogy, Wolfe explains. There will also be a trilogy, he adds, entitled *The Book of the Short Sun* . . . "—if I ever get it finished: *On Blue's Waters, In Green's Jungles,* and *Return to the Whorl*." Further suggestions regarding titles, Wolfe points out, will earn no points.